# Chronicles of Time: Seizing Freedom

By

Peter F Herring

# Whispers of Liberty: The Time Travelers' Pact

# TABLE OF CONTENTS


Chapter 1.................................................1

Chapter 2................................................14

Chapter 3................................................25

Chapter 4................................................39

Chapter 5................................................48

Chapter 6................................................59

Chapter 7................................................74

Chapter 8................................................92

Chapter 9...............................................103

Chapter 10..............................................118

Chapter 11..............................................137

Chapter 12..............................................170

Chapter 13..............................................186

Chapter 14..............................................203

Chapter 15..............................................218

Chapter 16..............................................232

Chapter 17..............................................242

Chapter 18..............................................256

Chapter 19..............................................271

Chapter 20..............................................286

Chapter 21..............................................301

Chapter 22..............................................326

Chapter 23..............................................336

Chapter 24..............................................351

# CHAPTER 1

The sun dipped low in the sky, casting long shadows across the ivy-covered Hawthorne House Boarding School walls. A grand and imposing structure, it stood tall against the backdrop of a dense forest, its ancient stone walls weathered by time yet still held firm. The air was thick with mystery, the whispers of the past echoing through the halls and staircases of the old-fashioned building.

Sarah Merriweather stepped out of the school's main doors and onto the courtyard, feeling slightly out of place in her neatly pressed uniform. She was a girl of about fourteen, with long blonde hair that tumbled down her back and bright blue eyes that seemed to hold secrets of their own. Her kind-hearted nature was evident in the gentle curve of her smile and the way she carried herself, with a softness that belied her inner strength.

"Hey Sarah, which way do you think we should go?" called one of her classmates from behind her. Sarah hesitated, glancing between the paths that led towards their dormitories and the ones that meandered through the gardens. She wished someone else would just decide for her. Her fingers toyed with the hem of her skirt nervously as she weighed the options, her mind racing with the possible consequences.

"Uhm, maybe we could take the path through the gardens? It's such a nice day," Sarah finally said, her voice barely audible above the chattering students around her. She internally scolded herself for not being more assertive but couldn't help the timid tone that laced her words.

"Are you sure, Sarah? The other path is shorter," another classmate chimed in, and Sarah felt her cheeks warming with embarrassment. She was never quite able to make decisions on her own, constantly second-guessing herself or letting others choose for her. It was something she knew she needed to work on, but the fear of making the wrong choice always held her back.

"Y-yes, I'm sure. The gardens are beautiful this time of day," Sarah managed to say with a bit more conviction, hoping it would be enough to sway her classmates. She took a deep breath and started walking in the direction she had chosen, praying that they would follow her lead.

As they strolled through the lush gardens, Sarah couldn't help but feel a sense of wonder at the vibrant colors and delicate fragrances that surrounded them. The beauty of nature was something that had always captivated her, and she found comfort in the knowledge that some things were constant despite the ever-changing world around her.

"Sarah, you were right; this is lovely," one of her friends said, and Sarah felt a small swell of pride at the compliment. Perhaps she could learn to trust herself more and find the strength to make decisions independently. And maybe, just maybe, she could become the person she always dreamed of being at Hawthorne House Boarding School, surrounded by the mysteries of the past and the hope for a brighter future.

As Sarah walked further into the garden, she saw two boys up ahead, immersed in conversation. The first boy, Charles Hamilton, had short dark hair that framed his face, highlighting his piercing blue eyes. Standing tall and poised, he exuded confidence as he spoke, his words carrying a sense of authority that seemed to come naturally to him.

"Look, Henry," Charles said, gesturing with one hand to emphasize his point. "We need to approach this logically. If we jump to conclusions without evidence, it's only going to cause more problems."

Henry Turner, the other boy, stood facing Charles with his arms crossed. He was taller than Charles, with a sturdy, athletic build that suggested he spent many hours on the sports field. His jaw was clenched, and the furrow in his brow indicated his growing impatience.

"Logical?" Henry scoffed. "You mean like how you didn't trust Paul when he offered to help us? How's that working out for us?"

Charles sighed and ran a hand through his hair, frustration creeping into his voice. "I don't have time to explain my reasons every time I make a decision, Henry. You need to learn to trust my judgment."

"Trust your judgment?" Henry shot back, his anger boiling over. "The problem is you don't trust anyone else's! We're supposed to be a team, Charles!"

Sarah watched the exchange from a distance, feeling curious and apprehensive. She knew that both boys were intelligent and capable, but the tension between them was palpable. It was clear that Charles's difficulty in trusting others was a source of conflict within their group.

"Alright, let's just take a step back," Charles suggested, taking a deep breath and attempting to diffuse the situation. "I know I can be stubborn, but we all want the same thing — to succeed here at Hawthorne House. We need to work together."

Henry's expression softened, and he uncrossed his arms. "Fine," he agreed begrudgingly. "But you need to start trusting us more, Charles. We're not your enemies."

"Agreed," Charles said, extending a hand for Henry to shake. As they shook hands, Sarah could see the determination in their eyes – a shared understanding that they needed each other to overcome the challenges ahead.

As Sarah continued to observe them, she couldn't help but admire Charles's leadership and Henry's strong sense of justice. Despite their differences, she knew they were bound together by their shared desire to make the most of their time at Hawthorne House. Perhaps, if they could learn to trust and understand one another, they could truly unlock the secrets hidden within the walls of the ancient boarding school.

As Sarah watched Charles and Henry walk away, she noticed another figure lingering in the shadows. With a gentle sway, the girl emerged into the sunlight like a deer from the forest. She was slender, with long brown hair that fell over her shoulders like a waterfall, framing a pair of round glasses perched on her small nose. Her name was Clarissa Jennings, and though she appeared timid, her mind was a treasure trove of intellect.

"Clarissa!" Sarah called out, waving her over. "Come join us!"

Clarissa hesitated for a moment before stepping toward them, her eyes flickering nervously between Charles, Henry, and Sarah. She toyed with the strap of her satchel, biting her lip as if contemplating whether to speak or remain silent.

"Hey, Clarissa," Charles greeted her warmly. "What's got you so deep in thought?"

"Um, well... I was just..." Clarissa stammered, her face flushing with color. "I was wondering if any of you had seen the article about the discovery of King Arthur's tomb. It's truly fascinating."

"King Arthur?" Henry asked, raising an eyebrow. "You mean the guy from all the myths and legends?"

"Exactly! Some historians believe they've found evidence of his existence," Clarissa explained, her voice gaining confidence as she delved into her passion for history.

"Wait?" Sarah questioned, intrigued by the idea. "But wasn't he supposed to be just a legend?"

"Many people thought so, but this new discovery could change everything," Clarissa replied, her eyes sparkling with enthusiasm. "It's incredible, don't you think?"

"Sounds interesting," Charles admitted, exchanging a glance with Henry. "You'll have to keep us updated on it."

"Of course!" Clarissa said with a smile, grateful for their interest.

"Alright, team," Charles announced, clapping his hands together. "We've got work to do to make our mark at Hawthorne House. Let's put our heads together and figure out how to tackle this place."

"Agreed," Sarah chimed in, smiling at Clarissa. "We're all in this together."

"Indeed," Henry grumbled, though he couldn't help but smile as well.

"Okay, then!" Clarissa exclaimed, her voice barely more than a whisper. "What should we do first?"

As the four friends huddled close, sharing ideas and debating strategies, Sarah marveled at their unique strengths. Charles's leadership, Henry's determination, and Clarissa's brilliant mind were all invaluable assets. And yet, she knew they each had their individual flaws — Charles's trust issues, Henry's temper, and Clarissa's quiet nature often holding them back.

But together, they could overcome anything.

The day had begun with a thick fog, making the ancient boarding school appear even more mysterious than usual. As Sarah walked through the damp courtyard, she could feel the weight of generations that had come before her. The whispers of the past seemed to linger in the air; secrets carried through time on the faintest breeze. She shuddered, pulling her cardigan tighter around herself.

"Did you see the schedule for next week?" Charles asked, his eyes scanning the notice board as they passed by. "We've got a history exam, a physics presentation, and a literature essay all due."

"Seriously?" Henry groaned, running a hand through his hair. "As if we didn't already have enough to deal with."

"Boarding school life isn't easy," Sarah murmured, her gaze drifting toward a group of students laughing and chatting by the water fountain, their camaraderie clear. A pang of longing struck her heart – she yearned for that sense of belonging, to be a part of something greater than herself.

"Hey, look on the bright side," Clarissa chimed in, adjusting her glasses. "At least we have each other. We can help one another study and prepare for everything."

"True," Charles agreed, a slight smile tugging at the corner of his mouth. "We can't let these challenges get the better of us."

"Speaking of challenges, here comes Headmaster Winters," Henry warned, nodding subtly toward the approaching figure.

A palpable shift swept through the courtyard as the enigmatic headmaster drew nearer. Archibald Winters was an elderly man with a long white beard that danced like wisps of smoke in the air. His piercing blue eyes cut through the fog, seeming to see into the very souls of those he observed. There was an air of mystery about him – a hidden depth beneath the surface that hinted at stories yet untold.

"Good morning, students," Headmaster Winters greeted them, his voice deep and resonant. "I trust you are all settling in well."

"Good morning, sir," they replied in unison, their voices tinged with nervousness.

"Remember, my young scholars," he continued, pausing to look each of them in the eye. "The challenges you face here will only serve to strengthen you, to mold you into the people you are destined to become. Embrace them, and learn from them."

"Thank you, sir," Sarah managed to say, her heart pounding in her chest. She could sense the genuine affection he held for the students, even if it was hidden beneath a veil of mystery.

"Carry on, then," Headmaster Winters said, nodding once before continuing on his way.

"Wow," Clarissa breathed as they watched him disappear into the mist. "He's... something else, isn't he?"

"Definitely," Sarah agreed, her mind racing with questions about the enigmatic headmaster. Who was he, really? And what secrets did he hold?

"Alright," Charles announced, determination etching his features. "We've got our work cut out for us, but we can do this. Together."

"Agreed," Henry said, cracking his knuckles. "Let's show Hawthorne House what we're made of."

As they walked back toward their dormitories, Sarah couldn't help but feel a flicker of hope. Despite the pressures, the social dynamics, and their own personal struggles, they had each other – and, she realized, that was all they needed to face whatever challenges the boarding school threw at them.

A golden beam of sunlight filtered through the heavy curtains, casting a warm glow over Sarah's face as she awoke to the sound of birds chirping outside her window. She blinked groggily, pushing aside her tangled blonde locks before sitting up, a sense of purpose filling her chest.

"Rise and shine," Charles called from across the hall, his voice filled with energy. "We've got a big day ahead of us."

"Can't... sleep... just a little longer?" Henry mumbled, burying his face in his pillow.

"Come on, Henry," Clarissa chimed in, adjusting her glasses as she peered at the book she was already reading. "We have to be prepared for our classes."

"Fine," Henry grumbled, rolling out of bed and rubbing his eyes. "Let's get this over with."

"Alright, team," Charles said, clapping his hands together. "Breakfast first, then we'll tackle our assignments. We can help each other out if we get stuck."

Sarah smiled, grateful for the support they provided one another. Knowing they faced them together made the boarding school's challenges seem more manageable.

"Sounds like a plan," she agreed, pulling back her covers and swinging her legs over the side of the bed.

The dining hall was a cacophony of noise and movement as students hurried to grab breakfast before classes began. The smell of freshly baked bread mingled with the aroma of sizzling bacon, making Sarah's stomach rumble with anticipation.

"Here," Charles said, handing her a plate piled high with scrambled eggs, toast, and fruit. "Eat up. You'll need your energy today."

"Thanks," Sarah replied, taking a bite of toast while they found an empty table to sit and eat together.

"Did you finish the history essay?" Clarissa asked, nibbling on a piece of bacon.

"Almost," Sarah admitted, feeling a pang of guilt. "I got stuck on the conclusion."

"Maybe I can help you with that," Charles offered. "We can work on it during our study break."

"Thanks," Sarah said, her heart swelling with gratitude. "I'd appreciate that."

"Hey, what are friends for?" Henry chimed in, his mouth full of eggs. "Besides, we're all in this together, right?"

"Right," Sarah agreed, her confidence bolstered by their camaraderie.

The morning went by in a whirlwind of classes, from arithmetic to literature, each proving more challenging than the last. Yet, amidst the academic pressures, Sarah found solace in the simple routines that structured their days — the quiet moments spent studying together in the library, the laughter shared over lunch, and the whispered conversations exchanged in the hallways.

"Almost done," Charles whispered, scribbling furiously in his notebook as they worked on their essays side by side. "How about you?"

"Getting there," Sarah replied, her brow furrowed in concentration. "Just a few more sentences..."

"Take your time," Clarissa encouraged, closing her book with a satisfied sigh. "You'll get there."

"Thanks," Sarah murmured, swallowing her doubts and focusing on the task at hand.

As the sun dipped below the horizon, casting long shadows across the grounds, the four friends gathered in the courtyard, savoring the crisp evening air.

"Another day down," Charles mused, stretching his arms above his head.

"Only a million more to go," Henry quipped, earning a chuckle from the others.

"True," Clarissa conceded, "but it's not so bad. Not when we have each other."

"No," Sarah agreed, gazing at the twilight sky and feeling a deep sense of belonging. "Not when we have each other."

As the days turned into weeks, the four friends became more attuned to each other's strengths and weaknesses. One afternoon, they found themselves gathered in their favorite corner of the library, surrounded by towers of books that seemed to stretch on forever. Sarah was caught up in a particularly vivid description of a far-off land when she noticed Clarissa fidgeting with the edge of her parchment.

"Clarissa, what's wrong?" Sarah asked, her blue eyes filled with concern.

"Nothing, really," Clarissa mumbled, pushing her glasses further up her nose. "It's just that... well, I've been thinking about how we can help each other grow."

"Go on," Charles said encouragingly, his confident demeanor making it clear he was eager to hear more.

"Perhaps we could teach each other something new or help

each other overcome our weaknesses," Clarissa suggested, her voice gaining strength as her idea took shape.

"Like a skill swap?" Henry chimed in, his sturdy frame leaning forward in anticipation. "I like it."

"Exactly!" Clarissa beamed, her intelligence shining through. "For example, Sarah, you could teach me to be more assertive while I can help you become more decisive."

"Sounds like a plan," Sarah agreed, the prospect of transforming herself filling her with equal parts excitement and trepidation.

"Alright," Charles declared, taking charge as his natural leadership skills dictated. "Let's make this official. Starting tomorrow, we'll dedicate an hour after dinner to our skill swap sessions. Agreed?"

"Agreed," the others echoed in unison, sealing their pact with determined nods.

That evening, as the sky outside their window turned from crimson to indigo, Sarah lay awake in her bed, contemplating the changes that awaited them all. She couldn't shake the feeling that something monumental lay just beyond the horizon, waiting to sweep them off their feet.

"Psst, Sarah," whispered a voice from the darkness, drawing her out of her reverie. It was Charles, his silhouette barely visible in the moonlit room. "I know it's late, but... I found something you might want to see."

"Really?" Sarah replied, curiosity piqued. "What is it?"

"Meet me at the library in ten minutes and get the others," Charles said, his voice low and conspiratorial. "You won't believe your eyes."

With her heart racing and her imagination running wild, Sarah tiptoed through the hushed corridors of the boarding school, anticipation mounting with each step. Running to Henry and Clarissa's rooms, she woke them for the anticipated development. As they rounded the final corner, they spotted Charles standing by the towering bookshelves, an enormous leather-bound tome cradled in his arms.

"Look at this," he whispered, opening the book to reveal intricate illustrations of fantastical creatures and cryptic symbols. "It's a hidden history of the school – one that I've never seen before."

"Whoa," breathed Henry, who had joined them along with Clarissa. "Where did you find this?"

"Hidden behind some dusty old volumes," Charles explained, a gleam in his eye. "I think... I think there's something more to our school than we ever imagined."

The four friends exchanged excited glances, each one feeling the pull of the unknown tugging at their hearts. Little did they know that in the days to come, this mysterious tome would be the key to unlocking a secret world – one that would test their courage, their friendships, and the very fabric of time itself.

# CHAPTER 2

"Quickly, everyone get to work. We need to find the answers as to what this book could be! Drop everything you're doing, Henry. Hurry and get me the encyclopedia from the other library across campus." Charles bellowed.

"Charles, you can't just barge in here and start ordering us around!" Henry's face was flushed with anger as he stood nose to nose with Charles in the dimly lit library. The tension between them crackled like a fire about to burst into flames, their conflicting personalities clashing once again.

"Someone has to take charge if we want to solve this mystery!" Charles retorted, his dark eyes flashing with defiance. "And I happen to be good at it."

Sarah Merriweather, her long blonde hair shimmering in the light of the flashlight, hesitated near the door, biting her lip nervously. Her gentle heart ached for her friends, and she wished she had the courage to step forward and intervene.

"Please," whispered Clarissa Jennings, her brown eyes wide behind her glasses. She reached out tentatively to touch Henry's arm, silently pleading with him to let go of his anger. "We're all in this together."

Henry shook off Clarissa's hand, his gaze never leaving Charles's. "You may be used to getting your way, Hamilton, but that doesn't mean the rest of us have to follow your every whim. We all have something to contribute."

"Exactly," agreed Sarah, finding her voice at last. "We can figure this out much faster if we work together." She took a deep breath and stepped closer to the boys, her blue eyes filled with determination. "Now, let's put aside our differences and focus on what's really important: figuring out what this could mean."

Charles crossed his arms but nodded reluctantly. "Fine. But we don't have much time. Let's get to work."

"Thank you," murmured Clarissa, her timid smile lighting up her face like the sun breaking through clouds. "I think we'll surprise ourselves with what we can accomplish when we stand united."

As the four young friends settled down around the ancient wooden table, their attention now focused on the mysterious leatherbound tome before them, the library seemed to come alive with a sense of purpose. The flickering candlelight cast playful shadows on the walls as if hinting at the grand adventure that awaited them. And though they faced an uncertain future, one thing was clear: together, they would face it head-on, ready for whatever challenges lay ahead.

The four friends barely had a chance to examine the volume when the library doors swung open with a creak, revealing the stern face of Mrs. Higgins, the school's librarian. Her gaze swept over them like a hawk circling its prey, and her voice cut through the air like a knife.

"Headmaster Winters wishes to see you in his office at once," she announced, her sharp tone leaving no room for argument.

As the children reluctantly abandoned their attempts to decipher the script, Sarah felt a shiver run down her spine. What could the headmaster want with them? She exchanged worried glances with Clarissa, who looked equally concerned.

"Come along now," Mrs. Higgins urged impatiently, gesturing for them to follow her as she marched out of the library.

"Whatever it is, we'll deal with it together," Charles whispered to Henry as they trailed behind the girls. Their earlier disagreement was momentarily forgotten in the face of this new development.

Sarah nodded silently, her stomach churning with nerves as they approached the formidable door to Headmaster Winters' office. It loomed before them like an ancient tree, its dark wood covered in intricate carvings that seemed to dance in the flickering torchlight.

The door creaked open to reveal the enigmatic figure of Headmaster Archibald Winters. He was an elderly man with a long white beard that cascaded down to his waist like a waterfall of snow. His piercing blue eyes seemed to bore into their very souls, and Sarah couldn't help but feel that he knew every secret she'd ever tried to hide. Yet there was something strangely comforting about his presence, as though he held the key to unlocking their true potential.

"Ah, my young scholars," he said softly, his voice a blend of gravel and silk. "Do come in."

The door to Headmaster Winters' office creaked open as if hesitant to reveal the secrets contained within. Charles, Sarah, Henry, and Clarissa exchanged nervous glances before stepping into the dimly lit room, their apprehension palpable in the air.

Charles hesitated at the threshold, his eyes scanning the ancient tomes and peculiar artifacts that cluttered the room. He could practically feel the weight of history pressing down on him, each dusty volume a testament to the knowledge and power wielded by the enigmatic headmaster.

With bated breath, the friends stepped into the shadowy office, their eyes drinking into the countless books and artifacts that lined the walls. The air was heavy with the scent of aged leather and parchment, a testament to the knowledge contained within these hallowed halls.

"Please, have a seat," Headmaster Winters gestured to a group of plush armchairs arranged around a crackling fireplace. The warmth emanating from the flames did little to soothe Sarah's nerves as she sank into one of the chairs, her fingers twisting the hem of her skirt in an unconscious gesture of anxiety.

"Sir, we were wondering—" Charles began, but Headmaster Winters raised a hand to silence him.

"Patience, young man," he said, his eyes twinkling with an unspoken secret. "All will be revealed in due time."

"Now, let me welcome you properly!" Headmaster Winters exclaimed from behind a towering mahogany desk, his voice rich with a blend of mischief and wisdom that set the children's hearts racing. "Do make yourselves comfortable."

"Is something the matter, Mr. Charles?" Headmaster Winters inquired, one bushy eyebrow arching in amusement as he took in the boy's wide-eyed expression.

"Uh, no, sir," Charles stammered, feeling the heat rise in his cheeks as he shuffled forward to join his friends, who had already settled into the plush armchairs arranged around the fireplace.

Henry shot Charles a disapproving look, but the tension between them seemed to have abated somewhat in the face of their shared anxiety. "We're sorry for our behavior earlier, Headmaster," he offered solemnly, his hands clasped tightly in his lap.

"Indeed," Winters replied, his piercing blue eyes studying each of them in turn. "Conflict is a natural part of life, my young scholars. The key is learning how to navigate it with grace and understanding."

Sarah swallowed hard, her fingers worrying the hem of her skirt as she ventured a question. "Sir, are we... in trouble?"

"Trouble?" The headmaster echoed, his lips quirked into a knowing smile. "That remains to be seen. You see, I have brought you here not to chastise you but to offer you an opportunity."

"An opportunity?" Clarissa echoed, her curiosity piqued despite her lingering unease.

"Indeed," Headmaster Winters confirmed, leaning back in his chair as he regarded the children with a gleam in his eye. "An opportunity to learn and grow beyond the confines of these walls. A chance to embark on a grand adventure like no other."

"An adventure?" Charles asked incredulously, the disbelief evident in his voice even as his heart raced at the thought.

"Ah, but I've said too much already," Headmaster Winters chided gently, tapping a finger against his lips as though to lock away any further secrets. "The choice is yours, my young scholars. Will you embrace this opportunity or let it slip through your fingers?"

The four friends exchanged a series of meaningful glances, their apprehension melting away under the weight of the headmaster's enigmatic words. As one, they nodded their agreement, their faces alight with newfound determination and excitement.

"Very well," Headmaster Winters declared, a note of approval in his voice as he rose from his chair. "Let the adventure begin!"

"Follow me," Headmaster Winters instructed his voice a blend of mystery and wisdom. With deliberate steps, he led the children to a dusty corner of the office where an aged wooden cabinet stood. Its surface was adorned with intricate carvings of mythical creatures and celestial symbols, creating an aura of enigma.

The headmaster retrieved an ancient-looking cryptex from one of the drawers, its metallic surface tarnished with age. The cylindrical object, roughly the size of a man's forearm, bore a series of rotating dials covered in cryptic letters, numbers, and symbols.

"Behold," he announced, his blue eyes twinkling as he presented the object to the children. "The key to your adventure lies within this cryptex."

"Wow," Sarah breathed, her fingers itching to touch the artifact. Henry leaned in for a closer look, his scientific curiosity piqued by the seemingly impossible construction of the device.

"Many have tried to unlock its secrets," Headmaster Winters

continued, his voice taking on a more solemn tone. "Some have succeeded, while others... well, let's just say they've learned valuable lessons along the way."

"Is there any clue to help us decipher it?" Charles inquired, his skepticism fading beneath the allure of the challenge before them.

"Ah, you see," the headmaster replied cryptically, a mischievous smile playing at the corners of his lips, "the clues are all around you. You need only open your eyes – and your minds – to find them."

"Are you saying the answers are here? In the school?" Clarissa questioned, her mind racing with possibilities.

"Perhaps," Headmaster Winters teased, tapping the side of his nose with a knowing wink. "Or perhaps not. The journey you're about to embark upon will require each of you to harness your unique strengths and talents. Remember, my young scholars, the greatest lessons come not from knowing the answers but from discovering them for yourselves."

The children exchanged glances, their minds whirring with questions and anticipation. The cryptex seemed to hum with potential, a tangible reminder of the adventure that awaited them.

"Take this," Headmaster Winters said, placing the cryptex into Sarah's outstretched hands. "And let the journey begin."

The cryptex felt heavy in Sarah's hands, its cold metal surface etched with intricate patterns that seemed to dance and weave around her fingers. She held it up to the light, watching as the dust motes swirled around the shadows it cast upon the floor.

"Look at these markings," she said, tracing a series of symbols that adorned the outer ring of the contraption. "Do you think they have anything to do with how we're supposed to open it?"

"Maybe," Charles replied, leaning in for a closer look. "But there must be thousands of them. It could take us years to figure out the right combination."

"Or just a few minutes," Henry countered, his eyes sparkling with excitement. "After all, Headmaster Winters said the clues are all around us. We just need to find them."

"Easy for him to say," Clarissa muttered, crossing her arms over her chest. "He's not the one who has to crack this thing open."

Their curiosity and confusion grew as the four friends continued to examine the cryptex. What secrets did it hold? And why had Headmaster Winters chosen them – of all people – to unlock its mysteries?

"Wait a minute," Sarah said suddenly, her eyes widening with realization. "Headmaster Winters said that what we're searching for can be found within the cryptex. What if he means... ourselves?"

"Like, a metaphor?" Charles asked, raising an eyebrow. "You think this is some sort of psychological exercise?"

"Perhaps," Sarah mused, her gaze thoughtful. "Or maybe it's more literal than that. Maybe what we're searching for is the key to understanding our own strengths and weaknesses."

"Interesting theory," Henry conceded, stroking his chin. "But how does that help us open the cryptex?"

"Good question," Clarissa agreed, her frustration mounting. "It's all well and good to talk about personal growth and self-discovery, but that doesn't get us any closer to solving this puzzle."

"Maybe we're overthinking it," Sarah suggested, her fingers absently tracing the grooves of the cryptex. "Headmaster Winters said the clues are all around us, right? Maybe we just need to take a step back and look at things from a different perspective."

"Or maybe we should sleep on it," Charles yawned, stretching his arms above his head. "I don't know about you guys, but I'm beat. We can pick this up again tomorrow with fresh eyes and clear heads."

"Sounds like a plan," Henry agreed, stifling a yawn of his own.

"Fine," Clarissa sighed, her shoulders slumping in defeat. "But we'd better get cracking first thing in the morning. I have a feeling there's more to this cryptex – and Headmaster Winters' challenge – than meets the eye."

As the friends left the headmaster's office, their minds still buzzing with questions and possibilities, they couldn't shake the feeling that they were embarking on a journey unlike any they had ever experienced before. And though they didn't yet understand the full scope of the adventure ahead, one thing was certain: the cryptex held the key to unlocking not only its secrets but the hidden potential within each of them.

"Guys," Sarah said, her eyes sparkling with excitement as she clutched the cryptex tightly. "Think about it. Headmaster Winters wouldn't have given this to us if it wasn't important. This could be the adventure of a lifetime!"

Henry's brows furrowed as he squinted at the mysterious object in Sarah's hands. The shadows cast by the lamplight outside of Mr. Winters's office building seemed to dance across its ancient surface, teasing him with hidden secrets and tempting promises.

"Sarah's right," Clarissa chimed in, her voice filled with determination. "We can't let this opportunity slip through our fingers. We've got to solve this cryptex and find out what lies within."

The friends exchanged charged glances, their hearts pounding with anticipation and nerves. Charles stepped forward, his previous exhaustion forgotten in the face of their newfound mission.

"Wait," Charles interrupted, his eyes darting between his friends and the door to Headmaster Winters' office. "We should do this somewhere else. We don't want to get caught snooping around in here."

"Agreed," Clarissa nodded. "Let's take this back to our dormitory. We can work on it there without any interruptions."

Gathering their belongings and carefully tucking the cryptex under Sarah's arm, the children stole one last glance at Headmaster Winters' office. The room seemed to hum with an energy that they had never noticed before as if the very air held whispers of secrets and stories untold.

As the friends stepped into the chilly night air, a gust of wind swirling around them like the fingers of fate beckoning them forward, they couldn't help but feel a mix of trepidation and exhilaration. They were on the precipice of something extraordinary, and there was no turning back now.

"Here's to the adventure of a lifetime," Charles murmured, his voice barely audible above the sound of their footsteps echoing down the dimly lit corridor.

"Alright then," he declared, cracking his knuckles for dramatic effect. "Let's get down to business."

As they gathered around the desk in the study room of their dormitory once more, poring over the cryptex with renewed enthusiasm, the children couldn't help but feel a sense of camaraderie and excitement that transcended their previous bickering. They were a team now, united in purpose and driven by the irresistible lure of adventure.

"Look," Henry said suddenly, his finger tracing a barely perceptible pattern on the cryptex's surface. "There's a series of symbols here, like some sort of code. Maybe that's our first clue."

"Good catch, Henry!" Sarah praised, leaning in for a closer look. "Let's see if we can decipher it."

"Indeed," Henry echoed, his eyes gleaming with excitement and anticipation. "I have a feeling we're in for quite the ride."

# CHAPTER 3

"Isn't it incredible?" Sarah murmured, turning the cryptex over in her hands, admiring the artistry and complexity of its design.

"Absolutely," agreed Henry, his excitement palpable. "I can hardly believe that Headmaster Winters entrusted us with something like this. It must be incredibly important."

"Whatever secrets it holds will surely guide us on our journey," said Clarissa, her face lit up with wonderment. "But how do we unlock it?"

After their clandestine meeting with Headmaster Archibald Winters, the children were left with a cryptex, an object that would lead them on a journey of a lifetime. The old man's eyes sparkled with mischief as he handed over the artifact, whispering about its significance and the great adventure that awaited them.

The cryptex itself was a marvel to behold. Made from ancient brass, it seemed to pulse with the weight of history in their hands. Intricate engravings of mythic creatures adorned its surface, each one seeming to come alive as they traced their fingers over the etchings. The cylindrical device was divided into several rotating rings, each featuring a myriad of letters that could be aligned to spell out a secret code. The skillful craftsmanship spoke of a bygone era, one where such puzzles were revered as sacred treasures.

"Headmaster Winters did mention that we'd have to work together to figure it out," reminded Charles, his voice tinged with apprehension. "He also said that it would require all of our strengths and skills."

As the children stared at the cryptex, their thoughts raced with possibilities, each one eager to contribute their talents and uncover the secrets within. They knew that this object held the key to their great adventure, and they couldn't wait to see what lay ahead.

"Let's put our heads together and give it our best shot," suggested Sarah, her eyes shining with determination. "We're a team, after all, and there's nothing we can't achieve when we work together."

"Right!" Henry agreed, his heart pounding with excitement. "Let's unlock the mysteries of the cryptex and embark on the journey that Headmaster Winters has set before us!"

With that, the children eagerly gathered around the cryptex, each one eager to play their part in solving the ancient puzzle, their anticipation building as they drew closer to unveiling its secrets and beginning their extraordinary adventure.

With the cryptex cradled in her hands, Sarah bit her lip nervously as she glanced around at her friends. Their eyes held a mix of determination and curiosity, all focused on the seemingly impenetrable object. The cryptex itself appeared ancient, with its weathered brass casing adorned with intricate engravings that seemed to dance and twist around the cylindrical body.

"Any ideas?" Clarissa asked, her fingers drumming against her thigh impatiently.

"Maybe it's a riddle we need to solve?" Charles suggested, his voice wavering slightly. "Or an anagram?"

"An anagram? That could be interesting," said Henry, rubbing his chin thoughtfully. "But where would we even begin?"

"Let's first try words that sound important or Latin," Sarah proposed, her heart pounding with excitement. "Like... 'Chronos' or 'Aeon.'"

"Good idea, Sarah!" encouraged Clarissa as the others nodded in agreement.

"Chronos" was entered first, and when the cryptex didn't open, Charles tried "Aeon" next. As each word failed to unlock the cryptex, the children exchanged looks of increasing concern, their initial excitement slowly being replaced by doubt.

"Any other suggestions?" Sarah asked, her voice barely above a whisper. She hated feeling so indecisive, but she knew that her friends were relying on her.

"Carpe Diem!" exclaimed Charles out of the blue, his bright eyes meeting Sarah's gaze. "It means 'seize the day' in Latin. It's worth a try."

"Carpe Diem," Sarah repeated softly, the words sending a shiver down her spine. She couldn't help but feel a deep connection to the phrase as if it held the key not just to the cryptex but also to unlocking her own courage.

"Go ahead, Sarah. Try it," urged Clarissa, her eyes alight with anticipation.

"Okay," Sarah agreed, taking a deep breath. Her hands

trembled slightly as she entered the letters C-A-R-P-E-D-I-E-M. The air seemed to crackle with energy, and as the final letter clicked into place, the cryptex emitted a soft but decisive click.

"Did it work?" Henry asked, his voice barely containing his excitement.

"Only one way to find out," said Sarah, her heart in her throat. With all eyes on her, she carefully twisted the two ends of the cryptex, holding her breath as she pulled them apart.

The moment the cryptex opened, a blinding light enveloped them, and their surroundings seemed to dissolve into nothingness. All at once, they were swept away by an invisible force, their bodies weightless and spinning through space. Sarah's heart raced as she felt herself being pulled apart and then stitched back together again, her very essence undergoing a metamorphosis she could hardly comprehend.

"Wha—what's happening?" gasped Charles, his voice barely audible over the roaring wind that tore through their ears.

Sarah's mind reeled, trying to process the impossible reality of what was happening to them. As the sensation of hurtling through the void intensified, she fought to hold onto her sense of self, her memories, and her connection to her friends.

"Stay close to me, Sarah," yelled Charles, reaching out his hand to grasp hers. "We'll get through this together."

"Charles... I'm scared," she confessed, her voice shaking as she clung to him for dear life.

"Me too," he admitted, his grip on her hand tightening. "But we're not alone. We have each other."

"Where do you think we'll end up?" asked Clarissa, her eyes squeezed shut against the dizzying whirlwind that surrounded them.

"Who knows?" replied Henry, a grim determination in his voice. "But wherever we are, we'll face it together."

As suddenly as it had begun, the maelstrom ceased, and they found themselves standing on solid ground once more. The abrupt shift left them breathless and disoriented, their senses struggling to adjust to their new environment.

"Is everyone okay?" asked Sarah, her heart pounding in her chest as she surveyed her friends, who all appeared to be relatively unharmed.

"Define 'okay,'" muttered Charles, rubbing his head in confusion. "I feel like I've been turned inside out and back again."

"Same here," agreed Henry, attempting to steady his wobbly legs.

"Where are we?" whispered Clarissa, her eyes wide with wonder as she took in the unfamiliar landscape that surrounded them.

"Or better yet, when are we?" added Charles, his voice tinged with both curiosity and trepidation.

"Only one way to find out," said Sarah, taking a deep breath and mustering every ounce of courage she possessed. "Let's explore this new world together and see what secrets it holds."

As they stepped forward into the unknown, their fears and

uncertainties were momentarily eclipsed by a shared sense of wonder and anticipation. Whatever awaited them in this strange land, they would face it together, united by friendship and the unbreakable bond forged in the crucible of time.

"Wait, what's happening?" gasped Sarah, her eyes wide as she took in the strange world around them. The air was thick with a mixture of woodsmoke and damp earth, and the sound of distant voices mingled with the clatter of wagon wheels on cobblestone streets. A sudden gust of wind carried the scent of fresh-baked bread and saltwater, teasing their senses and making their stomachs rumble in unison.

The air felt heavy, and the ground seemed to spin beneath their feet as the children blinked rapidly, trying to adjust to their new surroundings. They found themselves standing in the middle of a bustling cobblestone street, surrounded by people dressed in unfamiliar clothing and speaking with strange accents. The smell of horses and woodsmoke filled their nostrils while the cacophony of voices, footsteps, and the creaking of wooden carts threatened to overwhelm them.

"Where are we?" whispered Sarah, her eyes wide with a mix of fear and wonder.

"By the looks of it, we've gone back in time," Charles said cautiously, his voice filled with disbelief. "And by the smell, I'd say... colonial times?"

"Colonial Boston?" replied Sarah, her voice barely audible above the clamor. "But how did we get here?"

"Good guess," Clarissa murmured, her gaze fixed on a sign swinging above a nearby doorway. "'The Green Dragon Tavern,' that sounds familiar."

"Of course!" Henry exclaimed, excitement sparking in his eyes. "This is where the Sons of Liberty used to meet in Boston!"

"Are you saying we're in the middle of the American Revolution?" asked Clarissa, her voice barely audible.

"Seems like it," replied Charles, trying to maintain his composure. "But how are we supposed to survive here? We know nothing about this time or place!"

"More importantly," interjected Henry, his gaze darting around, "how do we blend in?"

"Let's just stick together and try to blend in," suggested Sarah, taking a deep breath to calm her racing heart. "We'll figure this out, I promise."

As they strolled toward the bustling town square, the children couldn't help but feel overwhelmed by the sheer intensity of the sights, sounds, and smells that assaulted them at every turn. Women in long, full skirts hurried past them, clutching baskets filled with produce from local markets, while men wearing tricorn hats engaged in animated discussions about politics and trade.

"Look at those clothes!" whispered Henry, staring in awe at a passing group of elegantly dressed men and women. "They're so... fancy."

"Focus, Henry," Charles reminded him. "We're here for a reason."

"Right," Henry mumbled, his cheeks flushing with

embarrassment.

"Guys, I think we should find someplace to hide while we figure out our next move," said Sarah, her voice filled with determination. "We can't just wander around like this; someone will notice us eventually."

"Agreed," Charles nodded, his eyes scanning the crowded square for any hint of danger or suspicion. "Let's head to the Green Dragon Tavern; it seems like our best option at the moment."

With their hearts pounding in their chests and their minds reeling from the sudden shift in time and place, the children made their way toward the tavern, hoping that they might find some answers within its walls. As they cautiously stepped through the doorway, they couldn't help but feel both terrified and exhilarated by the unknown world that lay before them and the challenges that awaited them in colonial Boston.

Sarah's heart raced as they entered the Green Dragon Tavern, its dimly lit interior offering a stark contrast to the bright, sunlit streets of colonial Boston. The air was thick with the aroma of roasted meats and pipe smoke, and she found herself coughing before her eyes adjusted to the haze.

"Where do we even start?" Clarissa whispered, her voice trembling with uncertainty. She clutched her skirts tightly as if they could anchor her in this unfamiliar world.

"Let's just find a table and sit down," Charles suggested, trying to maintain an air of confidence despite his own pounding heart. "We can talk about what we know so far."

As they settled into a corner booth, Henry leaned forward with furrowed brows, his voice barely audible above the murmur of the tavern's patrons. "So, we're really in the past? Like, actual colonial America?"

"Seems that way," Charles replied, nervously fidgeting with the cuffs of his shirt. "I mean, look at everything around us. It's like we stepped into a history book."

"Carpe Diem," Sarah whispered under her breath, recalling the phrase that had unlocked the cryptex. "Seize the day... but why here? Why now?"

"Maybe we're supposed to change something," Clarissa ventured, pushing her glasses up the bridge of her nose. "Or learn something important."

"Guys, I think we need to blend in as much as possible," Charles interjected, his gaze darting around the tavern. "That means figuring out what people do and say in this time period. We have to act like we belong here."

"Right," agreed Sarah, swallowing hard. "We don't want to draw attention to ourselves."

"Could you imagine the consequences if we messed up history?" Clarissa shuddered. "We have to be careful."

"Exactly," Charles nodded. "So let's try to learn as much as we can and keep a low profile."

"Agreed," the others chimed in, their determination growing with each exchange of words.

As they sat there, huddled together in the dimly lit corner of the Green Dragon Tavern, Sarah couldn't help but feel a thrill of excitement mixed with dread. They were truly in uncharted territory, and every decision they made could alter the course of history. But despite the overwhelming gravity of their situation, there was also a sense of camaraderie that bound them together, a shared determination to navigate this unfamiliar world and uncover the secrets that lay hidden within its depths.

"Alright, then," Charles said, leaning back in his seat with a steely look in his eyes. "Let's make the most of this journey and see what destiny has in store for us."

"Still, it feels like we're walking on a tightrope," Henry muttered, his eyes scanning the bustling street outside. "One wrong move, and everything could come crashing down."

The group's disorientation was palpable, with each individual attempting to recalibrate their senses to the unfamiliar sounds and smells of colonial Boston.

"Remember, it's about adapting," Charles said, trying to reassure himself as much as the others. "We'll find our footing soon enough."

"Look!" Sarah exclaimed, pointing at a passing group of children playing with a wooden hoop and stick. "Life back then must have been so simple." Her voice wavered, betraying her anxiety.

Clarissa adjusted her glasses and glanced around nervously. "It's strange, isn't it? Like stepping into a painting. I can hardly believe we're really here."

"Neither can I," admitted Charles, his confident demeanor

betraying a hint of vulnerability. "But we'll get through this together."

"Right," agreed Henry, rolling up his sleeves. "Let's start by asking around. We need to know who's who in this town."

As they sat there, feeling lost and out of place, a tall, distinguished gentleman in his late 30s approached them. His hair was neatly tied back, and his strong jawline framed a face that radiated warmth and intelligence.

"Good day, children," he said, his voice kind and soothing. "You seem lost. Can I be of assistance?"

"Who are you?" asked Sarah cautiously, studying the man's face.

"Dr. Joseph Warren, at your service." He extended his hand towards her. "I am a physician here in Boston."

Something about Dr. Warren's demeanor put the children at ease. It was as if his compassionate nature and dedication to others created an aura of trust and safety around him.

"Thank you, Dr. Warren," Sarah said, grasping his outstretched hand. "We would be grateful for your guidance."

"Let's start with proper attire," Dr. Warren suggested, steering the children out of the tavern and towards a tailor's shop adorned with colorful bolts of fabric. "You seem to be wearing clothes from... out of town, and to put it frankly, you stick out like a sore thumb. Let's fix that, follow me."

As they followed Dr. Warren through the crowded streets of colonial Boston, the children couldn't help but feel a sense of awe wash over them.

As they ventured further into the heart of the city, Sarah found herself captivated by the sights and sounds surrounding them. She marveled at the horse-drawn carriages that clattered along cobblestone streets, the vendors hawking their wares, and the women in bonnets gossiping outside shops.

Dr. Warren led the children into a small, dimly lit tailor's shop. The scent of beeswax candles and fresh fabric filled their nostrils as they gazed in wonder at the rows of colonial attire lining the walls.

"Wow, look at all these clothes!" Sarah exclaimed, her fingertips brushing over intricate lace and embroidered silk. "They're so different from what we're used to."

"Indeed," Dr. Warren replied, selecting a few items for each child as he explained the significance of various garments. "Men typically wear breeches, waistcoats, and tricorn hats, while women don dresses with petticoats, stays, and caps. You'll find that clothing serves not only a practical purpose but also reflects one's social status."

"Ah, Mr. Thompson," Dr. Warren greeted the shopkeeper with a warm smile. "I have a few young friends here in need of clothing befitting our town."

"Of course, Dr. Warren," Mr. Thompson replied, quickly taking measurements of the children. As they were fitted for their new garments, Dr. Warren began to explain the delicate state of affairs in colonial America, then stopped abruptly. "Actually, I think it would be best to fill you in on the goings-on from a place that might have less prying eyes and ears." "I dare say, Dr. Warren, my shop surely shouldn't be on your list," Mr. Thompson began, but then Dr. Warren cut in, "Now, Mr. Thompson, I meant no disrespect; it isn't for you or your shop. I am concerned about the heightened danger we live in, and I just want to take the children's safety into consideration." Mr. Thompson seemed appeased by the doctor's words and continued his work.

"Now, Mr. Thompson will house you all for the night; he is a good man, and you can trust him, and in the morning, I wish for you to join me in a little work of mine. Meet me in my office after you break your fast, and I will fill you in there. Mr. Thompson knows where it is; in the meantime, be on your guard, and of course, welcome to Boston!" Dr. Warren finished as he headed out the door and into the street.

Mr. Thompson fitted them with their new clothes and told them to be back before sundown and to stay out of trouble but that they were welcome to explore the town. As the group dispersed, Sarah felt her heart race with anticipation. There was still so much to learn about colonial Boston and their role within it. But as dangerous as their situation was, she couldn't help but feel the thrill of excitement coursing through her veins.

As the children tried on their new outfits, they couldn't help but marvel at how they transformed into colonial-era children before their very eyes.

"Look at us!" Charles said, adjusting his tricorn hat with a grin. "We fit right in!"

"Listen up, everyone," Charles instructed, pulling their attention back to the task at hand. "We've got to figure out how to blend in and learn more about this time period."

"Be careful how you phrase your questions," Clarissa warned. "We don't want to arouse suspicion."

"Got it," Henry replied with a determined nod.

"Alright, then," Charles whispered to himself, steeling his resolve. "Let's uncover the secrets this city holds and find our way back home."

With each step they took into the past, the children found themselves increasingly captivated by the mysteries that lay ahead. As they delved deeper into the world of colonial Boston, the threads of history began to intertwine, leading them on a journey they could never have anticipated.

# CHAPTER 4

Only a day had passed since Sarah, Charles, Clarissa, and Henry arrived in colonial Boston through the mysterious doorway of time. The city bustled with life as they quickly adapted to their new environment. But their journey into the past was about to take a darker turn.

"Are you sure this is where we're supposed to be?" Sarah whispered, her eyes darting around the dimly lit room. The space was small and cramped, with shelves lined with jars filled with unknown substances and ancient-looking medical instruments.

"Dr. Warren said to meet him here," Charles replied, trying to sound confident. Clarissa nodded, her gaze fixed on the unusual scene before them.

The children watched as Dr. Joseph Warren, a respected physician and revolutionary leader, stood over a cold, lifeless body. The young boy's face was pale, his eyes closed in eternal slumber. It was hard for them to believe that he was only a few years younger than they were. He had been killed by a British customs officer in a tragic act of violence. The injustice of it all sent shivers down their spines.

"Forgive me for the unsettling sight," Dr. Warren said, acknowledging the children's unease. "But this autopsy is crucial in our search for justice." His voice was firm with determination yet gentle enough to calm some of their fears.

Sarah blinked away her shock, steadying herself as she took in the gruesome scene. Dr. Warren carefully made an incision, his expert hands moving with precision. The gleam of the surgical blade caught the faint glow from the flickering candles, sending a shiver down her spine. The scent of blood, slightly metallic and overwhelmingly heavy, hung in the air like a dark cloud.

"Doctor, why did this have to happen?" Henry blurted out, unable to contain his curiosity any longer. The question echoed in the room, bringing a hush over the other whispered conversations.

"Ah, young Henry," Dr. Warren began, pausing his work momentarily to look at the boy. "This is the sad reality of life in the colonies under British rule. Tensions have been growing for years, and innocent lives are often caught in the crossfire."

"Can't we do something?" Charles asked, his voice barely audible as he clenched his fists in anger.

"Of course, my boy," Dr. Warren replied with a gentle smile. "That's why you're here, after all. Providence has brought you here for a purpose, and I believe it's to help us in our fight for independence."

The children exchanged glances, their initial skepticism slowly melting away as they listened to Dr. Warren's passionate words. They could see that this man truly cared about the cause – and about them.

"Will you teach us, Dr. Warren?" Sarah finally asked, her voice quivering with emotion. "Will you help us make a difference?"

"Indeed, I will," Dr. Warren promised, his eyes full of warmth and determination. The flickering candles cast a soft glow on his face, making him appear even more resolute. "Together, we'll stand up against tyranny and injustice. And together, we'll make history."

The somber atmosphere of the room pressed down on Sarah and her companions like a heavy fog, the flickering candlelight casting eerie shadows on the walls. The air was thick with tension and anticipation, as if the very room held its breath, waiting for something momentous to occur.

In the midst of this charged atmosphere stood Dr. Joseph Warren, a tall, distinguished gentleman in his late 30s. His dark hair was swept back from his strong jawline, and his eyes burned with the fire of unyielding determination. He seemed to be a beacon of hope in this grim setting, a man who carried the weight of their cause on his broad shoulders.

"Dr. Warren?" Sarah ventured hesitantly, her voice breaking the heavy silence. "What happens now?"

He looked at her with a reassuring smile, his gaze steady and comforting. "Now, we begin the journey that will change the course of history," he said softly, the conviction in his voice unmistakable. "We'll learn together, grow together, and fight for our freedom together."

A newfound sense of purpose surged through Sarah and her friends, their hearts swelling with pride and courage. As they stood beside Dr. Warren in that dimly lit room, they knew that they were no longer merely children lost in time — they were a part of something much greater, a force that would shape the fate of a nation.

The children huddled closer together, their eyes wide with a mix of wonder and fear as they watched Dr. Warren work on the lifeless body before him. They had never seen anything like this before, and their curiosity warred with the gnawing uneasiness that settled in their stomachs.

"Is he...?" whispered Clarissa, her voice barely audible as she trailed off, unable to finish her question.

"Dead? Yes," Dr. Warren answered softly, not looking up from his task. "But by examining him, we can learn more about what happened and perhaps even prevent it from happening again."

Despite their unease, the children leaned in closer, drawn by the macabre fascination of witnessing something so far beyond their realm of experience. They whispered among themselves, sharing theories and asking questions in hushed tones, their voices barely audible above the rustle of Dr. Warren's clothing as he moved around the table.

"See here," Dr. Warren said, pointing to a particular wound on the young boy's body. "This tells us something important about the weapon used, which could lead us to the perpetrator."

The children exchanged glances, their curiosity piqued by this new piece of information. Each of them felt a growing sense of determination, driven by the desire to uncover the truth behind the boy's tragic death and to bring those responsible to justice.

Dr. Warren's deft hands moved with precision over the boy's body, his fingers tracing the edges of each bruise and laceration as he explained their significance. He was not only skilled in his craft but also compassionate and understanding, treating the lifeless body before him with the utmost dignity and care. The room was filled with tension, the children holding their breaths, trying to make sense of the morbid scene before them.

"Notice how the angle of this cut shows that the attacker was right-handed," Dr. Warren said, his voice low and steady. "And this bruise here," he continued, pointing to a dark purple mark on the boy's torso, "indicates that a heavy object was used to strike him with great force."

The children leaned in closer, eyes never leaving the doctor's skilled movements. Sarah bit her lip, her thoughts racing. "But why would someone do this?" she asked, her voice barely audible.

Dr. Warren paused in his examination, looking up at Sarah. His gaze was gentle yet held a somber weight. "I wish I could tell you, my dear," he said softly, "but human nature can be cruel and unpredictable. What we can do, however, is use our knowledge to bring justice to those who have been wronged."

"Can we really make a difference?" Clarissa chimed in, her brow furrowed with concern.

"Absolutely," Dr. Warren replied, his eyes sparking with determination. "By understanding what happened to this young boy, we may be able to prevent similar tragedies in the future."

As the doctor continued his work, the children couldn't help but feel inspired by his unwavering commitment to uncovering the truth. Each meticulous observation, each careful note taken, fueled their own desire to learn and contribute to the cause.

"Remember," Dr. Warren said, looking at each child in turn,

"knowledge is power. And with power comes responsibility. It is our duty to use what we know to protect others and ensure that justice prevails."

As the candlelight flickered around them, casting shadows that danced on the walls, the children felt an unspoken bond forming between them and Dr. Warren. They were united by their shared hope for a better future and the determination to fight for it, no matter the cost.

Sarah bit her lip, casting a sidelong glance at Charles before hesitantly asking, "Dr. Warren, how do we know that you're truly on our side? We've only just met you, and we've been through so much already."

"Ah," Dr. Warren paused in his work, setting down the scalpel and wiping his hands on a cloth. "A fair question, my dear. I cannot expect your trust to be given freely, especially in these uncertain times."

He turned to regard them, his eyes filled with understanding. "Let me tell you a bit about what's happening here in the colonies; perhaps that will help you see where my loyalties lie."

"Go on," Sarah replied, folding her arms across her chest but leaning in slightly, curiosity piqued.

"Very well." Dr. Warren cleared his throat, adjusting his spectacles as he began to explain. "The British authorities have imposed unjust taxes upon us, colonists, without allowing us any representation in their government. This has fueled tensions between our people and the British crown."

Charles frowned, narrowing his eyes. "But why would they do

that? Isn't it better to keep everyone happy?"

"Indeed," Dr. Warren agreed, nodding solemnly. "But power and greed often cloud judgment, my boy. The British see the colonies as a source of wealth to exploit, not as fellow citizens deserving of equal rights."

As the children digested this information, their minds raced with questions. They knew they had to be cautious, but the doctor's words stirred something within them. Could they really trust him? Their thoughts tumbled like leaves caught in a whirlwind, seeking a place to land.

"Dr. Warren," Clarissa finally said, her voice quivering ever so slightly, "how can we be sure that helping you won't put us in even greater danger?"

"Nothing worthwhile comes without risk, Clarissa," he replied gently. "But I promise you, the cause we fight for is just, and I will do everything in my power to keep you safe."

"Alright," Henry conceded, his expression softening. "We'll help you, but we're still not sure about all of this."

"I understand," Dr. Warren said, a warm smile gracing his features. "In time, I hope to earn your trust completely. For now, let's focus on learning all we can and standing up for what's right."

As they listened to Dr. Warren speak with such conviction, the children felt something shift within them. It was as if the walls they had built around their hearts were beginning to crumble, allowing a small, flickering flame of hope to take hold.

"Trust is earned," Sarah thought to herself, watching the

doctor's face intently, "and perhaps, in time, we'll find that in Dr. Warren."

"Look here," Dr. Warren said, gesturing for the children to come closer. The group exchanged glances before stepping forward, curiosity winning over their lingering doubts.

Dr. Warren pointed at the small notebook he had been writing in, filled with detailed observations from the autopsy. "We must present this evidence to the people to show them the British customs officer's wrongdoing."

Sarah bit her lip, her eyes scanning the meticulous notes. Her heart swelled with admiration for Dr. Warren's dedication to finding justice for the young boy. His commitment to the cause of American independence was undeniable.

"Dr. Warren, you're truly doing everything you can for him, aren't you?" Clarissa asked, her voice tinged with a newfound respect.

"Indeed, Clarissa. It is our duty to stand up against tyranny and injustice," he replied, his eyes meeting hers with genuine warmth.

"Right," Henry chimed in, his tone reflecting his growing trust in the doctor. "If we don't stand up for what's right, who will?"

"Exactly, my young friend," Dr. Warren said, nodding approvingly. "Now, I believe it's time for us to move forward together as allies in the fight for freedom."

He rolled up the notebook and tucked it securely into his coat pocket, then turned to face the children. In the dim candlelight, determination burned in his eyes, igniting a sense of excitement and anticipation within them all.

"From now on, consider yourselves under my guidance. I promise to teach you all I know and help you navigate this new world that's unfolding before us."

"Thank you, Dr. Warren," Sarah replied, her chest swelling with pride and newfound purpose.

"Thank you, sir," echoed Charles, his previous skepticism melting away in the face of Dr. Warren's unwavering conviction.

"Let us forge ahead, my young friends," Dr. Warren declared, clapping his hands together with a sense of purpose and urgency. "There's much to be done, and time is of the essence."

As they followed Dr. Warren out of the dimly lit room, the children felt the weight of their new responsibilities settle upon their shoulders. But alongside it, a spark of excitement flickered in their hearts, fueled by the knowledge that they were no longer alone in their fight for justice and freedom.

# CHAPTER 5

"Presently, we are experiencing a great deal of tension between the American colonies and the British government," Dr. Warren said, his voice both engaging and charismatic. "Many colonists, myself included, feel that we are unfairly taxed and burdened by the Crown without any representation."

Sarah furrowed her brow in curiosity. "But why would the British do such a thing? Aren't we all on the same side?"

"An excellent question, my dear," Dr. Warren responded, his eyes twinkling with pride. "While it is true that we share many commonalities with our British brethren, the Crown has grown increasingly oppressive in its attempts to maintain control over the colonies. It is this very struggle for freedom and independence that drives us forward."

As Sarah and Charles exchanged glances, they could feel their hearts swelling with awe and respect for Dr. Warren and the cause he championed. In this unfamiliar world, they found themselves eager to learn more about the events unfolding around them.

"Dr. Warren," Charles piped up hesitantly. "Do you believe that there will be...well, a war?"

"War is never a desirable outcome, young Benjamin," Dr. Warren replied solemnly. "But it may prove necessary if we are to secure our liberties and protect the future of these colonies."

"Then we want to help," Clarissa declared with determination, her eyes meeting Dr. Warren's. "We may not understand everything that's happening, but we're willing to learn and do whatever it takes to make a difference."

"Your passion is both admirable and inspiring," Dr. Warren said, placing a hand on each of their shoulders. "Together, we shall navigate these tumultuous times and strive for a brighter tomorrow."

Under Dr. Warren's tutelage, they knew they would grow and adapt to this strange, new world - and perhaps even play a small part in shaping history itself.

"Come, children," Dr. Warren beckoned as they stepped out into the crowded streets of colonial Boston. "There are some people I would like you to meet."

The cobbled streets were filled with a cacophony of voices, smells, and sights that left the young time travelers in a state of sensory overload. As they followed Dr. Warren through the bustling town, they could not help but feel both exhilarated and intimidated by the world unfolding before them.

"Ah, here we are," Dr. Warren announced as they approached a group of men gathered outside a local tavern. Among them stood two individuals who commanded an air of authority that each one of the children's attention. One was a tall, handsome man with wavy brown hair, while the other was a middle-aged man with graying hair and piercing eyes.

"Allow me to introduce Mr. John Hancock and Mr. Samuel Adams," Dr. Warren said, gesturing towards the two men. "Both are prominent figures in our community and play significant roles in the fight for American independence."

"Mr. Hancock, Mr. Adams," Henry stammered, offering a

shaky hand to each of the men. "It is an honor to meet you."

"Likewise, young man," John Hancock replied with a warm smile, grasping Ben's hand firmly. "Dr. Warren tells us you children are eager to learn about our cause."

"Indeed we are," Clarissa chimed in, feeling a sense of awe wash over her as she shook hands with these historical giants. "We may be from...a different place, but we share your desire for freedom and independence."

"Such determination in one so young is commendable," Samuel Adams responded, his sharp eyes seeming to appraise the sincerity behind Clarissa's words. "Our struggle is not an easy one, but it is crucial if we are to protect the rights and liberties of our people."

As the conversation unfolded, the children each were captivated by the palpable sense of purpose that seemed to radiate from these men. The gravity of their mission began to sink in, and they felt a newfound determination to play their part in shaping history.

"Mr. Adams," Clarissa asked, her curiosity piqued, "what do you believe is the most important thing for us to understand about your cause?"

"Perseverance, young lady," he replied firmly. "This fight will not be won overnight. It requires patience, dedication, and an unwavering commitment to our principles."

As they listened to the passionate words of John Hancock and Samuel Adams, the young children knew they had much to learn from these remarkable figures. The weight of their responsibility was now clearer than ever before, and they resolved to face the challenges of their journey with courage and determination. With their hearts swelling with inspiration, the young time travelers eagerly embraced the opportunity to become a part of this pivotal moment in history.

With each step on the uneven cobblestone roads, they felt as though they were walking through the pages of a history book come to life. Horse-drawn carriages clattered by, their wheels crunching over the stones, while street vendors hawked their wares with boisterous enthusiasm. The air was filled with the aroma of freshly baked bread and the tangy scent of sea air, mingling with the earthy smell of hay from the nearby stables.

"Isn't this amazing?" Charles whispered to Sarah, his eyes wide with wonder as they took in the scene around them. "We're really here, in the middle of the revolution!"

"Indeed, we are in the thick of something changing if we can only get the rest of the colonies to understand that as quickly as you have," Dr. Warren agreed, leading the children down one of the narrow alleyways that branched off from the main thoroughfare. "But remember, our purpose here is not just to observe – we must learn from it and find ways to contribute to the cause."

"Dr. Warren," Clarissa said hesitantly, adjusting her glasses as she glanced around at the unfamiliar sights, "how do we know where to begin?"

"By asking questions and listening," Dr. Warren replied, his voice firm yet gentle. "The people you meet here will have much to teach you about their lives, their struggles, and their dreams for the future."

As they walked through the city, the atmosphere of tension and rebellion grew more palpable. They passed groups of men huddled together in a heated discussion, murmurs of discontent rising like a wave above the noise of the crowd. Clearly, the fight for independence was still an abstract idea or a distant goal. The people were working it all out in the open and in the streets through passionate dialog and arguments, but it is a real and present struggle for Boston's people if not fully realized.

"Can we really make a difference here?" Henry asked, his brow furrowed in thought. "We're just kids."

"Never underestimate the power of youth and determination," Dr. Warren said with a smile, placing a reassuring hand on Henry's shoulder. "You have a unique perspective and energy that can be harnessed for the cause."

"Besides," added Samuel Adams, who had joined their group as they continued exploring the city, "many young people are involved in the fight for freedom. It is our duty to inspire and educate the next generation so that they may continue our work."

As the children listened to the words of their mentors, they felt a renewed sense of purpose and resolve. They knew they had much to learn about the complex political and social landscape of colonial America, but they were eager to dive headfirst into this new world and do whatever they could to support the struggle for independence.

"I'm ready to learn everything I can about this place," Sarah declared, her blue eyes shining with determination. "And then, we'll find a way to help."

"Me too," agreed Charles, his confident demeanor returning as he squared his shoulders. "Let's get to work."

Dr. Warren led the children into a bustling marketplace, where merchants called out their wares and shoppers bartered for goods. The scent of freshly baked bread and roasting meat filled the air, making their stomachs rumble with hunger.

"Next on our list: food and dining etiquette," Dr. Warren announced, guiding them toward a nearby tavern. Inside, the warm glow of candles and the aroma of hearty fare enveloped them.

"Remember, always use your knife and fork when eating," Dr. Warren instructed, demonstrating the proper technique. "And never speak with your mouth full. Manners are important in polite society."

"I can do that!" Henry declared, eagerly digging into a steaming bowl of stew. "Mmm, this is delicious!"

"Agreed," Sarah added, savoring a bite of warm bread. "I've never tasted anything like it!"

"Food in town is quite different from what you're accustomed to, wherever that is," Dr. Warren explained between bites. "We rely on local artisans, if you will, who came from all over New England from their rural townships to grace us with their talent, so you know you're truly getting the best."

As the evening wore on, the children soaked up everything Dr. Warren taught them about colonial customs and norms. They practiced their curtsies and bows, learned to address their elders with respect, and even picked up a few phrases of colonial slang.

"By Jove, I think they've got it!" Dr. Warren declared, beaming with pride as he watched his young charges confidently navigate their new surroundings.

"Thanks to you!" Clarissa said, eyes shining with gratitude. "We couldn't have done it without your guidance, Dr. Warren."

"Indeed," Charles chimed in, his tricorn hat now perched jauntily on his head. "We're ready for whatever comes our way!"

"We'll make a difference, just like you said," Henry added, clapping Dr. Warren on the back. "Together, we'll make history!"

Dr. Warren led Sarah, Charles, Henry, and Clarissa through the cobblestone lanes, pointing out landmarks and sharing tales from the city's rich history.

"Over there," he gestured towards a grand red-brick building, "is Faneuil Hall, where many important meetings have taken place. It's often referred to as the 'Cradle of Liberty.'"

"Remarkable," Clarissa breathed, adjusting her glasses, her eyes scanning every detail of the architecture with rapt attention. "And to think we're walking on the very same stones as our founding fathers!"

"Indeed," Dr. Warren replied, beaming at her enthusiasm. He turned to Charles, who was carefully inspecting a curious-looking device in a shop window. "Charles, do you know what this is?"

"Um," Charles hesitated, furrowing his brow. "A... spinning wheel?"

"Close!" Dr. Warren chuckled. "It's a printing press! Quite revolutionary for its time."

"Wow," Charles said, his eyes widening in admiration. "So that's how newspapers and pamphlets were made back then!"

"Exactly, though I am not sure what you mean by back then, I assure you it is top of its class in technology." Dr. Warren nodded, pleased with their interest. "Now, come along. There's much more to see."

"Dr. Warren," Henry asked as they strolled along the harbor, watching ships unload their cargo, "how did you become involved in the fight for independence?"

"An excellent question," Dr. Warren replied, pausing to collect his thoughts. "For me, it was a gradual process. As a physician, I saw firsthand the suffering caused by unjust laws and heavy taxation. I realized that change was necessary, and I chose to use my skills and influence to make a difference."

"Like you're making a difference for us," Sarah interjected softly. "You're teaching us so much, Dr. Warren."

"Thank you, Sarah," he smiled warmly. "It's been a pleasure guiding you all on this journey."

"Speaking of journeys," Charles piped up, grinning mischievously at Henry, "we should probably start practicing our colonial accents, right? We don't want to stick out like sore thumbs!"

"Capital idea!" Dr. Warren agreed, chuckling at their antics. "You do sound as though you have just come into the city from some far-off farm somewhere.'"

"Ahem," Henry cleared his throat dramatically, adopting an exaggerated accent. "Prithee, good sir, might thou direct me towards the nearest apothecary?"

"Bravo!" Sarah clapped, laughing as her companions joined in the merriment.

"Very well done, Henry," Dr. Warren praised, his eyes twinkling with amusement. "With a bit more practice, you'll fit right in!"

"Dr. Warren," Sarah said earnestly, once the laughter died down, "we trust you completely. You've brought this world to life for us and shown us how important it is to fight for freedom. We won't let you down."

"Nor I, you," Dr. Warren replied, his voice filled with conviction. "Together, we will stand strong in the face of adversity, and we shall prevail."

The children stood at the town square with Dr. Warren, their eyes wide as they took in the sights and sounds around them. The infectious energy of the city buzzed in the air, mingling with the excitement that coursed through each of them.

"Remember," Dr. Warren said gently, placing a hand on Sarah's shoulder, "everything you've learned here will help you on your journey through life. Trust yourselves and trust each other."

"Thank you, Dr. Warren," Charles said, his voice filled with determination. "We won't forget everything you've taught us."

"Nor will we forget you," Clarissa added softly, her eyes shining with gratitude.

"Indeed," Henry chimed in, puffing out his chest. "We shall remain steadfast in our mission! For freedom!"

"Very eloquent, Henry," Dr. Warren chuckled, ruffling his hair playfully. "But perhaps save the dramatics for when we're not surrounded by townsfolk."

"Of course," Henry grinned sheepishly, rubbing the back of his neck. "Sorry, couldn't resist."

"Your enthusiasm is commendable," Dr. Warren told him warmly. "Just remember to channel it wisely."

"Speaking of which," Clarissa mused aloud, adjusting her glasses, "we should review the key points of what we've learned so far."

"Excellent idea, Clarissa," Dr. Warren agreed. "Let's see...first, we must always remember the significance of unity in the fight for independence—"

"Right!" Sarah interjected. "Like how John Hancock and Samuel Adams worked together despite their differences."

"Exactly," Dr. Warren nodded, smiling at her. "And the importance of perseverance in the face of adversity—"

"Like Samuel Adams said with his Sons of Liberty!" Henry exclaimed, his eyes alight with excitement.

"Very good, Henry," Dr. Warren praised. "And finally, the power of knowledge and understanding in times of turmoil—"

"Which is what you've given us," Charles said resolutely, clapping Dr. Warren on the back. "We won't let you or the cause down, I promise."

"Thank you, Charles," Dr. Warren replied, his eyes glistening with pride. "Now, we must prepare for our next steps. Remember to always stay true to your convictions, and never lose sight of the greater good."

"Dr. Warren," Sarah whispered, her voice quivering with emotion, "we'll make you proud. We'll do everything we can to help ensure a better future for everyone in this land."

"Sarah, my dear," Dr. Warren said, his voice thick with emotion as he embraced her, "you already have."

With renewed determination etched upon their faces, the children stood tall beside Dr. Warren, their hearts swelling with pride and purpose. As they looked out at the bustling streets of Boston, it was clear that their journey had only just begun.

Just then, a loud whirring sounded, the cryptex started spinning, and a great light emanated from within. A similar portal opened behind the children, and they were taken away again into the vortex without another sound; their last vision was of Dr. Warren walking off into the distance down the streets of Boston.

# CHAPTER 6

They were now transported to Boston again, but at a new point in time, a few years later. They looked around and saw the same office of Dr Warren and decided to go in. The cold, damp air hung over the hidden room like a heavy blanket as four children huddled around Dr. Joseph Warren in his office. The flickering candlelight cast shadows on their young faces, making them appear much older and more sardonic than their years.

"Listen carefully," Dr. Warren began in a hushed tone as though he hadn't missed a beat with them. "This message you are about to deliver is of utmost importance. A man named Paul Revere must receive it before nightfall, or the struggle for our independence may be altered forever. Do you know who he is?"

"Paul Revere? Like... the Paul Revere?" Charles gasped, his eyes widening with awe.

"Indeed, it seems his reputation precedes him; of course, that would be no surprise to him," Dr. Warren chuckled, his eyes twinkling with amusement.

An involuntary shiver ran through Sarah's spine as her heart raced with a mixture of fear and excitement. She glanced at her companions, who stared wide-eyed at Dr. Warren, hanging onto his every word. The tension in the room was palpable; even the slightest creak of the wooden floorboards seemed to echo loudly in the confined space.

"Remember," Dr. Warren continued, "you must remain inconspicuous and trust no one. This mission is not only essential for our cause but also dangerous. You have been chosen because

I believe in your courage, intelligence, and resourcefulness."

"Thank you, Dr. Warren," Clarissa replied, her voice barely a whisper yet filled with determination. "We won't let you down."

Sarah squeezed Clarissa's hand, feeling her friend's nerves mirrored in her own trembling fingers. She knew they were all putting on brave faces, but beneath the surface, they were terrified. Yet, this fear did nothing to quell their desire to help shape the future of their country.

"Is everyone clear on what they must do?" Dr. Warren asked, scanning each child's face for any signs of doubt.

They nodded in unison, their expressions resolute. Sarah couldn't help but feel inspired by Dr. Warren's unwavering faith in them. He saw something special in each of them, and she was determined not to disappoint him.

"Very well, then," Dr. Warren said, his eyes lingering on Sarah for a moment longer than the rest. "I trust you completely. Now, go and deliver the message to Paul Revere. Good luck, and may Providence guide your steps."

As the children prepared to leave the safety of the hidden room, Sarah drew in a deep breath, her lungs filling with the musty air. The weight of their mission pressed down on her like a heavy stone, but she knew that there was no turning back now. For better or worse, they were setting out on an adventure that would change not only their lives but the course of history itself.

"Remember," Dr. Warren whispered as he handed Sarah the sealed envelope, his dark eyes locked onto hers, "the fate of many rests within this message. Keep it safe and hidden until you reach Paul Revere."

Sarah felt her palms grow sweaty as she clutched the envelope, knowing the weight of the responsibility that had just been placed upon her and her young companions. The other children looked at her with a mix of admiration and concern, but she could see the determination in their eyes. They would not fail.

"Trust in yourselves, and trust in each other," Dr. Warren said softly, giving them a slight nod. "Now, go."

As Sarah stepped out of the hidden room, followed closely by the others, she blinked, adjusting to the sunlight that streamed through the cracks in the wooden shutters. She peered out into the bustling streets of Boston, taking in the sight of people scurrying about, utterly oblivious to the secret mission they were about to undertake.

"Are you ready?" Sarah whispered to her friends as they huddled together in the dimly lit corner, each one feeling the thrill of anticipation mingling with the fear of being discovered.

"Ready as we'll ever be," Charles replied, his voice wavering only slightly.

"Let's do this," Clarissa added, her chin lifted defiantly.

Sarah nodded, her heart pounding in her chest as she led her group out onto the cobblestone streets. The city was alive with activity, horses, and carriages rolling past, and the sounds of merchants calling out their wares filled the air. The aroma of freshly baked bread wafted from a nearby bakery, tempting Sarah's rumbling stomach even as she focused on the task before them.

"Stay close, and remember what Dr. Warren said," Sarah thought to herself, glancing back at her band of young patriots who followed her lead. "We must trust in each other."

"Stay vigilant," she whispered, her eyes darting around the crowd, searching for any sign of danger. The envelope seemed to burn a hole in her pocket, a constant reminder of the importance of their mission.

As they moved through the throng of people, Sarah couldn't help but marvel at the bravery and determination that had brought them all together. They were just children, yet they carried the weight of a nation's future on their small shoulders. As they pressed forward, one step closer to Samuel Adams, she felt her resolve strengthen, knowing they would not let Dr. Warren or their country down.

As Sarah and her companions stepped further into the crowded streets, the lively chatter of Bostonians enveloped them like a warm embrace. Yet underneath it all, an undercurrent of tension simmered, palpable in the air as wisps of unease.

"Keep your wits about you," Charles whispered, his eyes scanning the crowd with a furrowed brow. His hand brushed against Sarah's reassuringly, a silent reminder that they were in this together.

"Right," Sarah murmured, swallowing the lump in her throat. She drew in a deep breath, the scent of salt from the harbor mingling with the aroma of spices from the open market stalls. The clamor of voices and footsteps seemed to echo inside her head, amplifying her sense of urgency.

"Look!" Clarissa suddenly hissed, her voice barely audible above the din.

Sarah followed her gaze to see a group of British soldiers marching down the street, their red coats striking a stark contrast against the dusty cobblestones. The sight sent a shiver down her spine; the threat they posed was now more real than ever.

"Stick to the plan," Henry muttered, his jaw clenched tight as he watched the soldiers pass by. "We can't afford any mistakes."

"Agreed," Clarissa added, her green eyes flickering with determination. "We'll blend in with the crowd and make our way to Paul Revere as discreetly as possible."

"Remember," Sarah thought, her heart pounding in her ears, "we are the hope for our nation's future." Her fingers tightened around the sealed envelope hidden within her pocket, its contents holding the key to their success.

"Let's move," Charles said, giving her a nod. A silent understanding passed between them, a wordless promise to protect one another at all costs.

With every step they took, the children felt the weight of their mission bear down upon them. Yet, despite their fear, they pressed on, moving as one through the bustling streets of Boston, their eyes trained on the horizon and the unknown dangers that lay ahead.

"Wait!" Sarah whispered suddenly, her heightened senses picking up on something amiss. The other children froze in their tracks, turning to look at her questioningly.

"Did you hear that?" she asked, her voice barely audible as her gaze darted around the crowd, searching for any hint of trouble.

"Stay close," Charles urged, his hand closing around hers. Their fingers intertwined, a lifeline connecting them amidst the sea of uncertainty.

"Trust," Sarah repeated to herself, drawing strength from her friends' unwavering resolve. "We've come this far together, and together, we'll see it through to the end."

And with that, they continued onward, the looming presence of the British soldiers a constant reminder of the stakes at hand - the future of their nation resting on the shoulders of these brave and determined young souls.

Despite the beauty of the setting sun, the children couldn't shake the sense of danger lurking around every corner. With British soldiers patrolling nearby, their hearts pounded like drums in their chests.

"Quick, this way!" whispered Charles, gesturing for the others to follow him down a side street. The narrow path was less crowded, but the sight of two men in dark clothing leaning against a wall with suspicious expressions raised alarm bells in Sarah's mind.

"Charles," she whispered urgently, tugging at his sleeve. "Those men... I don't like the look of them."

"Neither do I," he agreed, his eyes narrowing as he assessed the situation. He then turned to Clarissa and Henry, speaking softly. "We need to blend in. Let's pretend we're discussing something, like where to buy groceries."

The four friends huddled together, feigning conversation about vegetables and baked goods as they passed the suspicious individuals. To their relief, the men paid them no mind, focused instead on their own secretive whispers.

Once out of earshot, Sarah breathed a sigh of relief. "That was too close," she murmured.

"Indeed," Charles replied. "But we have to stay sharp. Our mission depends on it."

As they continued down the crowded street, they noticed a heavily guarded area up ahead, blocking their path. Henry furrowed his brow, trying to think of a solution. "We can't go that way," he said, frustration evident in his voice.

"Wait," Clarissa interjected, her eyes lighting up with an idea. "I saw a cart selling flowers back there. We could buy some and pretend we're delivering them to someone. It might help us slip past unnoticed."

"Brilliant!" exclaimed Sarah, clapping her hands together. "That's a great idea, Clarissa."

"Quickly, then," Charles urged, leading the group back to the flower cart. After purchasing several bouquets, they each held one and resumed their journey.

"Remember, act natural," Charles whispered as they approached the guarded area.

"Excuse me, sir," Sarah said sweetly, flashing her most

innocent smile at one of the red-coated soldiers. "We're just delivering these lovely flowers to our dear aunt. May we pass?"

The soldier eyed them suspiciously for a moment but eventually nodded, allowing them to proceed with barely a second glance.

"Phew," Henry muttered under his breath as they moved away from the guards. "Nice work, everyone."

"Especially you, Clarissa," added Sarah, beaming at her friend. "Your quick thinking saved us."

"Thank you," Clarissa replied, blushing slightly. "But we're not out of danger yet. We still have a mission to complete, so let's keep moving."

With renewed determination, the children pressed on, their resourcefulness and teamwork propelling them forward in the face of adversity. The secret message, now tucked safely in Charles's pocket, served as a constant reminder of their purpose, and they vowed not to let Dr. Warren down. Together, they knew they could overcome any obstacle that stood in their way.

The crisp autumn air nipped at the children's cheeks as they ventured deeper into the shadowy labyrinth of Boston's narrow alleyways. Brick walls loomed overhead, casting eerie silhouettes on the cobblestone pathways beneath their feet. The sound of their footsteps echoed like whispers from the past, reminding them that they were walking a fine line between success and failure.

"Stay close and be quiet," Charles instructed, his voice barely audible. They moved swiftly yet cautiously, every nerve in their bodies alert to the slightest hint of danger.

"Look!" Sarah whispered, pointing to a group of British soldiers up ahead. "We can't go this way."

"Quick, in here!" Henry motioned toward an open doorway, and the children ducked inside just as the soldiers rounded the corner.

Pressed against the doorframe, they held their breaths, listening intently as the soldiers' footsteps drew nearer. Clarissa closed her eyes, praying silently that they wouldn't be discovered. She could feel her heart pounding in her chest, threatening to give away their hiding place.

"Did you hear something?" one of the soldiers asked, pausing outside the doorway.

"Probably just a rat," another replied dismissively, and the group continued on their patrol.

"Phew," Sarah exhaled, her eyes wide with relief. "That was too close for comfort."

"Let's keep moving," Charles said, peering out of the doorway. "We need to find another route."

They slipped back into the shadows, weaving through the dimly lit corners of the city. At times, the alleyways grew so narrow that they had to walk single file, their shoulders brushing against the brick walls on either side.

"Look, there's a crowded shop just up ahead," Clarissa observed, adjusting her glasses. "If we need to hide again, we can blend in with the customers."

"Good thinking," Henry nodded.

"Remember, we're almost there," Charles added, his eyes fixed on their destination. "Just a little further."

As they rounded the final bend in the alley, Sarah's foot caught on an uneven cobblestone, causing her to stumble and let out a small cry.

"Sarah!" Charles whispered urgently, reaching out to steady her. "We can't afford any more slip-ups."

"Sorry," she murmured, tears welling in her eyes. "I'll be more careful."

"Let's not forget why we're doing this," Clarissa said, trying to offer comfort. "Dr. Warren trusted us with this message. We can't let him down."

"Right," Sarah nodded, wiping away her tears. "We have to stay focused."

"Come on," Charles urged, leading them toward the crowded shop. "We're almost there."

The children knew that every step they took brought them closer to Paul Revere and the fulfillment of their mission. But with each narrow escape and close call, the stakes grew higher, and the weight of their responsibility became heavier. They would need all their courage and resourcefulness to see this journey through to its end.

Emerging from the dim alleyway, the children found themselves in a bustling marketplace. The vibrant colors and sounds enveloped them, providing both a sense of relief and urgency. Charles glanced back at his friends, giving them a determined smile before gesturing to move forward.

"Stay close," he mouthed, his eyes darting around for any potential threats.

The children weaved through the throngs of people, their senses attuned to every noise and movement. Clarissa held onto Sarah's hand, ensuring they didn't get separated in the crowd. Henry took the lead, scanning the sea of faces for any sign of recognition or suspicion.

"Three more streets," Charles thought to himself, feeling his heart race with anticipation. "We can do this."

As they navigated the crowded marketplace, the children relied on subtle cues to communicate with one another. A simple nod from Henry indicated a clear path, while a quick tug on Sarah's hand by Clarissa meant they needed to change direction immediately.

"Clarissa, two o'clock," Henry whispered under his breath, his gaze locked on a group of British soldiers.

"Got it," she replied, expertly guiding her friends away from the looming threat without drawing attention to themselves.

"Almost there," Charles reassured himself, his grip on the sealed envelope tightening. "Just a little further."

Despite their fear, the children pressed on, their hearts pounding in unison with every step they took. They knew that delivering the secret message to Paul Revere was crucial, and they couldn't afford to fail now.

"Two more streets," Charles thought, his eyes glued to the envelope in his hands as if it held the key to America's freedom.

"Charles!" Sarah suddenly cried out, her voice barely audible above the din of the marketplace.

"Soldier, six o'clock!" Henry added, his eyes wide with alarm.

"Quick, into that cart!" Clarissa commanded, pushing her friends toward a nearby vegetable cart.

As they huddled together under the cover of the cart, their breathing labored and hearts racing, they knew how close they had come to being discovered. But the thought of their mission and the trust Dr. Warren placed in them fueled their determination to see it through.

"Let's go," Charles whispered, leading his friends out of their hiding spot once the coast was clear. "We're almost there."

"Stay strong, everyone," Clarissa added, offering an encouraging smile. "Dr. Warren is counting on us."

With renewed vigor, the children pressed on, their eyes fixed on their destination and their minds focused on the task at hand. They moved in unison, silently communicating with each other as they navigated the final stretch of their journey. And, despite the ever-present threat of capture, the children knew that they were so much stronger together than they could ever be apart.

The sun dipped lower in the sky, casting long shadows across the cobblestone streets as Charles led his friends through a labyrinth of tight alleyways. The air was thick with anticipation, and their hearts hammered in their chests like drums of war.

"Almost there," Charles thought, gripping the precious envelope tightly. He glanced back at his companions, their determination mirrored in their eyes, and felt a swell of pride.

"Careful," Clarissa whispered as they neared a busy intersection. "There are more soldiers here."

"Stay close and blend in with the crowd," Sarah suggested, pointing at a group of townspeople heading in the same direction as them.

"Great idea," Henry agreed, nodding vigorously. "We'll be like ghosts, drifting through unseen."

As they merged into the throng, Charles's senses heightened. Every rustle of fabric, every whispered conversation, and every footfall seemed amplified. He knew that Paul Revere awaited them, just around the corner, but would they make it without being caught?

"Look!" Clarissa exclaimed softly, her excitement barely contained. "That's the shop and Paul Revere's house up ahead."

"Finally," Sarah breathed, her eyes wide with awe.

"Let's not celebrate yet," Charles warned, his gaze scanning the area for any sign of danger. "We still have to deliver the message."

"Right," Henry concurred, swallowing nervously. "No time to lose. Let's go."

As they approached the entrance of Paul Revere's shop, the tension between them was. Their mission was almost complete, but one wrong move could still cost them everything. They exchanged determined glances and steeled themselves for what lay ahead.

"Wait," Clarissa said suddenly, her hand on Charles's arm. "Do you hear that?"

"Footsteps," Sarah whispered, her eyes darting around. "They're getting closer."

"Hide!" Charles hissed, pushing his friends into a nearby alcove. They could see the entrance to the shop just a few feet away, but it seemed like miles.

The footsteps grew louder, and the children held their breath, praying they wouldn't be discovered. As the sound of boots on cobblestones echoed around them, a shadow emerged from around the corner.

"Who's there?" The voice was gruff and menacing, sending shivers down their spines.

"Show yourselves!" demanded another voice as the shadows drew closer and closer.

"Think fast," Charles thought, his heart pounding in his ears. "One chance, one move."

"Ready... now!"

And with that, the children sprang into action, darting out of the alcove and sprinting towards the entrance with all their might. Would they make it in time? Or would their daring attempt at delivering the message end in disaster?

"Paul Revere, here we come," Charles panted as the door to

the shop loomed before them, and the shouts of pursuit rang in their ears.

"Will we make it?" Sarah cried, her eyes wide with fear and hope.

"Only one way to find out," Clarissa shouted back, her face a mixture of pure determination and courage.

"Let's do this!" Henry roared, adrenaline pumping through his veins.

# CHAPTER 7

The sun was just beginning to set over colonial Boston, casting a warm golden glow on the cobblestone streets. The children huddled together in an alley, their hearts pounding as they tried to make sense of the dangerous mission they had stumbled into. The sights, sounds, and scents were simultaneously familiar yet foreign, leaving them feeling overwhelmed and lost.

"Where do we go?" whispered Clarissa, her voice trembling with uncertainty as her eyes darted around the bustling street just beyond the alleyway.

Henry squeezed her hand reassuringly, his own thoughts racing with equal anxiety. "We'll find a way, Clarissa. We've come this far."

As if on cue, the tinkling melody of a bell chimed from a nearby shop, drawing the children's attention. A tall man with striking features emerged, wiping his hands on a leather apron. His eyes met theirs, and he flashed a warm, knowing smile before beckoning them over with a wave of his hand.

"Come along, young ones. No need to be skulking about in the shadows," he said kindly, his voice rich and melodious like a well-tuned instrument.

"Who are you?" asked Henry, his voice steady despite the apprehension knotting his stomach.

"Ah, forgive my manners," replied the man, extending a hand towards him. "My name is Paul Revere, at your service. I'm a silversmith by trade, amongst other things, you could say."

"Oh, thank goodness, we found you," Clarissa said, her disbelief turning to hopefulness.

"Of course!" Paul said, nodding earnestly. "I can see you're a bit out of your element, and I'd be remiss if I didn't offer a helping hand. Besides, I have a feeling that our paths crossing may not be mere coincidence."

"Indeed," Charles began to explain, "We were sent to find you and deliver a message from Dr. Warren. We tracked across town and were hounded by the soldiers before you opened the door to us!"

"Then it's settled," Paul declared, clapping his hands together with a resolute gleam in his eye. "Come in, and let's hear about what ills have befallen you on your journey here to my shop. Though I would wait till we are out of earshot before we go any further into our conversation." He says as he looks up to see the soldiers passing by with an expression of pure disdain on their faces. He smiles and waves at them as they go by.

"Thank you, Mr. Revere," Henry said gratefully, his guarded demeanor softening under the weight of Paul's sincerity. "We could certainly use a friend in these uncertain times."

As they entered behind Paul Revere, they couldn't help but feel a sense of security and determination that had been missing since their second arrival in this unfamiliar time.

"First things first," Paul said, leading them through the winding cobblestone streets. "We should find you a safe place to stay while we plan our next steps. You can't go back to Dr. Warren just yet now that the lobster backs have marked you down."

They leave the shop from the back door and pass by the outer garden or Paul Revere's shop, where he stored his heavier tools and equipment, and into the street. As they navigated the vibrant marketplaces and busy thoroughfares, the children marveled at the sights and sounds of Boston, noticing how the air has been primed since they were pulled through the vortex a second time by the cryptex. The air was filled with the chatter of merchants hawking their wares, the heavy clip-clop of horses' hooves, and the ever-present sense of excitement as word of the growing tension spread from person to person.

"Wow, I still can't believe we are here; it's so different from what we've learned in history class," Clarissa whispered, her eyes wide as she took in the colorful array of shops and stalls.

"History has a way of simplifying things," Sarah replied, her voice tinged with wonder. "But there's no substitute for experiencing it firsthand."

"True, but we can't forget our mission," Charles reminded them, his focus unwavering. "We need to find a way back to our own home, and we have to do it soon."

"Of course, my young friend, I thought you children sounded as though you were from out of town, from one of the outer hamlets in New England?" Paul mentioned him, guiding them towards a small boarding house nestled between a bakery and a blacksmith's forge. "I promise you, I will help you in any way that I can; you are part of the Sons of Liberty, as Dr. Warren's note mentions. But for now, let's settle in and get some rest. Tomorrow is a new day, and we have much to accomplish."

With grateful nods, the children followed Paul Revere into the boarding house, eager to begin their journey toward unraveling the mysteries of time and discovering their roles in the great tapestry of American history.

The sun had barely risen the following day when Henry awoke, his back aching from the thin mattress and his mind racing with thoughts of their newfound ally. As he sat up on the edge of the bed, he couldn't shake the lingering feeling of skepticism that clung to him like a second skin. He trusted Paul Revere about as far as he could throw him, which wasn't very far considering the man's solid build.

"Can we really trust him?" he whispered, more to himself than anyone else in the room. Charles stirred on his cot, clearly still lost in slumber, while Clarissa slept soundlessly nearby.

"Are you talking about Mr. Revere?" Sarah mumbled, her eyes still closed, but her ears tuned to Henry's concerns. "He seems genuine enough to me."

"Of course we can! Dr. Warren said we could, and we trust Dr. Warren, right? Besides, Paul Revere hasn't given us any cause to mistrust him." Charles replied

"Appearances can be deceiving," Henry muttered, folding his arms over his chest. "We don't know anything about him other than what he's told us."

"Perhaps today's events will help put your mind at ease," Paul's voice carried through the open door as if he'd been listening just outside. Henry's cheeks flushed with embarrassment, and he quickly rose to his feet.

"Sorry," he mumbled, shuffling out into the common area where Paul stood near a small table laden with breakfast offerings - fresh bread, cheese, and some kind of porridge.

"Apology accepted. To be fair, I know nothing about you either," Paul said with a warm smile. "Now, let's break our fast and prepare for the day ahead. I've arranged for a tour of our current situation that should prove most enlightening."

As they ate, Henry couldn't deny the growing sense of curiosity that bubbled within him. The streets of colonial Boston held secrets and stories that no history book could ever capture, and perhaps Paul Revere was the key to unlocking them.

"Where are we going first?" Charles asked, his voice filled with enthusiasm.

"Ah, well, that would be telling," Paul replied, a mischievous glint in his eye. "You'll just have to wait and see."

As they made their way through the bustling streets of Boston, Henry couldn't help but marvel at the city's vibrant energy. Everywhere he looked, there were people going about their daily routines, completely unaware of the extraordinary events unfolding around them.

"See that building over there?" Paul asked, pointing towards a large brick structure with an imposing facade. "That's the Old State House, where some of the most important decisions regarding our fight against the tyrannical British Parliament have been made."

"Wow," Clarissa breathed, her eyes wide with awe. "It's amazing to think that we're standing on the precipice of something truly great happening in Boston, either for good or ill."

"Indeed," Paul agreed, leading them down a narrow cobblestone alleyway that opened up into a bustling market square. "But as you'll soon discover, there's far more to Boston than meets the eye."

Throughout the day, Paul guided them past historic landmarks and hidden treasures alike, his encyclopedic knowledge of the city and its people both captivating and disarming. It was hard for Henry to maintain his skepticism when faced with the undeniable passion and expertise that Paul possessed.

"Alright, Mr. Revere," Henry finally conceded, his voice tinged with admiration. "You've proven yourself to be quite the resourceful guide. I suppose I can trust you... for now."

"Thank you, Henry," Paul said, a genuine smile lighting up his face. "I promise that I won't let you down."

As they continued to explore the city, Henry couldn't help but feel a newfound sense of camaraderie with Paul and a deepening connection to the revolutionary cause. And while he still had much to learn, one thing was certain: he was ready to face whatever challenges lay ahead with Paul Revere by his side.

Paul led the children to a secluded rooftop overlooking the city. The wind whipped around them, bringing with it the scent of saltwater from the nearby harbor. With the entire city sprawled out before them, Henry couldn't help but feel a thrill at the thought of what lay ahead.

"Alright, then," Paul said, turning to face Henry, his eyes alight with determination. "If we're going to make a meaningful contribution to this struggle, we'll need to be strategic in our actions. And that starts with you, Henry."

"Me?" Henry asked, taken aback by the sudden focus on him. He shifted uncomfortably under Paul's expectant gaze.

"Indeed," Paul replied, nodding firmly. "You have a fire in your belly, lad. I can see it. But if we're going to succeed, you need to learn how to harness that anger and turn it into something productive."

Henry frowned, running a hand through his tousled hair. "What do you mean?"

"First things first," Paul explained, placing a hand on Henry's shoulder. "You must understand that fighting for what's right isn't just about brute force. It's also about strategy, cunning, and knowing when to hold back."

"Like a game of chess," Sarah chimed in, her own excitement apparent as she watched the exchange between the two.

"Exactly," Paul agreed, shooting her an approving smile. "Now, let's start with something practical. I want you to observe the people down there." He gestured towards the bustling streets below. "Tell me what you see."

Henry squinted, observing the men and women going about their daily routines. After a moment, he said hesitantly, "I see... people? Going about their business, buying goods, talking to one another."

"Good," Paul encouraged. "Now look deeper. Who are they? What do they want?"

Henry frowned, concentrating on the scene below.

Gradually, he began to notice patterns: the way certain individuals exchanged furtive glances or slipped coins into waiting palms. He felt a small thrill of satisfaction as he realized that these people were not just ordinary citizens—they were revolutionaries working in secret to undermine British rule.

"Ah," Henry said, his voice barely more than a whisper. "I see... spies. Smugglers. People fighting for freedom, right under the noses of the redcoats."

"Excellent," Paul beamed, clapping him on the back. "You're learning to see beyond the surface, Henry. That's the first step towards becoming an effective patriot."

Over the following weeks, Paul continued to mentor Henry, teaching him the art of strategy, deception, and diplomacy. Slowly but surely, Henry began to feel himself changing, growing into the role of a true revolutionary. Gone was the hot-headed youth who had started this journey; in his place stood a young man with a clear purpose and newfound determination.

"Thank you, Paul," Henry said one evening as they sat together on the same rooftop where their lessons had begun. The city spread out beneath them like a patchwork quilt, alive with the promise of revolution.

"Thank me?" Paul asked, raising an eyebrow. "For what?"

"For believing in me," Henry replied, his voice thick with emotion. "For helping me become someone who can truly make a difference."

"Never forget, Henry," Paul said, his eyes twinkling in the fading light. "The power to change the world has always been within you. I merely helped you find it."

Seated on a barrel in the bustling marketplace, Paul Revere leaned back, his eyes crinkling with amusement as he listened to Henry recount his latest attempt at espionage.

"Then, just as I was about to slip away unnoticed, I stepped on a stray cat's tail, and it let out a yowl that could have awakened the dead!" Henry exclaimed, his face flushed with embarrassment.

Paul laughed heartily, the sound echoing through the marketplace like the peal of a silver bell. "Ah, my young friend, we've all had our share of mishaps," he said, patting Henry reassuringly on the shoulder. "But each one is a lesson learned."

"Have you ever made any mistakes, Paul?" Henry asked, his curiosity piqued.

"Of course," Paul replied, his eyes growing distant as he recalled memories from years past. "One night, early in this struggle, I was tasked with delivering a crucial message to a fellow patriot. The moon was full, casting strange shadows across the uneven ground. My horse stumbled, and I dropped the message into a puddle, rendering the ink illegible."

Henry gasped, his eyes wide. "What did you do?"

"Fortunately, I had memorized the contents of the message," Paul said with a smile. "I recited it to my contact, word for word. It was a close call, but we managed to avoid disaster."

"Wow," Henry breathed, clearly impressed. "You're like a real-life hero, Paul."

"Hardly," Paul chuckled, shaking his head. "Just a man who believes in the cause of freedom, doing what must be done to secure it."

As they continued to converse, a profound sense of camaraderie settled between them. They swapped stories and advice, laughter and solemnity intertwining like the threads of a finely woven tapestry. The marketplace around them faded into the background, their connection growing stronger with each exchanged word.

"Paul," Henry said suddenly, his voice tinged with awe. "Do you think I could ever be as brave and resourceful as you?"

"Bravery and resourcefulness are not qualities one is born with, Henry," Paul replied, his eyes filled with warmth and understanding. "They are forged in the fires of experience and tempered by the desire to do what is right. Believe in yourself, and you will become the hero you wish to be."

As they rose from their makeshift seats, the sun long vanished behind the horizon. Henry felt a renewed sense of purpose coursing through him. With Paul Revere by his side, he knew that anything was possible. Together, they would fight for the future of their country – and change the course of history forever.

The soft morning glow bathed the cobblestone streets of colonial Boston, casting long shadows as Henry and Paul stood in a small, secluded courtyard. The air was crisp and cool, filled with the scent of dew-covered grass and the distant sound of a blacksmith's hammer.

"Alright, Henry," Paul began, his eyes scanning their

surroundings for any signs of eavesdroppers. "Today, I'm going to teach you some tactics that will be crucial in our fight against the British forces."

Henry nodded eagerly, his pulse quickening at the thought of becoming as adept as his newfound mentor. He stood tall and proud, ready to absorb every piece of wisdom Paul had to offer.

"First," Paul continued, his voice low and steady, "we must understand our enemy. The British soldiers are well-trained and disciplined, but they rely heavily on traditional formations and tactics. Our strength lies in our ability to adapt and think creatively."

As they spoke, Paul demonstrated various strategic maneuvers, explaining the advantages and drawbacks of each. Henry listened intently, his mind racing to keep pace with Paul's keen insights.

"Paul, this is incredible," Henry said, his eyes sparkling with excitement. "But how can we possibly remember all of these strategies?"

"Practice, Henry," Paul replied, a wry smile playing at the corners of his lips. "We'll practice until they're second nature."

Over the next several days, Henry and Paul trained together tirelessly. From dawn until dusk, they practiced their techniques, honing their skills and refining their understanding of the skills of a rebel. With each passing day, Henry felt his confidence grow stronger, his movements becoming more fluid and precise.

"Excellent work, Henry!" Paul exclaimed one afternoon, clapping him on the shoulder as they paused to catch their breath. "You've really come a long way in such a short time."

"Thanks, Paul," Henry panted, a mixture of pride and exhaustion evident on his face. "But I know I still have so much to learn."

"Indeed," Paul agreed, his eyes gleaming with admiration. "But you have the heart of a true patriot, and that is more valuable than any lesson I could teach you."

As they stood together in the waning sunlight, Henry felt an immense wave of gratitude wash over him. Through Paul's guidance and unwavering support, he had discovered a newfound strength within himself – one that would carry him through the battles yet to come.

"Thank you, Paul," Henry said quietly, his voice thick with emotion. "I promise that I won't let you down."

"Of that, I have no doubt," Paul replied, his hand resting firmly on Henry's shoulder. "Now, get some rest. We have a long day ahead of us tomorrow."

With renewed determination burning in their hearts, Henry and Paul prepared to face the challenges that lay on the horizon. Side by side, they would stand against tyranny, united in their quest for freedom and justice.

The sun dipped low in the sky, casting long shadows across the cobblestone streets of colonial Boston. Henry and Paul found themselves resting on a bench in a small park, their breaths coming in short puffs as they recovered from the day's training. The air was crisp and cool, carrying with it the scent of fallen leaves and woodsmoke.

"Paul," Henry began hesitantly, his eyes focused on the ground, "there's something I've been wanting to talk to you about. I haven't really opened up to anyone before, but I trust you."

Paul looked at him with concern, nodding for him to continue. "You can tell me anything, Henry. I'm here for you."

"I've always struggled with my temper, even back home," Henry confessed, his voice barely above a whisper. "I used to get into fights all the time, and sometimes, I couldn't control myself. I... I hurt people, Paul. And I regret it every day."

As he spoke, an image of a boy from his past flashed through his mind – a boy with a bloody nose and swollen eye, the result of one of Henry's uncontrollable outbursts. He winced inwardly, the guilt gnawing at him like a hungry wolf.

"Ah, I see," Paul murmured thoughtfully, his brow furrowed in sympathy. "It's never easy to admit our flaws, but by doing so, we take the first step towards growth."

Henry looked up at Paul, his eyes filled with uncertainty. "Do you think I can change? Can I be the kind of person who uses his strength for good?"

"Absolutely," Paul replied without hesitation, his eyes locking onto Henry's with unwavering conviction. "But it will require hard work and dedication on your part. You must learn to channel your anger, to harness it and direct it towards a noble cause."

"Like fighting for freedom and justice?" Henry asked, a spark of hope flickering in his eyes.

"Exactly," Paul affirmed with a warm smile. "And I will do everything in my power to help you achieve that goal, my young friend."

"Thank you, Paul," Henry said sincerely, feeling a weight lift from his shoulders as he shared his burden with his mentor. "I won't let you down."

"Remember, Henry, the path to change is not a straight line but a winding road filled with obstacles and setbacks," Paul advised, his voice gentle yet firm. "But if you persevere, if you hold fast to your convictions and keep your heart aimed towards the greater good, there's no limit to what you can achieve."

As the sun slipped below the horizon, casting the park in a soft twilight, the bond between Henry and Paul strengthened. Through their shared struggles and triumphs, they would forge a friendship that would withstand the test of time, and together, they would fight for the future they both believed in.

Henry stared at the glowing embers of their small campfire, the dancing flames casting flickering shadows across his face. He still couldn't believe the turn his life had taken since he and his friends found themselves in colonial Boston, fighting for a cause they never even knew existed until now.

"Paul," Henry began hesitantly, twirling a twig between his fingers. "I want you to know how grateful I am – for everything."

"Grateful?" Paul looked up from where he was stoking the fire, his eyes thoughtful as they met Henry's. "For what, my young friend?"

"Ever since we arrived here, you've been nothing but kind

and generous to us, teaching us about this world and how to survive in it," Henry confessed, warmth blooming in his chest. "You didn't have to take me under your wing, yet you did, and I'll never forget that."

"Ah, Henry, there is no need for thanks," Paul said softly, a fond smile gracing his face. "I saw potential in you – and I knew that with the right guidance, you could grow into a fine patriot and an even finer man."

"Still," Henry insisted, determination shining in his eyes. "I promise you, Paul, I won't let you down. I'll do my best to be the person you believe I can be."

"Your word is enough for me," Paul replied, patting Henry on the shoulder. "And remember, you don't have to face all of this alone. We're all in this together," he gestured around the circle, where their friends sat, listening intently.

"Right," Henry nodded, feeling a sense of unity and camaraderie wash over him. It was true – they were a team, all of them bound together by their shared experiences and the challenges they faced in this strange new world.

"Let's make a pact," said Clarissa, her eyes gleaming with determination. "No matter what happens, we'll face it together – as a team."

"Agreed," Charles chimed in, his voice steady and resolute.

"Count me in," Sarah added, a grin spreading across her face.

"Me too," Henry affirmed, his heart swelling with pride and gratitude. He knew that with the support of his friends and with Paul by their side, they could overcome anything life threw at them.

As the fire crackled and snapped, sending sparks spiraling into the night sky, the children clasped their hands together, sealing their pact. They were no longer just lost travelers struggling to find their way; they had become a family bound together by love, loyalty, and a fierce desire to fight for the freedom they all held dear.

As the stars twinkled overhead, casting their silvery light upon the group huddled around the campfire, Henry couldn't help but feel that they were watching over them, guiding them on their journey like celestial beacons in the darkness.

The first light of dawn crept over the horizon, casting a soft golden glow upon the sleeping forms huddled around the dying embers of the campfire. As the gentle rays of the sun-brushed against Henry's face, he stirred from his slumber, blinking away the remnants of sleep as he took in the peaceful scene before him. Beside him, Sarah's chest rose and fell with the steady rhythm of her breath. Her blonde hair fanned out like a halo on the makeshift pillow she'd fashioned from her cloak. Across the fire, Charles and Clarissa lay, their quiet snores a testament to the trust they'd forged during their time in colonial Boston.

"Rise and shine, young patriots," Paul Revere's voice cut through the morning air, jolting the children awake. Though his tone was light, there was a sense of urgency beneath the playful words, reminding them all that they had a mission to complete — and a limited amount of time in which to do so.

"Already?" groaned Clarissa, rubbing the sleep from her eyes as she sat up. "Feels like we only just closed our eyes."

"Time waits for no one," Paul replied, his eyes twinkling with a hint of mischief. "Especially not a group of out-of-town rebels."

Henry couldn't suppress a grin as he stretched, feeling the satisfying pop of his stiff muscles as they protested the sudden movement. It was true – their journey was far from over, and every moment spent lingering in this place put their futures at risk. But despite the danger and uncertainty that surrounded them, he couldn't help but feel a surge of excitement at the thought of what lay ahead.

"Where do we go next, Paul?" Charles asked, his expression serious as he looked to their newfound mentor for guidance.

"Today, we shall make our way to the outskirts of the city," Paul explained, his eyes scanning the horizon as if he could already see their destination. "There, we'll rendezvous with a group of fellow patriots who will aid us in our fight against the British forces."

"Are they trustworthy?" Sarah inquired, her blue eyes clouded with concern. "We've encountered more than our fair share of danger since arriving here."

"Trust me, dear girl, these are some of the finest men and women I have ever had the privilege to call my friends," Paul assured her, his voice steady and sincere. "They'll stand by us through thick and thin – just like we'll stand by each other."

His words seemed to reassure not only Sarah but the rest of the group as well. As they broke camp and began their journey towards the edges of Boston, Henry couldn't help but marvel at how far they'd come – both in distance and in spirit. They were no longer simply lost souls struggling to find their way through an unfamiliar land. They were a united front, bound together by their shared experiences and a newfound sense of purpose.

As they walked, Paul regaled them with stories of other daring acts of heroism he'd witnessed during his time with the Sons of Liberty. Each tale served to remind them of the importance of their mission and the strength that lay within them all. And as the sun climbed higher in the sky, casting its warm golden light upon the path they traveled, Henry knew deep in his heart that they were ready to face whatever challenges awaited them – together.

# CHAPTER 8

The world spun around them, a blur of colors and sounds merging into an indistinguishable whirlwind. Sarah clutched Charles' hand tightly, her other hand gripping the edge of the cryptex as if her life depended on it. Her heart pounded in her chest, her breath coming in short, ragged gasps. And then, just as suddenly as it had begun, the spinning stopped.

"Is... is everyone okay?" Charles asked, his voice shaky and uncertain. The ground beneath their feet felt solid again, but the air was heavy with tension and anticipation.

"Alive, at least," Henry grunted, rubbing his head. Clarissa nodded silently, adjusting her glasses as she surveyed their surroundings. They found themselves standing on a cobblestone street lined with quaint wooden buildings that leaned slightly towards each other. The smell of saltwater and fish filled the air, mixing with the distant scent of burning wood.

"What... where are we?" Sarah whispered, her eyes wide with awe and confusion.

"Look!" Clarissa exclaimed suddenly, pointing towards the old south meeting house. There, amidst the chaos and commotion, colonists gathered, attempting to discuss their next steps after the Governor refused to send the ships out of the Harbor.

"I wonder if this is where Paul Revere was referring to when he was going to bring us to his next mission before we got pulled away by the cryptex." Charles broke in.

"He was right when he said the people he was taking us to

could be trusted if that was the case; look!" Sarah chimed in.

Ahead at the center of the gaggle of people were Paul Revere, Samuel Adams, and Dr. Warren, listening to the crowd and, at the same time, bringing to their attention another man who looked to be a captain of a ship.

"Woah, there are so many people here. What are they all talking about?" Henry spoke up then.

"Tea, my boy, tea and taxes," A voice behind them chimed, and as the children turned around, they could see a familiar face, John Hancock, standing before them. He bowed to them, recognizing them after their first meeting with Dr. Warren.

"What is happening?" Asked Clarissa, adjusting her glasses and looking at the large crowd.

"They are discussing what to do with the tea on board the ship in the harbor and waiting to hear from the captain as to the Governor's decision if he will let them leave after the refusal of the local people to unload the tea brought from England." John Hancock started to fill them in.

"Why is everyone so upset?" Asked Charles, looking around from face to face.

"The British Parliament in all their brilliant splendor," John began giving this compliment the scorn he truly felt, "decided that the only tea we should be dealing with is British tea, but lowering taxes, while at the same time at a rate that would put everyone's profits at risk, as well as confirm to the Parliament that they have the ability to tax us without our consent."

"Oh, so this is kinda like a test to see if the colonists would conform to the will of Parliament," Charles replied

"Precisely right," John answered. "And precisely why we have gathered here today, I know what the Governor has decreed, and the captain is now telling everyone that he has been denied permission to leave the harbor, and once that happens, we Sons of Liberty will respond."

At that moment, the crowd flew into an uproar, hearing the news from the captain just as John Hancock had explained.

"So what is the response?" Sarah began to ask when John Hancock put up a hand to stop her. "Listen closely."

Samuel Adams' voice rose above the noise of the crowd. "This meeting can do nothing more to save the country!"

"That's the sign!" John Hancock said excitedly, "Come, children, follow me." He then guided the children down towards the dock where the ship was anchored in the night.

Thanks to the elaborate planning behind this seemingly spontaneous event, groups converge from at least ten different locations: taverns, shops, clubs, and even houses. Hastily disguising themselves, dressed as Native Americans, were hurling crate after crate of tea into the water. "It's the Boston Tea Party!" Clarissa chimed in, and at this exclamation, John looked down and replied, "The Boston Tea Party? Now, that is a good name for this." He began to laugh at the idea.

Awe and excitement shone on the children's faces as they took in the historical scene before them. In the midst of the turmoil, they saw men and women of all ages shouting and cheering, their voices blending together in a cacophony of defiance and rebellion.

"Can you believe it? We're actually here!" Henry shouted over the din, his eyes alight with the fire of revolution. "We've got to join them!"

"Wait!" Charles held up his hand, his expression serious. "We need to be careful not to interfere too much. We're here to learn, not to change history."

Sarah watched as the colonists continued to fling the tea into the harbor, their faces contorted with anger and determination. She felt a swell of pride rise within her as she realized the significance of what they were witnessing – the spark that would ignite the American Revolution.

"Charles is right," she said softly, her eyes never leaving the scene in front of them. "We need to observe and learn from this moment. Then, we can use our newfound knowledge and strength to face whatever challenges lie ahead."

The children huddled together, watching as history unfolded before their very eyes, knowing that they had been granted a rare and precious gift. They vowed to cherish this experience, taking with them the lessons they would learn from the brave men and women who fought for freedom so long ago. They noticed how meticulously planned this all was, like a choreographed dance; not a single item other than the tea was broken; the colonists were all very careful and deliberate in what they were doing so as to be very targeted in their protest. And as the last of the tea crates crashed into the waters below, they knew that their journey was only just beginning.

"Look!" gasped Clarissa, pointing toward a group of men

standing on the edge of the harbor, their faces obscured by the flickering shadows cast by the torches they held aloft. "It's Samuel Adams and Dr Warren. They are talking with John Hancock!"

The children exchanged excited glances, their hearts pounding in their chests as they realized the significance of meeting these iconic figures from history all in one place.

"Unbelievable," whispered Charles, his eyes wide with awe. "We're actually here, witnessing the Boston Tea Party."

"Be cool, be cool," Sarah muttered to herself, trying to calm her racing heart.

As the children cautiously approached the men, they couldn't help but feel a sense of reverence for the historical figures that stood before them. Dr. Joseph Warren, his now very familiar face, and Samuel Adams, a middle-aged man with graying hair and sharp eyes, had a strong presence that commanded attention even amidst the night's chaos. John Hancock, tall and handsome with wavy brown hair, exuded an air of sophistication that set him apart from the other colonists, who met them before the events of the night.

"Excuse me, sirs?" Clarissa said hesitantly, swallowing nervously as the men turned to regard her with surprise. "We're... we're here to support this historic event, if you don't mind us being here."

"Support, you say?" Samuel Adams replied, his voice carrying a hint of curiosity. "Well, it's not every day we have ones so young seeking to aid in the midst of a protest."

"Indeed," John Hancock agreed, giving the children a thoughtful look. "Perhaps you can learn a thing or two about standing up for one's rights and the power of unity."

"Ahh, my young friends, it's so good to see you, and on such an eventful night as this!" Dr. Joseph Warren put in with his arms open in greeting to the young children.

As the men spoke, the children became acutely aware of the vivid sensory details surrounding them. The smell of the damp tea leaves mingling with the salty sea air filled their nostrils, creating a heady scent that clung to their skin and clothes. The sound of wooden crates crashing into the water echoed throughout the harbor as colonists, their faces streaked with soot and paint, continued to hurl them overboard in defiance.

"Wow," breathed Charles, his eyes darting around the scene as he tried to take in every detail. "I never thought I'd be able to taste the saltwater in the air at the Boston Tea Party."

"Nor did I ever imagine smelling the tea as it's being thrown into the harbor," added Sarah, her eyes shining with excitement. "This is all so... real."

"It's one thing to read about history in a book," Clarissa mused, her gaze locked on Samuel Adams and John Hancock as they barked orders to the other colonists. "But to actually be here, meeting the people who shaped our nation's destiny... it's beyond anything I could have dreamed of."

"Agreed," Charles said softly, his voice filled with wonder. "We'll never forget this night — and we'll carry these memories with us wherever our journey takes us next."

As the children watched the spirited chaos unfold before them, they silently vowed to learn all they could from these courageous men and women who dared to stand up for their beliefs. They knew that by witnessing these historic events firsthand, they would gain a deeper understanding of the sacrifices made in the pursuit of freedom – and perhaps even find the strength to face their own challenges, whatever they may be.

As the crates of tea continued to splash into the cold harbor waters, Sarah couldn't help but recall her history lessons at the boarding school. She glanced over at Charles and Clarissa, who seemed to share her thoughts.

"Did you know," she began, her eyes wide with wonder, "that they're dumping over 340 chests of tea tonight? That's around 92,000 pounds of tea! And it's all because of the Tea Act of 1773, which was passed by the British Parliament to save the struggling East India Company."

"Really?" Charles asked, impressed by Sarah's knowledge. "I thought it was just about taxes."

"Partly," admitted Clarissa, adjusting her glasses. "The Tea Act lowered taxes on imported tea, but it also gave the East India Company a monopoly on tea sales in the colonies. The colonists saw this as another example of taxation without representation, which led to protests like this one."

"Exactly," Sarah nodded, feeling more confident now that she had shared this vital information.

"Hey, watch out!" Henry warned suddenly, grabbing Sarah's arm and pulling her behind him as a group of British soldiers approached. They were searching for any colonists responsible for the destruction of the tea. The children huddled together, their hearts pounding as the redcoats walked past them, barely noticing the inconspicuous group.

"Thanks, Henry," Sarah whispered, grateful for his quick thinking. The children exchanged tense glances but knew they had to keep moving.

"Stick together," Charles urged, taking the lead as they navigated through the chaos of the Boston Tea Party. "We can't afford to get caught."

"Right behind you," Henry replied, keeping an eye out for any approaching soldiers while Clarissa and Sarah followed closely.

The children worked seamlessly as a team, using their individual strengths to avoid detection. Charles led with confidence, making quick decisions on which path to take, while Henry protected the group physically, ready to step in if necessary. Sarah provided historical context and facts, ensuring they understood the significance of the event unfolding around them, and Clarissa used her intellect to find creative solutions when obstacles arose.

"Over there!" Clarissa pointed toward a stack of crates that offered temporary cover from the patrolling redcoats. They quickly darted behind it, holding their breaths as the soldiers passed by once more.

"Phew, that was close," Charles muttered, wiping sweat from his brow. "Good call, Clarissa."

"Thanks," she said shyly, feeling proud of her contribution to the team's success.

Together, the children continued their journey through the bustling harbor, witnessing firsthand the passion and determination of the colonists fighting for their rights. As they slipped past British soldiers and aided the patriots in whatever way they could, their understanding of the American Revolution deepened, and they grew closer as a team, united by their shared experiences and newfound appreciation for history.

"Wow, can you believe we were just part of the Boston Tea Party?" Charles exclaimed, his eyes wide with amazement.

"Unbelievable," Sarah agreed, brushing a stray strand of hair from her face. "I've read about it so many times, but being here, seeing it all happen right in front of us... it's a whole new perspective."

"Indeed," Clarissa chimed in, "The audacity of the colonists to stand up against the British Crown like that? It's inspiring!"

Henry nodded thoughtfully, his gaze scanning the harbor, where remnants of the protest still lingered. "To think they risked their lives for what they believed in... It really makes you appreciate the sacrifices they made to pave the way for America's independence."

"Absolutely," Sarah said, her voice filled with admiration. "The Sons of Liberty, led by Samuel Adams and John Hancock and our friend Dr. Joseph Warren, organized this protest as a direct response to Britain's unjust taxation policies, such as the Tea Act. They wanted to send a message that colonists wouldn't tolerate taxation without representation."

"Right," Charles added, "and the Boston Tea Party played a crucial role in sparking the American Revolution. The British retaliated with harsh measures, leading to further unrest and, ultimately, the fight for independence."

"Speaking of which," Henry interjected, sensing a sudden shift in the atmosphere around them, "it feels like something important is about to happen."

"Look!" Clarissa shouted, pointing to a man running through the cobblestone streets. "That's Paul Revere! He's helping everyone get to safety before the British start making arrests!"

"Quickly, let's follow him!" Henry urged, leading the group in pursuit of Revere. "This is our chance to do what we can to support the American Revolution!"

The children's hearts raced in sync with the rapid hoofbeats on cobblestones as they followed Paul Revere through the dark streets of Boston. The echo of each step resonated off the surrounding buildings, creating an eerie symphony of urgency. Henry, Clarissa, and Charles could hardly contain their excitement.

It was then that Dr. Warren ushered them over to another meeting house and then stated, "My dear young friends, what an eventful night this was; I am sure you are as elated as I."

"Yes! Dr. Warren, we are all too happy to be a part of this most auspicious moment!" Sarah replied

"Good, of course, there will be work to do from this fallout, and I will need your help in the coming days, but for now, we must all lay low and evade the eye of the retribution soon to follow this event." Dr. Warren warned them, "Go to the boarding house that Paul Revere set you up in, and I will send for you when the time is right."

With that, the children made their way to the boarding house that became their new home for the present until they could find their way back to their time and use the cryptex to do just that.

# CHAPTER 9

The sun peeked through the canopy of leaves, casting dappled light across the grassy clearing. Sarah and Charles found themselves alone for the first time in days, their breaths visible in the crisp autumn air. Dr. Warren had left them to gather supplies from a nearby village, trusting the two teenagers with the responsibility of continuing their training on their own.

"Alright," Sarah said, her voice soft but determined. "Let's see if I've got this right." She closed her eyes, focusing on the cryptic puzzle that was laid out before them. Charles observed her, his dark eyes filled with a mix of concern and admiration.

"Remember what Dr. Warren taught us," he encouraged, his voice steady and confident. "You need to let the images come to you, not force them."

Sarah nodded, her long blonde hair falling into her face as she did so. The seconds ticked by, and she could feel Charles's gaze on her. It made her nervous but also strangely comforted. Finally, the pieces began to click together in her mind, and she opened her eyes, excitement shining in their blue depths.

"I think I've got it!" she exclaimed, her fingers deftly working to align the symbols on the cryptex. When it clicked open, her face lit up with delight. "I did it!"

Charles grinned at her, his confidence infectious. "I knew you could do it," he said, clapping her on the shoulder. "I never doubted you for a second."

His words warmed Sarah's heart, and she blushed slightly, tucking a strand of hair behind her ear. "Thanks, Charles," she murmured. "I couldn't have done it without your help."

"Of course," he replied, waving off her thanks. "That's what friends are for."

Sarah glanced at him, hesitating for a moment before speaking. "Charles, can I ask you something?" she inquired, her voice filled with curiosity.

"Sure, what's on your mind?" he asked, a thoughtful expression crossing his face.

"Well," Sarah began, her eyes shining with admiration. "I just wanted to say that I'm really impressed with how well you lead us. You always make sure everyone is taken care of, and you never hesitate to step up when we need guidance."

Charles looked surprised by her words but smiled nonetheless. "Thank you, Sarah," he said, clearly touched. "That means a lot coming from you."

"Really?" she asked, her own surprise evident in her voice.

"Of course," Charles continued, his gaze steady and sincere. "You're incredibly caring and observant, not to mention intelligent. Your opinion means a lot."

Sarah blushed again, her heart fluttering at his words. She had never imagined that someone like Charles would think so highly of her. It made her feel seen in a way she hadn't experienced before. As they stood there together, the world around them seemed to fade away, leaving only the two of them bathed in the dappled sunlight.

"Thank you, Charles," she whispered, a shy smile tugging at

the corners of her lips. "That means more to me than you know."

Charles shifted his weight from one foot to the other, a rare vulnerability creeping into his eyes. "You know, Sarah," he began hesitantly, "I haven't always been this way."

"What do you mean?" she asked gently, her curiosity piqued.

"Being a leader... it's not easy, especially when you have trust issues." Charles looked away for a moment, his fingers absently twisting the hem of his shirt. "In the past, I've been let down by people I thought I could rely on. It's made me wary of opening up to others."

Sarah watched as a flicker of pain crossed his face, her heart aching for him. She reached out and placed a reassuring hand on his arm, her touch light but steady. "I can understand that," she offered softly. "But you're not alone in having fears and insecurities."

Charles raised an eyebrow, surprised at her admission. "Really? You seem so self-assured and kind-hearted."

Sarah laughed lightly, an ironic twist to her lips. "Well, appearances can be deceiving. I struggle with making decisions and asserting myself. Sometimes, I feel like I'm just following along, afraid to take the lead."

"Isn't that something?" Charles mused aloud, the ghost of a smile playing on his lips. "We both have our demons, don't we?"

"Indeed," Sarah agreed, her own smile returning, albeit tinged with melancholy. "But perhaps we can learn from each other and grow stronger together."

"Maybe you're right," Charles conceded, his eyes meeting hers again with renewed determination. "I think it would do us both good to work through these challenges."

"Absolutely," Sarah concurred, her grip on his arm tightening ever so slightly. "We'll figure it out together, one step at a time."

And as they stood there, beneath the dappled sunlight filtering through the leaves above, Charles and Sarah found solace in their shared vulnerabilities. It was a moment that would mark the beginning of a deeper understanding and connection between them - one forged not only by their individual strengths but also by their willingness to face their fears together.

The sun dipped low in the sky, casting a warm orange glow over the training grounds. The air hummed with the buzz of cicadas and the distant rustle of leaves, creating a serene backdrop for Sarah and Charles' conversation.

"Isn't it strange," Sarah mused aloud, her eyes focused on a small ladybug crawling across her hand, "how we've both been struggling in our own ways yet somehow found comfort in each other's company?"

Charles chuckled softly, watching the ladybug take flight before turning his gaze back to Sarah. "It is, isn't it? But maybe that's just what we needed — someone who understands the weight we carry."

Sarah nodded thoughtfully and sighed, the tendrils of her hair catching in the gentle breeze. "I never imagined I'd find someone who could truly understand my fears and insecurities."

"Nor did I," Charles admitted, his dark eyes meeting hers with warmth and honesty. He hesitated for a moment as if weighing his next words carefully. Then, with a deep breath, he took a step closer to Sarah and reached out to gently brush a stray lock of hair behind her ear. "You know, there's something I've been wanting to tell you, but I'm afraid..."

"Of getting hurt?" Sarah offered softly, her heart racing at his touch.

"Yes," Charles confessed, his voice barely more than a whisper. "But I think it's important that I say it anyway. Sarah, I've developed feelings for you. More than just friendship."

The confession hung in the air between them like a delicate thread, fragile and vulnerable. Sarah's cheeks flushed pink, and she looked down at her hands, suddenly very aware of how close Charles was standing. She searched for the right words, wanting to offer comfort and understanding without betraying her own fears.

"Charles," she began, her voice wavering slightly. "I want you to know that I appreciate your honesty, and it means a lot to me that you trust me enough to share this with me. We both have our challenges, but... maybe we can help each other navigate them."

"Maybe we can," Charles murmured, his eyes never leaving hers. It was as if searching for something hidden beneath the surface.

As they stood there, bathed in the golden light of the setting sun, Sarah and Charles found solace in their newfound understanding of one another. The air vibrated with possibility, charged with the electric connection that had formed between them. And though their journey was far from over, they knew they had each other's support to rely on – a bond that was stronger than any obstacle they might face.

The garden seemed to come alive with the colors of the setting sun, each flower cast in a warm, golden hue. Sarah could feel the heat on her cheeks as she watched the way Charles's eyes crinkled at the corners when he smiled. She drew a deep breath, inhaling the sweet scent of roses and lavender that filled the air.

"Charles," she began hesitantly, clasping her hands together as if they alone could hold the weight of her words. "I've been attracted to you too, but I'm scared... Scared of losing my independence."

He tilted his head, considering her words carefully. "I understand," he said softly. "We're both struggling with trust, and neither of us wants to lose ourselves in the process. So, let's take this slow. Let's support each other and overcome our fears together."

"Taking it slow... That sounds like a plan," Sarah agreed, a small smile playing at the corner of her lips. "But how do we start?"

"By being honest with each other," Charles suggested, his voice firm yet gentle. "By talking about what scares us and working through those fears one step at a time."

As they walked along the gravel path, their steps in sync, Sarah couldn't help but notice the way the sunlight glinted off Charles's dark hair, making it seem almost like a halo. The sight brought warmth to her heart, and she found herself smiling more freely than she had in a long time.

"Charles?" she ventured, her voice barely above a whisper.

"Yes, Sarah?"

"Thank you for understanding and for being there for me."

"Of course," he replied, his eyes meeting hers with an intensity that made her heart skip a beat. "And thank you for doing the same for me."

They continued walking, their conversation flowing easily between them. They shared stories of their past, their dreams for the future, and the obstacles they feared might stand in their way. And as they spoke, a newfound sense of trust seemed to weave itself around them, a silken thread that held fast against the uncertainties of the world.

"Sarah," Charles said suddenly, his hand reaching out to brush a stray lock of hair behind her ear. "I just wanted to say... I really believe in you, and I know that together, we can face whatever lies ahead."

"Thank you, Charles," Sarah whispered, her eyes shining with unshed tears. "I believe in us, too."

Sarah and Charles sat side by side on a fallen log, the cool evening breeze rustling through the tall grass around them. They had spent the day training with Dr. Warren, and now they were taking a moment to rest before continuing their journey.

"Charles, I've been thinking," Sarah began, her voice soft and thoughtful. "We've both been honest about our feelings and our fears. Maybe we should make a pact, you know, to be completely open with each other."

He turned his gaze to her, the fading sunlight reflecting in his dark eyes. "I think that's a great idea, Sarah. We can't let our fears hold us back, especially when there's so much at stake. Let's promise to communicate everything, no matter how small or insignificant it may seem."

"Agreed," she said, extending her hand. As he took it, their fingers entwined, she felt a warmth that went beyond the simple touch of skin. It was the warmth of trust, growing stronger with every shared experience.

As they continued their journey, the bond between Sarah and Charles deepened. A silent understanding settled between them as if they could sense each other's needs without speaking.

One morning, when the dew was still clinging to the grass beneath their feet, Charles noticed Sarah shivering in the crisp air. Without a word, he removed his jacket and draped it over her shoulders. She glanced up at him in surprise and gratitude, her blue eyes shining with appreciation.

"Thank you, Charles," she murmured, tightening the jacket around herself.

"Anything for you, Sarah," he replied with a gentle smile, the corners of his eyes crinkling ever so slightly.

As days turned into weeks, the world around them seemed to change and grow with them. The once-empty fields now burst with vibrant wildflowers, their heady scent filling the air. The once-barren trees now reached for the sky, heavy with ripe fruit and leaves that whispered secrets in the wind.

Sarah found herself more and more at ease in Charles's company. She began to assert herself, making choices and taking charge of situations that would have once left her paralyzed with indecision. In turn, Charles began to open up, sharing his thoughts and fears without hesitation.

"Sarah, I'm scared," he admitted one night as they sat beneath a canopy of stars, their faces illuminated by the flickering firelight. "I'm scared of losing you, of letting my guard down only to have it all come crashing down."

"Charles, I'll be honest too – I'm scared too." She took a deep breath, gathering her courage before continuing. "But I know that we can face these fears together because we trust each other, and that makes us stronger than our fears."

"Sarah, you're amazing," Charles whispered, his voice filled with admiration. "You've come so far, and I'm so proud of the person you've become."

"Thank you," she replied, her cheeks flushed with pride. "And thank you for being there every step of the way."

As they journeyed onwards, hand in hand, Sarah and Charles knew that they could face whatever challenges lay ahead. For in each other, they had found a strength that surpassed any obstacle - the incredible power of trust and love.

Sarah and Charles sat on the steps of an old church, its weathered stone walls offering a moment of reprieve from their tireless journey. A gentle breeze rustled through the leaves above them as if whispering secrets to the world below.

"Charles," Sarah began, her eyes fixed on the setting sun, "have you ever thought about what you want to do when all this is over? What kind of future do you hope to create?"

He looked at her, his dark hair dancing in the wind, and smiled. "I have, actually. I want to be some sort of leader — maybe even a politician, though, like the ones we see in Samuel Adams, Paul Revere, Dr Warren, and John Hancock. I've always admired people who can stand up for what they believe in and make a difference."

Sarah nodded, her blue eyes reflecting the fiery hues of the sky. "That suits you. You've always been so good at looking out for others and leading the group." Her gaze shifted downwards, and she played with the hem of her dress, feeling the coarse fabric between her fingers. "As for me... I'm not entirely sure yet. But I think I'd like to help people, too. Maybe as a nurse or a teacher."

"Both would be perfect for you, Sarah," Charles said warmly, placing a reassuring hand on hers. "You're such a caring and compassionate person. It's one of the many things I admire about you."

"Thank you," she murmured, her cheeks coloring with a hint of pink.

They sat there in companionable silence for a moment; each lost in their thoughts about the future. However, a sudden commotion down the street jolted them back to reality. The sound of hooves thundering against the cobblestones, angry shouts, and the unmistakable clang of metal echoed through the air.

"Looks like we've found our next challenge," Charles murmured, an edge of determination in his voice.

"Whatever it is, we'll face it together," Sarah declared, her gaze meeting his. "We've come this far, and we won't let anything tear us apart."

Charles met her determination with a resolute nod. "You're right, Sarah. We can handle anything as long as we believe in each other and communicate our fears. That's what makes us strong."

As they rose from the steps, ready to confront whatever lay ahead, Sarah felt a newfound sense of confidence surge through her. She glanced at Charles – his unwavering strength and faith in her were a source of comfort, a beacon in the darkness that guided her forward.

Together, hand in hand, they stepped into the fray, their hearts alight with love and trust. They knew that no matter the obstacles they faced or the challenges that awaited them, they would remain steadfast in their commitment to each other. And with the future stretched out before them like an untrodden path, they walked arm in arm, ready to embrace all the possibilities and dreams that awaited them just beyond the horizon.

The golden rays of the setting sun filtered through the leaves, casting a warm glow over the quiet alcove where Sarah and Charles found themselves. They sat on a fallen log, their backs against its rough bark, as they took a moment to rest from their latest adventure. The air was thick with the scent of fresh grass and wildflowers, creating a peaceful atmosphere that seemed almost magical.

"Sarah," Charles began hesitantly, his fingers tracing patterns in the soft earth, "I just wanted to say... thank you."

"Thank you?" Sarah echoed, tilting her head curiously. "For what?"

Charles looked at her earnestly, his eyes filled with gratitude. "For being there for me every step of the way. You've shown me what it means to trust someone, and I don't know if I would have made it this far without you."

Sarah felt her cheeks grow warm, but she met his gaze steadily. "And I couldn't have done it without you, Charles. You've taught me how to be brave and stand up for myself."

They shared a small smile, and the world around them seemed to be still; the only sounds were the gentle rustle of leaves and the distant call of a bird.

"Can I ask you something?" Charles ventured, his voice uncharacteristically timid.

"Of course," Sarah replied, intrigued.

"Would it be alright if I..." He trailed off, suddenly shy, before taking a deep breath and continuing, "If I kissed you?"

Sarah's heart skipped a beat, her pulse quickening at the thought. She didn't need to think twice. "Yes, Charles," she whispered, her eyes shining with anticipation.

Their faces inched closer, the space between them shrinking until their lips finally met in a tender, lingering kiss. It was a moment suspended in time, the electric connection between them palpable as they shared their first expression of love.

As they pulled away, Sarah couldn't help but smile, her heart overflowing with warmth and affection. "That was... incredible," she murmured, still trying to catch her breath.

"It was," Charles agreed, his own smile gentle and genuine. "And I think it's only the beginning of what we can overcome together."

The sun dipped lower in the sky, painting the world in shades of gold and amber, as they wrapped their arms around each other and leaned against the fallen log. There, amidst the beauty of nature and the magic of young love, they found solace and strength in each other's presence – a bond that could weather any storm, a connection that would last a lifetime.

"Promise me, Sarah," Charles whispered into her ear, "that no matter what happens, we'll always be there for each other."

"I promise, Charles," she replied softly, her fingers intertwining with his. "Together, we can face anything."

The air was crisp and cool as Sarah and Charles walked side by side through the bustling colonial streets of Boston. They moved with an easy grace, their newfound connection evident in the way they smiled at each other, laughter bubbling up like a secret shared between them.

"Charles," Sarah began, her eyes sparkling with curiosity, "have you ever had a moment where everything just felt... perfect?"

He glanced over at her, his dark hair falling into his eyes as he nodded. "Yes, I think so. When we help each other out or when we make progress on our mission – those moments feel pretty perfect to me."

Sarah's cheeks flushed pink, and she looked down at the cobblestone path beneath their feet. The sun cast long shadows across the ground, turning the ordinary stones into a mosaic of light and dark. In that instant, she realized just how far they had come — not only in their journey together but also in their personal growth.

"Me too," she agreed, her voice soft yet steady. "But I also think that overcoming our trust issues is part of what makes those moments so special."

Charles tilted his head thoughtfully, his eyes searching hers for understanding. "You're right, Sarah. We've both made mistakes, and we've both been hurt before. But we're learning from those experiences and growing stronger together."

"Exactly," she replied, her blue eyes shining with conviction. "And I believe that as long as we continue to support each other and communicate openly, there's no obstacle we can't overcome."

As they continued to walk, the lively sounds of the marketplace filled the air — the hum of conversation, the clatter of carts loaded with goods, the calls of merchants hawking their wares. Amidst the chaos, Sarah and Charles found a sense of tranquility in their newfound bond and in the knowledge that they could face any challenge that came their way.

"Speaking of communication," Charles said with a sly grin, "I wanted to tell you that I noticed how assertive you were during our last meeting with Dr. Warren. You made your opinion known and stood up for what you believed in — I was really impressed."

"Thank you, Charles," she replied, her heart swelling with pride at his words. "I've been trying to work on that, you know. Asserting myself and making decisions independently."

"I can see you're making progress," he encouraged, reaching over to give her hand a gentle squeeze. "And it's not just me who's noticing – the others are too. They respect your opinions and look up to you."

"Really?" Sarah asked, astonishment coloring her voice. "I never realized they felt that way."

"Trust me, they do," Charles assured her, a warm smile spreading across his face. "And I'm proud of you, too."

Sarah and Charles continued their journey together – side by side, heart to heart, conquering their fears and insecurities with love and support from one another. And in those moments, as they navigated life's challenges hand in hand, they discovered that the most powerful force of all was not an army or a weapon but rather the unbreakable bond that connected them – a bond that would guide them through the darkest nights and into the brightest days, a bond that would endure for all time.

# CHAPTER 10

The next morning in Dr. Warren's office, the thick tension in the air hung heavy as a cloud over the group of children huddled together, each casting furtive glances at one another. Sarah, with her long blonde hair cascading down her shoulders, chewed on her bottom lip and looked around, sensing the unease that had begun to creep into their once unified circle.

"Something's not right," whispered Henry, his eyes darting from one person to the next. "I can feel it."

"Me too," agreed Sarah, her heart pounding in her chest like a runaway horse. "We have to be careful about who we trust."

As the children continued to exchange uneasy looks, a stranger entered the room. There was a man, tall and lean, with sandy blond hair that fell just below his ears. He strode confidently towards Dr. Joseph Warren, who greeted him warmly. The doctor's charisma shone through as he introduced the newcomer to the group.

"Everyone, this is Mr. Hawthorne," Dr. Warren announced, clasping the man's hand firmly. "He has come to aid us in our cause."

"Please, call me Thomas," the man corrected with a charming smile, making his way around the circle and shaking hands with each child. His charm seemed to effortlessly blend him into the group, easing the children's suspicions for the moment.

"Nice to meet you, Thomas," said Sarah, her guard momentarily lowered by the man's disarming demeanor. She noticed how his eyes sparkled, almost as if they held a secret within them.

"Thank you, Sarah," Thomas replied, holding her gaze for a beat longer than necessary. "I'm looking forward to working with all of you."

As the children and Dr. Warren continued to engage in conversation with the charismatic stranger, none could shake the growing feeling that something was amiss. Sarah couldn't help but wonder if their trust in Mr. Hawthorne was misplaced. She decided to keep a watchful eye on the new arrival, her instincts telling her that this seemingly trustworthy man might not be all that he appeared to be.

"Come, let me show you around our makeshift headquarters," Dr. Warren suggested to Thomas, motioning for the children to follow. As they walked through the dimly lit corridors, Sarah continued to study Thomas' every move, trying to discern any hidden intentions behind his friendly exterior.

"Ah, your collection of books is impressive!" Thomas exclaimed upon seeing a small library in one of the rooms. The children watched as he ran his fingers along the spines of the books, his eyes lighting up with genuine interest. It was hard not to feel drawn to him, even as their unease persisted.

"Indeed, knowledge is power," Dr. Warren replied with a smile, clearly pleased by Thomas' enthusiasm. "We must understand our history and our world if we are to change it."

"Very true," agreed Thomas, nodding thoughtfully as he pulled a book from the shelf and flipped through its pages. "It's an honor to be here, among people who share my beliefs and passions."

As the tour continued, the children couldn't help but feel charmed by Thomas' presence. His intelligence and wit seemed to fit perfectly within their group. And yet, Sarah's instincts still nagged at her, urging her to remain cautious.

"Time will reveal all," she whispered to herself, clutching the locket around her neck. For now, she would keep a close watch on Mr. Hawthorne, hoping that her suspicions would prove unfounded and that their new ally could truly be trusted.

Sarah and the others gathered around the large oak table in Dr. Warren's study. Thomas Hawthorne took a seat at the head of the table, his eyes scanning the faces of the young patriots with an air of confidence.

"Let's discuss our plans," he said smoothly, tapping his fingers on the polished wood. "I've heard whispers of a British shipment arriving soon. I believe intercepting it could prove beneficial to our cause."

Charles raised an eyebrow, exchanging glances with Sarah. "What sort of shipment?" he asked cautiously.

"Arms, ammunition, supplies—valuable resources for their troops," Thomas replied, his eyes glinting with cunning. "If we can seize them, we'll gain an advantage and deliver a blow to the enemy."

Dr. Warren nodded thoughtfully, stroking his chin. "It's a bold move but risky. We'll need careful planning and precise execution."

"Leave that to me," Thomas assured them, his voice laced with charm. "I have connections that can provide us with useful information."

As they delved into the details of their plan, Sarah couldn't help but notice how effortlessly Thomas guided the conversation, steering them toward decisions that seemed to align with his own agenda. Each suggestion was met with approval, and before long, the group found themselves following his lead.

"I should feel excited about this mission," Sarah thought, biting her lip. "But something feels…off." The unease she'd felt earlier continued to gnaw at her, growing stronger as she observed the man's subtle manipulations.

"Sarah, what do you think?" Charles asked, snapping her out of her thoughts.

"Um…" She hesitated, feeling the weight of their gazes on her. "I agree that the mission is important. But we should be cautious, too. We don't know what traps the British might have set for us."

"Spoken like a true patriot," Thomas said with a smile, placing a reassuring hand on her shoulder. "Fear not, for we shall tread carefully and keep our wits about us."

"Indeed," Dr. Warren chimed in, his eyes twinkling with confidence. "With Thomas' connections and our combined skills, we have a strong chance of success."

Sarah forced a smile, but her stomach churned with unease. There was something about Thomas' smooth assurance that bothered her, yet she couldn't quite put her finger on it.

As the group continued to discuss the mission, Clarissa

remained quiet, her brow furrowed in concentration. Sarah noticed her friend's contemplative expression and wondered if Clarissa shared her apprehensions.

"Clarissa, any thoughts?" Dr. Warren asked, turning his attention to the shy girl.

"Um..." Clarissa hesitated, adjusting her glasses nervously. "I think the plan is sound, but I can't help feeling like there's something we're overlooking... something important."

Her words hung in the air, casting a shadow of doubt over the group. The children exchanged worried glances, their excitement dampened by the growing sense of unease.

"Trust me," Thomas said, smiling warmly at Clarissa. "We've covered all our bases. There's no need for concern."

"Perhaps you're right," Dr. Warren conceded, his voice firm yet gentle. "But it never hurts to be vigilant. Let's go over the plan once more, just to make sure we haven't missed anything."

Sarah watched as they dove back into the details, her heart pounding with trepidation. As Thomas began to recount the plan to the group, their concerns became dissuaded, and the plan was one that could be won. The children listened and thought back to what they had learned about trust, came together, and decided that this new charming ally could be an added piece to their cause.

As the group dispersed, Sarah wandered into the quiet and dimly lit library of their temporary headquarters. The gentle flicker of candlelight illuminated rows of dusty tomes that held the secrets of long-forgotten knowledge. She ran her fingers along the spines of the books, feeling a connection with the past as she searched for something – anything – to help ease her troubled mind.

"Looking for answers?" whispered a soft voice behind her. Startled, Sarah turned to see Clarissa, her eyes wide with worry.

"Something doesn't feel right," Sarah confessed, her voice barely audible. "I can't put my finger on it, but I think we're in danger."

Clarissa hesitated, then nodded in agreement. "I've been feeling the same way. But what can we do?"

"Maybe there's something in these books that can help us," Sarah suggested, her determination shining through her fear. Together, they scanned the shelves, hoping to find a clue that would unlock the mystery.

After several minutes of fruitless searching, Sarah pulled a heavy book from the shelf, its leather cover worn with age. As she opened it, a folded piece of parchment fell on the floor, catching her eye. Picking it up, she unfolded it and gasped, her eyes widening in horror at the words scrawled across the page.

"Clarissa, look at this!" she whispered urgently, holding the paper for her friend to see. It was a letter, written in an elegant, flowing script, detailing a Thomas Hawthorne, who was a Boston leader from years ago and had died and left no heirs. The letter is one from this Thomas Hawthorne to his distant family in England, stating his affairs and leaving all he had to their ownership. This showed that this ally they just met couldn't possibly be real as there was no other Hawthorne family in Boston.

"Impossible," Clarissa breathed, disbelief etched on her face. "He seemed so genuine..."

"Yet here it is, plain as day," Sarah replied, her hands trembling as she clutched the damning evidence. "We've been betrayed."

The two girls exchanged anguished looks, their hearts heavy with the weight of their discovery. The seeds of doubt sown earlier had blossomed into a dark, choking vine that threatened to strangle their trust in those around them.

"Dr. Warren and the others need to know," Clarissa said, her voice shaking. "We can't let him get away with this."

"Agreed," Sarah replied, her eyes hardening with resolve. "But who can we trust? If he could deceive us so easily, how do we know there aren't more spies among us?"

"Trust is a fragile thing," Clarissa murmured, her gaze fixed on the damning letter. "Once broken, it's difficult to mend. But we have no choice – we must put our faith in each other and confront this treachery head-on."

With heavy hearts and minds clouded by uncertainty, the two girls left the library, determined to unmask the betrayer in their midst and protect their friends from the consequences of misplaced trust. As they stepped into the hallway, the shadows seemed to close in around them, echoing the darkness that lurked within their own hearts.

As Sarah and Clarissa hurried through the dimly lit corridors of the safe house, their hearts raced with the urgency of their mission. They could hear the distant echo of laughter from Dr.

Warren's planning session, a group gathered in the parlor to strategize for the upcoming raid on the British supplies. The young girls exchanged a knowing glance, acutely aware of the impending danger.

"Dr. Warren," Sarah called out breathlessly as she and Clarissa burst into the room, "we need to speak with you."

"What's the matter, my dear?" Dr. Warren asked, his eyes filled with concern as he took in the girls' anxious expressions.

"May we speak in private?" Clarissa interjected, casting a wary eye over the assembled group.

"Of course," Dr. Warren replied, escorting them into an adjacent study. "Now, what's so urgent that it couldn't wait?"

"Someone among us is a traitor," Sarah blurted out, her hands shaking slightly as she revealed the letter they had discovered.

The color drained from Dr. Warren's face as he read the words on the parchment. "This can't be..." he whispered, disbelief clouding his features.

"Unfortunately, it's true," Clarissa said solemnly. "And we think he has already sabotaged tonight's mission."

"Impossible!" Dr. Warren exclaimed, but deep down, he knew they were right. In his haste to save lives and aid the rebellion, he had trusted too easily. And now, their cause was in grave danger.

"Is there any way to salvage the mission?" Sarah asked, her voice laced with determination.

"Perhaps," Dr. Warren mused, his mind racing with possibilities. "But we must act quickly."

"First, we have to identify the spy," Clarissa insisted, her gaze unwavering.

"Yes, and once we've done that, we must find a way to counteract his treachery," Dr. Warren agreed, the fire of resolve igniting in his eyes.

"Then let's do it," Sarah said, her voice firm. "We can't let him ruin everything we've worked for."

"Agreed," Clarissa nodded, her own determination mirrored in her friend's steely expression.

"Alright, my young friends," Dr. Warren said, clapping his hands together with purpose. "Let's set things right."

The three of them returned to the parlor, their steps quickened by the urgency of their task. Each person they passed became a potential suspect. Every smile now tinged with the possibility of deception.

"Remember," Dr. Warren whispered as they rejoined the group, "trust no one."

"Except each other," Sarah added, her gaze locked on Clarissa's, their friendship a beacon of hope amidst the sea of doubt.

"Indeed," Dr. Warren agreed, his eyes fixed on the faces around him, searching for any hint of betrayal. "Now, let's save our mission – and our cause."

As the clock ticked away the precious minutes, Sarah, Clarissa, and Dr. Warren worked tirelessly to identify the traitor among them. Every word spoken was scrutinized, every action analyzed, their determination unwavering. As they delved deeper into the shadows, the girls knew that their bond, forged in trust and loyalty, would be the key to dismantling the sabotage and preserving the fragile hope of their rebellion.

The crackling fire cast eerie shadows on the walls as Sarah, Clarissa, and Dr. Warren gathered in the dimly lit parlor, their eyes darting from one person to another. Their hearts raced with unspoken tension, and a heavy silence filled the room. It was time to confront the traitor.

"Tell me," Dr. Warren began, his voice steady despite the turmoil brewing inside him, "are you loyal to our cause?"

"Of course!" the man sent by Thomas Hawthorn, named George, replied, feigning innocence. "I'm as dedicated to American independence as anyone here."

"Then explain this!" Sarah blurted out, thrusting forward a crumpled letter that she had discovered hidden in the spy's belongings. Her hands trembled with anger and betrayal. "This letter is addressed to General Gage himself, detailing our plans!"

"Sarah, I can't believe you would go through my things!" George exclaimed, attempting to turn the tables. "This is an outrageous violation of trust!"

"Enough!" Dr. Warren interjected, his patience wearing thin. "It's clear that you are responsible for sabotaging our mission, putting everyone here in grave danger. You will answer for your actions."

"Or what?" the George sneered, defiance flashing in their eyes. "You have no proof beyond this letter, which could be easily forged."

"Your arrogance will be your undoing," Clarissa declared, her quiet voice echoing with newfound strength. "We know the truth, and we won't let you destroy everything we've worked for."

With a fluid motion, the spy suddenly lunged towards the door, desperate to make their escape. Dr. Warren reacted without hesitation, grabbing the nearest chair and swinging it in the path of the fleeing traitor. The chair collided with the spy, sending them sprawling onto the floor, gasping for breath.

"Charles! Henry! Help us!" Sarah shouted, adrenaline pumping through her veins as her friends rushed in to assist.

"Going somewhere?" Charles demanded, his eyes narrowed as he helped pin the spy down. "You really thought you could deceive us all and get away with it?"

"Let me go!" George snarled, struggling against the combined strength of Charles and Henry. But their determination held firm, refusing to let the traitor escape judgment.

"Your treachery ends here," Dr. Warren declared, his voice cold with finality. "You will face the consequences of your actions, and we will ensure that our cause remains strong."

As they stood united in the flickering firelight—Sarah, Clarissa, Dr. Warren, Charles, and Henry—their resolve solidified like iron. Betrayal had shaken them, but it had not broken them. Each knew deep within their heart that they would overcome this setback, driven by the unwavering belief in their mission and each other. Together, they would fight for freedom and restore hope to their ravaged land.

"Please," George begged, a note of desperation creeping into their voice. "You don't understand."

"Understand what?" Clarissa demanded, her eyes blazing with fury. "How you betrayed us? How you put our lives in danger?"

"Enough!" Dr. Warren commanded, his strong presence making everyone stop in their tracks. "We need to get this traitor secured and interrogated before they can cause any more harm." The others nodded, feeling a renewed sense of urgency.

As Charles and Henry tightened their grip on the spy, the room fell silent. It was Sarah who noticed it first: the faint rustling sound coming from the traitor's cloak.

"Wait," she whispered, her blue eyes widening with fear. "What's that?"

The spy smirked and, in a sudden blur of motion, pulled a small, concealed dagger from their cloak. With an almost unnatural speed, they slashed at Charles and Henry, forcing them to release their hold.

"Get him!" Dr. Warren yelled as the spy darted towards the open window. The children scrambled after the fleeing figure, desperately trying to catch up.

The streets outside were dark and slick with rain as they pursued the shadowy form of the spy. Their hearts pounded in their chests, each breath ragged and labored as they pushed themselves to keep up.

"Where did he go?" Charles panted, scanning the dimly lit alleys for any sign of the spy.

"Over there!" shouted Henry, catching sight of the traitor slipping around a corner.

As they rounded the bend, Sarah couldn't help but feel a sickening sense of dread building within her. Would they be able to capture the spy before he vanished into the shadows? And even if they did, how could they ever trust anyone again?

"Watch out!" Clarissa exclaimed just as the spy leaped out of the shadows, aiming a fierce kick at Sarah. The force of the blow sent her sprawling onto the cobblestone street.

"Sarah!" Charles cried out, rushing to her side. He glared at the spy, his fists clenched in anger. "You'll pay for that!"

"Charles, be careful!" Dr. Warren warned as he and Henry tried to corner the traitor.

As the spy desperately looked for an escape route, they suddenly produced another dagger, brandishing it menacingly. Their eyes locked with Sarah's, and she could see something dangerous lurking within those dark depths.

"Stay back," the spy hissed, jumping up and backing towards the edge of a nearby wall that gave way to a drop to another level below. "I won't hesitate to take one of you down with me." The children hesitated, unsure of what to do next.

"Listen to me," Dr. Warren said, trying to appeal to the spy's humanity. "There's still a chance for redemption. You don't have to choose this path."

For a moment, it seemed as if the spy might waver. But then their expression hardened, and with a cold, calculating smile, he stepped back off the edge of the wall and disappeared into the darkness below.

"NO!" Sarah screamed, rushing to the edge and peering down into the abyss.

"Is he...?" Clarissa asked fearfully.

"Can't be certain," Dr. Warren replied, his face etched with worry. "But either way, we've lost them—for now."

The children stood there, hearts pounding, as the rain began to pour down around them. They had failed to capture the spy, and the consequences of that failure weighed heavily on each of them. With the threat of the traitor still looming, there was no telling what dangers lay ahead. As their gazes met, a silent understanding passed between them: they must be prepared for anything.

"Come on," Dr. Warren said, his voice filled with determination. "We have a lot of work to do."

The group ran back to the meeting place and went over some of the papers from the spy's belongs to find whatever information they could to help salvage the night.

"It looks like this was all an elaborate ruse, and they are actually bringing troops into Boston to seize the gun powder stock held at Lexington!" Dr. Warren exclaimed, "This is worse than we thought. It also seems they will be making arrests of both Samuel Adams and John Hancock in the night as well. We need to warn them."

"How will we know where the British will be coming?" Henry asked, his anger seeming to bubble beneath the surface.

"We had a plan for just this circumstance, although admittedly, I didn't think it would truly come to this," Dr. Warren explained.

"What can we do to help?" Sarah chimed in, seeing Dr. Warren move behind his desk, and began writing several notes.

"I need you children to take this to Paul Revere instantly. He will know what to do. I will send out other riders, and I will need to get to the North church to have the signal sent out." Dr. Warren said, not looking up from his work.

"The signal?" Henry asked, puzzled.

"The North Church? A signal?" Clarissa questioned, and then her eyes flashed bright with recognition. "Oh! One if by land, two if by sea! To let the riders know how the British are coming to raid the land."

Dr. Warren abruptly stopped and looked up from what he was doing. "Yes, wait...how did you know that?! That was supposed to be a secret."

The children, one by one, started to understand the significance of the events that were transpiring, and Clarissa spoke up again, "It is Dr. Warren, it is; it was just something that came to our minds. This plan will work, and you can trust that we will deliver this message to Paul Revere. You will save this night."

"Well, we better, or else the British are going to swoop in and catch us unawares," Dr. Warren stated, shaking off his concern and going back to his letters. "It seems you already know what you need to do; I need you to carry out this most important mission and use your discretion, farewell my young friends. I will see you on the other side of this."

The children ran through the streets ever watchful for the enemy they had already faced that night, and the pressure of the moment seemed to hang on them. They ran through the now familiar streets and found themselves at Paul Revere's house.

"Mr. Revere!" Henry exclaimed, running to his friend and handing him the letter, "this is for you from Dr. Warren."

As Paul read the letter, his countenance dropped, and he quickly got up and told the children to follow him out back.

"We must ride at once, children," Paul Revere shouted, "here, there is a horse for each of you. Take one and follow me quickly!"

As they watched Revere saddle his horse and prepare for his famous midnight ride, the children could feel the urgency and tension in the air. The night was charged with a sense of impending danger and the need for swift action.

"Wow, history is unfolding right in front of us," Charles marveled, his heart racing with adrenaline.

As the children followed after the galloping horse, they knew that each step was taking them deeper into history. The Boston Tea Party had been an eye-opening experience, but they were eager to continue their journey and uncover more secrets of the past. And with Paul Revere's ride unfolding before them, their adventure was far from over.

"Can you believe it?" Charles shouted over the clatter. "We're witnessing Paul Revere's famous midnight ride!"

"Shout it a little louder, why don't you?" Clarissa teased, her eyes sparkling in the dim light. "Maybe the British will hear you too!"

"Quiet, both of you!" Henry hissed, although he couldn't help but grin at their banter. "We need to stay close to Revere without drawing attention."

As they rounded a corner, Revere suddenly pulled back on his horse's reins, bringing it to a stop just ahead of them. He checked for the children, his eyes full of wisdom and determination.

"Are you ready?" he asked in a hushed tone, studying their faces closely.

"Uh, we're –" Henry stammered, unsure of what to say.

"Ready," Clarissa interrupted confidently. "We're ready to help with your mission, Mr. Revere."

"Very well, but time is short," Revere replied, his voice steady and calm. "Listen closely, young ones. Tonight, we must warn the countryside that the British are coming. This information is crucial to our fight for independence."

"Wow, this is really happening," Charles whispered to himself, awe-struck by Revere's presence.

"Stay close, and remember – silence is key," Revere

instructed as they all were mounted on their horses. "Now, follow me."

"See that church there?" Revere said, pointing to a towering steeple. "The lanterns were hung in its belfry earlier tonight as a signal – one if by land, two if by sea. It's a secret message system we patriots use to communicate."

"Wow, so this is how you would know what to tell the people," Henry mused, looking over to Clarissa and smiling after she shocked Dr. Warren with that very comment.

"You lot catch on quick," Revere replied, a hint of a smile on his lips. "And remember, my young friends, our fight for freedom depends on people like you – brave, curious, and passionate about justice."

As they continued out of the city, the children felt a newfound sense of purpose and solidarity – not just with each other but with the countless individuals who had stood up against tyranny throughout history. Paul Revere's ride wasn't just a thrilling adventure; it was a lesson in courage, sacrifice, and the power of unity.

"Paul, how did you find the courage to ride like this?" Sarah asked, her eyes wide with admiration as they continued through the darkened streets. "I mean, it's one thing to speak out against injustice, but to literally risk your life for a cause...it's amazing."

"True bravery is not the absence of fear," Paul Revere replied thoughtfully, "but rather, the decision to face it head-on in the name of freedom and justice. It is something that each and every one of us has within us – you remember Dr. Warren's speech?"

"Oh, we remember," Henry chimed in, "we all have our roles to play in the fight for independence. Just look at us! We're kids who've managed to find ourselves right in the thick of things."

"Exactly," Revere agreed, nodding his approval. "And I am confident that, together, we can make a difference."

"Wow, I can't wait to tell my history teacher about this," Clarissa whispered excitedly, glancing around at the historical landmarks they had witnessed firsthand. "No more boring textbooks for me!"

"Same here," Sarah agreed, her voice barely a murmur as they darted between shadows to avoid detection. "It's incredible how much more alive history feels when you're actually here, experiencing it."

As they paused momentarily, hidden from view, Henry took a deep breath, inhaling the scents of saltwater and gunpowder that permeated the air. He could feel the energy and tension coursing through Boston — the impending clash of forces that would change the course of history forever.

"Guys," he said softly, his voice tinged with awe, "this has been a once-in-a-lifetime experience. The Boston Tea Party, Paul Revere's ride... It's shown me that history isn't just something to be read about or studied; it's something to be lived, to be felt."

"Agreed," Clarissa whispered, a fierce determination lighting her eyes. "And now that we've seen it for ourselves, we can't just sit idly by. We have a mission — and I, for one, am ready to do whatever it takes to succeed."

"Me too," Charles added resolutely, the others echoing her sentiment with determined nods.

As they slipped back into the shadows, following Paul Revere through the night, the children found their resolve strengthened by their experiences. The Boston Tea Party and Paul Revere's ride had taught them invaluable lessons about bravery, sacrifice, and the power of unity – lessons they would carry with them as they continued on their incredible journey through history.

# CHAPTER 11

The warm scent of cinnamon and cloves filled the air as Dr. Warren led the children into his study. The cryptex had pulled them through again as the world spun and whirled about them to take them to another time in this adventure; the feeling wasn't easy, but it became more familiar. The golden glow of candlelight flickered upon the shelves, casting shadows on the well-worn books that lined the walls. Sarah gazed around in awe, her eyes wide with curiosity.

"Please, gather 'round," Dr. Warren said, gesturing to the chairs near the fireplace. He stood tall and proud, his dark hair framing his strong jawline. There was a kindness in his eyes that immediately endeared him to the children.

"Friends," he began, "tomorrow marks the anniversary of the Boston Massacre, a tragic event that we must never forget. Our fellow citizens gave their lives for our cause, and it is our duty to honor their sacrifice. I have been asked to deliver a speech that will inspire and unite the people in our fight for freedom."

Henry leaned forward, his eyes shining with determination. "We want to help, Dr. Warren. We're ready to do whatever it takes."

"Indeed," Charles chimed in, his voice firm and resolute. "We may be young, but we understand the importance of this struggle."

Dr. Warren looked at each of them, his gaze thoughtful and deliberate. "I am grateful for your willingness to assist me. Your energy and enthusiasm will serve us well."

Sarah felt her heart swell with pride, and she knew Clarissa shared her feelings. They were part of something much larger than themselves, and the knowledge filled them with a sense of purpose.

"Your task, my young friends, will be to help me craft a message that speaks to the hearts of our people. We must remind them of what we are fighting for: liberty, justice, and the right to determine our own destinies."

"Let's show them that even though we've suffered, we're stronger than ever!" Sarah exclaimed, her mind racing with ideas.

"Exactly," Dr. Warren said, his eyes crinkling at the corners as he smiled at her. "I believe that together, we can make a difference."

The children exchanged glances, their determination mirrored in each other's faces. They knew the task ahead was daunting, but the fire inside them burned brighter than ever. And as Dr. Warren explained his vision for the speech, they began to realize just how important their role would be in shaping the future of their country.

"Right," Sarah said, her eyes bright with determination. "The best way for us to understand how people truly feel about the

Boston Massacre and its impact is to hear it from their own mouths, in their own words."

"Indeed, but we must be discreet," Dr. Warren cautioned. "We don't want to draw any unnecessary attention to ourselves."

"Perhaps we could visit some taverns or gathering spots frequented by patriots?" Sarah suggested, her heart beating faster at the thought of venturing out into the bustling streets of Boston.

"An excellent idea, Sarah," Dr. Warren praised, his gaze encouraging. "You four can split up into pairs and listen in on conversations, gather as much information as you can."

"Sounds like a plan," Charles replied, already thinking through the logistics. "Sarah, you can come with me; Clarissa, you'll go with Henry."

"Alright," Sarah agreed, trying to quell the nerves fluttering in her stomach. She glanced at Charles, hoping he didn't notice the slight blush that crept up her cheeks.

"Stay safe, children," Dr. Warren reminded them as they prepared to head out. "And remember, discretion is key."

"Of course, Doctor," Henry assured him with a confident nod.

Stepping outside, Sarah breathed in the crisp air, her senses immediately assaulted by the myriad sights, sounds, and smells of the city. Vendors shouted their wares. Horses clopped down the cobblestone streets, and the scent of freshly baked bread wafted from nearby shops.

"Let's head over to The Green Dragon Tavern first," Charles whispered to Sarah as they walked, keeping an eye out for any potential danger. "It's known to be a popular spot for patriots."

"Good plan," she agreed, her fingers fiddling with the edge of her shawl as they approached their destination.

As they entered the dimly lit tavern, Sarah and Charles seemed to blend in effortlessly with the boisterous crowd. They found a quiet corner where they could observe and eavesdrop on the conversations around them without drawing too much attention.

"Remember," Charles whispered, "we're just here to listen."

"Right," Sarah replied, her heart pounding in her ears as she focused on the low murmur of voices surrounding them.

"Did you hear about the new taxes?" one man grumbled to another at a nearby table, his voice full of frustration. "We can barely afford to put food on our tables as it is!"

"Indeed," the other man replied grimly. "But what can we do? The British have us by the throat."

"Maybe not for long," the first man said, leaning in conspiratorially. "There are those who say that change is coming."

"Change, huh?" the second man scoffed. "I'll believe it when I see it."

"Shh!" the first man hissed, glancing around nervously. "Not so loud! You don't know who might be listening."

Sarah felt her pulse quicken as she absorbed their conversation, realizing the weight of the information they were gathering. This was far more than just eavesdropping; it was a chance to truly understand the struggles and hopes of the people they sought to inspire. And with every word heard, every emotion felt, they were one step closer to crafting a message that would resonate with the hearts of their fellow patriots.

Clarissa and Henry, with their collars turned up against the chill of the evening, found themselves in a small, dimly lit tavern on the outskirts of town. The walls were adorned with worn maps and faded portraits of men whose names had been lost to time, and the air was thick with the smell of pipe smoke and spilled ale. As they slowly made their way through the crowded room, Clarissa couldn't help but notice the intensity of the conversations taking place around them. A fire burned low in the hearth, casting flickering shadows on the faces of the patrons.

"Over here," Henry whispered, nodding towards an unoccupied table tucked away in a shadowy corner. They sat down, trying their best to blend in with the boisterous crowd. Clarissa shifted uncomfortably in her seat as she strained to catch snippets of conversation from a nearby group of men huddled together over tankards of ale.

"Mark my words," one man declared, slamming his fist onto the table, "the Boston Massacre only strengthened our resolve to be free from British rule!"

"Indeed," agreed another, raising his mug in salute. "Those brave souls who perished that night will not have died in vain."

Clarissa felt a spark of determination flare within her as she listened, her heart swelling with pride for the convictions of these patriots. She caught Henry's eye and saw the same fierce resolve mirrored there.

As Sarah and Charles slipped into a bustling marketplace, they quickly realized that their best chance of eavesdropping would be to pose as shoppers. They approached a stall selling colorful ribbons and trinkets, their fingers brushing over the delicate materials as they pretended to browse. Their ears, however, were tuned in to the conversation between two merchants standing nearby.

"British taxation is crippling us," one merchant lamented, his voice heavy with worry. "I can barely afford to keep my shop open, let alone provide for my family."

"Same here," sighed the other, shaking his head. "It's as if they're trying to squeeze every last penny from us, regardless of the consequences."

"Something has to change," the first merchant said firmly. "We cannot continue like this."

Sarah exchanged a glance with Charles, her mind racing with the implications of what she'd just heard. It was clear that the economic hardships faced by their fellow colonists were yet another catalyst driving them towards revolution.

As the two pairs of young time travelers continued to listen and learn, they knew that they had a responsibility to not only inform Dr. Warren but also to help give voice to the hopes and dreams of a people yearning for freedom. The weight of their mission settled upon their shoulders, but it was one they would bear willingly, knowing that they were part of something much larger than themselves.

Sarah glanced at the door of the tavern, and as if on cue, Clarissa and Henry stepped out into the dimly lit street. The four friends converged in a nearby alleyway, away from prying eyes.

"Did you find anything useful?" Sarah asked anxiously, her heart racing with anticipation.

"Absolutely," Clarissa responded, her eyes gleaming with excitement. "We overheard a group of patriots discussing how the Boston Massacre has only strengthened their resolve to fight for independence."

"Good," Charles chimed in, his voice quiet but determined. "We also learned that British taxation is causing severe economic hardships for the people here. They're struggling just to survive."

The air was thick with tension as the young time travelers exchanged their findings. It was evident that the situation in Boston was dire, and they had a crucial role to play in crafting Dr. Warren's speech to inspire hope and unity among the colonists.

"Dr. Warren needs to know about this," Sarah murmured, her thoughts racing. "But we can't just present him with facts. We need something more powerful to drive the message home."

"Something personal," Charles suggested, his brow furrowed in deep thought. "What if we gathered stories from those directly affected by the Boston Massacre? We could use their experiences as an emotional element in the speech."

"Brilliant idea, Charles!" Clarissa exclaimed, her eyes lighting up with determination. "Those stories will resonate with everyone who hears them."

Henry nodded solemnly, adding, "It'll show the resilience of our people and the depth of their conviction. We must not let the sacrifices they've made go unnoticed."

"Then it's settled," Sarah declared, her heart swelling with pride at the thought of the important task ahead. "We'll gather these stories and make sure their voices are heard."

As the four friends set off on their mission, the streets of Boston seemed to pulse with a sense of urgency. They knew that every word they collected would carry the weight of history on its shoulders, and with each step, they felt themselves becoming more deeply entwined in the fabric of the past. The playful nature of their adventure was eclipsed by the gravity of their responsibility, but it only served to strengthen their resolve.

"Let's split up again," Charles suggested as they approached the crowded market square. "We'll cover more ground that way."

"Agreed," Sarah replied, her thoughts already turning to the questions she would ask and the stories she hoped to uncover. "Remember, we're doing this for them — for all those who have suffered and still dare to dream of freedom."

No longer mere observers, they were now active participants in the unfolding drama of history. As they set out to gather the tales that would shape the destiny of a nation, they couldn't help but wonder how their own lives would be forever changed by the events that had brought them together.

Sarah approached the cluster of solemn, weary figures

huddled together in a corner of the market square. A knot of fear twisted in her stomach, but she swallowed it down, reminding herself that she was here to give these people a voice.

"Excuse me," she began hesitantly, her voice barely audible above the murmur of the bustling marketplace. "My friends and I are collecting stories about the Boston Massacre for an important speech. We want the world to know what happened here and how it has affected you all."

The group seemed to pause for a moment as if weighing Sarah's words before a frail, elderly woman with a weathered face and sorrowful eyes stepped forward. "You must be a brave girl to take on this task," she said softly. "I'll tell you my story, but first, let me introduce myself. My name is Abigail."

"Thank you, Mrs. Abigail," Sarah replied, feeling a mixture of relief and determination as the woman began to speak.

"I lost my son that night," Abigail began, her voice trembling with emotion. "He had just turned twenty, and he was so full of life, so eager to make his mark on the world. But all that was taken from him when those soldiers opened fire. The memory of his lifeless body, lying there in the cold, blood-stained snow, haunts me every day."

Sarah could feel her heart breaking for the woman standing before her, as well as the others who had gathered around to listen. She glanced over at Charles, who was speaking with another survivor, while Henry and Clarissa listened intently to a man recounting his experience.

"Every time I look into the faces of my grandchildren, I see my son's eyes staring back at me," Abigail continued, tears streaming down her cheeks. "And I am reminded that they will never know their father, nor will he ever know the joy of watching them grow."

"Thank you for sharing your story, Mrs. Abigail," Sarah said gently, reaching out to grasp the woman's frail hand. "We promise to do everything we can to make sure your son's memory lives on."

"God bless you, child," Abigail whispered, her eyes shining with gratitude.

As the children made their way from one survivor to another, they absorbed each harrowing tale, internalizing the pain, anger, and determination for justice that echoed through every word. It was a heavy burden to carry, but Sarah knew it was a small price to pay for the chance to heal the wounds of a broken people.

"Sarah," Charles called out, his voice tinged with urgency. "I think we've got what we need. We should go."

"Alright," Sarah agreed, feeling the weight of their mission settling on her shoulders like a cloak. As they turned to leave, she took one last look at the faces of those who had suffered so much and silently vowed to bring their stories to life.

Huddled together in the fading afternoon light, Sarah and the others carefully transcribed the stories they had gathered. Charles's hand shook as he traced the curve of a letter, his eyes shining with unshed tears. Henry sucked in a quiet breath while Clarissa bit her lip, both immersed in the raw emotions that filled the pages.

"Are you sure we got everything right?" asked Clarissa, her voice barely above a whisper.

"Every word," Sarah assured her, her gaze never leaving the ink-stained paper before her. "We'll make sure Dr. Warren knows exactly what we heard and felt today."

"Good," said Henry, determination flickering in his eyes. "I don't want to let these people down."

As the sun dipped below the horizon, casting long shadows across the cobblestone streets, the children made their way back to Dr. Warren's hideout. The city seemed to hold its breath, waiting for night to fall and cloak the world in darkness.

"Is it just me, or are there more Redcoats around than usual?" Charles murmured, his eyes darting between the street corners and alleyways.

Sarah furrowed her brow, suddenly aware of the increased presence of British soldiers patrolling the streets. Their crimson uniforms stood out like streaks of blood against the gray buildings, a stark reminder of the violence that had taken place on these very streets.

"Stay close and stay quiet," she instructed the others, her heart pounding in her chest. "We can't afford to be caught now."

Silently, the children wove their way through the twisting maze of streets, avoiding the watchful gazes of the soldiers. As they neared Dr. Warren's hideout, Sarah couldn't help but feel an overwhelming sense of urgency. What if the speech didn't have the impact they hoped? What if the survivors' stories went unheard?

"Sarah, look!" Clarissa hissed, pulling her back into the present. "There's a patrol coming this way!"

"Quick, in here," whispered Henry, gesturing to a narrow alleyway. The children slipped into the shadows, holding their breaths as the soldiers marched past, their boots echoing against the cobblestones.

"Phew, that was close," Charles exhaled, wiping the sweat from his brow with the back of his hand.

"Too close," agreed Sarah, her pulse still racing. "Let's get to Dr. Warren and make sure these stories are heard."

Emboldened by their narrow escape, the children hurried through the streets, their hearts buoyed by the knowledge that they carried the hopes and dreams of so many on their shoulders. Together, they would ensure that the voices of those who had suffered would not be silenced but instead would ring out like a clarion call for justice and freedom.

Sarah's heart raced as she scanned the street, her eyes darting between the red-coated soldiers and her fellow conspirators. "We need to split up," she whispered urgently. "Meet at Dr. Warren's hideout in thirty minutes."

"Are you sure?" Charles asked, his voice trembling slightly.

"Positive," Sarah replied, determination shining in her eyes. "It's the only way we can avoid suspicion."

"Alright, let's do it," Henry agreed, clapping Charles on the back for reassurance.

"Stay safe," Clarissa murmured, her gaze lingering on each of them. Then, without another word, the children disappeared into the bustling crowd, blending in seamlessly with the people going about their daily lives.

Sarah slipped through the throngs of market-goers, feeling a mixture of exhilaration and fear coursing through her veins. Her thoughts whirled around like autumn leaves caught in a gust of wind: would they make it to the hideout unnoticed? Would the stories they collected be enough to inspire the people?

"Keep moving, dearie," an old woman muttered under her breath, jostling Sarah out of her reverie. She nodded gratefully, taking advantage of the anonymity provided by the crowded marketplace.

Minutes felt like hours as Sarah navigated the labyrinthine streets, ducking into narrow alleys whenever she sensed danger. It wasn't until she turned a familiar corner that relief washed over her like a wave crashing upon the shore. Before she stood at the unassuming door to Dr. Warren's hideout, she knocked twice, then once more, and waited with bated breath.

"Who goes there?" a muffled voice called from behind the door.

"Freedom's whispers," Sarah responded, her heart pounding in anticipation.

The door creaked open, revealing the familiar face of Dr. Joseph Warren. Relief flooded his features as he ushered Sarah inside. "Thank heavens you're safe," he whispered, his dark eyes filled with concern.

"Sarah!" Clarissa exclaimed, rushing to embrace her friend.

"We were so worried!"

"Didn't doubt her for a second," Henry chimed in, grinning from ear to ear.

"Did we all make it?" Sarah asked, scanning the room for any missing faces.

"Charles should be here any minute now," Dr. Warren reassured her, glancing at the door anxiously.

Just as the words left his lips, there was a soft knock at the door, and Charles slipped inside, breathless but triumphant. "I made it," he panted, leaning against the wall for support.

"Thank goodness," Sarah murmured, her heart swelling with pride and relief. Together, they had faced danger and emerged victorious, each keenly aware of the gravity of their mission. The weight of the stories they carried was both a burden and an honor, one that they would bear together, united by their common goal – to inspire the people and fan the flames of revolution.

Dr. Warren's eyes scanned the faces of the young heroes, each brimming with determination and courage. He took a deep breath, allowing the weight of their shared purpose to settle on his shoulders. "I cannot express my gratitude enough," he began, his voice steady despite the undercurrent of emotion. "The information you've gathered will significantly impact our cause, and your bravery is truly inspiring."

Sarah stood tall, her chest swelling with pride at Dr. Warren's words. The playful banter and camaraderie they had developed during their mission had forged a bond that went beyond friendship – it was a connection born of shared ideals and unwavering loyalty.

"Thank you, sir," Charles replied, meeting Dr. Warren's gaze with newfound confidence. "We're honored to be part of this fight for freedom."

Henry nodded in agreement, adding, "We'll do whatever it takes to help our people."

"Indeed, we will not sit idly by while our rights are trampled upon," Clarissa chimed in, her eyes shining with conviction.

As the room buzzed with the energy of their collective resolve, Sarah couldn't help but feel a sense of awe at the power they possessed when united. She glanced around at her friends, seeing their faces alight with passion and determination, and knew that they were capable of great things.

"Remember, my young friends," Dr. Warren said, his eyes gleaming with wisdom, "it is not just the information you've collected, but your resourcefulness and tenacity that will inspire others to join our cause."

"Your actions have already begun to shape our future," he continued, fixing a warm, approving gaze on Sarah. "I am confident that together, we can achieve our goal of freedom and create a brighter tomorrow for all. Now, I need you to do one last thing before the speech tomorrow; as you know, there are heightened patrols about, and there is a rumor of a plot they will unleash during the speech. I need you to find out what it is and put a stop to this. I know this is dangerous, but I truly trust that you can get it done."

Sarah's heart swelled with pride and gratitude as she looked into Dr. Warren's eyes. She felt a surge of determination, knowing that she and her friends had made a difference in the fight for liberty. The trust and faith Dr. Warren placed in them only fueled their desire to do even more.

"Let's show them what we're made of," Sarah whispered, her voice filled with steely resolve and her spirit ablaze with the fire of revolution.

The soft glow of candles filled the hidden room, casting flickering shadows on the somber faces of Sarah, Charles, Henry, and Clarissa. They huddled around a small wooden table, their expressions a mix of determination and anticipation as they prepared for Dr. Warren's upcoming speech.

"Alright," Sarah began, her voice a gentle whisper in the dimly lit space. "We all have important roles to play tonight. Dr. Warren is depending on us, and we can't let him down."

Charles nodded solemnly, his dark hair falling into his eyes. "I'll be keeping watch outside the meeting place, making sure no one suspicious gets too close."

"Good thinking," Sarah replied, her blue eyes shining with admiration. She turned to Henry, whose sturdy frame seemed to loom over the rest of the group. "Henry, you're strong and quick on your feet. Can you handle crowd control if needed?"

"Of course," Henry grunted, shifting uncomfortably at the thought of potential confrontation. He clenched his fists, trying to channel his anger into something productive. "I'll do whatever it takes to ensure Dr. Warren's message reaches our allies."

Clarissa, the quietest of the group, finally spoke up. "I'll be inside, near Dr. Warren. I've memorized the layout of the building, so I can help navigate any escape routes if necessary."

"Excellent, Clarissa," Sarah said, offering her friend a proud smile. "You always come through with vital information when we need it most."

As the children continued discussing their responsibilities for the evening, Sarah couldn't help but feel a surge of pride at how far they had come. Their individual strengths were now working together towards a common goal, pushing them closer to achieving their mission.

"Guys," Sarah interjected, her voice wavering slightly as she struggled to assert herself. "I just want to say… thank you. We've all grown so much during this journey, and I'm grateful for each and every one of you."

Charles looked at Sarah, his trust issues momentarily forgotten as he sensed the sincerity in her words. "We're a team, Sarah. We wouldn't be able to do any of this without each other."

"Here's to the success of Dr. Warren's speech," Henry added, raising an imaginary glass in the air.

"Cheers!" Clarissa chimed in, her glasses slipping down her nose as she grinned.

Despite the dangers that awaited them, the children found comfort in their camaraderie and shared purpose. As they made final preparations for the night ahead, their hearts swelled with hope and determination – ready to face whatever obstacles lay in their path.

Sarah spread the tattered map across the worn wooden table, her fingers tracing the familiar streets and alleys of their city. Charles, Henry, and Clarissa huddled around her, their breaths held in anticipation as they studied their route for the night.

"Alright," Sarah began, her voice barely above a whisper, "we'll start here, at the old mill, then follow this path that leads to the old south meeting house. We need to be cautious — there's been an increase in British soldiers patrolling the area."

"Look at those red dots," Charles pointed out, his brow furrowed in concern. "It's like they're everywhere."

"Exactly," Clarissa chimed in, adjusting her glasses. "We must avoid detection at all costs. One wrong move could jeopardize everything."

As the group continued strategizing, the room seemed to grow smaller, the air thicker with tension. The weight of their responsibility hung heavily upon them, fear gnawing at their insides like a relentless shadow.

"Okay, team," Sarah said, forcing a brave smile onto her face. "We can do this. We've faced worse before, right?"

"Right," Henry agreed, cracking his knuckles in determination. "We just have to keep our heads down and stay quiet."

"Stealth is our greatest weapon tonight," Charles added, his eyes locked on the map.

"Agreed." Clarissa nodded, her mind racing with possible scenarios and escape routes.

As they delved deeper into their plans, the children felt a mixture of excitement and dread. The stakes were higher than ever, and one misstep could lead to disaster. Their hearts pounded in their chests as they considered the challenges ahead, each silently renewing their commitment to the cause.

"Remember," Sarah whispered, her eyes meeting each of theirs in turn, "caution and stealth. We've come too far to let anything stand in our way."

"Let's do this," Charles said, his voice steady despite the fear that twisted his insides.

"Agreed," Henry and Clarissa echoed their expressions, a mix of determination and trepidation.

With their route planned and their roles established, the children took one last look at the map before folding it up and tucking it safely away. Sarah's heart pounded in her chest as she considered the many obstacles they would face, but she refused to let fear get the better of her.

"Alright," she said, her voice barely above a whisper, "we should head out now. The sooner we get started, the better."

The group nodded in agreement, each taking a deep breath to steady their nerves. They extinguished the candles that had illuminated their planning session, plunging the room into darkness.

As they navigated the dimly lit corridors of the hidden passageways within the city, the children felt a mixture of excitement and terror. Every sound - from the creaking floorboards beneath their feet to the distant murmurs of British soldiers patrolling nearby streets - sent shivers down their spines.

"Stay close," Charles whispered, his eyes darting back and forth as they crept through the shadows. "And remember, silence is our ally."

Clarissa clutched the map tightly, her eyes flicking between the parchment and their surroundings, ensuring they were on the right path. Meanwhile, Henry kept an eye out for any potential threats, his body tense and ready to spring into action if necessary.

"Almost there," Sarah breathed, her pulse racing at the thought of what awaited them. She knew they had to be cautious, but the anticipation was almost unbearable.

As the group rounded a corner, they halted abruptly, spotting a pair of British soldiers standing guard just ahead. Their hearts raced, the fear threatening to choke them as they quickly retreated into an alcove, holding their breaths and praying they wouldn't be discovered.

"Too close," Henry muttered, his anger simmering beneath the surface.

"Patience," Sarah reminded him, her voice quivering slightly. "We'll find another way."

"Clarissa, can you figure out an alternate route?" Charles asked, his eyes filled with concern.

"Give me a moment," Clarissa whispered, her fingers tracing

the lines on the map as she sought a new path for them to take.

As they waited in anxious silence, each child couldn't help but feel the weight of their mission pressing down upon them. The stakes were high, and the dangers were all too real. But together, they knew they could overcome whatever obstacles lay ahead and that their shared determination would see them through to the end.

With renewed resolve, the children continued on their perilous journey, driven by the hope that their actions would make a difference in the fight for freedom and justice.

The shadows danced on the walls, casting eerie patterns that flickered in tandem with the single candle's flame. Sarah could feel her heart pounding in her chest, a faint rhythm that mirrored the urgency of their mission.

"Alright, everyone," she said, her voice steady despite the nerves bubbling beneath the surface. "We need to be prepared for anything. Charles, I want you to keep an eye on our surroundings and watch for any changes in the soldiers' movements."

Charles nodded, his eyes dark with determination, but a flicker of uncertainty lingered. "I'll do my best, Sarah," he promised, his fingers tapping restlessly against his thigh.

"Clarissa, your knowledge of the city is invaluable. We'll need you to guide us through the streets and find us safe passage whenever possible," Sarah instructed, her gaze shifting to Clarissa's timid expression.

"I won't let you down," the young girl whispered, clutching

the map tightly in her hands.

Finally, Sarah turned to Henry. "You're strong, Henry. We may need your strength to protect us if we run into trouble. But remember, violence is a last resort."

"Understood," Henry replied gruffly, his jaw clenched as he tried to contain his frustration.

Sarah took a deep breath, feeling the weight of responsibility settle on her shoulders. She knew they had to trust each other completely if they were going to succeed.

"Are you sure about this, Sarah?" Charles asked quietly, pulling her aside. The vulnerability in his voice was something she hadn't heard before.

"Of course, I'm scared, Charles," she admitted, her blue eyes locking onto his. "But we have to believe in ourselves and each other. We can't let fear hold us back."

He hesitated, his gaze shifting away from her as he wrestled with his thoughts. "It's just...I've never been good at trusting others. I'm always afraid they'll let me down."

"Charles," she said gently, placing a reassuring hand on his arm, "you're not alone in this. We're all here for the same reason, and we need to rely on one another. Trust isn't something that comes easily, but it's essential for us to succeed."

His eyes met hers again, a mixture of gratitude and determination shining within them. "You're right, Sarah. Thank you."

As they rejoined the group, Sarah could feel the unity among them, a bond forged by their shared purpose and unwavering resolve. They were more than just friends – they were comrades, united in their pursuit of justice.

"Let's do this," she declared, her voice carrying through the alley like a battle cry. Together, they extinguished the candle, and the darkness embraced them as they set out into the night, ready to face whatever challenges lay ahead.

As the darkness enveloped them, Henry moved with surprising grace through the narrow alleyways of the city. His breaths came in short, controlled puffs, and his eyes scanned his surroundings with an intensity that belied his years. He had always been strong, a natural fighter, but now he needed to focus that strength inward to become a silent protector.

"Stay close," he whispered to the others, who huddled together in the shadows, their hearts pounding with anticipation. "We need to keep a low profile."

Clarissa, her glasses perched precariously on her nose, stepped forward hesitantly. She clutched a bundle of papers to her chest, her knuckles white from the effort. "I... I found something," she stammered, her voice barely audible. The others gathered around her, their faces illuminated by the faint glow of a nearby lantern.

"Show us," urged Sarah, her eyes locked on the trembling girl.

With a deep breath, Clarissa unfurled the papers, revealing detailed maps and charts that she had secretly obtained from one of the British soldiers' guard stations. They showed the movements and positions of the enemy troops, information that was crucial for their mission.

"Clarissa, this is amazing!" Charles exclaimed, his trust issues momentarily forgotten as he marveled at her resourcefulness. "It also shows the meeting house, and there is some writing here about an "egg plot" whatever that is."

"They are clearly planning to interrupt the speech, and I can only guess an egg is going to be involved," Clarissa mentioned. "we will need to be on guard for any British soldiers at the speech, and maybe one with an egg?"

"Good work," Henry grunted, studying the maps carefully. A small smile played on his lips, a rare sight on his usually stern face. "These will help us navigate through the city without attracting attention. And now we know what to look for during the speech. Maybe they are going to use the egg to start a distraction or use it as a signal. Either way, it can't be good, and we need to get to the speech without getting caught with these papers. Great job, Clarissa, you really went for it on this one!"

"Thank you," Clarissa murmured, her cheeks flushed with pride. It felt good to be acknowledged, to know that she was contributing to their cause.

"Alright, everyone," Sarah said, gathering the group closer. "Let's review our plan one more time. Remember, we need to work together and stay focused."

"Right," Henry agreed, his thoughts turning inward as he mentally prepared himself for the coming day's events. He knew that his greatest challenge would be to restrain his anger and impulsiveness, to keep a clear head when faced with danger. But he was ready. For the first time in his life, he felt truly connected to something greater than himself.

"Stay sharp," he whispered to Clarissa as they moved through the city, their footsteps muffled by the soft dirt beneath them. "We're in this together."

And for the first time, Clarissa felt a surge of courage course through her veins, a newfound confidence fueled by the faith her friends had placed in her. She nodded, her eyes shining with determination.

"Let's make history," she declared softly, and together they stepped into the night.

The moon cast its pale glow upon the city, veiling the streets in a cloak of shadows. Sarah's heart raced as she led her friends through the labyrinthian alleys, her breath coming out in short, quick puffs. The air was chilling, causing goosebumps to form on her skin, but fear kept her warm.

"Keep close," she whispered, leading them into a narrow passageway hidden behind a row of barrels. "We can't afford to be seen."

"Right behind you," Charles murmured, his eyes darting around nervously. He couldn't shake the gnawing feeling at the pit of his stomach, the constant worry that they would be discovered before they could reach Dr. Warren's meeting place.

As they turned a corner, Henry suddenly grabbed Sarah's arm, pulling her back against the wall. His hand shot over her mouth, stifling the gasp that threatened to escape her lips. She stared wide-eyed at him, the question clear in her gaze.

"Soldiers," he whispered, nodding towards the street ahead. A group of British soldiers were patrolling the area, their red coats stark against the darkness. Their laughter echoed eerily, sending shivers down the children's spines.

"Blend into the crowd," Clarissa suggested, her voice barely audible as she pointed to a small gathering of people nearby. "We'll make our way past them unnoticed."

"Good idea," Sarah agreed, her pulse pounding in her ears. They slipped into the throng of people, mimicking their movements and whispers while keeping a wary eye on the soldiers.

"Almost there," Charles said under his breath, his fingers brushing against Sarah's as they navigated their way through the crowd. The touch sent a jolt of reassurance through her, reminding her that they were all in this together.

"Wait," Henry hissed, spotting another group of soldiers ahead. "Take this alley," he whispered, guiding the group into a dark, narrow passage.

"Thanks to Clarissa's maps, we know there's a hidden exit right around here," Sarah reminded them, her voice filled with gratitude. "We just need to find it."

"Here," Clarissa whispered excitedly, pressing a brick at the base of the wall. A section of the wall shifted, revealing a small tunnel-like passage. The children exchanged quick glances before slipping through, their hearts pounding with every step they took. "The Sons of Liberty aren't the only ones with a few tricks up their sleeves." She quipped.

As they emerged, disguised in the shadows of a nearby building, Sarah couldn't help but feel proud of their progress.

They had managed to evade detection and navigate the city using their newfound knowledge and skills.

"Dr. Warren's meeting place is only a few blocks away," she reminded them, her voice steady and full of determination. "Stay vigilant and remember our plan."

"Right," Charles agreed, his trust issues momentarily forgotten as he focused on the task at hand. "Together, we can do this."

"Let's go," Henry added, his fierce eyes shining with a newfound restraint. "For the cause."

"Lead on," Clarissa said softly, her newfound confidence radiating like a beacon in the night. And so, they continued onwards, their hearts fueled by determination and the knowledge that together, they could change the course of history.

The sun dipped below the horizon as the children navigated through the labyrinth of cobblestone streets. Charles kept a watchful eye on the dispersing crowds while Henry and Clarissa scanned their surroundings for signs of British soldiers.

"Sarah," whispered Charles, noticing her hesitance to make decisions without input from the others. "We need you to trust your instincts. You're a natural leader, but you must believe in yourself."

"Charles is right," agreed Clarissa, surprising everyone with her self-assured tone. "We all have our strengths, and yours is guiding us through these dire times."

"Alright," Sarah said, straightening her spine and squaring her shoulders. "Let's stick to the plan. We'll use the alleys to avoid any encounters with the soldiers."

"Good call," said Charles, his eyes still scanning their surroundings for danger. He wanted to trust Sarah's judgement, but his own insecurities gnawed at him. What if they were discovered? The thought sent shivers down his spine.

"Charles, I can see that you're worried," Sarah said gently. "But remember, we've come this far together. Trusting each other is our best bet now."

"Sarah's right," Henry chimed in, clenching his fists in an effort to control his simmering anger. "We can't afford to lose our cool now. We need to stay focused on the task at hand, not give in to our fears or let our anger control us."

"Agreed," Clarissa added, adjusting her glasses and taking a deep breath to steady her nerves. She had never been so bold before, but she knew that now was the time to step up and face her fears head-on. "We need to keep moving. Dr. Warren is expecting us to fill him in on what we found before his speech tomorrow."

As the children continued forward, they found themselves confronted by a barricade of British soldiers. There was no way to reverse course now; they had to find a way past the blockade.

"Alright, everyone," Sarah said, her voice barely above a whisper. "We need to be creative and use our strengths. Clarissa, can you think of another route that will get us to Dr. Warren's location?"

"Give me a moment," Clarissa responded, her eyes darting

back and forth as she mentally retraced their steps. "Yes, there's a narrow alley to the left that leads behind the soldiers' barracks. We'll need to move quickly and quietly."

"Perfect," Sarah whispered, leading the group toward the alley. As they approached the entrance, she scanned the area for any signs of danger. "Henry, I know your instincts are to fight when cornered, but we need you to stay calm and follow our lead."

"Understood," Henry muttered through gritted teeth, forcing his anger to subside as they slipped into the shadows.

"Charles," Sarah continued, "I trust your instincts. Keep an eye on our surroundings and let us know if anything seems off."

"Will do," Charles replied, his reluctance slowly giving way to trust.

The children moved with renewed purpose, their determination growing stronger with each step. The danger loomed ever closer, the stakes higher than ever before. And yet, they knew that the future of the revolution hinged on their ability to overcome their individual challenges and work together as a team. For it was only in unity that they could hope to change the course of history.

With hearts pounding and breaths held, the children slipped through the narrow alley, their every step a silent prayer that they would remain undetected. Sarah, as always, led the way, her eyes scanning for any signs of danger while her mind raced with contingency plans. The weight of their mission bore down on her like a heavy cloak, but she refused to let it dampen her resolve.

"Almost there," she whispered to the others, her voice barely audible even to herself. "Just around this corner, and we'll reach the hidden meeting place."

It was then that they came to the place that Dr. Warren mentioned at the start of their mission. He was waiting for them with anticipation, and when he saw them, his face lit up with glee.

"My young friends, tell me, how successful was your venture? Did you find anything to substantiate the rumor?" Dr. Warren asked the group of children.

"Yes, we did," Sarah began, "though we aren't sure what it means exactly. Clarissa, can you show Dr. Warren what you found."

Clarissa boldly stepped to the table in the middle of the room and spread out the map she had taken from the guard station. "This is a map of Boston as it stands today. Here are some routes they typically cover, and if you look here," she now points to the location of Dr. Warren's speech, the old south meeting house, "they have marked with the term "egg plot." We aren't quite sure what it means, but Henry did have some thoughts."

"We think it's an obvious plot," Henry picked up the tale, "they know you are giving a speech to commemorate the Boston massacre as you did a few years ago in 1772, and it seems like they want to stop it. I think they are going to use an egg to either interrupt you and disrupt the speech, or worse; they could be using it as a signal and create a riot from the audience or even to the other soldiers to attack."

Dr. Warren pondered this news with grave concern and

began to pace about the room, thinking over what the young patriots had brought to him. "You surely were busy tonight, and I thank you truly for this information; you have given me a lot to think about." Dr. Warren stated

"What are you going to do? And is there anything we can do to help?" Charles asked.

"You have done so much already, true patriots for the cause," Dr. Warren beamed. "I must still give the speech, though I fear you are right, Henry, when you say this "egg plot" is something the British will use against us."

"We can be on the lookout during your speech, and now that we know what to look for, maybe we can put a stop to it also." Sarah put in.

"I think that may very well be the best course of action, Sarah," Dr. Warren said as his face began to show signs of relief. "with you all working behind the scenes, I will feel more comfortable giving the speech."

"You got it, Dr. Warren. We will be there; we wouldn't miss it for the world." Clarissa chimed in.

"We have your back, Dr. Warren; those lobsterbacks will have to get through us first," Henry added with renewed vigor in his voice.

"I thank you all again for all you have done tonight and for what you will do tomorrow, but for now, please get some rest, and I will see you at the old south meeting house tomorrow." Dr. Warren finished just before leading the children to where they would be sleeping that night.

As the sun rose, the children woke up to find their adventure the night before had worn on them. They each felt the weight of the coming day and wanted to get a head start on the day. They left their quarters and went down to the old south meeting house.

As they turned the corner, the sight before them took their breath away. A large oak tree stood sentinel over a small clearing, its gnarled roots providing natural benches for the overflowing crowd. Lanterns hung from the branches, casting a warm glow over the sea of determined faces below that spilled out from the old south meeting house.

"Look at all these people," Clarissa marveled, her previous timidity replaced by awe. "They're all here to support Dr. Warren and the cause."

Henry, his anger momentarily forgotten, allowed himself a small smile. "We're not alone in this fight."

"Indeed," Charles chimed in, finally allowing himself to trust those around him. "And together, we can make a difference."

Sarah nodded, her heart swelling with pride. She knew that each of her friends had confronted and overcome their personal challenges, and in doing so, they had forged an unbreakable bond. As they moved to join the waiting crowd, she couldn't help but feel a sense of anticipation tingling in the air.

"Dr. Warren's speech will change everything," she thought, her pulse quickening with excitement. "The time has come to take a stand."

"Are you ready?" she asked her friends, her gaze flicking

between their resolute faces.

"More than ever," Charles replied, his once-guarded expression now open and determined.

"Let's do this," Henry echoed, his fists clenched not in anger but in solidarity.

"Absolutely," Clarissa agreed the quiet strength in her voice belying her earlier self-doubt.

"Together," they whispered in unison, their voices melding into a single, powerful declaration of intent.

And with that, they stepped forward into the gathering crowd, their hearts swelling with courage and determination. The atmosphere was electric, charged with purpose, as they awaited the arrival of Dr. Warren. The future of the revolution rested on their young shoulders, and they knew that they would face unimaginable challenges in the days to come.

But for now, they stood as one, united by their shared convictions and the knowledge that together, they could change the course of history. As the first notes of Dr. Warren's voice rang out across the clearing, the children took a collective breath, ready to embrace their destiny.

The time had come. The revolution was on its precipice. And if providence had its way, nothing would ever be the same again.

# CHAPTER 12

The sun rose high in the sky, casting a bright glow on the cobblestone streets of colonial Boston. A hush descended upon the crowd as Dr. Warren took the stage, his Roman Ciceronian toga billowing around him like the wings of an angel. The sight was all at once majestic and unexpected, a perfect testament to the man's unique blend of wisdom and character.

"Friends, Romans, countrymen!" he boomed, drawing laughter from the gathering throng. "I jest, of course – though we gather today in the spirit of those ancient, great civilizations." He paused, allowing the anticipation to build before continuing. "But rather than discuss empires long past, I stand before you today to speak of our own colonies and the fight for freedom that lies ahead."

As Dr. Warren began his speech, the crowd leaned in, captivated by his voice and presence. His eyes glittered with conviction, and his words seemed to flow like honey, sweet and rich with meaning. "Trust," he declared, "is the cornerstone of any lasting union, and it is trust that shall determine the outcome of our struggle against tyranny."

He paced slowly across the stage, engaging with his audience as only a master orator could. "The British forces would have us doubt one another; they would have us question our brethren's commitment to liberty. But let me ask you this: What greater bond can there be than a shared love of freedom? What force mightier than the collective will of men and women who yearn to cast off the shackles of oppression?"

A murmur of agreement rippled through the crowd, and Dr.

Warren nodded, pleased with the resonance of his message. All were drawn in except for the British soldiers in the front row angrily staring at Dr. Warren. One of the soldiers was even toying with a group of musket balls in his hands in an obvious attempt to highlight his goal in today's affair. "In times of trial, we may be tempted to rely solely on our own strength, but such isolation breeds weakness. We must trust in each other, lean on one another, and forge a united front against the enemy."

"Remember," he implored, his voice heavy with emotion, "that our strength lies not in our numbers but in the bonds of trust we share. Together, we can overcome any obstacle, defeat any foe, and secure the blessings of liberty for ourselves and future generations."

Sarah's blue eyes were fixed on Dr. Warren, her heart swelling with each powerful word he spoke. She clutched the edge of her simple dress, feeling the fabric between her fingers as she considered the weight of his message. Trust was essential to their cause, but it was something she had always struggled with, even in her daily life.

"United we stand," Dr. Warren proclaimed, "divided we fall!"

The words brought Sarah's thoughts back to her unlikely group of friends - Charles, Henry, and Clarissa. They were all so different, yet they had come together for a common purpose. She knew that if they were to succeed in their mission, they would need to trust one another completely. But could she do it? Could she let go of her fears and embrace the trust that Dr. Warren spoke of so passionately?

"Trust is the key," Dr. Warren continued, "that unlocks our potential and enables us to achieve feats greater than any one of us could accomplish alone."

Beside her, Charles stood tall, his dark hair ruffled by the breeze as he listened intently to the speech. He had always been a natural leader, confident and sure of himself. Yet she knew that beneath his exterior, he too harbored doubts and struggled with trust.

"Dr. Warren's right, you know," Charles whispered, leaning in close as he shared his thoughts with Sarah. "We'll never be able to complete our mission if we can't trust each other."

Sarah nodded, feeling a warmth spread through her chest as Charles' words echoed Dr. Warren's sentiment. She realized that the trust they needed to cultivate wasn't just about relying on others but also about trusting herself and her abilities.

"Charles," she began hesitantly, "I... I want to try. To trust more. Not just in our mission, but in myself as well."

He looked at her, his eyes softening. "I do, too, Sarah. We're in this together, and I believe that together, we can overcome anything."

A newfound sense of determination filled Sarah's heart as she listened to Charles' words and the inspiring speech that continued to unfold before them. Their mission wasn't just about changing the past; it was about shaping the future of their country and their future. And it all started with trust – in themselves, in each other, and in their cause.

"Let us stand united," Dr. Warren declared, his voice resonating through the crowd, "and together, we shall prevail!"

As Dr. Warren's voice rang out across the sea of people,

Henry stood at the edge of the crowd, his arms crossed over his broad chest. The muscles in his jaw clenched as he listened to the passionate speech. He had always relied on his fists to solve problems and his brawn to protect those around him. But as Dr. Warren spoke, Henry found himself reconsidering his approach.

"Trust," Dr. Warren said, his gaze sweeping over the audience, "is the foundation upon which we build our future. It is the glue that binds us together, allowing us to face our enemies with a united front."

Henry's eyes narrowed, his mind racing as he considered the doctor's words. Was it possible that trust was just as important as strength? That unity could be as powerful as the force of a well-aimed punch?

"Clarissa, what do you think?" Henry asked, turning to the girl who stood beside him, her brown hair tucked neatly behind her ears.

Clarissa looked up from her place in the crowd, her eyes wide behind her glasses. She had been listening intently to Dr. Warren's speech, her mind filled with images of brave patriots standing up against the oppressive British rule. As Henry posed his question, she hesitated for a moment before answering.

"I... I think he's right," she said softly, her voice barely audible amid the murmurs of the crowd. "We can't fight this battle alone. We need each other, and we need trust in order to succeed."

Her cheeks flushed with color as she spoke, her usual reserve giving way to a newfound sense of bravery. Henry watched her transformation with surprise and admiration. For so long, he had viewed Clarissa as a quiet, timid girl – someone who needed protection rather than someone who could contribute to their cause.

"Thank you, Clarissa," he said gruffly, his voice thick with emotion. "You're right. We do need trust, and I'm grateful for the trust you've shown me."

"Trust doesn't come easily to me," she admitted, her eyes shining with determination. "But I see now that it's something we all need to work on – not just for ourselves, but for our mission and our country."

Henry nodded, his chest swelling with pride as he looked at the young girl beside him. In that moment, he understood that trust was more than just a word – it was a bond that could hold them together even in the darkest of times across all backgrounds and situations. And with Clarissa's bravery as an example, he felt ready to embrace the challenge.

"Come on," he said, placing a hand on her shoulder. "Let's find Sarah and Charles. Together, we'll show the world what trust can really do."

As they made their way through the bustling crowd, Henry felt a renewed sense of purpose coursing through his veins. Trust might not be an easy path, but it was one he was determined to follow for the sake of his friends, his mission, and the future of the nation.

Dr. Warren's voice boomed across the town square, his toga billowing as he raised a hand to emphasize his point. "Bravery, my friends, is not merely about physical strength or force of arms. It is about standing up for what is right, even when faced with the most daunting of challenges."

Sarah stood on her tiptoes, her blue eyes wide and focused, trying to take in every word. She could feel the passion in Dr. Warren's speech, and she knew she wasn't the only one. The crowd around her was captivated, hanging on to each syllable as though their very lives depended on it.

"Throughout our journey thus far," Dr. Warren continued, "we have seen bravery in many forms. We have witnessed acts of courage that defy explanation, and we have marveled at the resilience of the human spirit."

As Sarah listened, she couldn't help but think back to her own moments of bravery during their adventure. Standing up to the British soldiers who sought to arrest the Sons of Liberty, learning to trust Charles despite his complicated past, and pushing herself to solve the cryptex's puzzles - all of these experiences had tested her courage and shown her just how strong she could be.

"Indeed," Dr. Warren went on, "it is often in the face of great adversity that we discover our true selves. And it is through this process of self-discovery that we come to understand the importance of standing together, united by our shared belief in freedom."

Charles glanced over at Sarah, a small smile playing at the corners of his mouth. He, too, had been reflecting on their journey, recalling the times he had put his faith in others and found it rewarded. Henry's unwavering loyalty, Clarissa's quiet intelligence, and Sarah's gentle determination had all played a role in shaping him into the person he was now becoming.

"Remember," Dr. Warren said, his voice soaring above the murmur of the crowd, "true bravery is not about never feeling fear. It is about facing that fear head-on and refusing to let it hold you back."

Henry, standing at a distance, nodded in agreement. His fists clenched and unclenched at his side as he thought about the many difficulties they had gone through together, both physical and emotional. Every time he had faced danger or adversity, he had learned something new about himself - and about what true courage meant.

"Let us all be brave," Dr. Warren urged, "not just for ourselves, but for the generations yet to come. For we are fighting not only for our own freedom but for the future of this great nation."

At this, Clarissa, who had been listening intently from the edge of the crowd, felt a renewed sense of purpose wash over her. She knew she might never be as strong or as skilled as some of her companions, but she also understood now that her intelligence and resourcefulness were valuable in their own right.

"Bravery takes many forms," Dr. Warren concluded, his eyes sweeping across the sea of faces before him. "And each of us must find our own path to courage, our own way of contributing to this noble cause."

The crowd erupted into applause, and Sarah, Charles, Henry, and Clarissa exchanged glances, their eyes brimming with determination and a shared understanding of the significance of their mission. They were all in this together, bound by trust, united by bravery - and ready to face whatever challenges lay ahead.

It was then that a movement snapped them out of their revelry as Henry spotted movement from the edge of the crowd, and he watched closely. It was a British soldier attempting to make his way through the crowd and moving closer to the front.

"The egg plot!" Henry hissed to his friends, "they are still trying their plan. We have to do something."

"You're right!" Charles blurted out, noticing the soldier pushing through the crowd. "Can you stop him, Henry?"

Henry's eyes narrowed, determination beaming from his face, "Yes, I will," he said

"Be careful, Henry," Clarissa mentioned, "Remember a measured and controlled approach; we can't risk a riot breaking out."

A smile crept across Henry's face, breaking from his usual dower expression. "Trust me," is all he said as he disappeared through the crowd to stop the soldier.

As Henry crept closer to the soldier, he could see in his right hand an egg being protected but seemly ready to be used at any moment. Instead of charging headlong and fighting with the man and stopping the plot but then causing more problems, Henry thought differently; using what he learned about picking his fights and when to use his strength, he decided on a different approach. Coming up from behind the soldier in his wake, Henry moved to his side and cut off the soldier's path, pretending to get caught up in his path, tumbling into him, and both came crashing down. He made sure to land on the soldier's hand to make sure that the egg was crushed, and he got up and attempted to help the man to his feet.

"I'm so sorry, sir; I don't know what got into me; I must have two left feet. I hope I didn't cause you too much trouble," Henry said to the soldier with an innocent grin.

The soldier stood up and, noticing the egg crushed, showed a shock of rage across his face and shouted, "You'll pay for that boy when we get our hands on you," he began when Henry then cut him off to say.

"You'll have to find me first, and we Sons of Liberty are everywhere." he then ducked back out into the crowd and couldn't be seen until he reappeared next to his friends with a smile on his face.

"Well, that's all done with. Did I miss anything?" Henry said, looking proud of his accomplishments and reading the joyous expressions on his friend's faces.

"Henry, you did it!" Sarah beamed.

"Well done, Henry, you stopped their plan to ruin this speech!" Charles said with a broad smile on his face.

"I knew you had it in you!" Clarissa said, patting Henry on his shoulder.

As the warm glow of the setting sun bathed the bustling square in hues of orange and pink, Sarah felt her heart swell with determination. She glanced at Charles, Henry, and Clarissa, who were all listening to Dr. Warren's speech with rapt attention. They had come so far on their journey, overcoming incredible obstacles and learning valuable lessons along the way. Now, as they stood together, united by a common purpose, it was clear that their mission extended beyond just the past; it was about shaping their own future.

"Remember, my friends," Dr. Warren continued, his voice strong and resonant, "our fight for freedom is not only about breaking free from the British yoke. It is also about forging a new nation, one that is built on the principles of liberty, justice, and equality for all."

The crowd murmured in agreement, and Sarah couldn't help but think of her own experiences, traveling through time to witness history unfold before her very eyes, being carried out by everyday folk. She knew that their actions now would ripple through the ages, affecting the lives of countless generations yet unborn.

"Unity is our greatest weapon against tyranny," Dr. Warren proclaimed, his piercing blue eyes sweeping across the sea of faces gathered before him. "Together, we can stand strong against the forces that seek to oppress us, and together, we can create a brighter future for all who call this land their home."

Charles clenched his fists, feeling a surge of conviction course through his veins. He thought about the many trials he had been through alongside his friends, both physical and mental, and understood that their strength lay not in their individual talents but in their ability to trust and support one another.

"Let us join hands, brothers and sisters," Dr. Warren implored, stretching out his arms to emphasize his point. "For when we stand united, there is no force in this world that can break our spirit or extinguish the flame of freedom that burns within us all."

As Dr. Warren's passionate words washed over them, Henry felt a newfound appreciation for the power of trust and unity. He had always relied on his physical strength in combat, but now he understood that it was their bond as a team that truly made them strong.

"United we stand," Clarissa murmured to herself, her quiet voice barely audible above the noise of the crowd. She had always been more reserved than her friends, keeping her thoughts and feelings locked away deep inside. But as she listened to Dr. Warren speak, she felt a spark of bravery ignite within her heart and knew that she, too, had an important role to play in this fight for freedom.

"Remember," Dr. Warren finished, his voice tinged with both hope and urgency, "the future of our great nation rests in your hands. Let us stand together, united by trust, inspired by bravery, and driven by our shared love for this land we call home."

The crowd roared in agreement, and Sarah, Charles, Henry, and Clarissa exchanged glances filled with renewed determination. They knew that their mission was not just about the past but also the future of their country – and they were ready to face whatever challenges lay ahead together.

The wind gently fluttered the edges of Dr. Warren's toga as he concluded his impassioned speech. The sun, now lower in the sky, cast a warm amber hue across the gathered crowd. It was as if time itself had slowed down, allowing Sarah and her friends to fully absorb the weight of the doctor's words.

Sarah's blue eyes met those of Charles, Henry, and Clarissa in turn, each gaze meeting hers with equal intensity. The air around them seemed charged with purpose, an unspoken vow passing between them like an invisible thread. They were in this together, bound by their shared mission and newfound understanding of its significance.

"United we stand," Charles whispered, his voice barely audible yet filled with conviction. His dark hair ruffled lightly in the breeze, but his eyes remained locked on Sarah's. She felt her heart swell with a mixture of pride and affection for the boy who had challenged her to trust not only others but herself as well.

"United we stand," echoed Henry, his sturdy frame tensing with determination. Gone was the pugnacious young man who had once thought only of fighting. In his place stood a true patriot, ready to channel his strength into the pursuit of freedom and justice.

"United we stand," Clarissa agreed, her timid voice unwavering. A glimmer of confidence shone in her eyes, revealing a depth of courage that had been hidden beneath her quiet exterior.

"United we stand," Sarah affirmed, finally embracing the role she had been chosen to play in this pivotal moment in history.

As Dr. Warren's final words rang out, the crowd erupted into thunderous applause. The cacophony of clapping hands and stomping feet rose like a wave, sweeping over the children and drawing them into the tide of exhilaration and camaraderie that surged through colonial Boston. Through it all, they remained connected, their unbreakable bond a testament to the power of trust.

"Thank you, Dr. Warren," Sarah thought, her heart brimming

with gratitude for his inspiring words and guidance. She clapped her hands enthusiastically, reveling in the sense of unity that encompassed them all.

"Come on," Charles said, reaching out to gently grasp Sarah's hand. "We have work to do." His touch sent a shiver down her spine, a reminder that their mission and the challenges they faced together had only strengthened their connection.

"United we stand," Sarah repeated silently, her eyes shining with determination and newfound purpose as she joined her friends in stepping forward, ready to face whatever lay ahead in their journey through time.

As the applause resonated through the air, Sarah felt a warmth spread through her chest, invigorating her with a renewed sense of purpose. The sun dipped lower in the sky, casting a golden hue over the gathered crowd and bathing Dr. Warren in an ethereal glow as he descended from the stage.

"Dr. Warren," Sarah called out, catching his attention as he weaved through the throng of people. He strode towards them with an air of elegance, his toga billowing around him like the wings of an ancient Roman god.

"Ah, my young friends!" Dr. Warren exclaimed, his eyes alight with a mixture of pride and gratitude. "Your support means more to me than you know."

"Your words were truly inspiring, sir," Charles chimed in, his voice firm and steady. "We've been learning so much on our journey, but your speech... it brought everything into focus."

"Indeed," Henry added, flexing his arms subconsciously as if readying for battle. "We understand now that trust and unity are just as important as strength when fighting for freedom."

"Thank you, Dr. Warren," Clarissa whispered, her voice soft yet steadfast. "You helped us realize that we all have something valuable to contribute to this cause."

Dr. Warren's face softened, and he placed a gentle hand on each of their shoulders. "I am humbled by your dedication," he said, his gaze unwavering. "With such courageous hearts and strong minds, I have no doubt that you will continue to be instrumental in our fight for freedom. And I should be thanking you. I noticed the British soldiers were on edge as if waiting to hatch some sort of plot, but nothing seemed to come about; I believe that is all due to you four."

"Their egg plot was scrabbled," Henry stated with a grin.

"United we stand," Sarah breathed, feeling the weight of their shared mission settle firmly upon her shoulders. The others echoed her words, their voices blending together in a chorus of determination.

"United we stand," Dr. Warren repeated, his eyes glistening with unshed tears. "May the lessons you've learned here today carry you forward in your journey, wherever it may lead."

"Thank you, Dr. Warren," Sarah murmured, her heart swelling with gratitude for the man who had played such a pivotal role in their growth. "We won't let you down."

"Nor I you," he replied, his voice thick with emotion. As Dr. Warren turned to leave, he cast one final look over his shoulder, the pride and gratitude shining in his eyes like beacons of hope.

"United we stand," Sarah whispered once more, determined to uphold the promise they had made that day. Together, hand-in-hand with her friends, she stepped forward into the unknown, ready to face whatever challenges awaited them on their quest through time.

As the crowd dispersed, a cool breeze swept through the streets of Boston, carrying with it the echoes of Dr. Warren's impassioned words. Sarah felt the wind gently ruffling her hair as she walked beside Charles, their hands brushing against each other from time to time. The sun was setting, casting an amber glow on the cobblestones beneath their feet.

"Can you believe that we got to witness such an important moment in history?" Clarissa asked, her normally quiet voice filled with excitement. "Dr. Warren's speech... it was so powerful."

"Indeed," Henry agreed, his eyes shining with newfound determination. "I never thought trust could make such a difference. We were already a team, but now... now I feel like we're truly united."

"United we stand," Charles murmured, squeezing Sarah's hand briefly before letting go.

"United we stand," she repeated, feeling the words resonate deep within her soul.

As they continued to walk, the buildings around them appeared to be frozen in time, bearing witness to the struggles and triumphs of the people who had come before them. Sarah couldn't help but be reminded of Headmaster Winters' cryptic words about the cryptex: "The answers you seek lie not only in the past but also within yourselves."

"Hey, Sarah?" Charles asked, interrupting her thoughts. "Do you think we'll ever find all the answers we're looking for?"

Sarah considered the question for a moment, watching as a group of children played nearby, their laughter ringing through the air like a promise of hope. "I don't know if we'll ever find all the answers," she admitted, "but I do know that we've learned so much already – about ourselves, about each other, and about what it means to truly fight for something bigger than ourselves."

"Whatever challenges we face next," Clarissa chimed in, "I know we'll face them together."

"United we stand," Henry echoed, his broad shoulders squared and his expression resolute.

"United we stand," Sarah whispered once more, feeling the truth of their words settle deep within her heart. As they walked through the streets of Boston, hand in hand with her friends, she knew that their journey was far from over. But with a newfound sense of purpose and a deepened commitment to their mission, she was certain that whatever challenges awaited them in the past – or the future – they would face them head-on, united as one.

The children went back to their quarters, knowing that they would still need to solve the mystery of the cryptex and get back home. They would meet with Dr. Warren tomorrow and continue their journey.

# CHAPTER 13

The sun streamed through the tall windows of the quiet room, casting a warm, golden glow on the polished wooden floor. The children, Sarah, Charles, Clarissa, and Henry, eagerly arranged themselves around Dr. Warren and Headmaster Winters, who were seated in two comfortable armchairs. A feeling of anticipation hung in the air as they leaned in, ready to listen.

"Children, I believe it is time you learned about my own journey to fight for American independence," Dr. Warren began, his voice filled with determination and a hint of sadness. He looked at each of them, his gaze settling on Sarah, who shared his passion for justice. "It all started when I witnessed firsthand the injustices imposed by the British rule."

As Dr. Warren recounted his experiences, the children listened intently, their eyes wide with wonder and curiosity. They could picture the bustling, colonial Boston streets draped with the flags of King George III and teeming with Redcoats. They felt the tension between the colonists and the soldiers, fueled by years of animosity.

"Growing up, I saw how the British crown exploited our resources and stifled our liberties," Dr. Warren continued, his voice growing more urgent. "I knew that something had to be done, but I wasn't sure what until the Intolerable Acts were passed."

Sarah's heart raced as she imagined the courage it must

have taken for Dr. Warren to stand up against such powerful oppressors. She glanced over at the others, who appeared equally captivated by his words.

"Dr. Warren, how did you find the strength to fight?" asked Charles, his eyes shining with admiration.

"Ah, Charles," Dr. Warren replied, a small smile gracing his lips. "When you see your friends and neighbors suffer under the weight of tyranny, you find yourself driven by an unyielding desire to make things right. That's when you know it's time to take a stand."

As Dr. Warren spoke, Sarah couldn't help but feel inspired by his unwavering commitment to the cause of freedom. She knew that she and her friends had been brought together for a reason, and their journey was only just beginning. She felt a renewed sense of purpose, knowing they had the guidance and support of Dr. Warren.

In that quiet room, bathed in golden sunlight, the children felt a sense of kinship with Dr. Warren. Their mentor's stories of resilience and determination lit a flame within each of them, kindling their own desire to fight for justice and liberty. And as they sat there, listening to the echoes of history, they knew that they were part of something much greater than themselves.

"Growing up in a colonial family," Dr. Warren began, his voice soft yet resolute, "taught me the importance of self-reliance and community. My parents instilled in me the values that have guided my life ever since." He closed his eyes for a moment as if lost in memories of his childhood.

"The Stamp Act was the first time I saw how British rule could threaten our way of life. My father gathered us around the table one evening to explain what was happening, and even as a young boy, I understood the injustice of it all."

"Despite the challenges we faced, I was fortunate enough to receive an education," Dr. Warren continued, looking at each of the children with a mixture of pride and gratitude. "My parents sacrificed much so that I could attend Harvard College, where I studied medicine. It was there that I discovered my true passion: healing others."

"Helping people has always been important to me," he said, his eyes sparkling with enthusiasm. "As a doctor, I've had the privilege to serve my community by treating their illnesses and easing their pain. But when the injustices of British rule became too much to bear, I knew I had to do more than just heal bodies – I had to help heal our broken society."

"Dr. Warren," Sarah asked, her eyes wide with admiration, "how did you find the courage to stand up against the powerful British government? Weren't you afraid?"

"Of course, I was afraid," he admitted, his strong jawline set in determination. "But fear can be a powerful ally, pushing us beyond our limits to achieve great things. The revolutionary cause needed people who were willing to risk everything for the sake of freedom – and I knew that I couldn't stand idly by while others fought for a better future."

"Your dedication is truly inspiring, Dr. Warren," Henry chimed in, his voice filled with reverence. "We're honored to have you as our mentor and guide."

"Thank you, Henry," Dr. Warren replied, his smile both warm and humble. "But remember, it's not just about me. It's about all of us – working together for a common cause. Our journey is only just beginning, but I have faith that we will prevail."

As he spoke, the children couldn't help but feel the weight of history upon their shoulders. They were part of a larger struggle – one that spanned generations and would shape the course of their nation. As they listened intently, Dr. Warren went on to describe his early life, painting a vivid picture of his upbringing in a colonial family.

"Growing up in was both fascinating and challenging," he began, his eyes distant as he recalled the past. "I was fortunate enough to receive a solid education, and it was during my studies that I first became aware of the injustices that our people faced under British rule."

"Was that when you first got involved with the revolutionary cause?" asked Clarissa, her curiosity piqued.

"Indeed," Dr. Warren nodded. "The Stamp Act was a turning point for many of us – a clear sign that we could no longer tolerate the oppressive policies of the British government. We had to take action, and so we did."

As he shared his experiences, the children could almost see the young Dr. Warren, driven by passion and determination, joining forces with other like-minded individuals to fight for their rights and liberties. It was a stirring image, one that filled them with a sense of pride and purpose.

"Dr. Warren," Clarissa ventured, "you mentioned earlier that you had a passion for medicine. How did that come about?"

"Ah, yes," he smiled warmly, his eyes lighting up at the memory. "From an early age, I was fascinated by the human body and the incredible power of healing. I knew that if I could master the art of medicine, I could make a real difference in people's lives – easing their suffering and helping them recover from illness and injury."

"And so, you became a doctor?" Henry inquired, clearly impressed.

"That's right," Dr. Warren confirmed. "And it has been my great privilege to serve the community in that capacity. But as important as my medical work is, I've come to realize that there are many ways to heal – and sometimes, the most effective treatment is a healthy dose of freedom and justice."

As the children listened to Dr. Warren's words, they felt a renewed sense of purpose and determination. They had been given a rare glimpse into the heart and mind of a true hero – a man who was not only skilled in medicine but also dedicated to the greater cause of American independence.

"Thank you, Dr. Warren," Sarah said softly, her voice thick with emotion. "Your story has given us so much to think about – and we're truly grateful for your guidance and support."

"Indeed," Clarissa added, her eyes shining with admiration. "We'll do our best to follow in your footsteps and make a real difference in this world."

"Remember, my young friends," Dr. Warren encouraged them, his voice strong and steady, "the future is in your hands. Never doubt your ability to change the course of history – and never forget the power of unity, courage, and perseverance. Together, we can create a better tomorrow for all."

Dr. Warren leaned forward in his chair, his eyes distant as he recalled the moments that had forever changed his life. "It was the Boston Massacre," he began, his voice heavy with the weight of the memory, "that truly solidified my commitment to the cause of independence."

As the children listened intently, Dr. Warren painted a vivid picture of that fateful night. He described how he had been walking home after treating a patient when he stumbled upon the scene – a rowdy mob of colonists facing off against a small group of British soldiers. Tensions were high, and before he knew it, shots were fired.

"I watched in horror as five innocent men fell to the ground, their lives taken far too soon," Dr. Warren continued, his voice trembling with emotion. "It was a moment I will never forget – and one that made me realize just how high the stakes were in our fight for freedom."

He went on to tell them about the subsequent trials of the British soldiers, where he had served as a key witness. The experience had only strengthened his resolve to fight for justice and liberty, no matter the cost.

"From that day forward, I vowed to do whatever it took to secure our independence from tyranny – and I have dedicated my life to that cause ever since," Dr. Warren concluded, his eyes meeting each of theirs in turn. "But always remember: we don't fight this battle alone. There are others who share our passion for freedom – and who are willing to risk everything to see it achieved."

Just then, the door to the room creaked open, and the children turned to see Headmaster Winters enter. They looked at each other in surprise – they hadn't expected to see him here and now. They thought he would have been back at the boarding school in their own time.

"Ah, Dr. Warren, your story reminds me of my own experiences during those tumultuous times," Headmaster Winters began, his beard twitching as he smiled. "You see, I, too, fought for our nation's freedom – though my methods were perhaps less conventional than yours."

"Really? What are you doing here, Headmaster Winters?!" Sarah asked, her curiosity piqued. "What did you do, Headmaster?"

"How did you get here?!" Charles Exclaimed, completely taken aback at seeing Headmaster Winters in colonial Boston with them.

"Well," he replied, glancing around the room with a mischievous twinkle in his eye, "let's just say I had a knack for being in the right place at the right time – and for using my unique abilities to help shape the course of history."

The children exchanged puzzled glances, wondering what he could possibly mean by that. But as they looked into his wise, ageless eyes, they couldn't help but feel a sense of awe – and a newfound appreciation for the man who had been guiding them on their journey. They also understood that he must know that the cryptex was a time-traveling device and that he would know that it would bring them to this point in time.

"Sometimes," Headmaster Winters continued cryptically, "it's not just about fighting on the battlefield or in the classroom – but about knowing when to step in and offer a helping hand. That's what I've done throughout my life – and it's what I hope to teach each of you, as well."

As the children nodded in agreement, they couldn't shake the feeling that there was much more to this enigmatic headmaster than met the eye – and they were eager to learn all they could from him and Dr. Warren as they continued their journey toward independence and a brighter future.

Headmaster Winters leaned against a tall wooden bookcase, his blue eyes twinkling with the memories of his past. The children sat on the floor; their eager faces turned up to him as they awaited his tale.

"During the American Revolution," he began, his voice soft but clear, "I had the pleasure of crossing paths with some of the most influential figures - men like George Washington and Benjamin Franklin."

The children exchanged excited glances, imagining the headmaster as a young man rubbing shoulders with such legendary individuals.

"Of course, it wasn't all grand meetings and historic moments," he continued. "I also found myself in the thick of battle, fighting alongside brave soldiers who believed in the cause of liberty."

As Headmaster Winters spoke, Sarah could almost see him charging into battle, his white beard not yet grown, his eyes alight with passion and determination. The vivid imagery sent shivers down her spine.

"Tell us more about the battles you fought in, Headmaster Winters," asked Henry, his eyes wide with curiosity.

"Ah, well, I remember one particularly fierce battle at Concord," he replied, a far-off look in his eyes. "The British were relentless, but our men, driven by their love for freedom, held their ground."

The room grew quiet as the children digested the gravity of these memories. They could barely fathom the courage it must have taken to fight against such odds, and their admiration for Headmaster Winters grew.

"Through it all," he continued, "I learned valuable lessons about resilience, determination, and the power of unity. These are the very qualities that led me to oversee this fine boarding school and guide each of you on your journey."

As the children listened intently, they began to understand the deeper connection between their headmaster's past and their own present-day struggles. It was as if he had been preparing them for something greater, using his own experiences to shape their education and personal growth.

"Of course," Headmaster Winters said, glancing briefly at Dr. Warren, "it is important that we respect the confidentiality of our shared stories. We wouldn't want any unnecessary complications to arise, now would we?"

He winked at the children, who understood his subtle message – Dr. Warren was not to know of the time travel. Instead, they would carry the knowledge within themselves, inspired by the sacrifices and bravery of those who had come before them.

With renewed determination, the children thanked both Dr. Warren and Headmaster Winters for their guidance and wisdom. They couldn't help but feel a growing sense of purpose, fueled by the incredible history they were now a part of. As they left the quiet room, their hearts swelled with pride and resolve, ready to face whatever challenges lay ahead on their journey toward independence.

"Headmaster Winters, Dr. Warren," Sarah began, her voice filled with newfound awe and respect for the two men who stood before them. "Thank you for sharing your stories with us. We had no idea of all that you've done."

"Indeed," Charles chimed in, still reeling from the shock of finding Headmaster Winters in the room with them. "Your experiences have truly opened our eyes to the importance of our own journey."

Dr. Warren smiled warmly at the young teens, his eyes reflecting the depth of his commitment to their cause. "It's been my honor to share my story with you. I believe in each and every one of you, and I know that you have the power within yourselves to make a difference."

"Indeed," Headmaster Winters agreed, stroking his long white beard thoughtfully. "You are all capable of great things, my young scholars. Remember the lessons of our past and use them to guide your future actions."

"Your words resonate deeply with us," said Sarah, exchanging glances with her friends, who nodded in agreement. "We promise to honor the sacrifices you've both made by fighting for American independence with everything we have."

"Thank you," said Dr. Warren, placing a hand on Sarah's shoulder. "I can see the fire in your eyes, and I am confident that you will succeed."

"Headmaster Winters," Charles hesitated before continuing, "we were shocked to find you here with us today. And though we understand the need for secrecy, we want you to know how grateful we are for your guidance and for entrusting us with the cryptex."

"Ah, the cryptex," Headmaster Winters said with a

twinkle in his eye. "I knew from the moment I first met you that you all had the potential to unlock its secrets and discover your true purpose. You have not disappointed me."

The sun was setting, casting a golden glow over the quiet room as Sarah and her friends gathered around Dr. Warren and Headmaster Winters. The air was heavy with anticipation as they listened intently to the stories of their mentors' pasts.

"During my time as a young man," began Dr. Warren, his eyes distant as he recalled the memories, "I witnessed firsthand the cruelty of British rule. It was the Intolerable Acts that pushed us to the brink, the unreasonable taxes and restrictions on our liberties that made us feel like prisoners in our own land."

His voice trembled with emotion as he described the fateful day when British soldiers stormed into Boston, enforcing their authority with brutal force. "I remember standing in the town square, watching as the redcoats marched past, their bayonets glinting in the sunlight. I knew then that we could not let this tyranny continue."

Headmaster Winters nodded in agreement, his blue eyes sparkling with a mixture of pride and sadness. "I, too, have seen the horrors of war. My role during the American Revolution was one filled with danger yet also moments of great triumph. I met many remarkable individuals, from General George Washington to Paul Revere, and together, we shaped the course of history."

As Dr. Warren and Headmaster Winters recounted their

experiences, Sarah and her friends couldn't help but be in awe of the hardships and sacrifices their mentors had endured. They listened with bated breath as the two men spoke of secret meetings by candlelight, daring acts of rebellion, and the camaraderie that bonded them together in their fight for freedom.

"Despite the pain and loss, it was worth every moment," said Dr. Warren, his eyes meeting Sarah's. "For we fought for something greater than ourselves – the future of our country and the generations to come."

"Your journey is a continuation of ours," added Headmaster Winters, his voice gentle yet firm. "You carry the torch of liberty, and it is your responsibility to ensure that the flame never dies."

The room seemed to vibrate with the weight of their words as Sarah and her friends exchanged glances, understanding the gravity of their mission. The once-distant events of the past now seemed so vivid and real, as if they were witnessing them firsthand.

"Dr. Warren, Headmaster Winters," Clarissa said, her voice trembling with emotion, "we had no idea what you both went through to fight for our freedom. It's truly an honor to learn from you and follow in your footsteps."

Henry nodded vigorously. "We promise to do our best to make you proud and continue the work you started all those years ago."

"Your experiences have shown us the importance of

perseverance and unity," added Charles, his face set with determination. "We will stand up for what is right, just like you did."

Sarah couldn't help but feel a surge of pride and admiration for Dr. Warren and Headmaster Winters. Their stories had not only brought history to life but also ignited a fire within each of them – a desire to protect the hard-won liberties they enjoyed in their era and ensure that future generations would be able to do the same.

"Thank you," she said softly, her eyes shining with gratitude. "You've given us more than just knowledge; you've given us purpose and the courage to fight for what we believe in."

As Sarah watched Headmaster Winters take his leave, she noticed the way Dr. Warren's eyes lingered on the retreating figure, a mixture of admiration and curiosity in his gaze. The room seemed to shrink without the headmaster's towering presence, leaving the children feeling closer to their remaining mentor.

"Dr. Warren," Sarah began hesitantly, her voice breaking the silence that had hung in the air since Headmaster Winters' departure. "How did you find the strength to persevere through all those hardships?"

The doctor smiled warmly at her as he leaned against the wooden table in the center of the room. "Well, Sarah, I believe it was my sense of duty and love for my fellow man that kept me going."

"Did you ever feel afraid?" Charles asked, stepping closer to Dr. Warren.

"Of course," Dr. Warren admitted with a nod. "Fear is a natural part of the human experience. But when faced with challenges, we must choose either to let fear control us or to stand up and fight for what we believe in."

"Like you did during the Boston Massacre," Henry added quietly, his eyes filled with admiration.

"Indeed," Dr. Warren agreed. "It was a defining moment for me – one that showed me how fragile our freedoms are and how easily they can be taken away."

Sarah felt a swell of determination grow within her, fueled by the doctor's words and the knowledge that their mentors had gone through so much to help shape the world they now inhabited. She exchanged glances with Charles and Clarissa, seeing her own resolve mirrored in their expressions.

"Dr. Warren, we want to make a difference too," Sarah declared, her voice filled with conviction. "We want to honor the sacrifices you and Headmaster Winters made and ensure that your struggles were not in vain."

"Your passion and dedication are admirable, Sarah," Dr. Warren replied, placing a reassuring hand on her shoulder. "I have no doubt that you and your friends will make a lasting impact on the world."

"Thank you," Thomas murmured, his eyes glistening with gratitude.

"Dr. Warren, could you teach us more?" Charles asked eagerly. "We want to learn everything we can from you."

"Of course, my young friend," Dr. Warren responded with a chuckle. "But first, we must take some time to reflect upon all we have learned today. The road ahead is long and filled with challenges, so it is important to understand our motivations and the lessons of the past."

As the children sat down around the table, they each took a moment to let the weight of their newfound knowledge settle in their hearts. They thought of the sacrifices made by those who came before them, the bravery displayed in the face of adversity, and the unwavering belief in the cause for freedom.

With Dr. Warren's guidance and support, Sarah, Clarissa, Charles, and Henry knew they were ready to embrace their destiny – a journey filled with trials and triumphs, where the echoes of the past would inspire them to fight for a better future.

Sarah stood by the window, her breath momentarily fogging the glass as she gazed out at the courtyard. The sun had begun to set, casting a warm glow on the cobblestone paths and well-tended gardens. She could feel the hum of anticipation in the air; history was unfolding before their very eyes.

"Are you ready for what's to come?" Dr. Warren asked gently, joining her at the window. His dark eyes held a quiet determination that Sarah admired.

"I think so," she replied hesitantly. "It's all happening so quickly – the battles of Lexington and Concord, and now the British invading Boston." She paused, then added softly, "I'm scared, but I know we have a part to play."

"Your bravery shines through your fear," Dr. Warren assured her. "You are stronger than you realize."

"Thank you," Sarah whispered, feeling a surge of determination course through her veins.

"Psst, Sarah!" Charles called from across the room, waving her over. He huddled together with Henry and Clarissa, who were poring over a map of Boston. "We've been thinking about how we can help during the invasion. We need to take action now while there's still time."

"Dr. Warren," Sarah asked earnestly, "will you guide us as we fight for American independence?"

"Of course," he responded, his voice filled with pride. "Together, we shall stand against tyranny and injustice."

As they gathered around the map, laying out their plans, Sarah couldn't help but feel a sense of hope brimming within her. No longer were they simply students at a boarding school, caught up in the machinations of time travel and cryptic puzzles. They were actively shaping the course of history, guided by trusted mentors and fueled by their unwavering belief in the cause of freedom.

"Alright," Dr. Warren announced, looking into the eyes of each young patriot. "We have much to do and little time. Let us embark on this journey with courage and resolve."

"Ready when you are, Dr. Warren," Charles declared, his eyes shining with determination.

"Let's do this," Henry added, his strong hands flexing in anticipation.

"United we stand," Clarissa whispered, her voice steady despite her timid nature.

"Indeed," Dr. Warren agreed, a hint of a smile playing at the corners of his mouth. "Now, let us go forth and make our mark upon history."

As they stepped out into the golden light of the setting sun, Sarah knew that they were embarking on the most important journey of their lives. With Dr. Warren by their side and the spirit of Headmaster Winters guiding them from afar, there was no challenge too great, no obstacle insurmountable. Together, they would fight for American independence, leaving an indelible legacy for generations to come.

# CHAPTER 14

"Move, move!" Dr. Joseph Warren urged, his voice barely above a whisper as he led Sarah and the other children through the chaos of a Boston street. The air was thick with tension, the people around them hurrying on their way, their faces taut with fear. Word had spread that the British forces were ramping up their search for the young runaways and the doctor who had been so prominent in various protests and speeches around Boston. They were causing too much trouble, and now, with the failure of Lexington and Concord, the British weren't going to take any chances with these rebels and were bent on trying to capture them.

"Where are we going?" asked Henry, his voice trembling as they dashed across a cobblestone road, narrowly avoiding an oncoming carriage.

"Somewhere safe," Dr. Warren replied, his eyes scanning their surroundings for any sign of danger. He knew they couldn't afford to be spotted by the British soldiers, not when they were so close to discovering the truth about their time-traveling adventure.

"Are you sure we're going the right way, Dr. Warren?" Sarah inquired, her breath hitching as she tried to keep up with the doctor's long strides.

"Trust me, Sarah," he assured her, his dark eyes meeting hers for a moment before focusing back on their path. "I've lived in this city for years; I know its streets like the back of my hand."

As they turned down another alleyway, Sarah couldn't help but think how grateful she was for Dr. Warren's guidance. His intelligence and charisma had been essential in getting them this far, and she knew that without him, they would have been captured by now.

"Dr. Warren," whispered Charles, glancing nervously over his shoulder. "I think I heard something."

"Everyone, quickly," Dr. Warren commanded, motioning for the children to duck behind a stack of wooden crates. They pressed themselves against the cold, damp walls of the alley, each heart pounding in unison as they strained to hear any signs of approaching footsteps.

"Stay quiet," Dr. Warren instructed, his voice barely audible. "And whatever happens, don't move until I give the signal."

As they held their breath, Sarah couldn't help but think about the harrowing journey they had embarked on together. Their lives had been turned upside down in an instant, and as they crouched in the shadows, she knew that their only chance of survival lay in their trust and reliance on one another.

"Dr. Warren," she whispered, her eyes wide with fear. "What do we do if they find us?"

He looked at her, his expression a mixture of determination and concern. "We stick together," he replied softly. "No matter what."

Sarah nodded, her heart swelling with gratitude for the man who had become like a father to them all. As they huddled together in the darkness, waiting for the danger to pass, she knew that it was their unity and trust in each other that would see them through this ordeal—and whatever challenges lay ahead.

With the sound of British soldiers' boots pounding the cobblestone streets, Dr. Warren led the group of children through a labyrinth of narrow alleys and hidden passageways. The air was thick with tension, as they knew that one wrong turn could lead to their capture.

"Stay close," he whispered urgently, his eyes darting around every corner for any sign of danger. "We can't afford to be seen."

Sarah clutched her long blonde hair tightly in one hand as she followed closely behind Dr. Warren, her heart racing with each step. She could feel the weight of her own fear settling like a heavy stone in her chest, but she pushed forward, determined to stay strong for the sake of her friends.

"Oi! Did you hear that?" Charles suddenly hissed, stopping Sarah in her tracks. He pressed himself against a nearby wall, peering cautiously around the edge.

"See anything?" Henry asked, his sturdy frame tensed and ready for action.

"Soldiers," Charles whispered, his voice laced with dread. "They're getting closer."

"Quick, this way!" Clarissa motioned towards a narrow gap between two buildings. Her glasses glinted in the faint moonlight as she scanned the area for any signs of an escape route.

Dr. Warren nodded approvingly at her resourcefulness. "Good find, Clarissa. Let's move."

The group squeezed through the tight space, their clothes snagging on jagged bricks and splintered wood. As they emerged into a dimly lit alleyway, they could hear the muffled voices of British soldiers drawing nearer.

"Where do we go from here?" Sarah whispered, her blue eyes wide with fear.

"Leave it to me," Dr. Warren replied, his dark eyes scanning the shadows for a safe haven. "I think I see a cellar door just ahead. It should be concealed enough to keep us hidden."

"Are you sure, Doctor?" Clarissa asked nervously, her fingers twisting the hem of her dress.

"Trust me," he reassured her gently. "We've come this far together. We'll find a way out of this mess."

As they hurried towards the cellar door, Sarah couldn't help but marvel at the bravery and resourcefulness of her companions. Despite their youth and inexperience, they had risen to the challenge, proving themselves capable of navigating a world fraught with danger.

"Alright, everyone in," Dr. Warren instructed as he opened the creaky door, revealing a pitch-black space below. The children descended cautiously into the darkness, their hearts pounding with each step.

"Remember," Dr. Warren whispered, his voice echoing through the cramped chamber. "Stay quiet, stay strong, and above all, trust in each other."

As the door closed behind them, shrouding them in complete darkness, Sarah knew that no matter what lay ahead for them, they would face it together – as friends, as allies, and as a family united by the bonds of courage, loyalty, and determination.

Huddled together in the damp darkness of the hidden alleyway, Sarah could hear her companions breathing – a ragged symphony of determination and fear. Their bodies were streaked with grime and perspiration, but their eyes held a fierce resolve that belied their youthful countenance.

"Sarah," whispered Charles, his voice barely audible above the distant sounds of British soldiers searching for them. "Thank you for trusting me back there."

"Of course, Charles," she replied softly, feeling a flutter in her chest. "We're in this together, aren't we?"

Charles nodded, and Sarah saw a spark of gratitude light up his eyes. At that moment, she realized that trust was not just about relying on others but also allowing them to rely on you. As they continued to elude their pursuers, Sarah felt the bonds between them grow stronger, like the roots of a tree reaching deep into the earth.

"Doctor," said Henry, his brow furrowed with concern. "I think we should move further into the alleyway, just in case they come this way."

"Good thinking, Henry," Dr. Warren replied, smiling approvingly. "Your instincts are getting sharper. I'm proud of how much you've grown."

As the group moved cautiously through the narrow passage, Clarissa suddenly grabbed Henry by the arm. "Henry," she said, her voice quivering. "I don't know if I can do this."

"Clarissa," he replied, his tone firm but gentle. "You are braver than you know. We have faced so much together already, and I believe in you."

"Thank you, Henry," she murmured, her expression softening.

Just then, they heard voices approaching, and Dr. Warren signaled for everyone to stay silent and press themselves against the walls. As the footsteps drew nearer, Sarah struggled to control her racing heart, her chest tightening with each echoing step. She could see the other children's eyes widen with fear.

"Oi! Did you hear that?" one of the soldiers asked, his voice unnervingly close.

"Must've been a cat," another responded dismissively. "Let's keep moving."

Sarah held her breath as they waited for what felt like an eternity for the soldiers to pass by. It wasn't until their footsteps had faded into silence that she allowed herself to exhale, her entire body trembling.

"Is everyone alright?" Dr. Warren whispered, his concern evident even in the darkness.

"We're okay," Charles replied, his voice shaking slightly. "But we can't stay here for long. They'll be back."

"Agreed," said Dr. Warren, taking charge once more. "We need to find a better hiding place, and quickly."

As they prepared to venture out into the dangerous streets once more, Sarah knew that they were bound together not just by fate but by something stronger – the shared experience of fear, courage, and trust. And with each step they took, their bonds grew ever stronger, propelling them forward into the unknown with determination and hope.

The sky had darkened, and the dim glow of lanterns cast eerie shadows across the narrow alleyway. Sarah's heart raced as she pressed her back against the cold, damp brick wall, listening to the distant sounds of footsteps and shouting from the British soldiers. Her breath came in ragged gasps, the frosty air biting at her lungs.

"Stay low," Charles whispered, his voice taut with anxiety. "If they see us, we're done for."

The others nodded silently, their eyes wide with fear as they huddled together behind a stack of wooden crates. Dr. Warren placed a reassuring hand on Sarah's shoulder, his grip firm yet gentle. The warmth of his touch was comforting amidst the chilling unease that enveloped them.

"Remember, we've come this far," he murmured, his tone steady even as his eyes darted from shadow to shadow. "We'll get through this together."

Sarah swallowed hard, trying to quell the panic rising in her chest. She closed her eyes, took a deep, steadying breath, and focused on the sound of Clarissa's soft sniffling beside her. It was a small, human reminder that she wasn't alone in her fear.

"Charles is right," Dr. Warren continued, his voice barely audible above the bustling sounds of Boston outside their hiding place. "We can't afford to be found out now. Stay close and quiet, and we'll make it through this."

The group exchanged nervous glances, their faces etched with determination. As the sounds of soldiers grew louder, they clung to one another, each heartbeat a silent prayer.

"Dr. Warren?" Clarissa whispered, her voice trembling. "What if...what if we don't make it?"

"Then we will have done our best," Dr. Warren replied softly, his gaze meeting hers with unwavering conviction. "But I have faith in all of you. We'll see this through together."

"Faith," Sarah echoed, clinging to the word like a lifeline. She felt her fear begin to ebb, replaced by a newfound resolve. If they had come this far, there was no turning back now.

"Alright, everyone," Charles commanded, his voice low but firm. "We're going to move on three. One...two...three!"

As one, the group darted from their hiding place, their footsteps muffled by the slushy ground beneath them. They navigated the treacherous streets of Boston with quiet determination, each twist and turn a testament to their will to survive.

"Almost there," Henry panted, his breath visible in the frosty air. "Just a little further."

"Keep going," Dr. Warren urged, his eyes never leaving the path ahead. "We can make it."

And so they pressed on, their hearts heavy with fear yet buoyed by hope. For in that moment, they were united not only by their shared past but also by the unbreakable bond of determination that would carry them into an uncertain future.

Sarah's breath caught in her throat as they stumbled into an open square, the icy wind slicing through her thin cloak. Her heart pounded painfully in her chest, but she pushed herself to keep moving. She knew they couldn't afford to slow down, not with the British soldiers relentlessly pursuing them like wolves on the hunt.

"Wait!" Charles hissed suddenly, his hand shooting out to grab Sarah's arm. "Look."

Sarah followed his gaze and saw a group of British soldiers standing guard near the entrance to a narrow alleyway. Anxiety clenched at her stomach, and she could see the fear reflected in the faces of Henry, Clarissa, and Dr. Warren. They were so close, yet so far from safety.

"Maybe we should split up," Henry suggested, his voice tense. "It'll be harder for them to catch us all that way."

"Absolutely not," Dr. Warren replied firmly. "We stay together. We're stronger as a group."

"Stronger?" Henry scoffed, his anger flaring. "All we've done so far is run and hide! How is that strong?"

"Running and hiding have kept us alive, Henry," Charles pointed out, his eyes narrowing. "And it's been working so far."

"Could you two please stop arguing?" Clarissa pleaded, her eyes darting nervously between them. "We can't afford to waste any more time."

"Clarissa's right," Sarah chimed in, her voice wavering slightly. "We need to focus on getting out of here safely."

"Besides," Dr. Warren added, his voice calm and steady, "the strength I speak of isn't just in our ability to evade capture. It's in the trust we have for one another and our willingness to face these challenges together."

Henry and Charles exchanged glances, their anger dissipating as they acknowledged the truth in Dr. Warren's words. They both knew that they couldn't let their differences divide them, not when so much was at stake.

"Fine," Henry grumbled, his gaze dropping to the cobblestones. "But we still need a plan."

"Agreed," Charles said, his tone more conciliatory as he

looked back at the soldiers guarding the alleyway. "What if we create a distraction? That might give us enough of an opening to slip past them."

"Good idea," Dr. Warren nodded, his eyes scanning their surroundings for any possible diversion. "Clarissa, do you think you could—"

"Leave it to me," she interrupted, a small, determined smile playing on her lips. "I've got just the thing."

As Clarissa rummaged through her bag, the others watched with bated breath, their trust in one another stronger than ever. They knew that whatever lay ahead, they would face it together, united by their shared purpose and unbreakable bond.

"Ready?" Clarissa asked, holding up a small, makeshift noisemaker fashioned from pebbles and a tin can.

"Ready," they all whispered in unison, their hearts pounding with anticipation and fear.

A gust of wind whipped through the alley, making Sarah shiver as she pulled her cloak tighter around herself. She looked at the faces of her friends and their anxiety etched deeply in the shadows cast by flickering lamplight. After a moment's pause, Clarissa cleared her throat and gestured toward a map spread out on an overturned barrel.

"Alright," she began, her voice shaky but determined, "we need to figure out where to go from here."

"Let's find a place to hide for the night first," Dr. Warren suggested, his eyes scanning over the map. "The British will likely tighten their patrols soon, so we should keep our movements minimal."

"Agreed," Charles said, tugging at his collar nervously. "I hate to say it, but we could use an extra set of eyes. Henry, do you think you can scout the area for us?"

"Sure thing," Henry replied, cracking his knuckles. "Just give me a moment to get into character."

As Henry slipped away to change into a borrowed uniform, Sarah felt her stomach churn with worry. She knew that they were all doing their part, but the thought of being discovered was a constant weight on her mind. Her thoughts were interrupted by Dr. Warren's calming voice.

"Sarah, I know this is difficult," he said softly, placing a reassuring hand on her shoulder. "But together, we'll find a way out of this."

"Thank you, Dr. Warren," she whispered, blinking back tears. "I just wish we didn't have to be so... sneaky."

"Sometimes, my dear, a little deception is necessary to protect those we care about," he replied, giving her a gentle smile.

"Look!" Clarissa suddenly exclaimed, pointing at a section of the map. "There's a network of tunnels underneath the city. We could use them to move around without being seen."

"Brilliant!" Charles said, his eyes lighting up with excitement. "Let's gather our things and wait for Henry to return. We'll follow his lead and head for the tunnels."

As they prepared for their daring escape, Sarah couldn't help but feel a flicker of hope. Despite the danger that surrounded them, the friendship and trust they shared were stronger than any obstacle they faced. Together, they would find a way to outsmart the British forces and continue their fight for freedom.

"Here goes nothing," Sarah thought as Henry returned in his makeshift disguise, ready to lead them toward the hidden passageways below.

Sarah's heart raced as they followed Henry through the narrow streets of Boston, the wind tugging at her hair and the cobblestones cold beneath her feet. As they moved from shadow to shadow, she couldn't help but feel exposed, vulnerable. The air was tense with anticipation, and every creak or rustle made her jump.

"Stay close," Charles whispered to her, casting a wary glance at the darkened windows above them. "We can't afford any mistakes."

"Right," Sarah murmured, her voice barely audible. She clutched the map in her hands, the paper crinkling softly under her fingers.

They turned down an alleyway, the walls closing in around them like a vise, and Sarah felt a pang of fear. What if they were discovered? What if the British soldiers found them before they reached the safety of the tunnels?

"Everything all right, Sarah?" Dr. Warren asked quietly, concern etching lines across his face.

"I'm just... scared," she admitted, her eyes flicking to the shadows that seemed to encroach upon them.

"Keep your head up, dear," he advised. "Fear is only useful if we use it to keep us sharp."

As they neared the entrance to the tunnels, Clarissa stopped suddenly, her face pale. "Did you hear that?" she whispered, her voice trembling.

"Shh!" Charles hissed, pressing a finger to his lips. They all froze, listening intently to the sound of approaching footsteps.

"Everyone, hide!" Dr. Warren whispered urgently, and they scrambled to press themselves against the walls of the alley, hearts pounding in their chests.

"Please, don't let them find us," Sarah prayed silently, her breath coming in shallow gasps. Charles' hand closed around hers, gripping tightly as if to say, We're in this together.

The footsteps grew louder, and the flicker of torchlight danced at the entrance of the alleyway. Sarah's pulse thundered in her ears as they waited, eyes wide with panic.

"Oi! What do we have here?" a gruff voice called out, and the sound of laughter echoed down the alley. The shadows shifted, revealing several British soldiers, their red coats glinting in the torchlight.

Sarah felt her stomach drop, her vision blurring as terror threatened to overwhelm her. This was it. They were going to be captured. All of their plans, their hopes for freedom, gone in an instant.

But just as the soldiers began to advance toward them, a sudden commotion erupted from the street behind them. Shouts filled the air, followed by the sound of heavy footfalls and clashing weapons.

"Hey, you lot!" Another voice shouted, drawing the soldiers' attention away from the alley. "Over here!"

"Go!" Dr. Warren urged, seizing the opportunity, the children slipped into the darkness of the alley entrance. Sarah's heart soared with hope as they darted inside, the shouts of battle fading behind them.

"Who was that?" she wondered aloud, her breath catching in her throat as they hurried through the dimly lit alleyway.

"Doesn't matter," Charles replied, his grip on her hand unrelenting. "We're safe now. That's what counts."

Safe... for now, Sarah thought, as they continued deeper into the back alleys, the unknown stretching before them like a vast abyss. And yet, the spark of hope within her refused to be extinguished. Together, they would face whatever challenges awaited them, bound by their shared determination and trust.

"Let's go," she whispered, her voice steady and resolute. But as they pressed forward into the darkness, she couldn't shake the feeling that something - or someone - was watching them, waiting for the right moment to strike.

# CHAPTER 15

The air was thick with tension as Sarah, Charles, Henry, and Clarissa huddled together in the narrow alley, their breaths coming out in shallow puffs. The pounding of boots against cobblestones echoed through the darkness, growing louder by the second.

"Hide!" Charles whispered urgently, but it was too late; a group of British soldiers rounded the corner, their red coats shimmering like fresh blood under the moonlight. The children's hearts raced, their eyes wide with fear and despair.

"Look what we have here," sneered the leader of the troop, his eyes narrowed into slits. "A bunch of little rebels. You know what we do to rebels, don't you?"

Charles gritted his teeth, determination lighting his eyes like a bright flame. "You can't just take us," he declared, stepping forward bravely. "We've done nothing wrong!" He shot a glance at Sarah, who nodded her agreement, her hands shaking at her sides.

"Is that so?" the soldier laughed, his voice cold and cruel. "I don't think His Majesty would agree. Now, hold still—this will be easier if you don't resist."

Henry clenched his fists, a familiar fire igniting within him. "Like hell, we won't resist!" He lunged at the nearest soldier, only to be knocked back by the butt of a musket, sending him sprawling onto the ground.

"Leave him alone!" Clarissa cried out, her timid voice cracking with emotion. She summoned her newfound courage and tried to pull a soldier away from Henry but was quickly overpowered and pushed aside.

"Enough!" Charles shouted, his chest heaving with frustration. "Let's make a deal. Let the girls go, and we'll come quietly."

"Nice try, boy," replied the leader, grabbing Sarah's arm and pulling her toward him. "But you're all coming with us."

Sarah's heart sank as she exchanged terrified glances with her friends. She knew Charles' offer was a long shot, but the crushing reality of their situation hit her like a ton of bricks. Was there no way out? Could they not escape the iron grip of the British soldiers?

"Stay strong," she whispered to Clarissa as they were shoved forward by the soldiers. "We'll find a way out. We always do." The two girls locked eyes, drawing strength from one another, their spirits refusing to be broken.

Meanwhile, Charles and Henry continued to struggle against their captors, their bravery shining through despite the overwhelming odds. They fought for every inch, never giving up even as they were dragged away into the night, their fates uncertain.

"Mark my words," Charles spat at the soldier holding him. "You'll regret this."

"Save your threats, boy," the soldier replied, smirking. "You'll have plenty of time to reconsider your options in His Majesty's custody."

As the children were led away, their hearts heavy with

despair, a fierce determination burned within them. They would not let their captors win; they would fight for their freedom until their last breaths.

The flickering candlelight cast eerie shadows on the damp stone walls of the cramped cell. The children, bound and tired, huddled together for warmth and comfort. Sarah Merriweather glanced around at her companions, their once vibrant spirits now reduced to mere whispers of their former selves. They had fought valiantly in the name of independence, but as each day passed in captivity, their resolve began to waver.

"Sometimes I wonder if we were ever meant to make a difference," murmured Charles Hamilton, his voice echoing with doubt. "Maybe we're just kids who got caught up in something bigger than ourselves."

Henry Turner's brow furrowed as he considered Charles's words. "You really think that?" he asked, unable to hide the hurt in his voice. "After everything we've been through, you'd just give up now?"

"Give up?" Charles shot back defensively. "No, I'm not saying we should give up. It's just...sometimes, I can't help but wonder if we're in over our heads."

"Charles has a point," Clarissa Jennings chimed in, her glasses catching the glint of the flickering candlelight. "We are very young to be shouldering such heavy responsibilities. And there's no guarantee we'll succeed."

"Or that we'll ever return to our own time," added Sarah, her voice barely audible as she stared down at her hands, bound together by coarse rope. She felt a pang of guilt for voicing this fear, knowing it would only add to the burden her friends already carried.

"Look at us," Henry muttered, absently picking at a threadbare patch on his trousers. "Trapped like rats in a cage."

"More like mice," Charles countered half-heartedly, attempting to bring some levity into the gloomy atmosphere. "Rats are much too resourceful for this sort of predicament."

"Whatever we are," Sarah sighed, wrapping her arms around her knees as she stared blankly at the wall opposite, "we're not going anywhere anytime soon."

Clarissa, usually the one brimming with bright ideas, could only offer a resigned nod in agreement. As the oppressive silence settled upon the group, their thoughts turned inward, each grappling with the enormity of their responsibilities and the fear that they might never return to their own time.

"Guys," Sarah whispered, breaking the silence, "what if we don't make it back? What if we're stuck here forever?"

"Sarah, don't talk like that," Charles chided gently, though the tremor in his voice betrayed his own fears. "We've made it this far, haven't we?"

"Charles is right," Clarissa added, trying to convince herself as much as her friends. "We can't let ourselves be consumed by doubt. We have a mission to complete."

"Easy for you to say," grumbled Henry, his jaw clenched tight as he fought back the rising tide of despair. "You weren't the one who got into a brawl with a redcoat."

"We all make mistakes, Henry," Clarissa reassured him, placing a comforting hand on his shoulder. "The important thing is that we learn from them."

"Besides," Charles added with a sardonic grin, "you've made quite the impression on our captors. I have no doubt they'll remember your name for years to come."

"Very funny," Henry snorted, but he couldn't help the ghost of a smile that flickered across his face.

As the children sat huddled together on the damp, dank floor of their prison cell, their once vibrant spirits seemed to have faded into a gray pallor that matched the cold stone walls surrounding them. Their eyes, which had once sparkled with determination and curiosity, now appeared dull and listless, weighed down by the gravity of their situation.

As they sat in their prison cell, the weight of their responsibilities felt like a suffocating cloak that threatened to smother any lingering sparks of hope. Yet, even as fear and despair gnawed at the edges of their resolve, the children clung to one another - finding solace in the knowledge that they were not alone in their struggles.

"Enough!" Henry exclaimed, slamming his fist against the cold, hard floor. "We can't let our fears control us. Look at how far we've come! We've faced challenges that would have broken others, but we've managed to stick together and overcome them."

"Besides," Sarah said quietly, lifting her head to meet Charles's gaze, "we've learned so much about ourselves and each other along the way. We're stronger now because of this journey."

"Sarah's right," Clarissa agreed with a small smile. "We've all grown in ways we never could have imagined. And together, we've become a formidable force."

"Formidable" might have been a bit of a stretch, but as the children exchanged glances, their eyes betraying flickers of uncertainty mingled with determination, they couldn't deny that they had come a long way since their adventure began.

"Alright," Charles conceded, his voice still tinged with doubt but strengthened by the encouragement of his friends. "We'll keep fighting for independence and for each other. No matter what."

"Agreed," Sarah said, her heart swelling with pride at their collective resolve. "Together, we'll make a difference. I can feel it."

"Me too," Henry chimed in, a steely glint in his eye. "And even if we don't succeed, at least we'll know we gave it our all."

"Indeed," Clarissa nodded solemnly. "It's better to have tried and failed than to have never tried at all."

"We'll find a way out of this," Sarah said, her voice barely audible but firm. "We're stronger together, remember?"

"Right," Charles agreed, his gaze meeting each of his friends in turn. "Together, we can face anything - be it redcoats, cryptex puzzles, or even time itself."

With a collective nod, the children braced themselves for whatever challenges lay ahead, their spirits bolstered by their shared determination and the promise of a brighter future beyond the bleak walls of their captivity.

The small, dimly lit cell seemed to shrink around them as they huddled together on the cold stone floor, their breaths ghosting out in the chilly air. The harsh reality of their situation was like a vice grip around Sarah's heart, squeezing out hope with every passing moment.

"Remember when we first started this journey?" Henry asked his voice a desperate attempt at breaking the oppressive silence that surrounded them.

"Feels like ages ago," Charles sighed, rolling a small pebble between his fingers. "We were so naive back then, thinking we could just waltz into the past and change history."

"Maybe we were," Sarah admitted, her eyes downcast. "But we've learned a lot since then, haven't we? We've grown stronger, smarter."

"Definitely more resilient," Clarissa added, managing a feeble smile. "I mean, look at us now – captive in a prison cell, but still fighting."

"True," Henry said, nodding. "We've faced challenges we never thought possible, and we're still standing."

"More like sitting," Charles quipped, earning a weak chuckle from the others.

"Sometimes," Sarah began hesitantly, her voice barely a whisper in the stillness, "I worry that we'll never make it back home."

"Me too," Clarissa admitted quietly, her eyes downcast as she traced patterns on the dusty floor with her finger. "And I'm scared that if we don't succeed, everything we've done so far will have been for nothing."

"Or worse," Charles added, his brow furrowed in concern, "that our actions could somehow change history for the worse."

"Speaking of challenges," Sarah continued, attempting to steer the conversation towards a more positive direction, "remember when we had to decode that cryptex message?"

"Ah, yes," Clarissa mused, her eyes lighting up with excitement. "The way we worked together to solve those puzzles... it felt like magic."

"Or the time we managed to warn Paul Revere about the British army's movements," Henry added, a hint of pride in his voice.

"Without us, who knows what might have happened," Charles said, allowing himself a small grin.

As the children reminisced about their shared experiences, their spirits lifted ever so slightly, the shadows of despair retreating to the corners of the cell.

"Remember that time we had to sneak to find out the planes for the egg plot?" Clarissa whispered, a mischievous glint in her eyes as she recalled the daring escapade. "I never thought I'd be able to find that secret tunnel."

"Or how about when we managed to deliver Dr. Warren's message to John Hancock and Samuel Adams just in time?" Sarah added, biting her lip to stifle her laughter. The image of

Charles sprinting through the streets of Boston, parchment clutched tightly in hand, was an enduring memory etched into their minds.

"Oh! Don't forget our great escape from the redcoats on horseback," Henry chimed in, his chest swelling with pride. "We were like lightning, outrunning those blimey soldiers!"

As they reminisced, the children couldn't help but feel a sense of accomplishment—a newfound strength that came from overcoming obstacles together. Despite the darkness surrounding them, their shared determination ignited a flicker of hope within their hearts.

"Guys," Charles said, a determined gleam appearing in his eyes, "we've come so far and accomplished so much. We can't let this place break us. We're stronger than that."

"Right," Sarah agreed, nodding resolutely. Her once fragile demeanor now held an air of confidence. She reached out and squeezed Charles' hand reassuringly. "Together, we can face anything."

"Even if we're scared, even if it seems impossible," Clarissa whispered, her voice wavering but steadying with each word, "we'll find a way. We always do."

"Exactly," Henry grunted, his jaw set in a fierce scowl, yet the intensity in his eyes betrayed a fiery passion for justice. "We've got a mission, and we're going to see it through."

"None of us asked for this responsibility," Henry said gruffly, his hands clenching into fists at his sides. "But we're stuck here now. We can't just give up."

"Of course not," Sarah agreed, her blue eyes meeting his with determination. "But it's normal to be afraid, isn't it?"

"Absolutely," Charles chimed in, placing a hand on Sarah's shoulder. "Fear can be a powerful motivator, as long as we don't let it paralyze us."

"Easy for you to say," Clarissa muttered under her breath, her gaze flickering nervously between her friends.

"Hey," Henry insisted, his tone softer now. "We've all got each other's backs, remember? No matter what happens, we face it together."

"Right," Sarah nodded, a small smile breaking through her solemn expression. "Together, we're unstoppable."

"Exactly," Charles grinned, giving Clarissa's shoulder a reassuring squeeze. "Nothing can break the bond we've formed."

As they spoke, their fears and doubts laid bare, the children found solace in the knowledge that they were not alone in their struggles. Though the future was uncertain, they knew they could rely on one another to face whatever challenges lay ahead.

The children sat huddled together, their resolve hardening like steel as they drew strength from one another. The oppressive weight of their captivity seemed to lighten, if only for a moment, as they shared in the warmth of their unbreakable bond.

"Despite everything we've been through, I'm grateful," Sarah whispered, her gaze meeting each of her friends in turn. "Grateful to have all of you by my side."

"Likewise," Clarissa agreed, placing a small hand over Sarah's. "I don't think any of us could have come this far alone."

"Absolutely," Charles chimed in. "Together, we're stronger than any one of us could ever be."

"Remember when we nearly got caught by those British soldiers?" Clarissa asked, her voice trembling with a mix of fear and amusement. "I thought my heart would burst from my chest."

"Or when we had to climb that rickety ladder over the harbor," Sarah chimed in, shuddering at the memory. "I've never been so scared in my life."

The wind whispered through the bars of their darkened cell, rustling the straw beneath them as it carried the faint sounds of soldiers' laughter. Sarah shivered at the chilling breeze, hugging her knees tighter to her chest. She looked around at her friends, who were all deep in thought and reflection, their faces cast in shadows.

"Guys," she said softly, breaking the silence, "I know it seems like we're trapped here forever, but... we can't give up hope. We've come so far already, and we still have a purpose."

"Sarah's right," Charles replied, his eyes gleaming with determination as he met her gaze. "We've faced countless challenges and obstacles, but we always found a way to overcome them. Together."

"Even when it felt impossible," Clarissa added, a small smile spreading across her face as she recalled their past victories. "Like deciphering the cryptex or escaping from that ambush in the woods."

"Or standing up to Headmaster Winters," Henry chimed in, a fierce pride swelling within him. "We fought for what we believed in, even when it was hard."

"Exactly," Sarah affirmed, her voice steadying with newfound resolve. "And we'll continue to fight for our mission, no matter how uncertain our future may seem."

The others nodded, their eyes filled with the same unwavering determination. Together, they formed an unbreakable bond forged by their shared experiences and the lessons they had learned along the way.

"Each time we've faced danger," Charles mused, his eyes distant, "we've come out stronger for it."

"Here's to us, then," Henry declared, raising an imaginary glass. "To our indomitable spirit and the lessons we've learned along the way."

"Cheers," they all murmured in unison, their voices barely audible but resolute.

"It's true, though," Henry agreed, nodding solemnly. "The more we've been through together, the closer we've become. It's like... we're a family now."

"An odd, time-traveling family," Clarissa added with a chuckle, her earlier fears momentarily forgotten as she leaned into the warmth of her friends' embrace.

"Exactly," Sarah smiled, her gaze steady and filled with gratitude. "And no matter what happens, I wouldn't trade this family for anything in the world."

"Me neither," Charles murmured, the lines of worry on his face relaxing as he glanced around at his newfound siblings. "We're in this together till the end."

"Agreed," Henry nodded, his spirits buoyed by the fierce determination in his friends' voices. "Let's make history remember us."

As the children sat in the bleakness of their captivity, their hearts swelled with the love and unity forged through their shared experiences. Together, they faced an uncertain future – but with renewed strength, hope, and resolve.

"Let's make a pact," Charles suggested, extending his hand toward the center of their circle. "No matter what happens, we'll never give up on our mission or each other."

"Agreed," Henry declared, placing his own hand atop Charles', his calloused fingers gripping tightly. Clarissa hesitated for a moment, then joined in, her slender hand trembling slightly but her resolve firm.

"Then it's settled," Charles continued, his gaze meeting each of his friends' in turn, the fire of their shared purpose reflected in their eyes. "We're in this together until the very end."

"Until the very end," they echoed, their voices joining in a chorus of unwavering commitment.

"Until the very end," Sarah whispered, adding her own hand to the pile. "We'll see this through together."

"Until the very end," they echoed in unison, their voices

blending into a single vow of steadfast commitment.

As they pulled their hands away and exchanged resolute glances, a renewed sense of purpose surged through them. They knew the road ahead would be fraught with danger and uncertainty, but as long as they had each other, they could face whatever challenges lay before them.

For now, their hearts were filled with hope and determination as their shared mission carried them forward into an unknown future.

And with that, the children's spirits soared, fueled by the memories of their victories and the knowledge that together, they were unstoppable.

# CHAPTER 16

Dr. Warren hid in the shadows of a narrow alley, his breath coming in short gasps as he pressed himself against the cold brick wall. He could hear the British soldiers' footsteps echoing through the streets, their gruff voices growing louder as they closed in on his location. As a man intimately familiar with the winding paths and hidden shortcuts of the city, Dr. Warren knew he had to act fast if he wanted to evade capture.

"Think, Joseph," he whispered to himself, frantically racking his brain for any possible escape routes. He glanced up at the moonlit sky, the stars winking down at him as if encouraging him to take control of his own fate.

"Ah!" he exclaimed under his breath, suddenly remembering a series of interconnected rooftops that would lead him straight to St. Paul's Churchyard. With a surge of adrenaline, Dr. Warren leaped onto a nearby stack of crates, using them as a makeshift staircase to reach the first rooftop. His heart pounded in his chest as he sprinted across the uneven tiles, adrenaline fueling his agile movements.

As he jumped from roof to roof, he couldn't help but think about the children he had left behind—their frightened faces and desperate attempts to resist capture. The gravity of the situation weighed heavily on his shoulders, and he felt an overwhelming responsibility to save them from their captors.

"Their lives are in my hands," he thought grimly, gauging the distance to the next rooftop. "If I don't act, who will?"

He recalled Sarah's fiery determination and her unwavering

bravery, even in the face of danger. She reminded him of himself in many ways, a kindred spirit with a shared passion for justice and freedom. He owed it to her and to all the children to do everything in his power to ensure their safety.

"Failure is not an option," he vowed, his voice just a whisper in the wind.

Leaping onto the final rooftop, Dr. Warren surveyed the city below, his mind racing as he considered the risks and potential consequences of his daring rescue attempt. He knew that if he were caught, he would face severe punishment at the hands of the British soldiers—perhaps even death. But the thought of abandoning the children to their fate was unbearable, and so he steeled himself for the challenges that lay ahead.

"Courage, Joseph," he murmured, psyching himself up for the task at hand. "You can do this."

With renewed determination, Dr. Warren descended from the rooftops and disappeared into the night, prepared to face whatever obstacles stood between him and the captured children. The stakes couldn't be higher, but Dr. Warren knew that where there was hope, there was always a chance for victory.

Dr. Warren crouched behind a stack of wooden crates in a dark alley, catching his breath and mentally devising a plan to rescue the children. He knew he had to be resourceful and quick-witted if he wanted to outsmart the British soldiers who were guarding them. A sudden gust of wind carried the distant sounds of footsteps and laughter, and he froze, listening intently.

"Alright, Joseph," he whispered to himself as he began to

formulate his plan. "It's clear that a frontal assault would be suicide. We need to play to our strengths...and their weaknesses."

"First things first," Dr. Warren mused, his thoughts racing. "I need to gather some allies – people I can trust, who know the city like the back of their hands." He mentally listed a few names, including that of a local blacksmith and an innkeeper who had proven their loyalty to the cause in the past.

"Secondly," he continued, "we need a diversion. Something to draw the attention of the guards away from the children. Perhaps a small explosion or fire...just enough chaos to create an opportunity for us to slip in undetected."

He paused for a moment, considering the risks involved in such a daring move. But with each passing second, the children's situation grew more dire. There was no time for hesitation.

"Lastly," Dr. Warren decided, "once the guards are distracted, we'll need to move quickly and silently. We'll have to rely on stealth and cunning to free the children without drawing additional attention."

As he mulled over his plan, Dr. Warren felt a mixture of excitement and trepidation that sent shivers down his spine. This was a high-stakes game of cat and mouse, and one false move could mean disaster for all of them. However, he also knew that the children were depending on him, and he couldn't let them down.

"Alright," he murmured, determination seeping into his voice. "Let's do this."

Dr. Warren moved swiftly through the shadows, making his way to the homes of his trusted allies. As he explained his plan, they each agreed to help without hesitation, knowing that the lives of the children hung in the balance.

"Remember," Dr. Warren cautioned as they prepared their makeshift explosives and weapons, his voice barely above a whisper, "timing is everything. We must work together, synchronize our movements, and rely on one another if we want to pull this off."

The tension in the air was palpable as they made their final preparations, every member of the small group feeling the weight of responsibility resting on their shoulders. The stakes were high, but failure wasn't an option. In the distance, a church bell tolled, signaling midnight and the beginning of their daring rescue mission.

"May fortune favor the bold," Dr. Warren said, a fierce glint in his eyes as he led his band of unlikely heroes out into the night. Their hearts pounded with anticipation, each step bringing them closer to the moment of truth.

The moon cast a ghostly glow over the cobblestone streets, casting eerie shadows that seemed to dance and flicker in time with Dr. Warren's pounding heart. He moved through the city like a wraith, his dark coat blending seamlessly with the inky night as he ducked behind corners and slipped through narrow alleyways. Every muscle was coiled tight with anticipation, his breath coming in short, controlled bursts as he strained his ears for any hint of approaching danger.

"Easy now," he whispered to himself, his voice barely audible even to his own ears. "One step at a time."

He could feel the weight of the makeshift explosive tucked into his belt, its presence a constant reminder of the risk he was taking - not just for himself, but for the children who depended on him. With each passing moment, their fear and despair gnawed at his resolve, spurring him onward despite the ever-present threat of capture.

"Dr. Warren!" hissed a voice from the shadows, causing him to freeze mid-step. A familiar figure emerged, one of his trusted allies, his eyes wide and frantic. "They've taken them to an old warehouse by the docks. Heavy security - redcoats everywhere."

"Thank you," Dr. Warren replied, nodding grimly as he committed the information to memory. His ally disappeared back into the darkness, leaving him to continue his journey alone.

As he neared the waterfront, the scent of the harbor filled his nostrils - a mix of brine, fish, and damp wood that was both comforting and oppressive all at once. The warehouse loomed ahead, its dark form a stark silhouette against the pale moonlight. Just as his ally had warned, British soldiers stood guard outside the entrance, their muskets gleaming menacingly in the dim light.

"Of course, it couldn't be easy," Dr. Warren thought to himself, his jaw clenched with determination.

He crept closer to the warehouse, assessing the security measures put in place by the British soldiers. The windows were barred, and the door was locked tight, the heavy padlock glinting tauntingly in the moonlight. A small group of soldiers patrolled the perimeter, their boots crunching on the gravel as they moved with military precision.

"Timing," Dr. Warren reminded himself, his heart racing as he prepared to put his plan into action. "It's all about timing."

He crouched low behind a stack of crates, watching the soldiers' movements carefully, waiting for the perfect moment to strike. In his head, he could already hear the voices of the children, whispering words of hope and gratitude.

"Stay strong," he thought, the image of the children's brave faces filling his mind. "I'm coming for you."

As the soldiers marched past him, Dr. Warren took a deep breath, steeling himself for the challenge ahead. There was no turning back now - it was time to act, and the fate of the children rested squarely on his shoulders. With one last silent prayer, he leaped into motion, his every move calculated and precise as he embarked on the most daring mission of his life.

Dr. Warren's heart pounded like a blacksmith's hammer as he crouched behind a barrel, his eyes fixed on the warehouse where the children were being held captive. He could feel the night air brushing against his face, the scent of damp wood and sea salt filling his nostrils. Every sense was heightened, every nerve electrified, as he prepared to infiltrate the enemy stronghold.

"Alright, Joseph," he whispered to himself, mentally rehearsing the plan one last time. "You can do this."

With cat-like stealth, Dr. Warren began edging around the perimeter of the warehouse, pausing only when a group of soldiers passed by, their red coats casting eerie shadows against the moonlit walls. He didn't dare to breathe, his chest tightening with anxiety as the cold steel of the pistol he had obtained from a fellow patriot dug into his side.

"Focus," he admonished himself, shaking off the fear and pressing on.

As he neared the entrance, he spotted a lone sentry standing guard by the door. Dr. Warren's mind raced, calculating the possibilities, weighing the risks. He knew that the success of his mission depended on remaining undetected, but how could he dispatch the soldier without raising the alarm?

"Think fast, now," he urged himself, his gaze darting from the sentry to the surrounding environment.

His eyes fell upon a pile of ropes coiled nearby, and a daring idea took shape in his mind. With practiced ease, he looped one end around the soldier's ankles and secured it to a hook on the wall. Then, he picked up a nearby stone and tossed it across the courtyard, eliciting a startled reaction from the sentry.

"Oi, who goes there?" the soldier demanded, taking a step forward – and promptly tripping over the taut line, falling to the ground with a muffled thud.

"Brilliant!" Dr. Warren thought, unable to suppress a grin as he approached the fallen soldier, who was still struggling to break free from his unexpected binds. He swiftly bound the man's hands and gagged him, ensuring that he would not be able to alert his comrades.

"Apologies, my good man," Dr. Warren whispered, "but this is for a greater cause."

With the guard neutralized, Dr. Warren turned his attention to the warehouse door. Luck was on his side tonight – the key to the padlock had been left hanging from the soldier's belt. He slid it into the lock, holding his breath as the heavy iron mechanism clicked open, granting him access to the children's prison.

Stepping inside, he found himself in a dimly lit room filled with stacks of crates and barrels, the air thick with dust and the scent of stale tobacco. He could hear the muffled sounds of the children's frightened whispers, their voices trembling with fear and despair.

"Be brave, little ones," he murmured under his breath, making his way through the labyrinth of containers toward the source of the noise.

Suddenly, he spotted them – Sarah, Charles, Clarissa, and Henry huddled together in a corner, their eyes wide with terror as they stared at their captors: two burly British soldiers smirking with cruel satisfaction.

"Time for the grand finale," Dr. Warren thought, his heart pounding as he raised his pistol, aiming it squarely at one of the soldiers. He took a deep breath, then called out in a voice both authoritative and booming:

"Release the children, or prepare to meet your maker!"

The soldiers whirled around in shock, their faces paling as they beheld the sight of Dr. Warren, his weapon trained on them with unwavering resolve. In that moment, he was a force to be reckoned with – a man driven by love, duty, and an unyielding commitment to the cause of freedom.

As the British soldiers stared at Dr. Warren, frozen in place by his unwavering determination, Sarah's eyes met his, and she felt a surge of hope. "Dr. Warren!" she gasped, her voice shaking with relief. Her hands flew to her mouth as tears pricked at the corners of her eyes.

"Stay back," he ordered the children, his voice softened with compassion but laced with authority. They nodded, their hearts pounding in unison as they huddled closer together. At that moment, they were no longer time-traveling adventurers; they were vulnerable children, desperately clinging to one another for comfort.

With a swift motion, Dr. Warren disarmed the first soldier, delivering a solid punch to his jaw. The second soldier lunged at him, but Dr. Warren expertly ducked under the attack, swiftly sweeping the man's legs out from under him. Both soldiers lay on the ground, dazed and defeated.

"Are you all right?" Dr. Warren asked the children; concern etched into his handsome features. They nodded vigorously, their eyes wide with gratitude.

"Thank you, Dr. Warren," Sarah whispered, her voice cracking with emotion. "We didn't think we would ever get out of here."

"Never fear, my dear," he replied, a gentle smile playing on his lips. "I promised I'd protect you, and that's exactly what I intend to do."

"Let's get out of here," Charles said, his voice quivering with excitement and newfound courage. Dr. Warren nodded in agreement, guiding the children toward the exit with a protective arm around them.

As they emerged from the dank warehouse into the fresh air

and sunlight, the children took a collective deep breath, savoring their newfound freedom. Their hearts swelled with gratitude as they looked up at Dr. Warren, who stood tall and proud, his eyes shining with determination.

"Dr. Warren," Clarissa said, her hand gripping his tightly, "we'll never forget what you did for us today. You risked everything to save us."

"Remember, my dear," he replied, his voice full of warmth and wisdom, "our mission is far from over. We must continue fighting for the future — not just for ourselves, but for the generations that will follow in our footsteps."

Together, they walked away from the warehouse, their heads held high and their spirits renewed by the knowledge that they had triumphed against all odds. The challenges ahead were daunting, but with Dr. Warren by their side, the children felt confident that they could face whatever fate had in store for them.

The coming days would be a sharp turn in their adventure as the British were landing their men at Breed's Hill and as General Dr. Joseph Warren would be leading the militia to attack a fight against the oppressive might of the British regulars. The children all knew that what they had done before this was dangerous, but what lay ahead was still more dangerous. And as the sun shined out in the morning, war was on the horizon.

# CHAPTER 17

Smoke billowed from the mouths of cannons, and the deafening roar of gunfire echoed through the air. The ground shook with each explosion, sending tremors through the children huddled together on Breed's Hill. The battle raged around them as they ducked behind a makeshift barricade, their hearts pounding in their chests.

"Stay down!" Charles shouted at Sarah, who had risked a glance over the edge of their cover. Soldiers charged toward one another, their bayonets gleaming under the weak sun that struggled to break through the haze of gunpowder and smoke.

"Charles, what are we going to do?" Sarah's voice was barely audible above the chaos, her blue eyes wide with terror.

"Clarissa, can you see any way for us to escape this madness?" Henry asked, cursing under his breath as another explosion sent dirt flying onto their hiding spot.

Clarissa adjusted her glasses, scanning the battlefield with a determined expression. "I think there might be an opening if we head toward that abandoned house," she said, pointing at a structure partially hidden by smoke. "We'll have to be careful, but it's our best chance."

"Alright, everyone, listen up," Charles took charge, his confident demeanor cutting through the tension. "When I give the signal, we're going to make a run for that house. Stay low and follow my lead. Are we clear?"

The other children nodded, their faces set with determination. They knew that they needed to act quickly to survive this bloody clash between the British and American forces.

"Wait!" Dr. Warren called out as he limped toward them, blood staining his once pristine coat. "There's something important I need to tell you before you go."

"Dr. Warren!" Sarah cried, her concern for the injured doctor momentarily overriding her fear of the escalating battle.

"Never mind me," he said, grimacing in pain. "You must find John Hancock and Samuel Adams. They are crucial to the success of the revolution. Tell them... tell them that they need to work together for the greater good despite their differences. The battle is raging, and we need more men to fight, but we also need to get the innocent people out of the town and save lives to ensure our cause will continue. It can't all end here."

"Dr. Warren, we can't just leave you here," Clarissa protested, her voice trembling as new waves of gunfire erupted around them.

"Listen to me," Dr. Warren insisted, his eyes burning with urgency. "You have a mission to complete, and time is running out. You must go now!"

Charles exchanged a glance with Henry, who nodded grimly. "Alright, everyone, on my signal," Charles said, his voice betraying the weight of the responsibility he now carried. "One...two...three!"

The moment Charles yelled "Three," the group dashed from their hiding spot toward the dilapidated house. The chaos of battle raged on around them, making it difficult to hear each other over the cacophony of screams and gunfire. Sarah's heart pounded in her chest, a mixture of fear and determination propelling her forward.

"Stay close!" Henry shouted, his strong voice carrying over the din as they weaved through the battlefield. The children's eyes darted around, searching for any signs of danger, while their minds raced with strategies to navigate through the treacherous terrain.

"Look!" Clarissa exclaimed, pointing at a nearby alleyway as they neared the house. "That could be a safer route to reach Hancock and Adams!"

"Good thinking, Clarissa," Charles praised, his tone firm and decisive despite the chaos surrounding them. "We can't afford to waste any time. Let's take that path."

As they slipped into the narrow alley, Sarah couldn't help but marvel at the way her friends were adapting to their new roles. They had been thrust into this dangerous situation, yet they remained focused and resourceful, determined not only to survive but also to complete their mission.

"Time is running out," she whispered to herself, feeling the weight of Dr. Warren's words settling on her shoulders. They needed to find Hancock and Adams quickly, deliver their message, and somehow return to their own time before it was too late.

"Alright, everyone, stay alert and keep moving," Charles instructed, taking charge like a natural leader. "We don't know what we'll encounter, so we need to be prepared for anything."

As they pressed on, Sarah felt a newfound resolve bubbling within her. She knew that they faced many challenges ahead, but she was determined to honor Dr. Warren's sacrifice and help secure the future of American independence.

"Charles," she said, her voice stronger and more assertive than before. "I have an idea that might help us locate Hancock and Adams faster."

"Let's hear it," Charles replied, his eyes glinting with curiosity and admiration as he looked at her.

"Paul Revere knows Boston like the back of his hand," she explained. "If we can find him, he might be able to guide us to them."

"Excellent suggestion, Sarah," Charles agreed, a proud smile gracing his lips. "That could save us precious time. Let's do it!"

With newfound determination and resourcefulness fueling their actions, the children pressed on through the heart of the battle, prepared to face whatever challenges lay ahead in their quest for American freedom.

The roar of cannons and the sharp crack of muskets filled the air as the children darted through the smoke-filled battlefield. They could barely hear each other's frantic shouts over the cacophony of battle. Charles gripped Sarah's hand tightly, guiding her through the haze as they led their friends in search of Paul Revere.

"Look out!" Henry called out as a British soldier appeared from the fog, charging toward them with his bayonet poised. The children scattered, each instinctively seeking cover behind the nearest boulders and fallen trees.

"Quick, everyone, stay low," Charles whispered, using hand gestures to communicate as they caught their breath.

"Charles, we need a plan," Sarah said, her heart pounding in her chest. "The redcoats are everywhere!"

"Alright," Charles replied, taking a deep breath. "Clarissa, you're the best with maps. Can you find us a hidden route to Paul Revere's shop?"

"Let me think," Clarissa responded, squinting through the smoke as she tried to recall the layout of Boston. "If we head west along this ridge, there should be an alleyway that leads straight to his shop."

"Good thinking, Clarissa," Charles said, nodding in approval. "Alright, everyone, stay close and follow us. We've got to move fast and stay out of sight."

The children moved cautiously through the chaos, their hearts racing with suspense as they narrowly evaded detection by British soldiers. At one point, they found themselves trapped against a wall as a group of redcoats marched past, their voices raised in a menacing battle cry.

"Stay still," Henry whispered, his breath catching in his throat as he pressed himself closer to the cold stones. "Don't make a sound."

As the soldiers passed, the children exchanged relieved glances before continuing their journey. Finally, after what felt like an eternity of navigating through the battle, they arrived at the alleyway Clarissa had mentioned.

"Paul Revere's shop is just up ahead," Charles announced, wiping sweat from his brow. "Let's go, and remember – stay low and stay quiet."

With renewed courage and determination, the children crept toward their destination, prepared to face whatever challenges lay ahead – all in the name of American independence.

The children huddled together in the shadowy depths of the alley, the dim light reflecting off their eyes as they gazed at one another. They had come so far, and their experiences on this harrowing journey had forged new bonds between them.

"Alright, team," Charles whispered, his voice steady despite the palpable tension. "We've managed to avoid detection so far, but we need to be extra careful moving forward. We can't let our guard down for even a second."

As the group nodded in agreement, Sarah found herself reflecting on her own growth throughout this adventure. She was no longer the timid girl she had been prior; now, she was a leader, standing side by side with her friends in the face of adversity.

"Look," Henry said suddenly, pointing towards the top of the hill where Dr. Warren stood, engaged in fierce combat with a towering British soldier. The sight of their beloved mentor in such peril sent a jolt of fear through the children's hearts.

"Dr. Warren!" Clarissa cried out, her words barely audible over the din of battle. The others stared in horror as the British soldier delivered a crushing blow to Dr. Warren, sending him sprawling to the ground.

"Stay back," Charles commanded, gripping his friends' arms tightly. "If we rush in there, we'll only make things worse. We have to think this through." He swallowed hard, trying to quell his own terror.

"Charles is right," Sarah agreed, her voice shaking. "We need to find a way to help Dr. Warren without putting ourselves – or him – in more danger."

"Maybe... maybe we can distract the soldier?" Henry suggested hesitantly, glancing around for any possible tools they could use.

"Wait!" Clarissa exclaimed, her eyes lighting up with an idea. "I remember reading about a secret tunnel system beneath Boston. If we can find an entrance nearby, we might be able to sneak close enough through the trenches to get to Dr. Warren to help or to get him out of there."

"Brilliant, Clarissa!" Charles praised, the fire of determination returning to his eyes. "Alright, team, let's find that tunnel and save Dr. Warren!"

The children, spurred on by their burning desire to help their mentor, set aside their fear as they scrambled through the chaos of the battlefield. They moved with a newfound sense of purpose and unity, working together to locate the hidden entrance – all while keeping a watchful eye on the injured Dr. Warren.

"Dr. Warren!" Sarah cried out, bolting through the smoke and debris as she caught sight of their fallen mentor.

Her heart pounded in her ears, drowning out the cacophony

of battle as the other children followed closely behind her. They had to reach him before it was too late. As they neared Dr. Warren's crumpled form, Sarah's mind raced with thoughts of what could've happened. She prayed it wasn't as bad as it looked from a distance.

"Please be okay," Charles whispered, his voice barely audible over the explosive chaos around them.

"Is he breathing?" Clarissa asked urgently, her eyes wide with fear.

"Let me check," Henry said, his fingers trembling as he felt for Dr. Warren's breath.

Sarah knelt down beside Dr. Warren, her hands hovering above his blood-soaked shirt. The crimson stain seemed to be spreading rapidly, and her heart sank at the sight. How could they help him if they didn't even know where to begin?

"His pulse is weak, but he's alive," Henry reported, his voice wavering.

"Thank goodness," Clarissa breathed, relief washing over her.

"Can we do anything to help him?" Charles stammered, looking to Sarah for guidance.

Sarah hesitated, biting her lip as she racked her brain for any shred of medical knowledge she might have gleaned from her time with Dr. Warren. She thought of how he had always been so calm, collected, and wise when faced with a crisis. How would he handle this situation? What would he want them to do?

"First, we need to stop the bleeding," she said finally, her voice firm yet uncertain. "We can use our clothes or whatever we can find to make a makeshift bandage."

"Right!" Henry agreed, immediately tearing off a strip of fabric from the hem of his shirt.

"Here," Charles offered, pulling a handkerchief from his pocket and handing it to Sarah.

"Good. Now let's apply pressure to the wound," she instructed, taking a deep breath as she pressed the makeshift bandage against Dr. Warren's injury. She tried to ignore the warm, sticky blood that seeped through the fabric and onto her hands.

"Is it working?" Clarissa asked nervously, watching the blood continue to spread.

"I don't know," Sarah admitted, her voice barely audible as she fought to hold back tears. "I just don't know."

"Stay with us, Dr. Warren," Henry implored, his eyes brimming with unshed tears. "We need you."

"Please," Charles added, his voice cracking, "don't leave us."

For a moment, the world seemed to stand still — the chaos of the battle fading away as the children focused all their energy on saving Dr. Warren. But even as they struggled to comprehend the severity of his wounds, their determination never faltered. They knew they had to do everything in their power to help him, for his sake — and for the future they were fighting for.

"Keep applying pressure," Sarah whispered, her voice filled with resolve. "We won't give up on you, Dr. Warren."

The air was heavy with the acrid scent of gunpowder and sweat, thick with the tension of battle. Sarah's heart raced as she clenched her hands around the handkerchief pressed against Dr. Warren's wound. She glanced up at her friends, their faces a mix of fear and determination.

"Is he going to make it?" Clarissa asked, her voice trembling.

"His sacrifice won't be in vain," Henry replied, his jaw set with conviction. "He risked everything for us, for this mission."

"Then we have to see it through," Charles declared, his eyes blazing with resolve. "We owe it to Dr. Warren and to everyone fighting for freedom."

"Agreed," Sarah whispered, gently patting her hands on the blood-soaked fabric. "We'll do whatever it takes to ensure American independence."

As they stood there, surrounded by the chaos of war, a deep sense of unity and purpose took hold of them. They knew that their journey had been nothing short of miraculous, but now it was time for them to take charge and make their mark on history. The stakes were higher than ever, and they couldn't afford to let fear or doubt cloud their judgment.

"Alright," Sarah said, her voice steady despite the turmoil within her. "Let's get Dr. Warren to safety first. We can't leave him here."

"Good idea," Charles nodded, helping Henry lift Dr. Warren's limp form. "Clarissa, you keep watch for any British soldiers while we move him."

"Got it," Clarissa responded, scanning the battlefield with a newfound intensity.

As they carefully maneuvered through the smoke-filled battleground, Sarah's thoughts swirled with images of Dr. Warren's kind smile and gentle encouragement. He had believed in them, and now they would honor his legacy by completing their mission.

"Once we're safe, we need to strategize," Sarah said firmly, her grip on Dr. Warren's arm tightening with determination. "We have to be smart about this if we want to make a difference."

"Right," Henry agreed, his eyes narrowing in concentration. "We need to find allies and people out of the area and save as many people as possible if we want our fight for independence to continue."

"Let's not forget our ultimate goal," Charles chimed in, his voice filled with conviction. "We have to help secure support for the American cause."

"Exactly," Sarah nodded, her heart swelling with pride and purpose. "Together, we can achieve what all these great men and women have risked their lives for and make a better future for everyone."

As they moved through the chaos, shielding Dr. Warren from further harm, the children's resolve only grew stronger. They knew the path ahead wouldn't be easy, but they were ready to face whatever challenges lay before them. With the memory of Dr. Warren's sacrifice fueling their determination, there was no doubt that they would play a crucial role in securing America's independence.

With the backdrop of the battle of Bunker Hill painted in shades of gunpowder and fire, Sarah took a deep breath, her eyes filled with resolve. As she looked at her friends, each wearing expressions of determination, she knew they were ready to face whatever lay ahead.

"Alright," Sarah began, her voice steady despite the chaos around them. "First, we need to get Dr. Warren to safety. Then, we can focus on gathering support for the cause."

"Agreed," Charles said, his eyes darting around the battlefield as he calculated their next move. "We should head towards the outskirts of town; it'll be easier to avoid British soldiers there. We did all we could here and struck heavy losses on the British; they may have won this battle, but we will win the war."

"Good thinking," Henry chimed in, his muscles tense as he prepared to sprint through the chaos. "Let's go!"

As they navigated the battlefield, Sarah couldn't help but think about Headmaster Winters' words. She recalled his mischievous smile and gentle wisdom, which only fueled her determination to succeed.

"Remember, guys," Clarissa added softly, adjusting her glasses nervously. "We have allies like John Hancock, Samuel Adams, and Paul Revere who can help us take care of Dr. Warren and take the next step in saving lives and winning our independence."

"Right," Sarah nodded, feeling a surge of hope amidst the smoke and gunfire. "Together, we can make sure that Dr. Warren's sacrifice isn't in vain."

"Enough talking," Charles interrupted, his voice urgent. "We need to move now!"

The children exchanged quick nods before dashing through the chaotic battlefield, dodging explosions and incoming gunfire. Their hearts pounded in unison, driven by the shared purpose of furthering the American cause.

As they reached the relative safety of the town's outskirts, they paused to take stock of their surroundings. The scent of burning wood and distant screams still lingered in the air, but they couldn't let it deter them from their mission.

"Alright," Sarah said, wiping sweat from her brow. "Now that we're away from the battle, let's plan our next steps."

"First, we get the message to John Hancock, Samuel Adams, and Paul Revere," Charles suggested, his eyes filled with anticipation. "They'll know how to carry Dr. Warren's vision forward and get the people to safety."

"Then, we do what we can to spread the message and get the rest of the people on our side," Henry added, flexing his fists as if ready to fight. "If we are truly going to win, then we need all of the colonies to join in our struggle."

"Let's make to spread our message far and wide," Clarissa chimed in, her voice growing more confident. "The more people who join us, the stronger our chances of success."

"Exactly," Sarah agreed, her blue eyes blazing with determination. "We've come this far, and we won't stop until we've achieved what Dr. Warren fought so hard for – American independence."

As they set off into the unknown, their hearts swelled with a sense of anticipation and resolve. They were ready to face the challenges that lay ahead, united by friendship.

# CHAPTER 18

The first rays of sunlight crept over the horizon, casting a warm glow on the faces of the four friends as they stirred from their slumber. Sarah blinked away the remnants of sleep and marveled at the vivid hues of orange and pink that filled the sky. A sense of determination washed over her, like the waves crashing against the nearby shore, as she remembered the vital role they were to play in the upcoming battle.

"Up and at 'em, everyone," she whispered urgently to her companions, Charles, Henry, and Clarissa. "We've got work to do."

Charles groaned but sat up, rubbing his eyes. He knew the importance of their mission and couldn't let the others down. His natural leadership skills would be essential today. Henry, ever the strategist, was already awake and studying the terrain around them, mentally preparing for the tasks ahead. Clarissa yawned and stretched her arms above her head before gathering her wits and focusing on the day's challenges.

"Right, let's gather our things and meet Dr. Warren," she said, her brilliance shining through even in the early morning light.

As the children collected their belongings and prepared themselves, they chatted excitedly about their roles in the battle. Their youthful energy was contagious, and soon, they set off towards the predetermined meeting point with an air of enthusiasm and confidence.

"Remember," Sarah reminded them, "we need to stay focused and trust each other. We all have unique abilities that will help us, and we must use them to rally support for the American cause."

"Agreed," Charles nodded, his face serious but his eyes sparkling with excitement. "Let's make history together."

"Quite literally!" Clarissa chimed in with a grin, and the friends shared a laugh.

Upon reaching the rendezvous spot, they spotted Dr. Warren waiting for them, looking every bit the distinguished gentleman they had come to admire. His dark hair caught the sunlight, and his strong jawline seemed to be set in determination.

"Ah, my young friends," he greeted them warmly. "I'm glad to see you all here, ready for the day ahead."

"Dr. Warren, we're determined to help in any way we can," Sarah assured him, her eyes reflecting the same fire that burned within him. "Our strengths combined will make a difference today."

"Indeed," Dr. Warren agreed, smiling down at her. "It's time to rally our troops and take a stand. The Battle of Bunker Hill won't be an easy one, but with your help, I believe we can turn the tide in favor of freedom and independence."

As they stood together, their gazes fixed upon the city of Boston in the distance, the children felt a sense of unity and purpose stronger than ever before. They knew that the challenges ahead would test their courage, resourcefulness, and resilience, but there was no turning back now. They were ready to embrace their roles in history, side by side, with determination and hope in their hearts.

The morning sun cast a warm golden hue upon the grass, its dew glistening like a sea of tiny diamonds. Dr. Warren turned to address the children, his eyes glinting with resolve.

"Listen carefully," he said, his voice commanding their full attention. "The British forces will be arriving soon, and our troops are in need of support. We must ensure that they are well-informed and ready to fight for the American cause."

As the wind playfully tousled Sarah's long blonde hair, she held her breath, awaiting the task that would be assigned to her.

"Sarah," Dr. Warren said, looking directly into her blue eyes, which widened with anticipation. "You have a gift for connecting with people, and you possess a gentle heart that can inspire others. I need you to use these qualities as a messenger. Your mission is to deliver crucial information to the local militia and rally them to join our cause."

A flutter of nerves danced within Sarah's chest, but she pushed aside her doubts, focusing on the importance of her role in the battle. She nodded firmly, resolved to prove herself worthy of Dr. Warren's trust.

"Thank you, Dr. Warren," she replied, her voice filled with determination. "I won't let you down."

"Of that, I have no doubt," he smiled kindly, placing a reassuring hand on her shoulder.

With the warmth of Dr. Warren's touch still lingering, Sarah set off on her mission, her heart pounding in her chest as if it were trying to keep pace with the urgency of her task.

As she navigated the winding dirt roads, Sarah marveled at

the beauty that surrounded her - the vibrant green leaves rustling in the breeze, the gentle hum of bees collecting nectar from wildflowers. It was a stark contrast to the chaos and intensity of war that awaited them all.

"Excuse me, sir," she called out, approaching a group of men gathered by a wooden fence, their muskets resting against their shoulders. "I bring an important message from Dr. Joseph Warren. He requests your help in the upcoming battle at Bunker Hill."

"Dr. Warren, you say?" one of the men asked, stroking his beard thoughtfully. "Well, if he's in need of our assistance, then we'd best not keep him waiting."

"Thank you," Sarah breathed a sigh of relief, her heart swelling with pride as they prepared to march towards the battlefield.

As she continued her mission, Sarah's confidence grew with each successful encounter. She began to feel that perhaps she truly was making a difference - and that maybe, just maybe, they had a chance to change the course of history.

But deep down, amidst the whirlwind of emotions, she couldn't help but think about Charles, hoping that he, too, would find success in his role on this monumental day.

"Stay safe," she whispered to the wind, hoping her words would reach him. And with renewed determination, she pressed on, eager to ensure that the sacrifices made at the Battle of Bunker Hill would not be in vain.

Charles stood atop a small hill, surveying the scene before

him. The morning light cast long shadows across the uneven terrain as dozens of American soldiers milled about, their uniforms tattered and worn, yet their spirits undeterred. He took a deep breath, the crisp air filling his lungs, and felt an unfamiliar resolve settle within him.

"Alright, everybody, gather 'round!" Charles called out, his voice carrying across the field. The soldiers paused in their tasks, turning their attention to him with a mix of curiosity and respect. It was time for him to rise to the occasion and prove that he could be the leader they needed.

"Listen up," he began, carefully choosing his words. "I know we're all scared, and I know we're not exactly a well-oiled machine. But we have something the British don't – heart. And that's what's going to pull us through this battle. So let's show them what we're made of!"

A murmur rippled through the crowd, and Charles saw the flicker of determination ignite in their eyes. He knew he couldn't afford to let doubt creep into their minds despite the unease that still gnawed at his own gut. They were counting on him, and he couldn't let them down.

"Alright, Henry, let's get these defenses set up." Charles motioned for his friend to join him, relieved to see the familiar face amidst the sea of strangers.

"Right, Charles," Henry replied, the two boys exchanging a brief nod of understanding. There was no place for tempers or grudges on the battlefield; they had to rely on one another now more than ever.

Together, they turned their attention to the task at hand.

With Henry's newfound strategic knowledge and Charles' leadership skills, they began to guide the troops in setting up defensive positions, using the natural contours of the land to their advantage.

"Make sure to stagger the lines," Henry instructed, his brow furrowed in concentration. "We want to create as much confusion for the enemy as possible."

"Great idea, Henry." Charles praised him, knowing that encouragement was crucial in keeping morale high. He couldn't help but feel a swell of pride at how far they'd come since their journey began – not only as individuals but as a team.

As the hours passed, Charles and Henry worked tirelessly alongside the soldiers, the sun climbing higher in the sky. Sweat beaded on their foreheads, but they refused to let fatigue slow them down.

"Keep pushing, men!" Charles shouted, his voice hoarse from exertion. "We're almost there!"

"Charles," Henry called out, wiping sweat from his brow, "I think we've done all we can. The troops are in position, and the defenses are set."

"Then it's time," Charles replied, steeling himself for the battle ahead. He knew that the coming fight would test them all to their limits, but he also knew that they were ready. And as he glanced over at Henry, he realized that, for the first time in a long while, he truly trusted someone other than himself.

"Stay safe," he murmured under his breath, echoing Sarah's own silent plea. With one last look at the troops they had prepared for battle, Charles and Henry stood shoulder to shoulder, ready to face whatever challenges lay ahead.

Clarissa's heart pounded as she approached Dr. Warren, her thoughts racing like a hummingbird in search of nectar. The air buzzed with anticipation, soldiers preparing for the onslaught that was sure to come. She knew that communication would be vital in the upcoming battle, and she was determined to contribute her skills to the cause.

"Dr. Warren," she began, her voice wavering slightly, "I believe I have an idea for how we can make the most of our limited supply of ammunition and work with General Putnam to get the most out of our men and cannon."

"Let's hear it, Clarissa," Dr. Warren replied, his eyes reflecting the weight of their task.

"We wait until the British are charging up the hill and can't turn back, making the most of every shot," Clarissa stated, her confidence growing with each syllable. "We could then use cannon at a staggered pace to have a steady and consistent volley but also accurate then, relay messages about our positions or any changes in strategy."

"An excellent idea, Miss Jennings!" Dr. Warren exclaimed, his dark eyes lighting up, "And I have just the man who can help us with this—our powder expert, Mr. Baxter!"

Clarissa nodded eagerly, her mind already conjuring images of billowing clouds of smoke. She couldn't help but feel a twinge of pride at the thought that her intellect might play a part in shaping the outcome of the battle.

"Mr. Baxter," Dr. Warren called out, beckoning the stout man with unruly whiskers over. As the three of them discussed the details of the plan, the other children gathered nearby, lending their support and ideas where needed.

"Perhaps we should assign specific quantities to the different divisions; I believe Breed's Hill is a most suited choice to have more of the ammo as the British will attack there first," Sarah suggested, her eyes gleaming with determination. "That way, there will be no confusion among our forces as to how much each man has to fire with."

"Agreed," Charles chimed in, his natural leadership shining through. "We could use the British tactics against them. They don't believe that we few militia could stand up to them, let them come to us, and let's make it count."

"Brilliant thinking, all of you," Dr. Warren praised, the corners of his mouth turned up in a smile that seemed to infuse the group with renewed energy.

As they continued to refine their plan, Clarissa marveled at how seamlessly they all worked together. It was as if each of them had found a missing piece within themselves, and together, they formed a puzzle that was more than the sum of its parts.

"Are we ready?" Henry asked, his voice filled with the same mix of excitement and trepidation that coursed through Clarissa's veins.

"Ready as we'll ever be," Dr. Warren replied, his tone both comforting and inspiring. "Remember, children, trust in your abilities and in each other. We are a team, and together, we can accomplish anything."

With those words ringing in their ears, the four young time travelers steeled themselves for the coming battle, their hearts swelling with the knowledge that they were not only fighting for their own futures but for the future of an entire nation.

The first shots of the Battle of Bunker Hill rang out like thunder, shaking the very ground beneath their feet. Clarissa felt her heart pounding in her chest as she watched the chaos unfold before her. The acrid scent of gunpowder filled the air, mingling with the cries of men and the clash of metal against metal.

"Stay focused," Dr. Warren shouted above the din, his eyes scanning the battlefield. "Our mission is crucial to the success of this battle. We must not falter!"

Clarissa exchanged a glance with her friends, each of them nodding resolutely. Despite the terror that threatened to consume her, she knew they could not let fear win. They had a purpose, and they were united in their determination to see it through.

"Sarah, take this message to General Putnam," Dr. Warren instructed, handing her a hastily scribbled note. "It's imperative he receives it quickly."

"Understood!" Sarah replied, her blue eyes filled with resolve. She dashed off, weaving her way through the maze of tents and makeshift barricades.

"Charles, Henry - I need you to rally the troops near the eastern flank," Dr. Warren continued. "They appear disorganized and in need of strong leadership."

"Right away, sir!" Charles saluted, his natural confidence shining through. Henry followed suit, his strong sense of justice propelling him forward.

"Clarissa, come with me," Dr. Warren beckoned, leading her toward a group of soldiers struggling to decipher orders amidst the clamor of battle. Together, they put their heads together, using Clarissa's intellect and Dr. Warren's experience to make sense of the situation.

"Dr. Warren, do you think we have a chance at winning this?" Clarissa asked, her voice barely audible over the cacophony of war.

"Sometimes, it's not about winning or losing but about outlasting the enemy," he replied, his eyes never leaving the battlefield. "We fight for freedom and independence, and that is a cause worth fighting for, and the rest of the colonies will take up the cause, and we will truly outlast the British then."

As they pressed on, they encountered numerous obstacles – British soldiers attempting to flank their position, loyalist spies spreading disinformation, and even the occasional stray cannonball. But with each challenge, they faced it head-on, relying on their resourcefulness and bravery to carry them through.

"Look!" Sarah called out, her voice breathless as she returned from her mission. "General Putnam has received your message, Dr. Warren, and is adjusting his strategy accordingly!"

"Excellent work, Sarah," he praised, a smile of relief briefly crossing his face. "Now, we must continue our efforts. There's still much to be done."

Clarissa marveled at their resilience and the way they each rose to the occasion despite the overwhelming odds. They were no longer just children but vital contributors to a cause that would shape history. And though the outcome remained uncertain, one thing was clear: they would do everything in their power to ensure victory for the American cause.

As the sun climbed higher in the sky, casting an eerie glow over the smoke-filled battlefield, Clarissa couldn't help but feel a surge of pride as she watched the fruit of their labor taking effect. She stood atop a small hill, her eyes scanning the scene below, taking in the American troops that had joined them on the front lines. Their faces were etched with determination and conviction, and she knew that it was their collective efforts that had inspired such resolve.

"Look at them," Charles said, joining her on the hill, his voice filled with awe. "We did this. We rallied them together."

"Indeed," Dr. Warren agreed, his gaze never leaving the battlefield. "And now we must continue to support them in any way we can."

Down below, Sarah could be seen darting through the chaos, delivering messages and rallying more men to their cause. Henry, who had been assisting in setting up defensive positions, now stood tall among the ranks of soldiers, shouting orders with newfound authority. And Charles, ever the natural leader, moved from group to group, motivating the troops and ensuring they were prepared for what lay ahead.

"Keep your heads down!" Henry bellowed, his voice carrying over the din of musket fire. "Wait for my signal!"

"Steady now, boys," Charles urged, his tone calm yet firm. "Remember what we're fighting for!"

Clarissa's heart hammered in her chest as she took in the scene unfolding before her - the British charge, a sea of red coats advancing like a storm across the field. But she knew fear would do her no good now; she had a job to do, just like the others. With a deep breath, she focused her thoughts, remembering the plan she'd helped devise with Dr. Warren to communicate with key figures in the battle.

"Dr. Warren," she said, turning to him with determination in her eyes. "I think it's time we send a message to General Putnam."

"Agreed, Clarissa," he replied, giving her a nod of approval. "Let's ensure our forces are ready for their counterattack."

The two hurried down the hill, Clarissa clutching the small, makeshift signal flag they'd created for this very purpose. As they reached the base, she unfurled it and began waving it with all her might, sending the prearranged code to General Putnam's position.

"Come on," she whispered under her breath, watching as the general studied her message through his spyglass. "Please understand."

"Look!" Sarah cried out, sprinting toward them, her face flushed with excitement. "General Putnam is waving back! He's received the message!"

"Fantastic work, Clarissa!" Dr. Warren exclaimed, clapping her on the back. "Now, we must prepare ourselves for the next phase."

As the American troops launched their counterattack, the battlefield erupted into a cacophony of sound - musket fire, cannon blasts, and cries of victory and defeat. And amidst it all, Clarissa and her friends fought alongside their newfound allies, each playing their part in turning the tide of the conflict.

Though the outcome remained uncertain, one thing was clear: they would do everything in their power to secure freedom and independence for the colonies. And as they stood together on that smoke-filled battlefield, they were no longer just children but heroes, bound together by a shared purpose and an unyielding determination to succeed.

Sarah, Charles, Henry, and Clarissa stood shoulder-to-shoulder with Dr. Warren on the front lines. The air was thick with the acrid scent of gunpowder and sweat while the taste of fear and determination lingered on their lips.

"Are you ready?" Dr. Warren asked them, his voice steady and reassuring despite the chaos around them.

"We're ready," Sarah replied, her eyes gleaming with resolve. "We've come this far, and we won't back down now."

"Good," said Dr. Warren, nodding firmly. "Remember, stay close and watch each other's backs. We are in this together."

As they charged forward, Charles shouted to be heard over the din of battle. "Keep your wits about you! And remember what we've learned!"

Henry nodded, gripping his musket tightly. "Right. Stick to the plan and trust in our abilities. We can do this."

Clarissa, her heart pounding wildly in her chest, took a deep breath and focused on the task at hand. "Fear won't stop us. We're fighting for something far greater."

"Stay close, everyone!" Sarah yelled as they advanced, bullets whistling past them. Her thoughts raced with images of the friends she'd made and the people they were fighting for. This battle wasn't just for them — it was for all those who believed in a better future.

"Dr. Warren!" Charles called out as they ducked behind a fallen tree. "How can we best support the troops?"

"Help them hold the line!" Dr. Warren instructed. "We must not let the British advance any further!"

"Understood!" Henry replied, his mind racing with strategic calculations as he scanned the battlefield, looking for the best way to offer assistance.

"Look out!" Clarissa cried, pulling Sarah back just as a British soldier lunged at her. With a surge of adrenaline, she managed to disarm him, her intellect and reflexes working in tandem.

"Thank you, Clarissa," Sarah breathed, her heart pounding. "I owe you one."

"Save it for after we win," Clarissa replied with a grin, her fear momentarily banished by the camaraderie she felt with her friends.

Together, they fought on, trusting in their individual strengths and the bond that united them. And though the battle raged around them and the odds seemed insurmountable, their spirits never faltered.

"Freedom!" Dr. Warren bellowed, his voice rising above the clamor. "For independence!"

"Freedom! For independence!" the children echoed, their voices joining together as one.

As the sun shone above the horizon, its golden light giving way to the scene of the hills below them, the young heroes stood strong.

# CHAPTER 19

"Down!" Charles shouted, his voice barely audible over the cacophony of gunshots and terrified screams as the young group found themselves in the midst of the Battle of Bunker Hill. Smoke filled the air, clouding their vision, while the metallic scent of blood mingled with the acrid burn of gunpowder.

"Stay together!" Sarah yelled back, her gentle heart pounding as she struggled to assert herself amidst the chaos. She grabbed Clarissa's hand, trying to seek comfort in the presence of her friend. The unfamiliar weight of a musket hung from her shoulder, the responsibility it represented pressing down on her like a mountain.

"Sarah, behind this barricade!" Henry called out, motioning frantically toward a makeshift wall of barrels and crates. They were no soldiers, but they knew the importance of finding cover during an onslaught like this.

"Alright, I'm coming!" Sarah stammered, her long blonde hair whipping around her face as she sprinted towards safety. Her blue eyes were wide with fear but also determination – she would not let her friends down, not now.

As she ducked behind the barricade, her chest heaving from the adrenaline coursing through her veins, she couldn't help but think about how they'd gotten here. What had started as a simple curiosity about the mysterious amulet had led them to travel through time itself, thrown headfirst into one of the most pivotal battles in American history.

"Are you alright?" Clarissa asked, her brilliant mind already working on strategies to help the Patriots. She could see the weak points in the British lines, and if they could just relay that information...

But Sarah was too focused on the advancing British soldiers, her chest tightening in anxiety as she watched them draw closer. She knew she wasn't a leader like Charles or strong like Henry, but she had to do something – anything – to help. She bit her lip, her mind racing, searching for a way to make a difference.

"Charles," she whispered, her voice trembling with the weight of her words. "I think I see an opportunity... a chance to slow them down. We can't just hide here – we have to fight."

"Alright, Sarah," Charles replied, his dark eyes filled with trust and admiration. "Show us what you've got."

Sarah took a deep breath, steeling herself for what was to come. At that moment, she knew that despite her fears and doubts, she had the power within her to stand on her own and change the course of history. And with her friends by her side, nothing could hold her back.

"Let's do this," she said, gripping her musket tightly and readying herself to face the enemy head-on.

Charles scanned the battlefield, his usually confident demeanor now marred by the harsh reality of war. His dark eyes searched for an opportunity amidst the chaos, a chance to rally their fellow patriots and make a stand against the advancing British soldiers.

"Men!" he shouted, his voice surprisingly strong and steady amidst the cacophony of gunfire and shouts. "We must hold our ground! The fate of our nation rests on this very moment!"

As if summoned by his words, a group of beleaguered patriots gathered around him, their faces etched with determination and hope. Charles locked eyes with each one of them, his natural leadership shining through the grim situation.

"Look at us," he said, his words laced with both pride and urgency. "We are but children, yet we stand here ready to fight for our freedom. Let no man doubt our resolve or our courage. Together, we can turn the tide of this battle!"

The patriots nodded in agreement, their spirits lifted by Charles's impassioned speech. As they prepared to defend their position, Charles caught sight of Henry, his broad-shouldered friend, clenching his musket tightly.

"Alright, Henry," Charles called out, confident in his friend's strength and fierce sense of justice. "It's time to show these redcoats what we're made of!"

With a determined nod, Henry charged forward, his powerful legs propelling him towards the enemy lines. He fired his musket with deadly precision, each shot like thunder rumbling across the battlefield. His heart raced, adrenaline coursing through his veins as he pushed himself to the limit.

"Take that, you bloody lobsterbacks!" he bellowed, his short temper igniting with every pull of the trigger. In the midst of the chaos, he found a sense of purpose, a desire to protect his friends and his homeland from the oppressive grip of the British.

As Henry fought on, Charles remained steadfast in his command, orchestrating their small band of patriots with the skill and wisdom of a seasoned general. Together, they stood against the onslaught. Their youthful faces were streaked with sweat, dirt, and gunpowder.

"Remember," Charles shouted above the roar of battle, "we are fighting for our future, for the generations that will come after us. Let us show them what it means to be free!"

With those words, Charles, Henry, and their fellow patriots charged headlong into the fray, their hearts brimming with courage and hope, each one determined to make a difference in the fight for America's independence.

The thick smoke of gunfire billowed around them, obscuring the battlefield as Clarissa squinted through her glasses. She could barely make out the forms of Charles and Henry in the distance as they dove into the fray, courage, and determination fueling their actions. But it was not brute force that would win this battle - it was strategy.

"Clarissa! We need your help!" a patriot soldier called out to her while ducking under a hail of bullets. He hurried to her side, his eyes pleading for guidance.

"Alright," she murmured, her heart pounding with equal parts fear and anticipation. "Give me a moment to think." She closed her eyes, picturing the layout of the terrain in her mind's eye, searching for any weakness in the enemy lines.

"Come on, Clarissa, you can do this," she whispered to herself, remembering Dr. Warren's encouraging words. Drawing upon her newfound confidence, she opened her eyes and looked out at the battlefield with renewed clarity.

"Over there," she pointed towards a small hill on their left flank. "We can use that to our advantage. It'll provide us with both cover and higher ground."

"Brilliant!" The soldier beamed, hope flickering across his weary face. "Let's rally the others and get moving!"

As the patriots moved into position, guided by Clarissa's keen strategic insight, the children began to work in unison. They communicated through hand signals and quick glances, ensuring each of them knew where the others were at all times.

"Charles, take your group up on the left!" Clarissa shouted, motioning in the direction of the hill. "Henry, provide cover fire and keep the redcoats distracted!"

As Charles led his band of fighters up the hill, Clarissa formulated the next steps in her head. She bit her lip, watching as Henry unleashed a volley of gunfire, buying them precious time.

"Alright, once we have the high ground, we can rain down fire on their exposed flank," she thought, her mind racing with tactical possibilities. "We just need to hold out a little longer."

The air was electric with tension, the sharp scent of gunpowder filling their nostrils. Clarissa's glasses fogged up from the smoke and heat, but she didn't dare wipe them clean - every second counted.

"Ready! Aim!" Charles shouted from atop the hill, his voice confident and commanding. The patriots raised their muskets, taking aim at the unsuspecting British soldiers below.

"Fire!" Charles ordered. A deafening roar erupted as they

unleashed a hailstorm of bullets upon the enemy, sending the British forces into disarray.

"Keep up the pressure!" Clarissa cried out, her voice strong and unwavering. She could see the tide turning in their favor, the determination of her friends and fellow patriots shining through the chaos.

"Freedom!" Henry roared as he continued to fire relentlessly, his fierce spirit inspiring those around him.

"By George, I think we're doing it!" Charles grinned, his eyes sparkling with excitement and hope. "This is for our future!"

Clarissa allowed herself a small smile, filled with pride not only in her friends but also in herself. For the first time in her life, she felt truly alive, her brilliant mind put to use for a cause greater than she could ever have imagined. Together, they would make history.

Amidst the smoke and cacophony of battle, Sarah's eyes were drawn to a flash of red amidst the churned earth. A wounded patriot lay crumpled on the ground. His breathing labored, hands desperately trying to staunch the flow of blood from his leg.

"Help!" the soldier cried weakly, his eyes clouded with pain.

"Stay here!" she called out to her friends, her voice barely audible above the roar of muskets and cannons. With a quick glance at Charles, who nodded in agreement, she dashed across the battlefield, her heart pounding wildly in her chest.

"Please," the man pleaded, his voice cracking as he looked up at her. "I don't want to die."

"Shhh," Sarah soothed, her fingers trembling as she applied pressure to the gash on his thigh. "You'll be all right." She bit her lip, fighting back tears, her thoughts racing. Can I save him? How much time do I have?

"Sarah!" Charles shouted from afar, urgency lacing his tone. Her gaze shifted to him, and she saw him gesturing frantically at a group of British soldiers attempting to flank their position. His eyes conveyed a message she couldn't ignore: We need to act now.

"Okay," she whispered to the injured man, offering him a smile that masked her own fear. "I'll be back soon."

"Thank you," he whispered, tears welling in his eyes as she rose and sprinted back to her friends.

"Charles, what's going on?" she asked breathlessly as she joined him behind a makeshift barricade.

"Those Redcoats are trying to flank us," Charles replied, his face set in determination. "We can't let them succeed. We need to hold the line."

"Right," Sarah agreed, swallowing hard. "What's the plan?"

"Listen closely," Charles instructed, his eyes darting between their friends and the approaching enemy. "We need to organize a counterattack. Henry, you keep firing at them from here. Clarissa, go with Sarah and take out those Redcoats on the right."

"Got it!" Clarissa nodded, her hands shaking as she adjusted her glasses. She looked at Sarah, her gaze steady and resolute. "Let's do this together."

"Okay," Sarah whispered, nodding in determination. The fear that had gripped her only moments before began to recede, replaced by a fierce desire to protect their newfound comrades. For the first time in her life, she felt truly capable of taking charge.

"Good luck," Charles said, his voice soft yet filled with confidence. "I believe in you."

"Thank you," Sarah replied, her cheeks flushing with warmth. With a final glance at Charles, she turned and sprinted after Clarissa, their hearts racing in time with the drumbeat of battle. Together, they would face the unknown, their actions shaping the course of history itself.

The sun cast an eerie glow over the battlefield as gunpowder smoke hung heavy in the air. Henry found himself face-to-face with a British soldier, their eyes locked in a deadly dance of determination and desperation.

"Give up, lad!" the soldier snarled, lunging forward with his bayonet. Henry's heart pounded in his chest, but he refused to back down. He dodged the thrust, his muscles tensing as adrenaline coursed through his veins.

"Never!" Henry spat, his voice laden with defiance. Time seemed to slow as he remembered his father's words: 'In battle, you must use your strengths to protect those who cannot protect themselves.'

With that thought in mind, Henry summoned all his strength and launched a powerful punch at the soldier's jaw. The impact echoed like thunder, and the Redcoat slumped to the ground, unconscious.

"Nice one, Henry!" Clarissa cried out from behind a pile of rocks nearby. She quickly emerged, her glasses askew and her brow furrowed in concentration. "But we've got bigger problems."

"Tell me," Henry replied, panting as he tried to catch his breath.

"Charles told us to counterattack," Clarissa explained, her voice steady despite the chaos around them. "I think I know a way to outmaneuver the British. There's a hidden path just beyond this ridge. If we can lead a group of patriots through it, we'll be able to hit the enemy from behind."

"Sounds risky," Henry mused, wiping sweat from his brow. "But if you think it'll work..."

"Trust me," Clarissa insisted, her eyes flashing with resolve. "We may be young, but we're not helpless. We can do this."

"Alright," Henry agreed, nodding firmly. "Let's gather some patriots and take the fight to those Redcoats."

Together, Clarissa and Henry rallied a small group of determined patriots, their faces etched with the same fiery resolve that burned within their own hearts. As they stood at the entrance to the hidden path, Clarissa hesitated for just a moment, her thoughts racing.

"Is everything alright?" one of the patriots asked, concern lacing his voice.

"Absolutely," Clarissa replied, her voice tinged with determination. "I was just thinking about how far we've come and how much we still have to learn. But right now, let's focus on turning the tide of this battle."

"Lead the way, Miss Jennings," another patriot said, his voice filled with respect.

Clarissa nodded, swallowing her fear as she stepped onto the narrow path. The shadows swallowed them whole as they snaked their way through the rocky terrain, but Clarissa's knowledge of the land guided them safely to their destination.

As they emerged from the darkness, the British soldiers were caught completely off guard. The element of surprise worked in the patriots' favor, and Clarissa watched with pride as their ragtag group gained the upper hand.

"Perfect timing, Clarissa!" Henry shouted over the din of battle. "You really saved us."

"Thank you," Clarissa replied, smiling despite the chaos around them. "But remember, we're in this together."

As the young time, travelers continued to fight alongside their new comrades, they knew that they had found a purpose greater than themselves – a purpose that would not only define their journey but help shape the course of history.

Sarah ducked behind a wooden barrel, her heart pounding in her chest. The musket fire was deafening, and she could hardly catch her breath. Around her, the patriots fought with a fierce determination that she had never witnessed before.

"Keep up the good work!" Charles shouted to a group of tired but determined soldiers. "Your bravery is inspiring!"

"Charles! Message from Dr. Warren!" Sarah called out to him

over the gunfire, holding out a hastily scribbled note.

"Thanks!" Charles replied, taking the note and quickly scanning its contents. "We need to pass this on to General Putnam immediately!"

"Got it!" Henry yelled, snatching the note from Charles' hand as he sprinted toward Putnam's position.

"Stay safe!" Clarissa called after him, her eyes filled with concern.

"Always!" Henry replied, grinning despite the perilous situation.

"Clarissa, how are we doing?" Sarah asked, seeking reassurance from her brilliant friend.

"Better than I expected," Clarissa admitted. "Our flanking maneuver was successful, but we can't let our guard down."

"Right," Sarah nodded, steeling herself for what lay ahead.

"Attention!" Charles called out to a group of nearby soldiers. "I have important information from Dr. Warren. We need to change positions and reinforce the left flank!"

"Understood!" one of the soldiers replied, his eyes wide with respect for the young leader.

"Let's move!" Charles commanded, leading the group toward their new destination.

"Keep your wits about you, Charles," Sarah thought, worry filling her mind. But she knew that he would do anything to protect those around him.

"Are you okay, Sarah?" Clarissa asked, noticing her friend's tense expression.

"I'm just worried about everyone," Sarah admitted, her voice barely audible over the cacophony of battle.

"Me too," Clarissa said, her eyes shining with determination. "But we're doing everything we can. We'll see this through together."

"Right," Sarah agreed, her resolve growing stronger by the moment.

As the battle raged on, the children continued to deliver crucial messages and relay important information to the patriots. Their actions inspired those around them as they witnessed the bravery and determination of these young fighters who had seemingly come out of nowhere. And though the outcome was uncertain, one thing was clear: Sarah, Charles, Henry, and Clarissa were making a difference, using their unique skills and unwavering courage to help turn the tide in favor of the American colonies.

The smell of gunpowder and sweat filled the air as Sarah, Charles, Henry, and Clarissa found themselves at the forefront of the battle. The deafening boom of cannons echoed in Sarah's ears while her heart pounded in her chest.

"Charles, I'm scared," she admitted, her eyes scanning the battlefield for any signs of danger.

"Me too," Charles replied, his voice strong but gentle. "But we've got to face it head-on. Together."

"Right," Sarah agreed, taking a deep breath to steady herself.

"Look there!" Henry shouted, pointing to a group of patriots being overtaken by British forces. "We need to help them!"

"Agreed!" Charles responded, a determined gleam in his eye. "Henry, lead the charge. Clarissa, find us an advantage. Sarah, stay close."

"Got it!" they all chimed in, adrenaline coursing through their veins.

As Henry sprinted toward the fray, Clarissa surveyed the battlefield. "There! That rocky outcropping will give us cover and a vantage point!"

"Excellent!" Charles commended, guiding Sarah toward the rocks. "Sarah, keep watch and signal if you see anything."

"Will do," she replied, her gaze focused and unwavering.

"Ready... fire!" Henry commanded, rallying the nearby patriots with his booming voice. The sound of gunfire rang out as they fought back against the British onslaught.

"Great shot, Henry!" Charles praised, watching as one of the enemy soldiers stumbled backward. "Keep pressing them!"

"Isn't he amazing?" Sarah thought, unable to tear her eyes away from Henry's fierce determination. She refocused her attention on the battlefield, looking for any signs of trouble.

"Charles! More British soldiers approaching from the west!" she called, pointing toward the advancing redcoats.

"Understood!" he shouted, quickly devising a plan. "Henry, take half the men and flank them! Clarissa, stay here and defend our position!"

"Got it!" Henry bellowed as he and his troops charged forward, their muskets at the ready.

"Let's do this," Clarissa whispered, her eyes sharp behind her glasses.

As the children fought alongside the patriots, their individual contributions began to make a significant impact on the outcome of the battle. Through their bravery and quick thinking, they successfully pushed back wave after wave of British soldiers.

"Look!" Sarah cried out, her voice filled with hope. "The British are retreating!"

"Thank goodness," Charles breathed, his shoulders sagging in relief. "We did it...for now, it looks like they may be regrouping for another effort."

"Couldn't have done it without you, Charles," Sarah said, her hand resting on his arm. "You're an incredible leader."

"Thank you, Sarah," Charles replied sincerely, a warm smile spreading across his face. "And thank you for always being there for me."

As the tide turned in favor of the American colonies, the British forces faced fierce resistance from the determined patriots who had found new strength in the young fighters among them. Amidst the chaos, the bonds between Sarah, Charles, Henry, and Clarissa grew stronger, each one feeling grateful and inspired by the others' unwavering courage and determination.

"Let's finish this," Sarah thought, her heart swelling with pride. "Together."

# CHAPTER 20

The sun hung low in the sky, casting a blood-red hue over the chaotic scene unfolding before Sarah's eyes. The sounds of cannon fire and musket shots rang out as American colonists charged headlong into battle with the formidable British forces. Despite their recent failure at Breed's Hill, the redcoats were regrouping with renewed determination and fury.

"Stay together!" Sarah yelled over the deafening noise, gripping the arm of her closest friend. Her heart pounded wildly in her chest, and she felt a mixture of fear and exhilaration course through her veins. As the young time-travelers navigated the chaos, their mission was clear: protect their newfound friends and defend the ideals that had brought them to this pivotal moment in history.

"Sarah, stay close to me!" Charles shouted, his eyes darting from one threat to another. Their small group of friends moved as one, dodging explosions and the deadly trajectories of musket balls.

"Charles, wait!" Sarah called out, but it was too late. In the heat of battle, she found herself separated from her friends and surrounded by British soldiers. She could feel her heart racing as adrenaline surged through her body, her mind racing to find a solution. Ducking behind a fallen tree, she took a deep breath and steadied herself.

"Oi, you there!" a gruff voice barked, and Sarah realized she'd been spotted. "What are you doing here?"

"Um, I got lost," she stammered, trying to appear innocent

and confused. "I was looking for my family."

"Lost, eh? Well, you'd better come with us then," the soldier sneered. "We'll take care of you."

As they led her away, Sarah racked her brain for a way to escape and reunite with her friends. She couldn't let herself be captured – not when so much was at stake. "Think, Sarah, think," she whispered under her breath.

"Wait!" she exclaimed suddenly, feigning distress. "I think I left something important back there! Can we go back for just a moment?"

The soldiers exchanged glances, clearly annoyed but also wary of leaving a potentially valuable prisoner unattended. "Fine," one of them grumbled, "but make it quick."

Seizing her chance, Sarah led the soldiers back to the fallen tree and, in a burst of resourcefulness, pretended to trip on a loose branch. As the soldiers rushed forward to help her up, she deftly slipped out of their grasp and darted into the nearby brush.

"Hey! Get back here!" the soldiers shouted, but Sarah was already gone, her heart pounding as she wove through the chaos of battle in search of her friends.

Charles scanned the battlefield, his eyes darting between the flashes of gunfire and plumes of smoke that clouded the air. He could feel the weight of responsibility settle on his shoulders as he thought about Sarah, separated from the group and in danger. He knew he couldn't waste any time worrying – he needed to act.

"Listen up!" Charles shouted, gathering a small group of nervous-looking patriots around him. "We need to outflank the British soldiers. Follow me, and keep low."

He led his makeshift squad through the thick smoke, relying on his instincts and natural leadership skills to guide them. As they moved, Charles realized that he had no choice but to trust these strangers with their lives – and his own. This realization brought a newfound sense of camaraderie, and he found himself working in sync with the others as they carefully maneuvered around the enemy lines.

Meanwhile, Henry's keen eyes caught sight of a British officer threatening a group of innocent civilians. His weapon raised menacingly. Rage bubbled up inside him, but he knew he couldn't let his temper get the better of him this time. There had to be a way to stop the officer without resorting to violence. His mind raced, searching for a solution.

"Oi!" Henry bellowed, drawing the attention of both the officer and the civilians. "You look like you've got something important to say. Care to share it with all of us?"

The officer hesitated, clearly thrown off by Henry's boldness. In that moment of distraction, one of the civilians seized the opportunity to escape, followed quickly by the others. The officer's face turned red with anger, but before he could react, Henry closed the distance between them and grabbed the officer's gun.

"Let's keep things civil, shall we?" Henry said, his voice steady even as adrenaline coursed through his veins. He held onto the weapon, not as a tool of violence but as a symbol of restraint – proof that he was learning to channel his strength effectively.

As the chaos of battle continued to swirl around them, Charles and Henry focused on their individual tasks, determined to make a difference in the fight for freedom. Little did they know that their paths would soon cross once more as fate – and friendship – drew them back together.

In the midst of gunpowder clouds and the deafening cacophony of battle, Clarissa huddled behind a fallen tree, her heart pounding as fast as the drumbeats that echoed through the air. Her fingers were trembling, but she clutched the intercepted message tightly, determined to decipher its contents.

"Think, Clarissa. Think," she murmured to herself, squinting at the smudged ink on the crumpled paper. The letters seemed to dance before her eyes, taunting her with their coded secrets. "Time is running out."

As she struggled to decode the message, she couldn't help but feel a pang of envy for Charles's natural leadership skills and Henry's strength. But she reminded herself that her intellect was just as valuable – perhaps even more so in this dire moment.

"Got it!" Clarissa exclaimed, her eyes lighting up with triumph. She hastily scribbled down the translated message and set off through the chaos, determined to deliver the crucial information to the right hands.

"Clarissa!" A familiar voice called out amidst the smoke and noise. It was Sarah, her blonde hair streaked with dirt and sweat, yet her blue eyes shone with relief upon seeing her friend.

"Sarah!" Clarissa cried, rushing into her arms. "I've deciphered the message. We have to find Charles and Henry!"

"Look!" Sarah pointed towards a group of patriots led by Charles, who was barking orders with newfound confidence and trust in his comrades. Nearby, Henry stood tall, exercising restraint as he faced off against the British officer, armed only with the weight of his convictions.

"Charles! Henry!" Clarissa shouted, waving the decoded message above her head. The two boys turned towards their friends, their faces breaking into smiles at the sight of Sarah and Clarissa safe and sound.

"Clarissa, what did you find?" Charles asked urgently. His gaze fixated on the paper in her hands.

"Listen," Clarissa said breathlessly, her voice barely audible over the din of battle. "The British forces are planning a surprise attack from the east. We must warn the others!"

"Great work, Clarissa!" Henry praised, clapping her on the shoulder. "We knew you could do it."

"Quickly, let's relay this information to the commanders," Charles urged, his eyes filled with determination as he led the group through the chaos.

Together, Sarah, Charles, Henry, and Clarissa navigated the battlefield, their bond strengthened by their shared purpose and mutual support. Each one had faced their own challenges that day, but now they stood united, ready to fight for freedom – and each other.

"Remember," Sarah shouted above the clamor, her voice steady and strong, "we're stronger together than we are apart!"

"Right!" The others echoed, their expressions resolute as

they charged forward into the fray, armed with the knowledge
that they were not alone in their struggle. They were a team, and
together, they were unstoppable.

"Colonel Prescott!" Charles called out as they approached the
commander. "We have important information!"

Prescott turned to face them, his face lined with concern and
weariness. "What is it, lad?"

"Clarissa deciphered a message from the British forces,"
Sarah explained, her newfound confidence shining through.
"They're planning a surprise attack from the east."

"Excellent work," Prescott praised, nodding at Clarissa, who
beamed with pride. "We must prepare our defenses
immediately."

"Allow us to help, sir," Henry offered, his eyes burning with
determination. "We've come this far, and we want to see this
through."

"Very well," Prescott agreed, clapping Henry on the shoulder.
"But stay together and watch each other's backs."

"Of course, sir," Charles replied, exchanging a determined
glance with his friends. "We won't let you down."

As the young heroes prepared for the impending battle, they
couldn't help but feel a deep sense of camaraderie and trust in
one another. It was at that moment that they realized the true
power of their friendship – a force that could withstand even the
most trying of circumstances.

With renewed energy and unwavering resolve, Sarah,

Charles, Henry, and Clarissa stood side by side, ready to face whatever challenges lay ahead. And though the battle raged on around them, they knew that they were stronger together – an unbreakable team fighting for the future of their newfound nation.

The smell of gunpowder and sweat filled the air as the cacophony of battle raged around them. Sarah, Charles, Henry, and Clarissa stood back to back, their breaths coming in quick, shallow bursts. They exchanged worried glances as British forces surged forward with a fierce counterattack.

"Can we really do this?" Sarah breathed, her hands shaking as she clutched her musket. "We're just kids. How are we supposed to hold off an entire army?"

"Remember what Dr. Warren said," Charles reminded them, his eyes scanning the battlefield for any signs of weakness. "We're fighting for our future – for the freedom of generations to come."

"Easy for him to say," muttered Henry, gritting his teeth as he stared down a charging British soldier. "He's not the one staring down the barrel of a musket."

"Enough!" Clarissa snapped, her voice cutting through the din of battle. "We can't afford to doubt ourselves now. We have to believe in each other and in the cause we're fighting for."

As if on cue, the booming voice of Dr. Warren echoed across the battlefield: "Hold your ground, men! Show them the mettle of American patriots!"

Sarah felt a fire ignite within her, fueled by Dr. Warren's

words and the trust she shared with her friends. She knew that they were stronger together and that their determination could overcome even the most insurmountable odds. With newfound confidence, she raised her voice, addressing the weary colonists around them.

"Listen to me, all of you!" she shouted, her blue eyes blazing with passion. "We may be young, but we are strong! We are the future of this great nation, and we will not let fear or doubt stand in our way!"

Her words seemed to resonate with the soldiers, who straightened their backs and tightened their grips on their weapons. Charles, Henry, and Clarissa exchanged proud smiles, knowing that their friend had truly come into her own.

"Remember why we're fighting!" Sarah continued, her voice steady and clear despite the chaos surrounding them. "We're fighting for our families, our homes, and our freedom! We will stand together, and we will prevail!"

As the colonists rallied around Sarah's impassioned speech, a renewed sense of determination spread through their ranks. Though they were low on ammunition and facing a formidable enemy, they knew they could not – would not – back down.

"Sarah's right," Charles declared, his voice full of pride and admiration. "Let's show these redcoats what we're made of!"

"Charge!" Henry roared, leading the colonists in a fierce counterattack against the British forces.

Together, the four friends charged into battle, their hearts pounding in unison as they fought for their lives and the future of their beloved country. No longer weighed down by doubt and fear, they pushed forward with unwavering resolve, knowing that they could rely on each other and the power of their friendship to see them through.

Despite the chaos and smoke surrounding them, Charles felt a newfound sense of clarity and purpose. His friends had shown their bravery and growth, and it was now his turn to prove himself worthy of their trust. He scanned the battlefield, searching for any threats that might endanger his friends.

"Get down!" he yelled as he spotted a group of British soldiers taking aim at them. With no time to spare, Charles threw himself in front of Sarah and Clarissa, shielding them from the barrage of gunfire. Bullets whizzed past him, some grazing his clothes, but he stood firm, refusing to let fear overtake him.

"Charles, you're crazy!" Sarah cried out, her eyes wide with concern.

"Maybe," he replied with a grin, "but I'd do anything to protect you guys."

"Thanks, Charles," Clarissa added, her voice trembling slightly. "We owe you one."

"Make that two," Henry chimed in, clapping Charles on the back before turning his attention to a skilled British soldier advancing toward them. The soldier wielded his bayonet with precision and confidence, clearly experienced in hand-to-hand combat.

In the past, Henry's temper would have gotten the best of him, blindly charging into battle without a plan. But his experiences with Paul Revere and his friends had taught him the value of patience and restraint. Taking a deep breath, he carefully observed the soldier's movements, searching for an opening.

"Alright, Henry," he muttered under his breath, "you've got this. Just stay calm and focused."

"Give it your best shot, redcoat!" he taunted, feigning bravado while internally calculating his next move.

"Ha! Foolish rebel," the British soldier sneered, lunging forward with his bayonet.

Henry dodged the attack with surprising grace, his mind clear and focused. As the soldier prepared for another strike, Henry found the opening he was looking for. Channeling all his strength and newfound skill, he disarmed the soldier with a swift, calculated move.

"Guess you underestimated us, huh?" Henry said, panting, as the enemy soldier crumpled to the ground.

"Nice work, Henry!" Charles called out, his admiration clear in his voice. "You've really come a long way."

"Thanks, Charles," Henry replied, trying to catch his breath. "Couldn't have done it without you and the others."

As they exchanged a grateful glance, the sounds of battle continued to rage around them. The scent of gunpowder hung heavy in the air while the cries of the wounded pierced through the chaos.

"Let's regroup with Sarah and Clarissa," Charles suggested,

scanning the battlefield for their friends. "We're stronger together."

As they raced toward their companions, bullets whizzed past them, sending puffs of dirt into the air. Determination and fear mixed within them as they knew that their fight was far from over.

"Stay close!" Charles shouted, his natural leadership shining through as he guided Henry through the chaos. The trust between them had grown stronger throughout their journey, and now, each of them relied on the other to survive this harrowing encounter.

Together, the four friends reunited amidst the pandemonium, their bonds solidified by the events that had unfolded. They may have been young and inexperienced, but they had proven themselves to be resourceful and resilient in the face of adversity.

"Remember," Sarah said, her confidence bolstered by her impassioned speech earlier, "we can do this as long as we stand together."

With renewed determination and a fierce sense of camaraderie, the friends prepared to face whatever challenges lay ahead, ready to fight for their cause and for one another.

Clarissa knelt down beside a wounded soldier, her hands trembling as she carefully removed the blood-soaked cloth from his leg. The sight of the deep gash made her wince, but she knew she had to remain calm in order to help him. She glanced up at the chaos surrounding them, soldiers fighting and falling, their cries echoing through the battlefield.

"Stay with me," Clarissa whispered to the soldier, her voice soft and reassuring. "I'm going to clean your wound."

As she worked, Clarissa tried to block out the sounds of battle, focusing instead on the task before her. Her knowledge of medicine, gained from Dr. Warren's mentorship, now proved invaluable. With careful precision, she cleaned the wound, her compassion shining through each gentle touch.

"Clarissa, we need to do something!" Sarah's voice interrupted her concentration. "We can't just stand here while the British forces continue to advance!"

"Sarah is right," Charles added, his eyes scanning the battlefield. "We need to come up with a plan."

"Let's think this through." Henry chimed in, his newfound patience evident as he resisted the urge to charge headfirst into the fray.

Gathering around a makeshift map drawn in the dirt, the four friends began to strategize. Despite the chaos surrounding them, they focused on devising a plan that would outmaneuver the British forces and secure a strategic advantage for the colonists.

"Perhaps we could create a diversion over here," Clarissa suggested, pointing at one section of the map. Her intellect, once hidden behind shyness, now gave her the confidence to speak up.

"Great idea!" Sarah agreed. "Charles, Henry and I could draw some of the British soldiers away, giving our side an opening to break through their lines."

"Then it's settled," Charles said, taking charge of the group.

"We'll execute the plan as soon as Clarissa finishes tending to the wounded."

"Are you sure this will work?" Henry asked, doubt creeping into his voice.

"Of course it will," Sarah responded with a smile. "We're stronger together, remember?"

As Clarissa finished her task, she looked up at her friends, their faces set with determination and faith in one another. At that moment, she knew they had become an unstoppable force.

"Let's do this," she said, rising to her feet. "Together."

With their plan in place, the four friends ventured back into the chaos of battle, ready to outmaneuver the British forces and change the course of history. Through teamwork, trust, and individual growth, they had become an essential part of the fight for freedom, proving that even the youngest among them could make a difference.

The air was thick with gunpowder and the deafening sound of cannon fire, but Sarah stood tall amidst the chaos, her eyes fixed on the battlefield before her. Charles, Henry, and Clarissa took their positions, ready to execute the plan they had devised together. As a unit, they had grown stronger, and now it was time to put their newfound strengths to the test.

"Ready?" Charles shouted over the din, his voice steady and commanding.

"Ready!" they all responded in unison, determination etched onto their faces.

"Then let's make history!" he cried, and with that, they sprang into action.

Henry, harnessing his newfound patience, charged forward with precision and restraint, his every move calculated and deliberate. Beside him, Charles led a group of patriots, guiding them skillfully around the outskirts of the British forces in a daring flank.

"Stay focused," Charles called out, keeping his eyes trained on the redcoats as he maneuvered his group into position. "We can do this!"

Meanwhile, Sarah used her wit and resourcefulness to create a diversion, drawing the attention of several British soldiers and leading them away from the main line of attack. She darted between trees and ducked behind rocks, always staying just out of reach, her heart pounding in her chest.

"Keep up if you can!" she taunted, feeling a surge of confidence and pride at her own cleverness.

Clarissa, her intellect as sharp as ever, relayed crucial information to the colonial commanders, helping to coordinate their movements and exploit the weaknesses in the British formation. Her once-timid voice rang out clear and strong across the battlefield as she shared her valuable insights.

"Attack from the left!" she instructed, her voice unwavering. "That's where they're weakest!"

As the American colonists pressed forward, bolstered by the actions and strategies of the four friends, the tide of battle began to turn. The British forces, once a formidable and seemingly unstoppable force, now found themselves on the defensive, struggling to maintain their ground.

"Push them back!" Charles cried out, his voice filled with passion and determination. "We have them on the run!"

And suddenly, as if in response to his words, a great cheer rose up from the colonial troops. The British soldiers, battered and beaten, had begun to retreat, leaving behind a trail of redcoats fleeing the battlefield.

"Look!" Sarah exclaimed, her eyes wide with disbelief. "We did it! We really did it!"

Charles, Henry, and Clarissa gathered around her, their faces mirroring her own amazement and joy. Together, they had helped change the course of history, proving that even the youngest among them could make a difference.

"See?" Charles said with a grin, looking down at the others. "I told you we were stronger together."

As the triumph of the moment washed over them, they exchanged a look of unspoken understanding. No matter what challenges lay ahead, they knew they could face them head-on – as long as they had each other.

# CHAPTER 21

As the day came to a close and their message spread throughout the city, they laid Dr. Warren to rest with the Sons of Liberty. The sun dipped low in the sky, casting warm hues of orange and pink across the horizon as Sarah, Charles, Henry, and Clarissa stepped through the portal and found themselves back at the familiar gates of their boarding school. The ivy-covered brick walls seemed to welcome them home, and the scent of freshly cut grass filled their nostrils.

"Whew! We made it," Sarah sighed, her blue eyes glistening with a mix of relief and excitement.

"Indeed," Charles agreed, running a hand through his dark hair. "That was quite an adventure."

As they walked towards the main building, the memories of their time-traveling escapades swirled around them like leaves caught in a gust of wind. They had faced challenges and dangers beyond their wildest dreams, and yet, they had also discovered newfound strengths within themselves.

"Can you believe everything we've been through?" Henry asked, his sturdy frame showing no sign of weariness. His short temper had been tested during their journey, but he now walked with a sense of purpose that hadn't been there before.

"I know, right?" Clarissa chimed in, adjusting her glasses as she glanced around the familiar courtyard. "It feels like we were gone for ages, but everything here looks exactly the same."

"True," Sarah said, her heart swelling with gratitude for the lessons she'd learned on their adventure. "But we're not the same. We've all grown so much."

Charles nodded, his confident demeanor tempered by the realization of how much trust had played a role in their success. "I used to think I could handle everything on my own. But now, I know that I need to rely on others sometimes. We couldn't have done this without each other."

"Let's not forget the people we met along the way," Clarissa added, her voice stronger than before, as her newfound confidence had given her the courage to speak up. "Dr. Warren and Paul Revere... They changed our lives too."

"Absolutely," Henry agreed, his thoughts drifting back to the mentorship he'd received from Revere. "They showed us that there are different ways to fight for what's right."

"Exactly," Sarah chimed in, determination shining in her eyes. "Now, we need to use what we've learned and face our own challenges with the same bravery and unity we had in Boston."

The four friends exchanged knowing glances, understanding that their journey was far from over and that they would carry the memories of their adventure and the lessons they'd learned with them for the rest of their lives. As they walked through the school's halls, their laughter rang out like a promise – a vow to embrace their newfound strengths and face whatever challenges lay ahead together.

Sarah, Charles, Henry, and Clarissa stepped away from the time-traveling device that had brought them back to their present. Shadows danced across the well-manicured lawns and ivy-covered walls of the boarding school, creating an atmosphere of both nostalgia and renewal.

"Let's gather in our favorite spot," Sarah suggested, her voice soft yet full of newfound determination. "We should talk about our journey and what it means for us going forward."

"Great idea," Charles agreed, his eyes meeting Sarah's with a hint of vulnerability, reflecting the trust he was learning to embrace.

Once settled on the bench, their senses were filled with the familiar scents of the courtyard – fresh grass, damp earth, and the faint floral perfume of nearby blossoms. The comforting sounds of rustling leaves and distant laughter from other students provided a backdrop for their heartfelt conversation.

The warm sunlight filtered through the oak leaves above, casting dappled shadows on the four friends seated in a circle beneath its mighty branches. Sarah tenderly plucked a blade of grass from the ground and twirled it between her fingers, her blue eyes shining with determination.

"During our adventure," she began, her voice steady and sure, "I realized how important it is to believe in myself and seize opportunities when they present themselves. I don't want to live with regrets or wonder what could have been." She looked at each of her friends in turn, feeling a newfound sense of independence that surged through her like an electric current.

"Sarah, that's wonderful!" Clarissa beamed, her eyes alight with pride for her friend's growth.

"Thank you," Sarah replied, meeting Charles's gaze with a small, meaningful smile. "What about you, Charles? What have you learned?"

Charles leaned back against the rough bark of the ancient oak, his dark hair ruffling in the gentle breeze. He took a deep breath, inhaling the earthy scent of the courtyard, before speaking.

"Trust has always been...difficult for me," he admitted, his words slow and deliberate. "But during our journey, I discovered that it's necessary to rely on others sometimes. I can't control everything, no matter how hard I try." He looked at Sarah, Henry, and Clarissa, his confident facade giving way to vulnerability for a brief moment. "You all showed me the importance of teamwork and delegating responsibilities."

His friends exchanged supportive smiles, touched by Charles's openness. Sarah reached over and gave his hand a reassuring squeeze, their connection deepening as they shared in each other's growth.

"Who would have thought time travel could teach us so much about ourselves?" Henry mused with a chuckle, his eyes twinkling with mischief.

"Indeed," Clarissa agreed, her own confidence shining through in her assertive tone. "It's been quite the journey."

The sun's warm rays filtered through the branches of the old oak tree, casting dappled shadows on the ground. Henry glanced around at his friends, feeling a newfound sense of camaraderie and understanding. He took a deep breath, inhaling the scent of freshly cut grass and damp earth, before speaking up.

"Y'know," he began, his voice slow and thoughtful, "I've realized something during our adventure." The others leaned in slightly, their expressions attentive and supportive. "I used to think that being strong meant always fighting back, never backing down. But now, I understand that true strength comes from controlling my anger and using it for what's right instead of just... resorting to violence."

Sarah smiled warmly at him, her eyes reflecting pride and admiration. "That's a powerful lesson, Henry. It takes courage to admit that and even more to change."

"Thanks, Sarah," he replied, his cheeks coloring slightly. "Paul Revere helped me see that there are better ways to stand up for justice – ways that don't involve fists."

"Speaking of change..." Clarissa chimed in, her voice steady and self-assured. She pushed her glasses up the bridge of her nose and straightened her posture, embodying the confidence she now felt. "I want to make a difference in this world, not just by using my intelligence but also by raising my voice for what's right. Dr. Warren showed me that my voice is a powerful tool, and I'm determined to use it."

"Bravo, Clarissa!" Charles exclaimed, clapping his hands together with genuine enthusiasm. "We all know you have so much to offer, and it's wonderful to see you embracing your abilities."

Clarissa blushed but held her head high, her newfound assertiveness shining through.

As the four friends sat beneath the wise old oak, their hearts swelled with pride and determination, united by their shared journey and the lessons learned along the way. They were no longer the same individuals who had first embarked on that fateful time-traveling adventure – they had grown stronger, wiser, and more resilient.

"Guys," Sarah said softly, her eyes glistening with unshed tears, "I just want you all to know how grateful I am for this experience and for each of you. We've come such a long way together, and I can't wait to see where life takes us next."

"Here's to our future," Charles declared, raising an imaginary glass in tribute. "Whatever it may hold, we'll face it as a team."

"Cheers to that!" Henry and Clarissa chimed in unison, their voices ringing out with confidence and conviction.

As laughter and heartfelt words filled the air, the sun dipped below the horizon, casting a warm glow on the faces of four friends who were ready to embrace whatever challenges awaited them with bravery, unity, and a newfound understanding of themselves.

"I'll never forget Dr. Warren," Sarah said, her voice filled with wonder. "He taught us so much about resilience and courage."

"Indeed," Charles agreed, his face lighting up at the memory. "Dr. Warren was always there for us – guiding, teaching, and believing in our abilities."

"His kindness and wisdom made it easier to face the unknown," Clarissa chimed in, her eyes sparkling with gratitude. "And I'll never forget how he helped me find my voice."

"Nor will I forget Paul Revere," Henry added with a grin, his muscles tensing as he recalled their encounters. "He showed me that true strength comes from within and that fighting for what's right is a noble pursuit."

As they reminisced, the teachers at the boarding school observed the children from a distance. They exchanged glances, marveling at the transformation that had taken place during their time-traveling adventure. Smiling, they approached the group, eager to offer their congratulations.

"Sarah, Charles, Henry, and Clarissa," Mrs. Hughes began, her voice full of warmth and pride, "you all look...different."

"Indeed," Mr. Thompson agreed, nodding his head in approval. "You normally run around like you are all late for something, but now it's almost like you are in total control, and that's great."

"Thank you," Sarah replied, her cheeks flushed with happiness. "We feel different."

"We truly thank you for your kind words," Charles added earnestly, looking at the teachers with gratitude. "We promise to live up to the new standards we are making for ourselves."

"Good," Mrs. Hughes smiled, her eyes shining with affection. "Remember, the key to success is embracing these newfound strengths and facing life's challenges head-on."

"Absolutely," Mr. Thompson affirmed. "And never forget that you all have the power to make a difference in the world."

As the teachers departed, leaving the children with their encouragement and wisdom, the four friends sat in companionable silence beneath the wise old oak. The shadows grew long, but the warmth of their bond remained – a testament to the transformative power of friendship and shared experiences.

As days turned into weeks, the children gathered at their familiar spot; the soft breeze rustled the leaves above, casting dappled sunlight across the courtyard where Sarah, Charles, Henry, and Clarissa sat on the worn stone benches. They had just finished their end-of-year exams when Headmaster Winters appeared, accompanied by several of the other teachers from the boarding school.

"Ah, there you are," Headmaster Winters said with a warm smile, his lively blue eyes twinkling beneath bushy white eyebrows. "I truly embraced your opportunity and wanted to commend each of you for your remarkable growth."

"Thank you, sir," Sarah replied, her heart swelling with pride as she looked up at the headmaster.

"Sarah," Mrs. Hughes began, her voice gentle yet firm, "your newfound independence and determination to trust yourself are truly inspiring. Continue to take risks and seize opportunities, and you will undoubtedly make a difference in this world."

"Charles," Mr. Thompson chimed in, resting a reassuring hand on the boy's shoulder, "you have shown tremendous progress in learning to trust others and delegate responsibilities. Keep nurturing these skills, and you'll see just how much stronger you and those around you can become."

"Thank you, Mr. Thompson," Charles murmured, his dark eyes shining with gratitude and resolve.

"And you, Henry," Headmaster Winters said with a twinkle in his eye, "I see you have become a gentle giant of sorts around the boarding school, someone everyone can look to and trust.

The wind picked up slightly, carrying with it the faint scent of lilacs as Henry responded to the praise he received from the teachers. "I appreciate your kind words, and I promise to continue working on controlling my temper and using it for noble purposes."

"Clarissa," Mrs. Parker said, her soft voice filled with admiration, "your confidence and assertiveness have blossomed during your journey. Never doubt your intelligence and the power of your voice. You, too, can change the world."

"Thank you, Mrs. Parker," Clarissa whispered, her glasses glinting in the sunlight as she beamed at him.

"Let us not forget," Headmaster Winters added, his voice carrying across the courtyard like a conductor's baton, "that these newfound strengths must be embraced and nurtured. You are all capable of great things."

"Thank you," Sarah repeated, her voice firmer this time as she locked eyes with each teacher in turn. Her thoughts raced with gratitude and determination. We've come so far and grown so much... But there's still more to learn, more to discover about ourselves and the world around us.

"Your praise means the world to us," Charles added earnestly, looking at the teachers with gratitude. "We promise to continue working hard and applying what we've learned."

As the teachers departed, leaving the children with their encouragement and wisdom, the four friends sat in companionable silence beneath the wise old oak. The shadows grew long, but the warmth of their bond remained – a testament to the transformative power of friendship and shared experiences.

Sarah could feel the sun's rays caressing her face, bathing her in warmth as she gazed at her friends. Their eyes sparkled with excitement, and their smiles held a newfound confidence. They were no longer the same children who had left for their time-traveling adventure; they had grown, evolved, and emerged stronger.

"Can you believe how much we've changed?" Henry grinned, his hands idly playing with a fallen autumn leaf, its edges tinged with gold. "We've been through so much together."

"Indeed," Clarissa chimed in, adjusting her glasses before pushing a stray curl behind her ear. "And I have a feeling this is just the beginning. There are still countless lessons to learn and experiences to be had."

"Absolutely!" Charles agreed, his voice resolute. "I mean, if we could survive colonial Boston, I'm sure we can handle whatever life throws at us now."

"True," Sarah mused, her fingers tracing the rough bark of the wise old oak tree that sheltered them. She couldn't help but notice that its deep roots mirrored the unbreakable bond that had formed between them throughout their journey.

"Hey, guys," she said, her blue eyes dancing with anticipation. "Promise me something?"

"Of course," Charles replied, his gaze meeting hers with unwavering loyalty. "Anything."

"Promise me that no matter where our individual paths take us, we'll always make time for each other." Her words echoed the hope that filled her heart, a hope that their friendship would withstand the test of time and distance.

"Absolutely," Henry nodded a determined glint in his eyes. "We're family now."

"Agreed," Clarissa added, her voice steady and strong. "We'll always be there for one another, no matter what."

"Then it's settled," Sarah smiled, her heart swelling with pride and affection for her friends. She felt a surge of excitement coursing through her veins, the promise of future adventures and discoveries beckoning them forward.

"Here's to us," Charles raised an imaginary toast, his eyes shining with enthusiasm. "To our growth, our friendship, and to all the incredible experiences that await us."

"Cheers!" they echoed in unison, their voices ringing out like a triumphant anthem. As they shared a moment of camaraderie and determination, Sarah knew that together, they could face whatever challenges lay ahead with bravery and unity.

The sun hung low in the sky, casting a warm golden light on the familiar grounds of Hawthorne House Boarding School as the children arrived at the main entrance. Their hearts swelled with relief and excitement, the sturdy brick buildings and neatly trimmed lawns welcoming them back like old friends. Sarah glanced around, her blue eyes wide with wonder as if seeing the place for the first time.

"Home sweet home," Charles said, grinning at his companions as they stepped through the iron gates. They had been away for what felt like an eternity, and the familiarity was comforting.

Hawthorne House Boarding School stood tall and proud amidst a lush landscape. The main building, a grand Victorian structure, loomed over the grounds with its red bricks and imposing towers. Surrounding it were well-tended gardens filled with vibrant roses, dahlias, and marigolds, their colors dazzling in the sunlight.

"Everything seems so...different now," Clarissa mused, adjusting her glasses as she took in the scene. "I guess our journey changed the way we see things, huh?"

Indeed, as they walked along the cobblestone paths that crisscrossed the school's grounds, the children couldn't help but notice details they had previously overlooked or taken for granted. A row of ancient oak trees standing sentinel along the western edge of the property, their leaves rustling softly in the breeze, now seemed to hold the wisdom and secrets of centuries past. The statue of the school's founder, Sir Reginald Hawthorne, perched on a pedestal near the entrance, appeared more alive than ever – his stern expression a reminder of the importance of courage and determination in the face of adversity.

"Remember when we thought these gardens were just for decoration?" Henry asked, a wistful smile tugging at his lips as he traced a finger along the petals of a nearby daffodil. "Now, they seem like a living testament to the beauty of nature and the passage of time."

"Everything seems so much more alive now," Sarah agreed, her thoughts drifting to Dr. Warren and the vivid world of colonial Boston they had left behind. "It's as if our eyes have been opened to the magic hidden in plain sight."

As they made their way toward the main building, the children passed groups of students lost in lively conversations or engrossed in their studies beneath the shade of leafy trees. These scenes, once mundane and unremarkable, now held new meaning for the young time travelers.

"Seeing everyone so focused on their education," Charles mused aloud, "makes me think about how lucky we are to have access to this kind of knowledge – and it's all thanks to the people we met on our journey."

"Like Dr. Warren," Clarissa added softly, her brown eyes shining with admiration. "I never thought I'd find such a powerful role model, but now I know that there are countless extraordinary individuals throughout history who've shaped the world we live in today."

"Speaking of which," Henry said, his voice filled with determination, "we've got some serious catching up to do. Let's make the most of the lessons we learned from those great men and women and show Hawthorne House what we're really capable of!"

With renewed passion and purpose, the children entered the school's grand hall, ready to embrace the challenges and opportunities that awaited them, forever changed by their incredible adventure through time.

The morning sun filtered through the tall windows of the classroom, casting a warm glow upon the rows of wooden desks. Sarah took her seat in the front row, her heart pounding with anticipation as she felt the weight of her history book in her hands. She looked around at her classmates, who were chatting animatedly and settling into their places. The familiar scent of chalk dust and polished wood brought an unexpected rush of nostalgia, and she realized just how much she had missed this place.

"Good morning, everyone," said Mrs. Williams, their history teacher, as she entered the room with a stack of papers in her arms. "I hope you're all ready for today's lesson on the American Revolution."

Sarah couldn't help but smile as she exchanged glances with Charles, Henry, and Clarissa. If only their teacher knew the extraordinary journey they had taken, the remarkable people they had met, and the incredible lessons they had learned. But those experiences were theirs to cherish and draw strength from, and they were determined to do so.

As Mrs. Williams began the lecture, Sarah found herself hanging on every word, her mind racing with images of Dr. Warren, Paul Revere, and the other heroes of the revolution. Gone were the days when she would merely memorize dates and names – now, she understood the true meaning behind those events and the sacrifices that had been made for freedom.

"Sarah," Mrs. Williams called upon her suddenly, "can you please explain the significance of the Boston Tea Party?"

"Of course, Mrs. Williams," Sarah replied confidently. "The Boston Tea Party was a political protest organized by the Sons of Liberty, led by men like Samuel Adams and John Hancock. They were fighting against British taxation without representation, and their actions helped to spark the American Revolution."

"Very good, Sarah!" Mrs. Williams beamed with pride. "It seems your time away has done wonders for your understanding of our nation's history."

Sarah couldn't help but feel a wave of gratitude wash over her as she thought of Dr. Warren and the others who had shaped her newfound perspective. It wasn't just in history class where she and her friends were excelling – their experiences had enriched their entire academic lives.

"Charles, can you tell us about the role Paul Revere played in the revolution?" Mrs. Williams asked, turning to him expectantly.

"Absolutely," Charles said with a grin, eagerness shining in his eyes. "Paul Revere was not only a skilled silversmith but also an important patriot. He played a key role in the events leading up to the revolution, including the Boston Tea Party and the famous midnight ride to warn the colonists of the approaching British troops. His bravery and resourcefulness were crucial to the success of the American cause."

"Excellent work, Charles!" Mrs. Williams praised, her eyes twinkling with delight. "You all seem to have returned with quite the passion for history."

"Thank you, Mrs. Williams," Charles replied, his chest swelling with pride.

As classes continued throughout the day, the children's newfound knowledge shone in every subject. In science class, Clarissa astounded her classmates by explaining intricate details about the medicinal practices of colonial times, and her teacher, Mr. Thompson, couldn't help but marvel at her sudden growth.

"Clarissa, your understanding of the scientific principles

behind these early medical practices is truly impressive," he commended as she adjusted her glasses and smiled shyly.

Meanwhile, Henry found himself excelling in physical education, where he showcased his newfound strength and agility—skills honed during their daring adventures in colonial Boston. Even Coach Davis noticed the change in him, clapping Henry on the back and declaring, "Turner, you've certainly come back stronger than ever! Keep up the good work!"

As the days went by, Sarah, Charles, Clarissa, and Henry reveled in their academic triumphs, humbled by the praise they received from their teachers and motivated to continue learning. Their time in the past had given them not only a deeper understanding of history but also a newfound appreciation for the power of knowledge and the importance of personal growth.

The sun cast a warm glow through the library windows as Sarah, Charles, Clarissa, and Henry huddled around a table laden with books, maps, and parchment. The scent of ink and leather filled the air, mingling with the soft whispers of their new-found dedication to learning.

"Look at this," Sarah said excitedly, pointing to an illustration in a book about colonial fashion. "This is the exact style of dress I saw Abigail Adams wearing when we met her!"

"Really?" Clarissa leaned in closer, her eyes widening in fascination. "How incredible it must have been to see the clothing of that time firsthand."

"Indeed," Charles agreed, carefully studying a map of revolutionary Boston. "I would never have thought I'd be so interested in history, but now it feels like every page holds a new discovery."

"Speaking of discoveries," Henry chimed in, his finger tracing a passage in a book on military strategy, "did you know Dr. Warren was actually a key figure in organizing the early stages of the American Revolution? His courage and leadership made such a difference."

As they delved deeper into the pages of history, Sarah couldn't help but reflect on the profound impact Dr. Warren and their journey had on each of them. They had grown not only in knowledge but also in character, having seen firsthand the sacrifices and determination of those who shaped the course of history.

"Dr. Warren's bravery has been an inspiration to us all," Sarah mused aloud, her voice tinged with admiration and nostalgia. "One can only imagine what it must have been like for him to risk everything for the sake of freedom."

"Indeed," Charles nodded solemnly. "Meeting him and the others has made me realize just how much we owe to the past and to those who fought for the rights and liberties we enjoy today."

"Absolutely," Clarissa agreed, her fingers brushing against the spine of a book on the shelf. "But it's not just about what they did for us, but also what we can learn from them. The way Dr. Warren and those historical figures persevered in the face of adversity is something we can all strive to emulate."

"True," Sarah added thoughtfully. "Their actions show that even in the darkest of times, there's always a light we can follow – a cause worth fighting for. It makes me want to be better, to make a difference in our world just like they did."

Henry looked up from his book, his eyes shining with determination. "You know what? Let's make a promise right here, right now. Let's promise that we'll use our newfound appreciation for history and education to better ourselves and help others. That we'll be leaders in our own right, just like Dr. Warren was."

"Agreed," Charles said, his voice firm.

"Count me in," Clarissa chimed, her enthusiasm contagious.

"Me too," Sarah nodded, feeling a surge of hope and purpose fill her heart.

And so, surrounded by the dusty pages of history and the echoes of their time-traveling adventure, the children pledged themselves to a future filled with learning, growth, and the unwavering determination to make a positive impact on the world — just as Dr. Joseph Warren and the countless other historical figures they had encountered had done before them.

Charles leaned back in his chair, gazing out the window at the school's lush green campus. The sun cast a golden light over the grounds, and the leaves on the trees seemed to dance in the breeze as if they shared the children's excitement for the future.

"Can you believe what we've been through?" Charles asked, breaking the silence. "I still can't wrap my head around it all."

"Neither can I," Clarissa admitted, twirling a strand of her hair. "But one thing I do know is that our experience has truly changed me. I mean, look at us! We're actually enjoying our studies now."

Henry laughed, nodding in agreement. "You know, I've been thinking about Paul Revere lately. How he risked everything for the cause he believed in. It takes an immense amount of bravery to do what he did, and I can't help but feel inspired by him."

"Absolutely," Sarah chimed in, her eyes distant as she recalled their encounter with the famous silversmith. "And remember Abigail Adams? She was so intelligent and strong-willed, even though she lived in a time when women had very little say in matters. Her determination to fight for equality – it's something we should all strive for in our own lives."

"Definitely," Charles agreed, his gaze shifting to the worn pages of his history book. "Their stories remind us that heroes come in all shapes and sizes and that each of us has the potential to make a difference."

"Speaking of heroes," Clarissa said, a fond smile spreading across her face, "Dr. Warren was such an incredible person, wasn't he? I'll never forget how he helped us navigate our way through colonial Boston or how he taught us that understanding history is key to making a better future."

"His kindness and wisdom really left a mark on me," Sarah agreed, her voice filled with gratitude. "I'll always cherish the bond we formed with him and the others. They may be gone, but their legacies live on through us."

"True," Henry added thoughtfully, staring at a sketch he had made of Dr. Warren in his notebook. "I think it's important that we remember the lessons they taught us, the friendships we forged, and how those experiences have shaped who we are today."

"Here's to carrying on their legacy," Charles proposed, raising an imaginary toast.

"Cheers," the others echoed, their voices resolute as they clinked their pencils together and returned to their studies, their hearts warmed by the memories of their time-traveling adventure and the powerful bonds they had formed with the historical figures who had inspired them to be better versions of themselves.

"Did you ever imagine we'd be back here, sitting in the courtyard and applying the lessons we learned from those heroes?" Clarissa asked, her brown eyes filled with wonder as she gazed around the familiar surroundings of the boarding school.

"Dr. Warren's words about understanding history really resonated with me," Sarah said thoughtfully. "It's become more than just a subject for me now - it's a way to understand people and their motivations."

"Exactly," Charles agreed. "We've all grown so much since our journey. I think we owe it to ourselves and to them to share our experiences with the others here at school. Maybe our story could inspire them too."

"Great idea, Charles!" Henry exclaimed, his excitement contagious. "I bet Paul Revere would be proud to know that his courage is still motivating people today."

"Let's start by sharing our adventures during lunch," Clarissa suggested, adjusting her glasses with newfound confidence. "We can take turns telling stories about the historical figures we met and the lessons we learned from them."

"Sounds like a plan," Sarah nodded, her blue eyes shining with determination. "I hope that through our stories, we can keep their memories alive and pass on the inspiration they gave us."

As the group of friends walked towards the dining hall, they couldn't help but feel a sense of responsibility and pride in sharing their incredible journey with their fellow students. After all, the knowledge and inspiration they had gained from their time-traveling adventure were gifts that deserved to be shared, and who knew how many lives could be touched by the tales of bravery, dedication, and friendship they had experienced firsthand?

The sun streamed through the windows of the boarding school's library, casting a golden glow over the rows of bookshelves. Sarah sat at a large wooden table, surrounded by her friends and fellow students. They were all engrossed in various extracurricular projects inspired by their time in colonial Boston.

"Look at this," Charles said excitedly, holding up a meticulously drawn map of the city. "I've been studying cartography so I can better understand how Boston has changed over time." His dark eyes sparkled with enthusiasm as he traced his finger along the winding roads, pointing out key locations from their journey.

"Wow, that's amazing, Charles!" Sarah exclaimed, admiring the level of detail in his work. She glanced down at her own project, a series of delicate watercolor paintings depicting scenes from their adventure, and felt a swell of pride. Her brushstrokes had grown more confident, and she knew it was thanks to the lessons she'd learned about determination and self-reliance.

"Hey, everyone," Henry called out from across the room, where he was practicing fencing moves with a group of students. "Paul Revere taught me these techniques during our time together. Who wants to join us for a lesson?"

A few eager hands shot up, and soon, the library was filled with the sounds of laughter and friendly competition. Sarah smiled as she watched Henry patiently teaching the others, his strong sense of justice now tempered by restraint and empathy. It was clear that he had taken Paul Revere's mentorship to heart and was eager to share his newfound knowledge.

Meanwhile, Clarissa sat nearby, her brown hair falling in front of her glasses as she scribbled furiously in a notebook. She had been captivated by the political debates they had witnessed and was now researching the philosophies behind the birth of the American Revolution. As she discussed her findings with a rapt audience of classmates, she radiated confidence and intelligence.

"Isn't it incredible how much our lives have been enriched by our experiences in colonial Boston?" Sarah mused aloud, pausing in her painting to glance around at her friends.

"Yes," Clarissa agreed, looking up from her notebook. "I never thought I'd be so passionate about history, but meeting people like Samuel Adams and John Hancock has completely changed my perspective. I feel so grateful for the opportunity we had."

"Me too," Henry chimed in, taking a break from his fencing lesson. "And I think the best way we can express our appreciation is by sharing what we've learned with others. That's what Dr. Warren would want us to do."

As the group continued their projects, they couldn't help but reflect on the transformative journey that had shaped their lives. They knew they owed a debt of gratitude to Dr. Warren and the historical figures they had encountered, who had opened their eyes to new possibilities and inspired them to grow as individuals.

"Thank you," Sarah whispered under her breath, her blue eyes glistening with emotion. "Thank you for showing us that our potential is limitless and for giving us the courage to chase our dreams."

With renewed determination, the young friends dove back into their projects, eager to honor the memories of those who had so profoundly impacted their lives.

Sunlight streamed through the tall windows of the boarding school, casting a warm glow on the group of students huddled together in animated conversation. Their faces were lit with excitement as they discussed their experiences in colonial Boston and their plans for the future.

"Imagine what we could do if we applied the same determination that Dr. Warren and the others had," Sarah said, her eyes shining brightly. "We could make a real difference in the world."

Charles nodded, his once-guarded demeanor replaced with an openness that was much more inviting. "That's true. We've learned so much from them, not just about history, but about ourselves too. I never thought I could trust people the way I do now."

"Neither did I," Henry admitted, his hand resting on the fencing foil he had become so skilled with since returning from their journey. "I used to think that strength meant dominating others, but Paul Revere showed me that it's about standing up for what's right and protecting those who can't protect themselves."

Clarissa adjusted her glasses and smiled gently. "And I've learned that even someone quiet like me can have a powerful impact. Samuel Adams taught me that it's our ideas and convictions that matter most, not how loudly we shout them."

The friends exchanged glances, each of them aware of the growth they had experienced and the potential they now possessed. As they sat together in the sunlit room, the air seemed to hum with possibilities.

"Let's make a promise," Sarah suggested, her voice filled with hope. "Let's promise to keep learning, to keep growing, and to use everything we've gained from our time with Dr. Warren and the others to make a positive impact on the world."

"Agreed," Charles declared, extending his hand towards the center of the circle. One by one, the others joined him, their hands connecting in a symbol of unity and commitment.

"Here's to our future," Henry said, his voice strong and steady.

"May we never forget the lessons we've learned," Clarissa added, her eyes sparkling with newfound confidence.

As their hands remained clasped together, the friends looked out at the world beyond the windows, filled with determination to honor the memories of the historical figures they had encountered. With hope in their hearts and dreams of a brighter future, they knew that their journey was far from over—indeed, it was only just beginning.

# CHAPTER 22

The warm glow of the fire flickered and danced, casting playful shadows on the walls of the cozy common room. Sarah Merriweather, with her long blonde hair and sparkling blue eyes, stared into the flames as if trying to decipher a hidden message within their depths. The others were gathered around her - Charles, Henry, and Clarissa - all reminiscing about their experiences in colonial Boston and how it had shaped them.

"Who would've thought that time travel could teach us so much?" Charles mused, his fingers absentmindedly fiddling with the worn edge of a woolen blanket draped over his lap.

"Indeed," agreed Clarissa, her quiet voice filled with warmth. "We've come a long way since we first arrived, haven't we?"

Sarah leaned back into the soft cushions of the armchair she occupied, allowing herself a moment to reflect on her own journey. She remembered the timid girl she had been when they first arrived in this foreign time and place. Her heart swelled as she acknowledged the remarkable transformation she had undergone. No longer was she the fragile, indecisive girl who struggled to assert herself; now, she stood tall and confident, ready to face life's challenges head-on.

"I know I've certainly changed," she said, pulling herself from her reverie and meeting the gaze of her friends. "When we first arrived here, I was terrified of making decisions on my own. But now...now I feel like I can do anything."

Charles grinned at her warmly. "You're not the only one who's grown, Sarah. We've all learned so much from our time here."

"Even me?" teased Henry, flexing his muscles playfully.

"Especially you!" Clarissa chuckled, rolling her eyes good-naturedly.

As the laughter died down, Sarah felt a surge of gratitude for these people who had become more than just friends; they had become her family. They had seen her at her weakest, and yet they had never given up on her. Instead, they had encouraged her to find her own strength – and she had.

"Thank you," Sarah said softly, her eyes shimmering with unshed tears. "For everything."

"Hey, we're in this together," Charles replied, reaching across the space between them to give her hand a reassuring squeeze. "We always have been."

At that moment, surrounded by the warmth of the fire and the love of her friends, Sarah knew deep within her heart that they would continue to grow and learn together, united by the incredible experiences they had shared in colonial Boston.

Charles stared into the dancing flames as they flickered and cast playful shadows on the walls, allowing himself to get lost in his thoughts. He couldn't believe how much he had changed since their arrival in colonial Boston. He used to have trouble trusting others, always trying to carry the weight of the world on his shoulders, but things were different now.

"Samuel Adams really taught me a lot, you know," Charles said, his voice filled with admiration. "When we first met him, I was so hesitant to trust anyone, but he showed me the power of loyalty and friendship."

"Speaking of loyalty," Henry chimed in, leaning back in his chair and stretching his legs out in front of him. "I've been thinking about my little scuffle with that Redcoat a while back. I used to be all about throwing punches first and asking questions later, but now, I think I understand what it means to fight for something bigger than myself."

"Like liberty and justice, right?" Sarah asked, her eyes twinkling with curiosity.

"Exactly!" Henry exclaimed, pounding his fist against his palm for emphasis. "Paul Revere helped me see that there's more to fighting than just brawling. It's about standing up for what you believe in, defending those who can't defend themselves, and making a difference in the world."

Charles nodded, understanding completely. "We've all grown so much during our time here. If we hadn't come to that time period, who knows what kind of people we would have become?"

"True," Sarah agreed, smiling warmly at her friends. "But I think no matter where or when we are, we'll always find a way to learn and grow together."

"Absolutely," Henry added, placing a hand on Charles' shoulder. "And I don't know about you, but I'm grateful for every single lesson we've learned here, even the tough ones."

"Me too," Charles said, feeling a surge of gratitude for his friends and their shared experiences. "You know, I used to have a hard time trusting people. I always felt like I had to do everything on my own." He glanced at Sarah and Henry, his eyes filled with appreciation. "But now, I've learned that having friends you can rely on makes all the difference."

"Samuel Adams taught me that," Charles continued, remembering how the older man had taken him under his wing, showing him the value of loyalty and collaboration. "He's not just a great leader for the cause of America's freedom; he's also a true friend."

"And Dr. Warren!" Henry said, "I think he's been a great mentor for all of us in different ways. He's shown us that we're capable of making an impact on history, even though we're just a bunch of kids from the future."

"Who would have ever thought," Sarah mused with a laugh, "that we'd be there, in colonial Boston, learning life lessons from none other than Dr. Joseph Warren?"

"I certainly wouldn't have," Charles admitted, chuckling along with her. "But I'm so grateful for all the adventures we've had and the friendships we've forged along the way."

The warm glow of the fireplace cast flickering shadows across the cozy common room of the boarding school, illuminating the animated faces of the young time travelers. They were gathered together, sharing stories and laughter as they reminisced about their experiences in colonial Boston.

"Isn't it incredible how much we've changed since our time in colonial Boston?" Clarissa mused, her brown eyes reflecting the dancing flames. "I never thought I'd be capable of doing the things I've done."

Sarah smiled at her friend, noting the newfound confidence in Clarissa's voice. "It's true. You've come such a long way, Clarissa. We all have, really."

"Indeed," Charles agreed, leaning forward with his elbows on his knees. "I mean, look at us now – we're practically seasoned revolutionaries!"

"Ha! Speak for yourself, Charles," Henry joked, playfully punching his friend's shoulder. "But seriously, I think we've all learned valuable lessons from our time there."

Clarissa nodded, her fingers nervously fidgeting with her glasses as she considered her own personal growth. "I used to be so afraid of speaking up, even when I knew I could make a difference. But now... I feel this quiet strength within me, a determination to stand up for what I believe in."

"Dr. Warren has been a great influence on you, hasn't he?" Sarah asked gently, knowing how much the brilliant physician had encouraged Clarissa to embrace her own talents.

"Definitely," Clarissa replied, her cheeks warming with a blush. "He taught me that my intelligence and quick thinking can have a real impact on the world around me. It's a lesson I'll carry with me for the rest of my life."

"Speaking of lessons, I've learned a lot from Paul Revere," Henry chimed in, his eyes shining with admiration. "He's taught me the importance of strategy and critical thinking – skills I didn't even know I had."

"Isn't it amazing how these people we've met have changed us so profoundly?" Charles mused, taking a sip of his hot chocolate. "It's as if our lives were destined to intertwine, even though we come from entirely different times."

As the laughter died down, Clarissa glanced around the room at her friends, feeling a deep sense of gratitude for the shared experiences that had bonded them together. She couldn't help but wonder what adventures awaited them in the future.

"After leaving that time period, I think we should all share a dream or aspiration we have for our lives going forward," Clarissa suggested, her eyes shining with excitement. "Something that reflects the growth we've experienced during the time we spent in colonial Boston."

"Great idea, Clarissa!" Sarah exclaimed, always eager to engage in thoughtful conversation. "I'll go first. My dream is to continue standing up for what I believe in and to never let fear hold me back again. What about you, Charles?"

Charles leaned back in his chair, a thoughtful expression on his face. "My dream is to become a true leader – someone who can inspire others through loyalty, trust, and understanding."

"Wow, Charles, that's really powerful," Henry said, nodding in approval. "As for me, I want to channel my passion for justice into making a real difference in the world. I want to be known as someone who fights for what's right, no matter the cost."

The room fell silent as everyone turned their attention to Clarissa, waiting for her to share her own dream. She took a deep breath, gathering her thoughts before speaking.

"Throughout our journey, I've discovered that my greatest strength lies in my intelligence and quick thinking," she began, her voice steady and resolute. "My dream is to use these gifts to help others and make a meaningful impact on the world around me."

Her friends smiled proudly at her, their eyes filled with admiration and respect. The cozy common room seemed to hum with hope and anticipation as each of them contemplated the bright futures that lay ahead.

"Whatever challenges we may face, I know that we will overcome them together," Sarah declared, her eyes glistening with determination. "For we have learned that it is through friendship, growth, and the pursuit of our dreams that we become our truest selves."

"Sarah," Clarissa said softly, "you've also shown incredible bravery. Like the time you stood up to that British spy. I'll never forget the fire in your eyes when you confronted him."

"Me?" Sarah's cheeks flushed with warmth as she remembered that harrowing encounter. "I suppose I did surprise myself then... I never thought I'd have it in me to stand up to someone so dangerous."

"Yet you did it with such grace and conviction," Charles added, his eyes meeting Sarah's with admiration. "Your actions that day showed us all that you are capable of great courage and standing up for what you believe in."

"Thank you," Sarah whispered, feeling a renewed sense of pride in herself and her abilities. The memory of facing that British spy now served as a reminder that she had grown tremendously since the beginning of their journey.

Henry chuckled, his muscular arms crossed over his chest. "I knew you had it in you all along, Sarah. You've got a fire in your heart that even the most deceitful spy can't snuff out."

"Indeed," Charles agreed, his dark hair falling into his eyes as he nodded emphatically. "You were magnificent, Sarah. Your bravery and determination saved us all."

Sarah blushed at the praise, but her heart swelled with pride. Her fingers traced the edge of her glass, remembering how they had trembled that day. Yet, she had faced her fear and, in doing so, discovered a strength she had never known she possessed.

"Your courage has inspired us all," Henry added, his voice sincere. "It's a reminder that no matter our size or age, we each have the power to make a difference."

"Speaking of making a difference," Charles said, leaning forward, his face illuminated by the firelight, "do you recall the time I trusted you, Henry, to have my back during that dangerous mission? Honestly, I was terrified. But trusting you turned out to be the best decision I could have made."

"Ah, yes!" Henry exclaimed, grinning widely. "That was quite the adventure, wasn't it? I'll never forget the look on your face when I swooped in and helped you disarm that trap. You were genuinely surprised that I had your back."

Charles laughed, a genuine, warm sound that filled the room. "I was! But you proved to me that day that we are stronger together and that teamwork is truly powerful."

"Your friendship has been one of the greatest gifts of this journey," Sarah chimed in, her heart warmed by their camaraderie. "I've learned that when we stand together, we can overcome any obstacle."

The four friends shared smiles and nods, feeling the strength of their bond as they reminisced on their adventures. They knew that together, they could face any challenge that came their way.

As the fireplace crackled, casting a warm glow over the cozy common room, Henry cleared his throat. He couldn't help but recall a particular adventure that had changed his perspective on life.

"Remember when we were trying to find the British's secret plot?" Henry began, his eyes gleaming with excitement. "I never thought I'd learn so much from someone like Paul Revere. He taught me how to strategize and think critically in difficult situations."

Sarah nodded, her smile wide. "Ah, yes. The night we snuck through the narrow streets of Boston, avoiding the Redcoats at every turn."

"Exactly," Henry continued a hint of pride in his voice. "Paul showed me how to analyze our surroundings and make split-second decisions. I've always been one to fight first and think later, but he helped me see that there's more to winning battles than just physical strength."

"Indeed," Charles chimed in, grinning at Henry. "You've come a long way from the hotheaded brawler we first met."

Henry chuckled, rubbing the back of his neck sheepishly. "I have you all to thank for that. Your friendship means everything to me."

A quiet cough interrupted their conversation, drawing their attention to Clarissa, who sat nervously on the edge of her seat. Taking a deep breath, she spoke up. "I also have a story to share, though it may not be as thrilling as yours, Henry."

"Please, do tell," Sarah encouraged, leaning forward with interest.

"Dr. Warren entrusted me with delivering a crucial message," Clarissa said, her voice barely above a whisper. "At first, I was terrified. I mean, I'm not exactly the most courageous person among us. But then, I realized that my intelligence and quick thinking could actually make a difference in this world."

"Of course, it can," Charles assured her, beaming. "You have a brilliant mind, Clarissa, and we're lucky to have you on our side."

"Was it the message about the reinforcements?" Henry inquired, his brow furrowed as he tried to recall the details.

"Yes," Clarissa confirmed, growing more confident with each word she spoke. "I had to navigate through a maze of winding alleys and evade enemy soldiers. It was exhilarating and terrifying all at once. But I made it, and the message reached our allies in time to prepare for the British attack." Clarissa's eyes shone with pride as she recounted her harrowing adventure.

"See, you're braver than you think," Sarah said, smiling warmly at Clarissa. "We each have our strengths, and they all contribute to our cause in different ways."

"Absolutely," Charles agreed. "Our experiences in colonial

Boston have shaped us all in different ways. We've grown stronger, wiser, and more determined to make a difference in this world."

The room fell quiet for a moment as they each reflected on their own personal growth, acknowledging the impact their experiences had wrought upon their young hearts.

"Speaking of change," Charles mused, breaking the silence, "it's amazing to think about all the possibilities that lie ahead of us. Who knows where our future adventures will take us?"

"I hope we'll continue to make a difference," Sarah said earnestly, her gaze fixed on the dancing flames. "Helping others and fighting for justice, just like the heroes of the Revolution."

"Absolutely," Henry agreed, flexing his brawny arms with determination. "We'll use our strengths to defend those in need and stand up for what is right."

"Perhaps we can even inspire others," Clarissa suggested quietly, her eyes shining with ambition. "By sharing our knowledge and experiences, we might encourage future generations to follow in our footsteps."

"Whatever the future holds," Charles declared, his voice resolute, "I know that together, we can face any challenge that comes our way. We've already accomplished so much, and I have no doubt that our journey is just beginning."

## CHAPTER 23

The ancient wooden doors of the boarding school creaked open, revealing a labyrinth of dimly lit hallways that seemed to stretch on forever. Every step echoed through the corridors, accompanied by the soft whispers of the wind that seeped through the cracks in the old walls. The air was heavy with the scent of musty leather and centuries' worth of dust.

"Wow," whispered Sarah, her blue eyes wide as she took in their surroundings. "It's like stepping into another world."

"Indeed," agreed Headmaster Winters, his long white beard rustling as he stroked it thoughtfully. "This place has a certain...mystique about it, wouldn't you say?"

As they ventured further into the heart of the building, it became clear that this was no ordinary boarding school. Intricate tapestries adorned the walls, depicting scenes from what appeared to be some of the most pivotal moments in history. A group of visionary educators founded this institution many years ago. Their aim is to create a unique learning environment where students cannot only study history but also come face to face with its mysteries.

"Headmaster, how is it that this school has managed to stay so...well, hidden?" Charles asked, his voice betraying his curiosity.

"Ah, my boy," chuckled the elderly man, pausing to adjust his spectacles. "That is just one of the many secrets this place holds. You see, our founders believed that knowledge is power – and in the case of our illustrious history, perhaps even more so."

"Knowledge is power," mused Clarissa, her fingers absently tracing the ornate frame of an oil painting on the wall. "I like that."

"Good!" exclaimed Headmaster Winters, clapping his hands together. "You'll find that there's much to learn here, young ones. And as you explore the depths of our vast library, you may just discover secrets that have been hidden away for centuries."

"Like a treasure hunt!" Henry's eyes sparkled with excitement at the prospect. "I can't wait to get started!"

"Patience, Mr. Turner," the Headmaster cautioned, his eyes twinkling mischievously. "You'll find that some things are worth waiting for."

As they continued their tour of the school, it became increasingly evident that this place was steeped in history and mystery. The students couldn't help but feel as though they were standing on the precipice of greatness and that if they dared to look closely enough, they might just catch a glimpse of the extraordinary.

"Alright, everyone," Headmaster Winters announced, stopping before a set of large double doors. "Behind these doors lies your first true test as students of this esteemed institution. Are you ready?"

The four young friends exchanged glances, excitement, and anticipation radiating from their faces. They nodded in unison, ready for whatever challenge awaited them.

"Very well," Headmaster Winters said, pushing the doors open with a flourish. They stepped inside, revealing a grand library that seemed to stretch on forever. Shelves upon shelves of ancient books towered over them, casting long shadows across the dimly lit room. The air smelled of aged parchment and polished wood, and there was an almost palpable sense of reverence that hung heavy in the atmosphere.

"Welcome to the heart of our school," Headmaster Winters whispered, his voice taking on a hushed tone as if he were sharing a secret. "This library contains the collected knowledge of generations – not just books, but manuscripts, maps, and artifacts from all corners of the globe."

"Wow," breathed Sarah, her eyes wide with wonder as she took in the sheer scale of the room. Charles, too, looked around in awe while Henry couldn't help but let out a low whistle of appreciation.

"Remember what I told you earlier," Headmaster Winters reminded them, pointing to the inscription above the entrance: 'Knowledge is power.' "That is the guiding principle of our founders, who envisioned this place as a haven for those who seek to learn and grow. And it is my hope that during your time here, you will come to appreciate the importance of history and how the actions of individuals can shape the course of events."

The students listened intently, their minds already racing at the thought of the countless hidden treasures that awaited them within this hallowed space. As they ventured deeper into the library, each carrying a lantern to light their way through the labyrinthine stacks, they couldn't help but feel the weight of the past pressing down upon them, whispering secrets and beckoning them to explore further.

"Let us begin our journey," said Headmaster Winters, his eyes shining with the promise of adventure. "There is much to discover, and I have no doubt that you will find your place in the grand tapestry of history that surrounds us."

With those words echoing in their ears, Sarah, Charles, Henry, and Clarissa embarked on their quest for knowledge and enlightenment, eager to uncover the hidden mysteries of the boarding school and its storied past. And as they delved into the library's ancient tomes, little did they know that their own lives would soon become intertwined with the very history they sought to understand.

"Headmaster Winters, may I ask you something?" Sarah inquired hesitantly as they perused the library's vast collection. The other students paused, curious to hear their headmaster's response.

"Of course, my dear," he replied with a warm smile, beckoning her closer. "What is it that you wish to know?"

"Your stories of the founding educators are fascinating," she began, her curiosity overcoming her initial hesitation. "But what about your own history? How did you come to be involved with the school and, well, time travel?"

The headmaster's eyes twinkled with mischief as he leaned in conspiratorially. "Ah, now that is a tale worth telling." He settled into a nearby armchair, his beard brushing against the worn fabric. "You see, many years ago, during the tumultuous days of the American Revolution, I stumbled upon a powerful artifact: a cryptex that allowed me to traverse the currents of time."

"Remarkable!" Charles exclaimed, his eyes wide with amazement. "And how did you decide to use this incredible gift?"

Headmaster Winters' expression grew solemn. "I realized

that by using the cryptex, I could help guide the course of history, ensuring a brighter future for generations to come. And so, I became embroiled in the events of the American Revolution, working alongside some of its most influential figures."

"Like who?" Henry asked eagerly, unable to contain his excitement.

"Ah, that's a story for another time, young man," the headmaster replied with a wink. "But let us return to the matter at hand: our beloved school here in northern Virginia. You see, it played a crucial role in the revolution, serving as both a refuge and a meeting place for those who sought to forge a new nation."

"Wow," Clarissa breathed, her imagination alight with visions of clandestine meetings and daring escapes. "So, is the school's history intertwined with that of the revolution?"

"Indeed," Headmaster Winters confirmed. "And it is my hope that by sharing these stories with you, I can inspire you to recognize the importance of your own actions and how they might one day shape the course of history."

As Sarah, Charles, Henry, and Clarissa continued their exploration of the library, their minds raced with thoughts of the headmaster's past adventures and the extraordinary legacy they had unwittingly become a part of. As they pored over dusty volumes and examined weathered maps, they couldn't help but feel a growing sense of wonder at the world they had been thrust into and an eagerness to uncover the secrets that lay within its storied halls.

"Headmaster," Sarah murmured thoughtfully, her eyes scanning the pages of a book on the American Revolution, "I think we're just beginning to understand the true significance of this place and our role in its history."

The sun began to set, casting an amber glow over the library's ancient shelves and illuminating the dust particles that danced in the air. The sounds of creaking floorboards and rustling pages created a symphony unique to the aged boarding school.

"Headmaster Winters," Charles ventured, "you've mentioned the school being a hub for historical knowledge, but how have you managed to keep all this information so accurate and alive?"

"Ah, my boy," the headmaster chuckled, his eyes sparkling like sapphires in the fading light, "it is all about curating the curriculum with great care. We are fortunate to have access to first-hand accounts and primary sources, thanks to my own adventures through time. Through these experiences, I've been able to instill in you all a deep appreciation for history and the importance of individual actions."

"Speaking of your adventures, Headmaster," Clarissa chimed in, her curiosity piqued, "you mentioned meeting some historical figures like Benjamin Franklin and George Washington. What was that like?"

Headmaster Winters leaned back in his chair, a nostalgic smile gracing his lips. "Ah, yes. My encounters with those great men were truly remarkable. You see, when I first discovered my ability to travel through time, I found myself drawn to the events of the American Revolution. I couldn't resist the opportunity to witness history unfold before my very eyes."

"Benjamin Franklin," he continued, "was as brilliant and witty as the stories suggest. I had the privilege of engaging in numerous lively debates with him at his home in Philadelphia. His insights on science, politics, and human nature were truly fascinating."

Charles raised an eyebrow, unable to contain his excitement. "And George Washington? What was it like meeting the Father of our country?"

"Ah, George Washington," Headmaster Winters mused, his gaze distant as he recalled the memory. "I first encountered him during the harsh winter at Valley Forge. Despite the suffering of his troops, he remained steadfast and resolute in his commitment to their cause. Time and again, I saw him inspire hope and courage in the hearts of his soldiers. It was an honor to be in the presence of such a leader."

The children exchanged awestruck glances, their minds racing with visions of what it must have been like for their headmaster to stand alongside such legendary figures. As they delved deeper into the night, exploring the hidden corners of the library and unearthing the secrets of the past, they couldn't help but feel a newfound sense of purpose and an unquenchable thirst for knowledge.

"Headmaster," Sarah whispered, her voice filled with determination, "we want to learn more. To know everything you can teach us about this incredible history and your role in it."

"Very well," Headmaster Winters replied, his eyes twinkling with pride and mischief. "I believe there is much to be discovered within these walls and even more to be learned from the lessons of the past. Together, we shall embark on a journey of discovery that will shape not only your understanding of history but also your place within it."

The air was thick with the scent of old parchment and the gentle hum of whispered secrets. The children wandered through the dimly lit corridors of the boarding school, their eyes lingering on the artifacts and relics that adorned every shelf and alcove. Each object held its own story, a connection to a specific historical event or figure that had shaped the world as it knew it.

"Look at this!" Charles exclaimed, carefully lifting a tarnished silver goblet from a dusty display case. "It's said to have been used by King Louis XVI during his final meal before the French Revolution."

"Remarkable," Clarissa murmured, her fingers tracing the delicate etchings along the rim. "And this," she continued, pointing to an ancient-looking scroll, "is a first edition of the Declaration of Independence, signed by John Hancock himself."

Sarah felt a shiver run down her spine as she imagined the hands that had held these items, the minds that had crafted the words that shaped history. She couldn't shake the feeling that there was more to discover within these walls, secrets that lay hidden just beyond their reach.

"Headmaster Winters mentioned something about another cryptex," Henry mused, his brow furrowed in thought. "Could you imagine if we found it? Think of the adventures we could have, the people we could meet!"

"Indeed," Charles replied, a mischievous glint in his eye. "We might even find ourselves face-to-face with the likes of Napoleon Bonaparte or Queen Elizabeth I."

"Or maybe even witness the building of the Great Wall of China," Sarah added, her eyes sparkling with excitement.

As they spoke, their imaginations ran wild with the possibilities that lay ahead. The knowledge that Headmaster Winters had once been a time traveler only fueled their curiosity and desire to uncover more hidden truths within the school's archives.

Clarissa, ever the diligent scholar, began leafing through stacks of dusty books and scrolls, searching for any hint of another cryptex. "There has to be something here," she murmured, determination etched on her face. "If only we knew where to begin..."

"Maybe it's not just about searching the books," Henry suggested. "Perhaps there's a clue hidden somewhere around the school itself."

"An excellent idea, Henry," Charles agreed. "We should start exploring every nook and cranny, from the attics to the cellars. Who knows what secrets this old building holds?"

With renewed purpose, the four friends set out to uncover the mysteries of their beloved boarding school, each eager to embark on new adventures and delve deeper into the annals of history. Little did they know that their journey would bring them closer together, forging bonds that would stand the test of time as they continued to learn valuable lessons about trust, courage, and the power of friendship.

The sun cast golden rays across the library's towering bookshelves, casting shadows that danced over the worn wooden floorboards. Clarissa stood on her tiptoes, reaching for a particularly old-looking tome on the top shelf while Charles steadied the ladder below her.

"Got it!" she declared triumphantly, carefully cradling the heavy volume in her arms as she descended. Sarah and Henry gathered around eagerly, their eyes wide with anticipation as Clarissa carefully opened the ancient book to reveal beautifully illustrated pages detailing key moments of the American Revolution.

"Look at this!" Sarah exclaimed, pointing to an intricate drawing of soldiers huddled around a campfire. "It says here that Headmaster Winters was with General Washington during the harsh winter at Valley Forge. Can you imagine what it must have been like?"

"Indeed," Charles mused, his fingertips tracing the edges of the fragile parchment. "To have witnessed such pivotal moments in history firsthand... Headmaster Winters must have so many stories to tell."

Henry furrowed his brow in thought as he flipped through another dusty volume. "All this time, we've studied history from books and scrolls, but the headmaster actually lived it. I wonder what else he experienced during his time travels."

As the children continued to explore the vast collection of historical texts, their curiosity about Headmaster Winters' past only grew stronger. The library seemed to hold endless secrets, each book a portal into the past. As their fascination with the boarding school's history intensified, so did their desire to uncover more about their enigmatic headmaster.

"Let's see if we can find anything else about his role in the

American Revolution," Clarissa suggested, her eyes scanning the shelves for any hint of information about Headmaster Winters' time-traveling adventures.

"Here's something!" Sarah called out, holding up an old journal bound in cracked leather. "It looks like it belonged to someone who knew Headmaster Winters during the war."

The children huddled together, carefully turning the pages and reading aloud as they discovered accounts of secret meetings between Headmaster Winters and prominent figures like Benjamin Franklin and George Washington. They marveled at how their headmaster had played such an instrumental role in shaping the course of history.

"Wow," Henry whispered, awe-struck by the revelations before them. "Headmaster Winters wasn't just a bystander in the American Revolution; he was an active participant."

"Imagine the things he must have seen... and the risks he took," Charles added, his mind racing with images of battlefields and clandestine rendezvous.

"Should we ask him about it?" Clarissa pondered, biting her lip nervously. "I mean, he's always been so kind and supportive of us. Maybe he'd be willing to share some of his stories."

"Or maybe," Sarah chimed in, a glint of mischief in her eyes, "we could try to find out more on our own. There's still so much we don't know about this school and its history. Who knows what other secrets might be hidden within these walls?"

With a shared sense of excitement and determination, the children embarked on a mission to uncover the full extent of

Headmaster Winters' extraordinary past. Little did they know, their journey would take them deeper into the annals of history than they ever could have imagined.

The children gathered outside the library, their breaths visible in the crisp autumn air. A sense of adventure bubbled within each of them, fueled by the countless secrets they'd uncovered in the ancient tomes. As the last rays of sunlight vanished over the horizon, Sarah took the lead, her fingers brushing the cold stone wall as she guided her friends down a dimly lit corridor.

"Remember that draft we felt earlier near the eastern wing?" Sarah asked, excitement lacing her voice. "I think it might be coming from a hidden chamber."

Henry's eyes widened, his curiosity piqued. "A hidden chamber? You really think so?"

"Only one way to find out," Charles grinned, clapping Henry on the back. "Let's go exploring."

As they reached the end of the corridor, Clarissa hesitated. "What if we get caught snooping around?"

"Then we'll have an interesting story to tell," Sarah replied with a mischievous wink.

With bated breath, the children pressed against the cold walls, searching for any signs of a hidden entrance. Suddenly, Charles felt a subtle shift beneath his fingertips. With a triumphant grin, he pushed against the stone, revealing a narrow passage shrouded in darkness.

"Nice job, Charles!" Henry whispered, his heart pounding in

anticipation.

One by one, they filed into the secret chamber, their eyes adjusting to the dim light cast by flickering torches. The room was filled with artifacts, maps, and journals piled high on dusty shelves, each item bearing witness to the school's rich history. The air was thick with mystery, and the children couldn't help but feel awed by the treasures before them.

"Look at this," Clarissa breathed, holding up a faded map of colonial Boston. "It shows key locations from the Revolution. Do you think Headmaster Winters used this when he was traveling through time?"

"Maybe," Sarah mused, carefully examining a journal filled with intricate drawings of cryptexes and complex mechanisms. "It seems like we've only just scratched the surface of what our headmaster has been involved in."

As they continued to explore the chamber, Henry stumbled upon a small envelope tucked between two leather-bound books. His eyes widened as he read the names written on the front in elegant script: Charles, Clarissa, Sarah, and Henry.

"Guys, look at this!" He called out, his voice shaking with excitement. "It's a letter from Headmaster Winters addressed to us!"

The children gathered around, their hearts pounding as Henry carefully unfolded the parchment. The words revealed not only Headmaster Winters' knowledge of their journey to colonial Boston but also his pride in their growth and bravery.

"Dear children," the letter began, "I have watched you grow

and learn throughout your time at this school, and I could not be prouder of your achievements. Your curiosity and determination have led you to discover a world beyond the confines of these ancient walls, and I believe you are ready for greater adventures..."

"Headmaster Winters knew all along," whispered Sarah, her eyes shining with awe. "He knew we'd find this place, and he believes in us."

"Then let's not disappoint him," Charles declared, determination settling in his chest. "Let's keep exploring, learning, and uncovering the secrets of our school and its incredible history."

With renewed resolve, the children delved deeper into the hidden chamber, eager to unlock the mysteries of the past and embrace the challenges that awaited them, for each child knew, deep down, that they were a part of something much larger than themselves – a story spanning centuries, bound by courage, and shaped by the indomitable spirit of adventure.

# CHAPTER 24

As Sarah Merriweather rounded the corner of a dimly lit hallway, she caught sight of her friends huddled together, their faces illuminated by the glow of Charles Hamilton's flashlight. The others—Henry Turner and Clarissa Jennings—were peering with wide-eyed curiosity at a dusty old bookcase that concealed a hidden door. With a gentle push, the bookcase swung open, revealing a secret room that had remained undisturbed for who knows how long.

"Wow," whispered Henry, his breath catching in his throat. "I never knew this place existed."

"Neither did I," admitted Clarissa, pushing her glasses up the bridge of her nose as she stepped inside the room, her eyes widening as they adjusted to the dim light.

Sarah hesitated for a moment, then followed her friends into the hidden chamber. The air was thick with dust and the scent of old parchment, sending a shiver down her spine. All around them, ancient books and artifacts lay strewn about on shelves and tables, each one beckoning to be explored.

"Look at all this stuff!" exclaimed Charles, his voice barely above a whisper as he picked up an old compass from a nearby table. "There must be hundreds of years' worth of history in here."

"Maybe even more," added Clarissa, carefully leafing through the pages of a moth-eaten tome. She glanced excitedly at her friends, her fear momentarily forgotten. "Can you imagine what we might learn from these?"

"Only one way to find out," declared Henry, his strong hands eagerly rummaging through a pile of yellowed maps and scrolls. A faint smile played on Sarah's lips as she watched her friends explore the dusty treasures. Their excitement was contagious, and it wasn't long before she found herself drawn to a shelf in the far corner of the room.

As she brushed aside cobwebs and layers of dust, Sarah's fingers brushed against something that felt different from the other objects on the shelf. It was an ornate wooden box, its surface adorned with intricate carvings and faded gold leaf.

"Guys, come take a look at this," she called out, her voice barely audible in the hushed atmosphere of the hidden room.

Her friends gathered around her, their eyes wide with curiosity as they examined the mysterious box. The carvings that adorned its surface seemed to tell a story of adventure, with images of ships, battles, and strange creatures dancing across the wood.

"Wow," breathed Charles, reaching out to touch the box with an almost reverent hand. "This must be something really special."

"Open it!" urged Henry, his impatience getting the better of him. Sarah hesitated for a moment, her blue eyes darting between the eager faces of her friends before she took a deep breath and carefully lifted the lid of the box.

As the children peered inside, their excitement grew, overtaking the room like a wave crashing against a rocky shore. Their hearts pounded in their chests, and their minds raced with possibilities. What secrets did this hidden chamber hold? What new adventures awaited them within the pages of these ancient books and artifacts?

"Whatever we find in here," whispered Clarissa, her brown eyes shining with wonder behind her glasses, "it's going to change our lives forever."

As the children continued their exploration of the hidden room, each lost in their own thoughts and imaginations, one thing was certain: the world beyond the walls of the boarding school would never look quite the same again.

With a creaking sound, the lid of the box opened, unveiling the cryptic treasure hidden within. The children gasped in unison as they beheld a cylindrical object nestled among soft velvet. Intricate carvings covered its surface, and a sense of mystery radiated from it.

"Look at this," Sarah breathed, carefully lifting the object from the box with trembling hands. "It's a cryptex."

"Whoa," murmured Henry, leaning closer for a better look, his eyes wide with admiration.

"Remember when we were in colonial Boston?" Charles asked with excitement, adjusting his stance to get a closer view. "We learned so much during our time there. Maybe the secrets inside this cryptex can help us even more!"

"Exactly!" chimed in Clarissa, her glasses glinting with newfound confidence. "We must unlock this cryptex. There could be clues about our future adventures or even answers that could change the course of history."

"Let's try to open it!" Sarah declared, her blue eyes sparkling with determination.

The group huddled around the cryptex, each eager to contribute their knowledge from their previous journey to unravel the mystery before them. As they manipulated the intricate engravings, they couldn't help but reminisce about their time in colonial Boston, where they had met remarkable figures like Dr. Joseph Warren, Paul Revere, and Samuel Adams. They had grown so much since then, overcoming personal challenges and forging strong friendships along the way.

"Remember when Dr. Warren taught us about the importance of unity and standing up for what we believe in?" Sarah mused aloud, her thoughts drifting back to the kind-hearted doctor who had been like a mentor to them all.

"Or when Paul Revere showed us how to navigate the city with his resourcefulness," Henry added, a note of admiration in his voice as he recalled the skilled silversmith who had taken him under his wing.

"Let's not forget Samuel Adams," Clarissa chimed in. "His passion and dedication inspired us to be brave in the face of adversity."

The children shared knowing glances, each remembering the lessons they had learned and the bonds they had formed during their time in colonial Boston. As they continued to examine the cryptex, their hearts swelled with determination, eager to unlock its secrets and apply the knowledge gained from their previous adventures to their current quest.

"Let's work together and use what we've learned to open this cryptex," Charles proposed, his eyes meeting those of his friends. "Who knows what other amazing experiences await us?"

With renewed vigor, the group focused on deciphering the cryptex, their memories of colonial Boston serving as a guiding light and a testament to their growth as individuals. The air was thick with anticipation and excitement as they worked tirelessly, eager to unravel the secrets hidden within the mysterious artifact before them.

"Perhaps some of these engravings are clues," Sarah suggested, her eyes scanning the mysterious symbols that adorned the cryptex. The twinkle in her blue eyes betrayed the excitement she felt as her fingers traced the intricate patterns.

"Wait a minute!" Charles exclaimed, pointing to a word carved on the side. "This is one of the phrases we saw in Dr. Warren's office, remember? He said it was an important principle during the fight for independence."

"Ah, yes! 'E pluribus unum' – 'Out of many, one,'" Clarissa recalled, adjusting her glasses as she gazed at the engraved phrase. "Let's try that!"

The children worked together, rotating the dials on the cryptex until they had aligned the words. However, when they attempted to open it, the cryptex remained stubbornly closed.

"Maybe it's a phrase or code associated with Paul Revere's work," Henry suggested, his brow furrowed in thought. "He mentioned something about a secret network of riders and signals, right?"

"True, but it doesn't seem likely that he would have used a

Latin phrase for that purpose," countered Clarissa, her mind racing to recall other significant words and phrases they had encountered.

"Guys, what about the words John Hancock spoke to us?" Sarah interjected, her voice soft but insistent. "He said, 'Liberty must at all hazards be supported.' That really stuck with me."

"Sarah, that's brilliant!" Charles exclaimed, his face lighting up. "It embodies the spirit of their struggle, and it's a concept we've seen time and again throughout our journey."

"Alright, let's give it a try," Clarissa said, her hands shaking slightly with anticipation as she carefully turned the dials to spell out the new phrase.

As soon as the last letter clicked into place, a soft but unmistakable sound filled the air. The cryptex had finally unlocked, revealing a hidden compartment within. The children gasped in unison, their hearts pounding with excitement and awe.

"Sarah, you did it!" Charles cried out, his eyes shining with pride and admiration, the trust issues that once hampered their relationship now a thing of the past.

"Thank you, John Hancock," Sarah whispered, her own eyes shimmering with gratitude for the man who had inspired them to fight for liberty and justice.

The children exchanged proud glances, beaming at one another as they marveled at the unlocked cryptex before them. Their journey had taught them the significance of perseverance, collaboration, and trust — and now, they held tangible proof of their growth in their hands.

"Let's see what secrets this compartment holds," Henry said, his voice full of anticipation as he reached out to open it. Little did they know what wonders awaited them next.

Henry's fingers trembled as they hovered above the hidden compartment, beads of sweat forming on his brow. The sense of anticipation was palpable, each child holding their breath in unison as they waited for him to reveal the cryptex's secrets. With a final deep breath, Henry carefully lifted the small parchment from its resting place, the delicate paper crinkling beneath his touch.

"Quick, let's gather 'round," Sarah urged, her excitement bubbling over as she motioned for the others to huddle closer. The children eagerly obeyed, forming a tight circle around the parchment as their eyes widened with anticipation, their earlier struggles momentarily forgotten.

"Alright, here goes," Henry said, unrolling the parchment with utmost care. As he began to read the cryptic message out loud, the children leaned in closer, curiosity lighting their faces like a thousand twinkling stars.

"Whispers in time, whisperers of fate / Onward you travel, your destiny awaits / Through trials and lessons, you'll shape history's bend / Hold fast to your courage, and fight to the end."

"Wow," Charles breathed, his confident demeanor momentarily faltering as his eyes scanned the parchment once more. "This must mean that we're meant to go on even more historical journeys and somehow play a part in shaping history itself."

"Indeed," Clarissa chimed in, her intellect shining through her timid exterior. "This message seems to imply that our adventures are far from over."

"Can you imagine?" Sarah whispered, her blue eyes sparkling with excitement. "More chances to learn about history firsthand and maybe even make a difference in the world?"

"Think of all the amazing people we met in colonial Boston," Henry mused a hint of awe in his voice. "Dr. Warren, Paul Revere, John Hancock, Samuel Adams... What incredible experiences await us next?"

"Whoever left this cryptex for us knew what they were doing," Charles said thoughtfully, stroking his chin as he contemplated the parchment's words. "We've grown so much already, not just as individuals but as a team. Just think of what we can accomplish together."

"Then let's make a promise," Sarah suggested, her voice full of determination. "No matter where our journey takes us or what challenges we face, we'll stick together and do our best to follow the course of history."

"Agreed," the others chorused, their voices resolute as they pledged themselves to the cause. The sense of anticipation and excitement in the air was electric, each child more determined than ever to embrace their newfound purpose.

"Let's keep this parchment safe," Henry said, carefully rolling it back up and placing it securely within the cryptex. "We don't want to risk losing it."

"Time to put the cryptex back in its hiding place," Charles

declared, leading the group back to the hidden room's dusty shelves. As they replaced the ancient relic, their hearts swelled with a sense of adventure, knowing that their story was far from over.

"Let's go," Sarah urged, taking one final glance at the hidden room before ushering her friends out. "We have so much to prepare for, and who knows when our next journey will begin."

As the door closed behind them, the children felt a surge of excitement course through their veins, each step forward tinged with the anticipation of what lay ahead. And so, they embarked on the next chapter of their incredible adventure – ready to learn, grow, and forever change the course of history.

With the cryptic message on the parchment fresh in their minds, the children huddled together in a secluded corner of the school's courtyard, where the ivy-covered walls shielded them from prying eyes. The gentle rustling of leaves overhead was the perfect soundtrack to their animated discussion.

"Imagine all the different time periods we could visit!" Sarah exclaimed, her blue eyes sparkling with excitement. "I've always wanted to witness Queen Elizabeth I's reign."

"Or what about the French Revolution?" Charles suggested, his dark hair ruffling in the breeze as he leaned forward eagerly. "We could meet people like Robespierre and Marie Antoinette!"

"Let's not forget Ancient Rome," Clarissa chimed in, pushing her glasses up her nose. "There's so much we could learn from their art and architecture, not to mention their political system."

"Or the Wild West!" Henry interjected, pounding his fist into his palm for emphasis. "We could help tame the frontier and bring justice to lawless towns!"

Sarah hugged her knees closer to her chest, lost in thought. "The possibilities are endless," she mused, her mind racing with images of grand palaces, daring revolutions, and fierce battles. "But we have to be careful. We're not just observers; our presence can change the course of history."

"Sarah's right," Charles agreed, his brow furrowing as he considered the weight of their responsibility. "We need to be cautious in our actions but also seize the opportunities to make a difference where we can."

"Absolutely," Clarissa nodded, adjusting her glasses once more. "We'll need to use our knowledge and skills to navigate each time period, all while learning from the people we meet along the way."

"Speaking of which," Henry said, a determined glint in his eye, "we should prepare ourselves by studying more about different eras. Who knows what challenges await us?"

The group exchanged excited glances, their hearts racing at the prospect of new adventures and the lessons they could learn from history. They knew that their journey would be fraught with danger and uncertainty, but the potential impact they could have on the world far outweighed any fear.

"Let's make a pact," Sarah suggested, extending her hand toward the center of their circle. "No matter what obstacles we face or how difficult things may become, we promise to continue our journey, learning from history and shaping it for the better."

"Agreed," Charles said, placing his hand atop Sarah's.

"Count me in," Clarissa added, followed by Henry's strong, calloused hand.

United by their determination and shared purpose, the children vowed to embrace the challenges and opportunities that lay ahead. With the cryptex safely hidden away, they returned to the secret room – their minds filled with wonder and anticipation, ready to embark on their next historical journey.

The warm glow of the setting sun painted the hidden room in shades of gold and amber, casting intricate shadows across the dusty floor. Sarah leaned against a bookshelf, her mind racing with the endless possibilities that lay ahead of them. Her gaze fell upon the wooden box containing the cryptex, now safely hidden on the highest shelf.

"Can you believe how much we've grown since we first stumbled upon this room?" she mused, blue eyes sparkling with gratitude. "I never thought I could be this brave or make such a difference in the world."

"Nor did I," Charles admitted, a rare vulnerability creeping into his voice. "It's funny how our friendships have made us stronger, more open to change."

"Indeed," Clarissa chimed in, adjusting her glasses. "I've discovered that there's so much more to me than I ever realized. And it's all thanks to you guys and our adventures together."

"Same here," Henry said with a smile. "I've learned the value of patience, and I owe it all to you. I'm grateful for the experiences we've had and the person I've become because of them."

As they stood in the secret room, basking in the warmth of their friendships and personal growth, Sarah felt a profound sense of gratitude wash over her.

"Friends," she said softly, "we must keep our discovery of the cryptex and our future journeys a secret. We have a responsibility to protect the delicate balance of time and space. Are we all in agreement?"

"Absolutely," Charles nodded firmly. "If word were to spread about our abilities, it could jeopardize everything we've worked for – and potentially alter the course of history in unforeseen ways."

"Agreed," Clarissa whispered, the weight of the decision settling on her slender shoulders. "We must proceed with caution and care, always mindful of the consequences."

"Right," said Henry, his expression resolute. "We'll keep this our secret – for the sake of history and for ourselves."

United by their shared understanding of the immense responsibility that lay before them, the children formed a pact of secrecy. The hidden room, once a symbol of mystery and discovery, now became a sanctuary for their secret adventures.

"Let's promise each other," Sarah said, her blue eyes shining with determination. "No matter what happens, we'll always be there for one another and protect this secret."

"Promise," Charles echoed, extending his hand toward the center of their circle.

"Promise," Clarissa added, her voice stronger than before, as she placed her hand on top of Charles's.

"Promise," Henry affirmed, completing the circle with his own hand.

With their pact made, the children knew that they had forged a bond that could withstand the test of time. Their gratitude for the experiences they had shared thus far only fueled their excitement for the journeys yet to come.

"Okay, everyone," Sarah said, taking a deep breath. "Let's put everything back in its place and make sure this room remains hidden."

Working together, they carefully returned the dusty books and artifacts to their original positions, ensuring that no trace of their presence remained. With one last look around the hidden room, they left, their hearts filled with a sense of adventure and newfound purpose.

As they closed the door behind them, the cryptex resting safely within its wooden box, the air seemed to hum with anticipation. Little did they know, their next historical journey was just around the corner, waiting to unfold in the pages of their story.

"Alright, it's time to close the cryptex," Sarah said, her eyes sparkling with excitement. The others nodded in agreement, their hearts racing with anticipation.

"Here goes nothing," Charles remarked as he carefully closed the cryptex, hearing the satisfying click of the mechanism locking into place. With the cryptex now secured, they knew that their next adventure was only a secret phrase away.

"Let's put it back in the box and hide it again," Clarissa suggested, her voice steady and filled with determination. They worked together to place the cryptex inside the ornate wooden box, their fingers lingering on its intricate engravings for just a moment longer.

"Where should we hide it? We can't risk someone finding this room and discovering our secret," Henry mused, his brows furrowing in concentration.

"Behind that stack of books," Sarah pointed out, her gaze locked onto a pile of dusty old tomes that looked as though they hadn't been touched in centuries. "No one would ever think to look there."

"Good thinking," Charles agreed, placing the box behind the books with great care. As he stepped back, he couldn't help but feel a thrill of exhilaration at the thought of their future adventures, knowing that they had so much more to learn from history.

"Is everyone ready?" Sarah asked, looking around the hidden room one last time. Their eyes drank in every detail, from the cobwebs that hung in the corners to the musty smell of ancient knowledge that permeated the air.

"Ready as we'll ever be," Henry replied, his face set with newfound courage. He could already feel himself growing stronger, more patient, and more resourceful, thanks to the lessons they had learned throughout their journey thus far.

"Let's go, then," Charles said, holding the door open for the others as they filed out of the room. Before he closed it, however, he took one last look at the cryptex's hiding place and whispered, "Until next time."

"Until next time," Sarah echoed, a smile playing on her lips. She could feel the adventurous spirit of Dr. Warren, John Hancock, Samuel Adams, and Paul Revere coursing through her veins, fueling her newfound confidence and determination. With a final glance at the hidden room, she followed Charles out, closing the door behind her.

"Can you imagine where we'll end up next?" Clarissa asked excitedly as they made their way back down the dimly lit hallway. "There's so much history left for us to explore."

"Who knows?" Henry mused, grinning. "Maybe we'll find ourselves in ancient Rome or medieval England. The possibilities are endless."

"Wherever we go," Sarah said, her blue eyes shining with excitement, "I know we'll learn something invaluable. It's amazing how our journey has changed not only the course of history but each of us as well."

"Indeed," Charles agreed, his trust issues slowly fading away as he felt more connected to his friends than ever before. "We've all grown stronger and wiser from our experiences. I can't wait to see what lies ahead."

"Neither can I," Clarissa murmured, adjusting her glasses. She felt a newfound sense of purpose, knowing that Dr. Warren believed in her abilities and encouraged her intellectual pursuits.

As they exited the darkened passageway and stepped back

into the brightly lit halls of the boarding school, the anticipation and excitement in the air were palpable. They knew that their story was far from over, and with every step they took, they carried the knowledge of their past adventures and the promise of those yet to come.

"Let's stick together," Charles suggested, glancing at his friends with a grin. "After all, we're a team now."

"Agreed," said Sarah, beaming. "Together, we'll face whatever challenges come our way and protect the delicate balance of time and space."

As the children prepared to leave the secret room, their eyes lingered on the peculiar artifacts and dusty volumes that had once seemed so ordinary but now held the promise of countless adventures. The air buzzed with energy as they shared one last glance at the cryptex's hiding place, feeling a mix of excitement and fear for the future.

"Alright," Charles said, taking a deep breath. "We should head back before someone notices we're gone."

"Right," Sarah agreed, her heart racing at the thought of what lay ahead. She couldn't help but smile as she remembered her time in colonial Boston and the incredible people she had met. Who would they encounter on their next journey?

"Wait!" Clarissa suddenly whispered, her gaze fixed on a small, tattered book lying on a table near the door. She picked it up carefully, her fingers tracing the faded lettering on the cover. "This... this might be something important."

"Let me see," Henry murmured, leaning over her shoulder as

she opened the book to reveal an old, hand-drawn map. Intricate lines and symbols covered the worn parchment, hinting at far-off lands and hidden treasures. "This looks like it could be our next clue," he mused, his eyes sparkling with curiosity.

"Where do you think it leads?" Sarah asked, peering over their shoulders to get a better look at the map.

"Hard to say," Charles replied, studying the markings thoughtfully. "But it's definitely not Boston."

"Maybe it shows another time period we'll visit," Clarissa suggested, her voice filled with excitement. "Just imagine all the amazing things we'll learn on our next adventure!"

"Could you imagine if we end up somewhere like ancient Egypt or medieval England?" Henry chimed in, grinning wildly. "The possibilities are endless!"

"Or even meeting some of the greatest historical figures!" Sarah added dreamily, thinking of the friendships they had formed during their time in colonial Boston. "I can't wait to see who we'll meet next."

"Whatever it is," Charles declared, his voice full of determination, "we'll face it together. We've been through so much already—we can handle anything that comes our way."

"Right!" the others agreed, their eyes shining with anticipation.

"Let's go," Charles whispered as he carefully closed the tattered book and tucked it under his arm, ensuring its safety. The children filed out of the secret room, leaving its mysteries behind them for now. As they stepped out into the dimly lit corridor, the door clicked shut, sealing their secret within.

"Ready for our next adventure?" Charles asked, his eyes twinkling with excitement.

"More than ready!" Sarah responded, feeling her heart swell with courage and newfound purpose.

"Let's go!" Clarissa exclaimed, her once-timid voice now full of confidence.

"Lead the way," Henry said, a determined grin spreading across his face.

"Alright then," Charles whispered, clutching the tattered book tightly. "Here's to the next chapter in our journey!"

As they walked away from the hidden room, the air seemed to hum with anticipation and excitement, their laughter echoing through the halls as they dreamt of the endless possibilities that lay ahead.

But little did they know, the greatest adventure of their lives was just about to begin...

9 781963 295719